Alexandra Raife has lived abroad in many countries and worked at a variety of jobs, including a six-year commission in the RAF and many years co-running a Highland hotel. She lives in Perthshire. All her previous novels, *Drumveyn*, *The Larach*, *Grianan*, *Belonging*, *Sun On Snow*, *The Wedding Gift*, *Moving On* and *Among Friends* have been richly praised.

Praise for Alexandra Raife:

'A welcome new storyteller'

Rosamunde Pilcher

'An absorbing story with a perfectly painted background'
Hilary Hale, *Financial Times*

'Scotland's answer to Rosamunde Pilcher'

South Hams Newspapers

'[a] readable love story full of emotion, pain and despair'
Coventry Evening Telegraph

Also by Alexandra Raife

Drumveyn

The Larach

Grianan

Belonging

Sun on Snow

The Wedding Gift

Moving On

Among Friends

RETURN TO DRUMVEYN

Alexandra Raife

CORONET BOOKS
Hodder & Stoughton

First published in Great Britain in 2002 by Hodder & Stoughton
First published in paperback 2002
A Coronet paperback
A division of Hodder Headline

2 4 6 8 10 9 7 5 3 1

A CIP catalogue record for this book
is available from the British Library.

ISBN 0 340 82235 X

Typeset in Centaur by Hewer Text Ltd, Edinburgh
Printed and bound in Great Britain by Clays Ltd, St Ives plc

Hodder & Stoughton
A division of Hodder Headline
338 Euston Road
London NW1 3BH

RETURN TO DRUMVEYN

Chapter One

Coming back to Drumveyn shouldn't have been like this, Cristi thought, still shaken by the information the lawyer's letter had contained, as she left Muirend behind and headed with relief up into the hills. Was it because of this startling news, throwing her whole future into uncertainty, that the glen seemed more beautiful today than ever?

Don't be a fool, she told herself, trying to focus on normality to dispel the dread which had gripped her since reading that letter. The glen looking gorgeous is more likely to have something to do with the mild winter and weeks of sunshine in April, then rain exactly when we needed it. But the appalling thought that all this might be lost to her could only only heighten her awareness of the glories of early summer, the majesty of spreading copper beeches, white of bird cherry, yellow of broom and laburnum, clematis smothering porches, rhododendrons beside the road trimmed back by passing traffic into walls of massed bloom. The clarity of light and definition of shadow, the freshness of varied greens and vigour of growth seemed almost too much to absorb.

Yesterday, briefly, in the first stunned moments, it had seemed to matter that hard-earned end-of-term fun, the parties, the euphoria of exams being over, the plans for the summer, had been sliced away. Now it felt as though they already belonged to a distant, unreal world, like the exciting possibilities for the autumn which she had intended to talk over with Archie and Pauly.

Trepidation rushed back. Doubts and uncertainties which had disturbed her from time to time as she grew up, but which had been firmly banished by one or other of the strangely linked group she thought of as her family, rose up with a new and terrifying power. Her family? Not one of these people at Drumveyn was related to her at all. Perhaps even her technical adoption when she was a child, by Archie's sister Lisa, might not be valid now that she was over twenty-one. She'd never thought of that.

Her actual family consisted of these strangers in Brazil, strangers who through the years had remained silent, hostile and inaccessible, their rejection of her total. Her mother's family, who had now communicated to her, via their lawyers, this incredible development.

'I still don't think we should have forwarded the letter,' Pauly said worriedly, glancing at the kitchen clock for the umpteenth time, cocking her head to listen for the sound of a car in the courtyard. 'We should have kept it here and let her see the term out. It couldn't have made any difference.'

Archie, running through the heap of mail Postie had left on the kitchen table, most of it expendable, dragged his mind away from the thorny subject of legislation on the right to roam, which with its complex rulings was probably going to end up giving campaigners less freedom than they'd had in the first place, and looked up frowning at Pauly's agitation, so unusual for her.

He tossed down the densely printed pages and came to put an arm round her. 'Pauly, come on. We couldn't have held the letter back. It could have been anything. And Cristi's not a child any more. We've no right to make decisions of that sort on her behalf, you know that.'

'Then I should have gone down with it, so that she wasn't alone when she opened it. It was bound to bring some ghastly news after all these years of silence.'

Archie hugged her, hiding a wry smile. Not everyone would consider such news ghastly.

'You'd have gone down if you could,' he said. 'So would I, come to that. But you know you'd promised to look after Tom. Mum would never have gone for her appointment if you hadn't been here to do that, and if she'd cancelled God knows how long she'd have had to wait for another. And I had to be here for the Water Authority meeting. If the mains supply is going to run across Drumveyn I do have to be in at the planning stage.'

'Oh, I know,' Pauly assented, rubbing her head against his shoulder, taking comfort from his hug. 'We were both stuck here, as usual. When aren't we? But at least it meant Cristi could get me on the phone the moment she heard.

Only, how must she have felt last night, and how must she be feeling driving up now?'

She glanced again at the clock, and then at her watch, as though it might tell her something more acceptable.

'She's always had plenty of resilience,' Archie tried to console her. 'And with student days behind her we have to try and see her as an adult, if we can.'

'Twenty-three's not grown up,' Pauly protested. 'And sometimes she still looks exactly like that eight-year-old I fell for the day I first arrived.'

'Yes, well, don't let her hear you say so,' Archie warned. 'Remember the problems she had when she started at university. And speaking of being grown up, just how old were you, may I ask, when you became a wife and instant mother of two, shortly to become four?'

'Thank goodness at least that Nicholas and the little girls are at school.'

Pauly, who had been twenty when she married Archie, swung onto a different tack, flashing a grin at him. He had a point.

Though brought up by Archie and Pauly, Cristi had been legally adopted by Archie's sister Lisa, because she was the daughter of Lisa's first husband, Howard Armitage. He, abandoning his marriage and his life in England with ruthless completeness, had vanished with Cristi's mother with whom, it appeared, he had long ago established a second household in Brazil. They had never been heard of since. With a callousness which could still appal the family when they were reminded of it, the pair had jettisoned Cristi, whom they hadn't wanted in the first place, despatching her to Lisa like a spare piece of luggage, with the technicalities of adoption already in place as part of Howard's meticulous planning.

Taken into the Napier family, Cristi had been brought up along with Nicholas, nine years younger than she was and Archie's son by a previous marriage, and the two small girls Archie and Pauly had later adopted.

Just as Cristi's parents had never been heard of again, so her Brazilian family had been obdurate in their rejection of her. Archie had once and once only made contact with them, soon after Cristi's arrival, when the obvious course had seemed to be to return her to them.

The meeting with her grandfather had been brief, its tone harshly uncompromising. The arrogant and embittered old man, an aristocrat of a previous era accustomed to wielding unquestioned power over his family, the employees on his ranch in the southern state of Santa Catarina, and even the nearby cattle town, had refused to acknowledge the existence of his daughter's child. A child not only illegitimate but being brought up as a non-Catholic.

Since that terse and unsatisfactory encounter Archie had had contact only with the family lawyers, writing to them when Cristi was eighteen, and again when she was twenty-one, in an attempt to establish some link. He did it because he believed Cristi should not be arbitrarily deprived of this genetic inheritance, but on neither occasion had he received the courtesy of a reply. He had not told Cristi of these abortive attempts, seeing no point in reopening the wound only to have her hurt by rejection yet again.

But now her grandfather had died. And, out of all his considerable family, he had left to Cristi not only a startling sum of money but the cattle ranch itself, the Estancia dos Tres Pinheiros.

Nearly there. The driver of a dusty pick-up coming down from the village greeted Cristi as he passed with a laconic lift of a finger from the steering wheel. Cristi waved back, but for one blank moment couldn't place vehicle or driver. It was as though the familiar things of home had already become strange, no longer part of safe, known territory. It was an absurd relief when the name clicked up.

It was an even greater relief to turn at last into the Drumveyn drive, and wind down its curves towards the river. Still shaken by the moment's disorientation, Cristi pulled up on the hump of the bridge and switched off her engine. In the moment of adjusting from sound to silence she heard a curlew call, the sweet ripple of notes the very voice of home, and she caught the distinctive silhouette above the hayfield that lay between the drive and the loch. Beyond, swathes of gorse blazed bright on the lower swells of the moor; here by the river the scent of hawthorn drifted into the crammed car.

How she had longed to be back. And how much she had hoped for from this summer, here at Drumveyn. Would this strange and scary news take all that from her? Fear filled her, and for a second, leaning her forehead on the wheel, she almost gave in to it. This was the thought which had lurked behind all others in the shock and flurry of yesterday, behind the effort to concentrate on the tying of loose ends, the hasty sorting out of the contents of the flat with the help of the others, returning books, arbitrarily disposing of possessions, informing anyone who needed to be told – winding up the life of four years in a single day. Leaving that self behind for good.

There had been no time to think. Well, she'd hardly been able to think, and the brief hours when she'd tried to sleep had produced nothing but the confused tatters of bad dreams mixed with churning waking fears.

Now she faced the fact which she'd been doing her best to displace by this urgent activity. To go away from Drumveyn, as had been demanded of her (the word did not seem too strong for the terms of that communication from the Brazilian lawyers), for however short or long a time, no matter what was ultimately decided, meant leaving Dougal, meant missing out on this chance to be together again to which she had looked forward so eagerly. How could she face these alarming new claims on her without his support and calm good sense?

Dougal had looked after her since the first day of her arrival here, somehow seeming to grasp, though he was only three years older than she was, the magnitude of the step from her sheltered life in the tropical heat of Rio de Janeiro to the winter cold and starkness of Glen Ellig.

He had protected and patiently instructed her, and kept an eye on her in those early days when they were both still at the glen school. Though there had been rocky times with his sister Jill, nearer to Cristi in age, his

7

friendship had never wavered through all the years as they grew up. It had survived her departure to boarding school but, to her dismay, not her subsequent departure to college.

The change had not been immediately apparent, and in fact at the beginning she had depended more than ever on the link between them which she took so much for granted. But, somewhere in her second year at Edinburgh, constraint had begun to creep in.

No, not constraint, she amended quickly. Constraint was too strong a word. It was merely that their separate worlds had drawn them apart, that they had been growing up. It was more surprising, really, that the easy, unquestioning companionship had lasted as long as it had.

She had been hoping that with university behind her their former easy closeness might be re-established, and this summer, before she embarked on any future career, had seemed the ideal opportunity. She knew Dougal had problems of his own, that he had had to forego any chance of university for himself, and that work and responsibilities took up most of his time, but at least these very problems meant that he was still living at home, in the shepherd's cottage at the home farm where he had grown up.

But everything had been thrown into the melting pot now. Cristi's face screwed up in dismay as reality returned. The only thing to do was get through each step in turn. Now she must start the car, follow the drive up through the trees to the big house, park in the courtyard and go calling along the kitchen corridor in the accepted manner.

Suddenly, more even than seeing Dougal, she wanted to hear Pauly's voice calling in reply, wanted to find herself wrapped in one of Pauly's warm, enveloping hugs.

Chapter Two

'Darling Cristi, it's lovely for us to have you home sooner than we expected, you know it is. But it's hard on you to have to come back in such a scramble, missing out on all the fun at the end of your last term, just because these wretched people say jump. And after saying nothing for practically the whole of your life.'

Archie grinned at the mixture of loving pleasure and protective wrath — with a little exaggeration thrown in — which Pauly managed to achieve. The flurry of arrival was over, the top layer of things in the car brought in, the first reaction to the news behind them.

Though Archie saw no reason to comment on Cristi's running for home in such blind haste — she was here, and he was delighted to see her — his view, almost the first thing he said to her, that there was no need to make any decision then and there had been definitely soothing. In any case no panicky questions about what lay ahead could mar Cristi's delight to be back.

They had had tea at the kitchen table, seeing off most of a feather-light lemon sponge which Pauly had thrown together as soon as she knew Cristi was coming. She had thrown together half a dozen, in fact. Even with the family away at school Pauly found it hard to think in terms of one cake. Since cooking was one of her passions, this kitchen was where she was usually to be found, and most discussions of any moment took place here. The big bay of the window looked west, over the tips of the conifers crowding the gorge of the burn, across the moor to the peak of Ben Breac, and its cushioned seat was a comfortable and popular spot.

'I had to come,' Cristi said, in answer to Pauly, though back once more in this familiar setting the urgency was harder to believe in. 'Everything around me seemed somehow to fall to pieces, once I'd read the letter, as though it wasn't real any more. And I couldn't bear to be on my own, with this to think about. Well, the others were there, of course, and they were great, they did everything they could think of, but it wasn't the same as being with you, here . . .'

She broke off, startled to find her voice wavering, a lump in her throat. The aspect Torie and Isa had seized on, naturally enough, had been the thrill of Cristi's exotic background suddenly re-emerging, and of her becoming overnight an heiress and the owner of a South American cattle ranch. What did a few days at the end of term matter compared to that? Any thoughts of how her life might change, of what she might have to leave behind, had been cheerfully glossed over, even by Torie. They had applied themselves to dispersing, or acquiring, any of her belongings which in their estimation she wouldn't need again, and had helped her to pack what was left with casual goodwill. Kindly meant as this had been, and Cristi was grateful to them, it had made her long even more for the step to be taken, the break behind her, and to be safe at home with the people on whose understanding and support she could always rely. Driving home she had found herself longing for smaller, apparently trivial things which were part of the whole, hardly defined — such as the comfort of sitting in this very spot, Broy the current Dandie Dinmont warm against her thigh, the air drifting in at the window carrying the evening scents of the summer garden, the sound of the burn, birdsong, and the occasional far-off call of the cuckoo.

To be with these dear people again. How good it had been to read in Archie's eyes, in the second before he hugged her, his message of reassurance that he would do everything in his power to help her, as he always had and always would.

Archie, now in his early forties, was unequivocally the father figure for Cristi. Nowadays his brown hair, though as thick as ever, showed signs of greying, and hard work and responsibility had carved deep lines into a face which had in any case matured early. His square figure carried heavy muscle, and he looked what he was, a man of strength and dependability, sure of his values and immovably conscientious.

In a flash of adult perception, Cristi saw how blessed

she had been to have had always in the background that kindness and even-handed integrity.

The same was true of Pauly, yet Pauly had a different place in her heart, a place all her own. Since Cristi's first sight of her, when to a child's eyes she had so clearly been 'not a real grown-up', a special bond had existed between them. Pauly had fulfilled a mother's role, her authority taken for granted, yet often had seemed more an elder sister – and a sister who could be outrageously scatty and frivolous into the bargain. There had been a tie between them which the younger children didn't share, and Cristi, on this day of sharpened vision, recognised it as love which needed no label or specific relationship.

'It suddenly seemed so unimportant,' she repeated, as though still coming to terms with the discovery. 'I mean, I'd loved it all, being in Edinburgh, the course, sharing with Torie and Isa, but it was as though it suddenly became – well, childish almost.'

She gave them a glance of deprecation, aware that to use the word could bring a smile, however kindly, to adult faces. But she wanted to convey these feelings to them, seeking the assurance of being understood to help her through whatever was coming.

Neither Archie nor Pauly felt like smiling. Though Archie, eyeing Cristi's undeveloped figure, her narrow shoulders and the slim neck on which the shapely head with its glossy blue-black hair was so elegantly poised, found it hard to believe that her twenty-fourth birthday was coming up.

In her skimpy lime-green top and yellow dungarees she

looked to him, still, very like the endearing child, brimming with enthusiasm for the new life so magically offered to her, whom Lisa had brought to Drumveyn fourteen years ago. He felt a stab of mingled protectiveness for her and anger towards the strangers who by carelessly claiming her in this way seemed so likely to bring her pain. But he couldn't deny that, indifferent and arrogant as they might be, they had a right to the claims of kinship. Cristi's dark strong-textured hair, the creamy skin which was an exotic gold in summer, the delicate bone structure – though it had to be said she was as tough as old boots, he amended with loving possessiveness – proclaimed her origins. A bright and alien bird indeed, to have migrated to the chilly north.

'I know what you mean,' he said, and found his voice gruffer than he had expected. 'Play-time over. But still, a couple of days couldn't have made too much difference.'

He knew he was echoing what Pauly felt, wanting to resist the bleak truth that Cristi could be summoned away in this manner, and they had no grounds for protest.

'Well, it doesn't matter now,' Cristi said. 'Loads of people left the minute exams were over. But the lease on the flat ran till the end of the month, and we'd just thought it would be fun to have a few days unwinding.'

'Surely you didn't manage to squeeze everything into the car,' Pauly said. 'Is there more to fetch?'

Cristi shrugged. 'I gave the rest away.' She'd known a journey back to fetch it would be unthinkable.

Pauly and Archie exchanged a glance. This told them so much. Pauly nobly bit back a question about Cristi's work, sad to think that she would never see much of what she had produced in this final year.

'Heavens, look at the time,' she exclaimed instead. 'We're supposed to be having dinner at the barn to save Tom and Madeleine coming down. Is that all right with you, Cristi? I thought you wouldn't mind.'

Would Cristi have preferred to go and find Dougal? Suddenly, in these new circumstances, Pauly was unsure of everything, and hated the feeling.

'Of course I don't mind,' Cristi said. 'I'm longing to see them. But won't it be a lot for Madeleine if we go up there?'

'No problem, I'm taking a lasagne with me. Not that I remembered to get it out of the freezer in time. You know me. I'd better bung it in the mike for a bit first, then Madeleine won't fuss.'

'Why any member of this family is still above ground beats me,' Archie remarked, but the look in his eyes as he watched Pauly hurry off to the utility room, lifting the soft mass of her toffee-coloured hair away from her neck in a habitual gesture as she went, was one of love.

Cristi, seeing it, smiled to herself. It was the essence of home.

And she was to go from it. She stood up quickly, tipping Broy, who had been fast asleep and didn't think much of this ruthlessness, onto the floor. He had been christened Rob Roy, in the tradition of Scott names for the Dinmonts, but Tom's elder son was Rob, and the nursery contraction of Broy had been convenient.

Cristi, her mind following this track, knew she was

seizing on trivia to keep dread at bay. Every facet of home seemed precious and significant. She wondered wryly how she was going to get through the days before her departure, strung up like this.

But she knew that what she was really asking, above and beyond everything else, was how she was going to deal with seeing Dougal – with saying goodbye to Dougal. How could she go away with everything between them so out of kilter?

But that must wait. First came Madeleine, Archie and Lisa's mother, and Tom her husband. Madeleine had been the first person to look after Cristi at Drumveyn when, bewildered and frightened, sent halfway across the world with only a stranger to deliver her to other strangers, she had arrived in the winter darkness at this unknown house. How cold and gloomy it had been then, draughty, meagrely heated, tree-shrouded, ordered by the unbending rules of the past. Yet Cristi had found in it a warmth, humanity and balanced good sense to which she had responded with instinctive appreciation.

Suddenly she couldn't wait to see Madeleine.

'I'll go and change,' she said, but paused beside Archie for a moment, linking her hands on his shoulder. His arm went round her, and she leaned there, shutting her eyes, and for them both it was reclaiming a moment from the past.

'You're our eldest, Cristi,' Archie said, pulling her close. 'Nothing will ever change that.'

She nodded, unable to speak, dropped a kiss on the top of his head and fled away to her room.

It had been the dressing-room of Madeleine's first husband, Charles, and was a dull slit of a room, but Cristi had clung to it in spite of offers of larger and more comfortable quarters as she grew up. Though the first room she had ever slept in alone, it had adjoined Madeleine's and she had felt safe there. That had mattered. Also it satisfied a scarcely recognised need in her for functional simplicity, and through all the changes which had overtaken the house she had never wanted anything else. It was very small, but a munificent twenty-first birthday present from Archie and Pauly — the conversion of the old laundry across the courtyard into a studio — had provided space for many of her belongings, though she continued to sleep in the house.

When Archie and Pauly married neither of them had wanted to use the dark and formal room which Archie remembered first as the scary habitat of his repressive grandmother, then as the equally unwelcoming bedroom of his parents. Pauly had got around to redecorating it in time and, with its turret windows and wide views, not forgetting the Victorian splendours of its bathroom, which Cristi mostly had to herself, it had become a much-favoured guest room.

Walking into her own little abode after the weeks away was always a pleasure but now, with the sun streaming in through the window which took up most of the end wall, its light hazing the treetops with gold and gilding the ridges of Ben Breac as it began its leisurely mid-summer descent, her delight in it was almost too acute to bear.

Don't think, get on with the next thing. It was bliss to sink into the enormous bath, where if she wanted to keep her hair dry she had to take some trouble not to float away, and let the pressures of the last thirty or so hours wash away. Thirty hours. She had picked up the letter yesterday at lunch-time and had phoned Pauly at once. Since then a whole life had ended.

Archie's words came back: 'You don't have to do anything you don't want to do.' Was that true? Did she have a choice? Could the whole thing be seen as some sort of fabulous adventure?

But the memory, more a settled idea in her mind than any direct personal experience, of the way that her mother's family had denied her existence, came disturbingly back, and with an exclamation of exasperation to find her moment of peace destroyed, she hauled herself out and wrapped herself in the bathsheet comfortably warm from the antique heated rail. Padding back to her room she pulled on briefs, top and skirt over her still damp skin. There were going to be no easy answers, she warned herself grimly.

They walked to the steading, catching up on news, enjoying the perfect evening, Archie with the lasagne in a basket, Broy trotting at their heels. He'd given up chasing rabbits, and cats, or anything at all really. Quiet life now.

In the upper room of the converted barn the French windows that ran across the gable end were open, and the impression was of light and space. Tom came bowling towards them in his wheelchair across the floor of rich red Paraná pine, his face alight with pleasure to see Cristi. Madeleine, busy at the kitchen end of the open living space, left what she was doing and hurried after him.

'Darling, darling girl!'

She had promised herself she would be matter-of-fact and accept sensibly whatever must happen, but at the sight of Cristi, to her eyes so young and vulnerable, so dearly cherished, tears she could do nothing about rose in her eyes. Cristi, her own eyes prickling, went thankfully into her soft embrace.

Later, as the shadows of the infinitely slow Highland dusk filled the glen, they were able to talk in practical terms of all that had to be decided.

'I can't not go,' Cristi said. 'That's the bottom line, isn't it?'

'Only if it's your choice.' Tom was as definite on that as Archie had been.

'It's something I can't dodge, though, isn't it?' This was what Cristi kept coming back to. 'Even apart from obligations or responsibility or the need to sort things out – God, owning a cattle ranch, I can't even begin to imagine it – apart from any of that, this is something I have to do, isn't it? Do for me, I mean.'

They waited as she searched for words, each knowing in some sense what was coming.

'I mean, it's about who I am.'

There was suddenly an edge almost of defiance in her voice, and it brought from Madeleine an involuntary stir of protest. Tom's hand reached for hers and gave it a warning pressure. They mustn't let their own feelings get in the way here.

'You know, I never give it a thought for months on end, years on end,' Cristi said awkwardly, dreading hurting them. 'You must realise that. You *are* my family. Only, sometimes, things remind me. Somebody talking about the way I look, that kind of thing.'

Such comments had been a totally unforeseen feature of her first term at Edinburgh, and were one of the reasons why it had been a rare unhappy period for her. 'It's this thing of not being really related. Even Lisa, who was supposed to be my guardian, on paper I mean, isn't strictly speaking anything to do with me, is she?'

Lisa, the member of the family to whom Cristi was least close, had been, until her divorce from Cristi's father was finalised, her stepmother, but it had never been anything more than a formality.

Cristi drew a deep breath. 'It's just that — well, sometimes I feel I need to *know* . . .'

Catching something close to desperation in her voice, Archie moved quietly to sit on the arm of her chair, his arm along its back. He didn't touch her — he wasn't sure if he could deal with that himself, let alone making it harder for her to go on — but he wanted to tell her that he was there for her, that they all were.

Broy half thought of moving to where the action was, but he'd had too much dinner. He sank back into slumber.

Cristi twisted round to give Archie a quick smile before plunging on. 'It's a lot to do with the way I look, if that doesn't sound too far-fetched.' She had never tried to talk about this before. 'If I'd looked like my father, English, I mean, with his colouring, it would be different. But look at me. It's quite obvious I don't belong.'

'Oh, Cristi, how can you say that?' Madeleine began in distress, but once more Tom warned her to silence.

'You know I don't mean—' Cristi wasn't sure she could go on with this, but tried again. 'I know it must sound hideously ungrateful after everything you've—'

'Hey, come on.' It was Archie who interrupted this time. Unthinkable to go there. 'Cristi, we know what you mean. Don't worry about all that side of things, just say whatever you want to say. We all know how we feel, no doubts on that score.'

Cristi nodded, grateful, then pressed her fingers to her forehead, marshalling her thoughts. Archie found himself noticing her hands, as if to give point to what she had been saying. They were unlike the hands of any other female he knew, including his mother's, and hers had been beautiful when she was younger. These were hands of someone belonging to another race, delicate and fine-boned.

'There have always been the questions.' Cristi was speaking almost to herself now. 'I realised there was a part of me I knew nothing about, almost didn't have control over. Then I'd wonder about my – my parents.' It was hard to use the word meaning Howard and Justina. 'About what they did, why they did it. Where they went. Where they *are*.' It was invariably a fresh shock to think of them as still existing, living their lives somewhere, perhaps with other children, growing older.

'But I'm not sure you'll discover more about any of that,' Pauly couldn't help breaking in anxiously. She dreaded the thought of Cristi facing more pain on this, the hardest aspect of the whole awful business. 'I mean, this is more about Justina's family, isn't it? About her father dying.'

She broke off, shooting a guilty look at Archie. Justina's father, but Cristi's grandfather. How could she have been so tactless? But it was hard to imagine that Cristi could feel much at such news about the hostile and implacable old man who had dealt so summarily with Archie during their single encounter.

Archie shook his head at her, then pulled a little face to tell her that he understood, and she felt better.

'Cristi, look.' Archie decided a more practical tone was called for. 'You know that if you feel you should go then whatever has to be arranged will be arranged – flights, making contact with the lawyers when you get there, somewhere to stay, whatever. There'll be no difficulty with any of that. The only thing is, I'm not sure who'll be able to go with you.'

He hated to say it, but since Tom's disablement, in the accident which had also brought about the first of the strokes which had killed Dougal's father, Archie had been busier than he had ever been before. Madeleine couldn't leave Tom, and she counted on a good deal of day-to-day help from Pauly, who in any case would soon have the younger children home.

Lisa, who in theory might also be called on, would no doubt find it impossible to take time off from the kennels. And would she be the ideal companion anyway, with her breezy lack of perception and her impatience with anything she categorised as 'sentimental twaddle'?

'Archie, no,' Cristi was protesting, 'it's really, really kind of you to think of it, but this is something I should handle on my own. Have to handle on my own,' she added, sending him a look which begged him to understand and accept this without further argument.

Archie did understand. She needed to discover that part of her heritage, of herself, in which Drumveyn had no share, and to do that she was probably right in insisting that she make the long journey alone.

Chapter Three

It was only a couple of hundred yards from the barn to Steading Cottage. The light was still on in the kitchen, as Cristi had expected. Jean was always a late bird, and in any case it barely felt like night, for dusk hadn't yet turned to dark up here on the open hillside.

Tom never stayed up late now, tired after exerting himself always a little more, a little more, every day, building up the muscles with painful slowness and resolve. Taking him down for physio had been a big demand on Madeleine, particularly through the winter months when she had had to drive all the way down to Ninewells. Now that Tom could go to bi-weekly sessions at the hospital in Muirend things were easier, and the fact that he had made sufficient progress to move between chair and bed without being lifted had made an immense difference. Then those first steps he had taken; how excited they had all been, and how proud Madeleine was of his achievement. She'd handled it all incredibly bravely, but there was no doubt that the shock of the accident, the fear of losing Tom, and the long haul back to this limited mobility had had its effect on her. Her dark hair was now silver, and she was much thinner than she used to be. Thinner than Tom liked, as he didn't fail to say, doing his best to get her to eat more, do less, indulge herself a little.

Cristi found herself smiling. She always enjoyed seeing them together, valuing their quiet contentment, their dislike of being apart, and the way they had shaped their existence in the old barn to suit their needs. Their happy relationship had been a satisfying and enriching element in the background of her life as she grew up.

At first, when Tom was still in hospital, it had looked as though it might be impractical for them to go on living in the barn, and Madeleine had steeled herself to face a move, either back to the big house or even to somewhere 'more convenient' lower down the glen. But Archie had seen no problem in making any modifications required to allow them to stay where they were, in the simple surroundings Tom had designed for himself when he came to Drumveyn as factor, in the year when Cristi herself had arrived.

A ramp had been built at the downstairs entrance and a lift installed, and the lower floor bedrooms, originally intended for Tom's sons, were now used by Tom and Madeleine, and a shower designed for wheelchair use was added. The open spaces of the upper room, with its hardwood floors, had needed no modification other than some rearrangement of the furniture. A nurse had stayed down at the house when Tom first came home, and after he left Archie and Pauly had given Madeleine the necessary help with lifting. There were many other willing hands on tap on the estate, however, not least Dougal, who at Steading Cottage had been one of the closest, and he had done more than his share. Lisa was not far away at Achalder, formerly an estate cottage, and her husband Stephen, if prompted, was more than willing to be of use. By this time Tom was not only a bit more mobile, but was also equipped with an electric buggy in which he could buzz about the estate roads on his own, restoring to him a degree of freedom and independence which made a huge difference to his life – and to Madeleine's.

Tonight Archie would put Tom to bed, and Pauly was helping Madeleine to tidy up after dinner, and no one had minded Cristi slipping away.

Delighted as she had been to find Tom looking so well, clearly in less pain than when she had last been at home, and reassuring as it was to see the matter-of-fact way in which he and Madeleine had adapted to a day-to-day existence limited by his disability, it was impossible as she approached the shepherd's cottage to avoid a wry comparison.

Money. Money could provide care and equipment, modify houses, smooth all paths. Money, of which she herself now appeared to possess large quantities – though Tom and Archie had both been anxious to warn of the fool's gold potential of dazzling inheritances. There would be many people ready to pounce on whatever there was, they predicted. There was no way of knowing what condition the ranch was in, or what obligations and possibly debts and encumbrances it might bring with it. No way of knowing either what claims other members of the family might make, what objections might be raised to what could only be seen as the bizarre, if not vindictive, decision her grandfather had made.

However, Cristi's thoughts ran on, even if this un-looked-for legacy did turn out to have little or no substance, the truth was that it wouldn't make much difference to her. Her father had amply provided for her when he had disappeared, just as he had for Lisa. Archie had not only ably managed these funds for Cristi over the years, but had also made her a generous allowance on his own behalf. Though Cristi fully intended to earn her own living, and it was accepted that she should do so, she couldn't pretend that Napier money wouldn't always be there in the background, hers without question if ever she needed it.

Money. She knew why that stir of reluctance, almost of guilt, had made itself felt as she covered the short distance to the steading. It was all about contrasts, contrasts endemic in society, in all societies, which were beginning to make her more and more uncomfortable, and which seemed to have no solution.

And yet, she reminded herself, focusing once more on the particular, almost as much had been done for Donnie Galloway after the accident as had been done for Tom, though in different ways. While Donnie was recovering from his first stroke Archie had continued to pay his full wages, and had seen to it that Jean received all the immediate practical help that she needed.

Donnie had recovered a degree of fitness and had returned to shepherding, but whatever he said it had been obvious that he couldn't manage on his own, and part-time help had been provided. Not that Donnie had welcomed it, or made the life of his assistant very agreeable, Cristi recalled with a fleeting grin. As he suffered two more, though still minor, strokes the gaps had gone on being discreetly filled by one means or another, but even though in the end Donnie could barely make a pretence of doing his job, Archie had made it clear to Jean that she need feel no fears about her security of tenure in the cottage.

But of course such fears had never been out of Jean's mind. Living in a tied house, her man sick, forever trying to do more than he was able, but at the end of the day past managing his job. And knowing it, saying nothing, burning himself up with fury at his own uselessness, looking at a future trapped in some wee box of a house, nothing to occupy him, his strength wasted, his hands idle. Washed up, underfoot, bored out of his mind.

When Donnie had died last February, almost the first thing Archie had said to Jean was that the house was still hers for as long as she needed it.

So Donnie and Jean had been looked after, in the traditional way not often found on estates today. Looked after as Tom had been. Yet with this telling difference. They had been cared for as employees. They had needed help, having barely made provision for retirement beyond relying on the customary move to a council house, never attempting to save what it would cost to own a house of their own, not even aspiring to it. Jean had never worked to boost their income. She had been a housewife, bringing up a family; but also a busy shepherd's wife who helped with the lambing as a matter of course, cooked mounds of mince and tatties for the men at clipping time, fed calves, kept hens, grew vegetables, made jam, supported the WRI, fought against the closure of the glen school, and almost never managed a holiday.

Now she lived every day in this house knowing that she had no right to be in it. She lay awake every night in the lonely bed staring at the ceiling and wondering what to do for the best, her troubles black as the bats slicing and wheeling through the half-dark of summer.

Cristi paused with her hand on the doorknob, suddenly aware that she needed to collect her resources against what she might find. For this was not just about Jean. In her own life too, money and all it could bring had the power to drive wedges and open gulfs. And now, at this moment, in a faraway country which she could barely remember, it seemed there were startling amounts of it waiting to be claimed. A grotesque vision of coffers spilling out screes of gold arose from nowhere, and she shivered, seeing the image as evil and destructive. It was time for a dose of Jean's prosaic good sense.

She turned the knob, calling, 'Hi, Jean! It's only me, don't get up.'

But Jean was in the kitchen doorway at once, her smile

of welcome twisted out of shape by the rush of other emotions, her arms held out.

'Oh, lassie, but it does me good to see you. How are you keeping – and what's all this I've been hearing about you? Oh here, take no notice of me, I'm just being daft, and at my age too.' For Cristi's answering hug had made her sniff and scrabble under her apron for a handkerchief. 'Come away in, don't stand there. You'll have a cuppie wi' me? Of course you will . . .'

Jean was alone. One of the cats surveyed Cristi from the safety of the dark vault under the dresser, the other squirmed and stretched on the beaten-down cushions of the old wooden-armed chair, digging in with its claws, inviting attention. Donnie's chair. Cristi saw with piercing vividness his strong, broad-shouldered body filling it, the weathered skin of his neck and arms, the faded check shirt, the dark blue dungarees he always wore, the mug of tea on the chair arm where innumerable pale rings still showed. Her eyes stung, and she went quickly to where Jean was plugging in the kettle.

No old blackened kettle simmering on the edge of the hob now, ready to be drawn over the flames and brought to the boil on demand. No whistling kettle either, on the blue-enamelled gas cooker Jean used to use if the fire wasn't lit. Steading Cottage had long ago acquired the modern fitted kitchen Jean had dreamed about, put in by Archie to her own specification.

'How are you?' Cristi asked softly, coming close, and Jean gripped her arm for a second with a still strong hand, and gave a couple of vigorous nods.

'I'm just fine,' she said. 'Don't you be worrying about me.'

'And how are Dougal and Jill?' Easy to slip past the moment by asking about both at once.

'Ach, they're just the same as ever they were. I've nothing to complain about wi' Dougal anyway.' Jean's lips folded tightly, and Cristi accepted their message: this welcoming moment was not to be spoiled by discussing the disaster Jill had made of her life. 'Now,' Jean went on, her tone clearly implying that they'd got that safely behind them, 'are you for cake or biscuits or what? Not that you'll have long finished your dinner. Me, I couldn't sit down to a meal like yon at this time of night.' And never would approve of the idea. 'Still, I daresay you're used to it.'

'Thanks, but you're right. I couldn't eat another thing,' Cristi admitted. 'But you have your supper.'

'Well, I'll mebbe have a bite.' And Jean went back and forth assembling a simple meal.

A bit of meat pie, cheese and crackers, gingerbread maybe, or a slice of whatever cake was on the go. It was what Donnie had always liked, a good snack, since he'd have had his tea at the back of five. Jean often thought in his words, in his voice, and sometimes when she did he would seem so close that she couldn't remember any more what she had set out to do, and would find herself standing at mid-floor, staring confusedly at whatever she was holding. Such moments were hard to bear.

Cristi, watching the movements of Jean's hands, so much less sure and deft than formerly, was also struck by how shabby Jean looked, something new for her, as though she didn't care about herself any more. It was hard to pin down where the change lay, for Jean had never been much interested in clothes. She had her things for best, scrupulously adhering to glen fashion, a floral print with a fancy neckline for parties and ceilidhs, a dark coat for funerals, a pleated skirt and nice blouse and cardigan for the rare occasions when visitors were expected. But her everyday clothes she wore to their last gasp of usefulness, and she had never forsaken the old-fashioned but convenient habit of covering everything up with a wrap-around pinafore. Trekking back and forth across the steading yard in all weathers at this windy height her hair had usually been untidy, and her hands had always shown unmistakable evidence of hard use. But now her skin looked grey, her hair needed washing, and there was a sag to her shoulders, a downturn to her mouth, which struck Cristi with dismay.

'So you've had some exciting news yourself, I'm hearing,' Jean prompted, putting down on its stained wooden stand the big brown teapot which she always filled as though still feeding a family of five. In her view tea never tasted the same if you made it in dribs and drabs. 'Sit in about,' she ordered.

Donnie had always preferred to sit at the table for his supper. Even if she only had a cuppie to herself at this time of the evening she always sat there too.

'I don't know whether it's exciting or just plain terrifying,' Cristi confessed, sitting down across the familiar red chenille cloth, which always covered diamond-wise by a smaller white tablecloth for proper meals. Though she had never seen Jean's table without this red cloth, she knew it had always been shaken out of the door and put back after every meal. Now crumbs and what looked like traces of egg yolk clung to its ribs. She looked away. The house-proud Jean of her childhood would never have countenanced such a thing.

Jean looked at her over the cup she was nursing in both hands. She didn't drink from it, nor did she take any of the food she had laid out.

'It'll no' be easy, hearing from your folks after all this time,' she said.

The forthright words brought instantly back the Jean Cristi remembered, the sensible, capable, active housewife and mother, always welcoming, always good-natured, who had been happy with her life in the crowded little cottage. The glimpse of the past was steadying, banishing for the moment half-apprehended concerns.

It also made it possible to open up to Jean the mixed bag of doubts and fears, but also of excitement and curiosity, which the news from Brazil had produced. Talking about it with the family there had been the dread of hurting them. Now wild speculations could be aired without being given undue weight, or raising questions which would then be tactfully suppressed. There was no risk of giving pain as she tried to sort out, for her own benefit as much as anything, her immediate reactions to what had happened, and acknowledged for the first time the startlingly keen longing which had seized her to get to know this part of her heritage.

It would put Jean neither up nor down, as she herself would say, if Cristi summoned up the fragmented memories of her early years in Rio, when she had spent her days enclosed and isolated in a small but beautiful and luxurious house, rarely seeing her frivolous socialite mother, stability and company provided by servants and in particular by her own maid, Isaura.

But then a jarring note was struck. Cristi, still finding it hard to take in, went on to talk about what she saw as something of a joke – the amazing fact that her grandfather had left her his cattle ranch.

'The Ranch of the Three Pines,' she quoted with relish. 'Doesn't that sound a bit romantic? Or a bit Laurel and Hardy? Anyway, can you imagine it having anything to do with me?'

'Aye well, you'll be getting too grand for us now altogether,' Jean commented sharply, getting up and rattling together the cups and saucers and the plate she hadn't used. 'Owning land and the lord knows what besides.'

Cristi was horrified at her own tactlessness. Fine to talk about going back to her roots, perhaps at last meeting the family who had refused all recognition of her existence till now, or to indulge in dipping into memories usually kept locked away, but she should never have referred to her actual inheritance.

Of course Jean couldn't help being tart on the subject. Why should she hide her resentment? But Cristi had sense enough to know that the reaction had less to do with her personally than with a deep-seated disillusionment at Jean's own situation and prospects for the future, and the general unfairness of fortune.

Flushing, Cristi knew that to attempt an apology would only cause deeper embarrassment. Jean, busy emptying the teapot at the sink, was saying over her shoulder, 'So when is it you're to be off?'

Not the dismissal it sounded like, as Cristi fortunately understood.

'We'll have to start thinking about that tomorrow,' she replied, and felt a cold clutch at her heart. Was she really going to leave here? 'But I can't be off right away. I may have to have inoculations and things, and there's the journey to organise and so on.'

Jean sniffed. Such things were outside her ken. 'We'll be seeing something of you before you go then.'

'Of course you will. Only, Jean, you didn't say very much before but – can I ask – where is Jill these days? Is she all right?' She found it beyond her to enquire about Dougal again, but hopefully, she did so much hope, she would be seeing him soon anyway.

'That one.' Jean turned to face her, twisting the ragged old towel on which she had just dried her hands. 'Don't be asking me about that one.' She glanced at the clock, her mouth grim. 'She'll be in when it suits her and not before.'

So Jill was living at home. That answered one question.

'Dougal should be back any minute, though,' Jean added in a different tone. 'He's been over at Riach, seeing Ed Cullane about some part for the Land Rover. Though

I'd not put anything I got from Ed Cullane into any vehicle of mine. Not if I wanted it to go.'

So Dougal too was still at home. Relief filled Cristi. She hadn't found herself able to ask the simple question during the evening, and his name hadn't been mentioned. Had people avoided it, aware that the solid friendship of years was foundering?

But relief was succeeded by panic. Dougal might come in, and finding her there think she was waiting for him. Then both feelings were overtaken by disbelief that she should be going through such hoops over Dougal.

'He'll not be best pleased to hear you're off abroad so soon,' Jean remarked and Cristi looked at her quickly. But the comment clearly held no overtones, and the little flurry of eager hope died.

'We're all going to miss you,' Jean added as they said goodnight at the door, and with that Cristi supposed she must be content.

Chapter Four

Starting down towards the house, Cristi saw a single downstairs light on at the barn. Madeleine reading. She admitted to not having slept well since Tom's accident, and seeing that light Cristi felt a hungry longing for everything to be as it used to be, no one hurt, no one lonely or grieving. She knew the wish was childish, part of an instinctive resistance to the changes so suddenly looming in her own future.

Was there a chance she'd meet Dougal as he came up? From here she could see clear across to the glen road. No lights. If she went slowly . . . She at once went faster, ashamed of being tempted to such a strategy, then demanded aloud, 'What are you *doing*?' If she wanted to meet Dougal then make it happen. Waylaying him on the drive was exactly what she would have done in the past, before this odd, uncomfortable distance widened between them, and neither of them would have thought anything of it. But now, hanging about on the off-chance of seeing him seemed all wrong. No, better to go up to Steading Cottage tomorrow evening when he was back from work. Phoning first, to make sure it was all right.

Odd that Jean hadn't talked of him more tonight. She was always so proud of Dougal, and particularly now, when she relied on him at every turn. But of course the chief topic had been Cristi's own news; she shivered as the scale of it came home to her again.

Where the drive divided, one fork looping left to keep farm traffic away from the house, she firmly took the other, which led past the old game larder, greenhouses and garden sheds to the courtyard with its garages, log shed, workshop and now her own studio. Archie had left the door to the kitchen passage open as usual, but as she was closing it behind her she changed her mind again.

Why shouldn't she wait for Dougal? He was her friend, and the friend she cared about and trusted most in the world. Nothing could change that. What could be more natural than to want to see him, especially now when everything in her life was flung into turmoil?

She went out again, across the courtyard, round the end of the north wing and down the main drive. Among the sheltering trees it was darker, but she didn't slow down. She would never sleep if she went in without seeing Dougal. She thought of his tough, muscular build, the heavy shoulders like his father's in his old worn jacket, his look of total concentration when some job threatened to defeat him, his half-hidden smile when he was teasing her, the big grin she could so easily provoke; the images brought a longing whose violence shook her.

She wanted the safety of being with him, the reassurance that something which had been fundamental to her existence since her very first day at Drumveyn was still there for her.

A memory not thought of for years bobbed up, clear in every detail. It belonged to that first day. The terrors of the journey fading, but everything still strange and alarming, names, faces, voices, food, clothes, new things expected of her, the cold, and the great grey house among the empty white hills.

Madeleine had taken her up to Steading Cottage – to return clothes of Jill's temporarily borrowed; she'd forgotten all about that – and Dougal and Jill had carried her off to see some new puppies. They had raced away ahead of her, crossing the mud of the yard without a thought, and for an alarmed moment she had hung back, unsure, conditioned by a very different environment and very different rules. And Dougal had turned to look for her, had come back, and had seemed to understand her doubts, stretching out a hand for hers, leading her by the best route to the byre. The air of that day seemed to be in her nostrils now, scent of snow on the wind, scent of fir trees, of wet stone and bruised straw. All things which had become so infinitely familiar, which meant home.

Waiting on the hump-backed bridge, not sure that moment of piercing nostalgia had been what she needed just now, Cristi tried to let the quiet night sounds soothe her, the call of an oystercatcher, a tawny owl somewhere across the hayfields, sheep. At this time of year, no matter how late or early, there would always be the hoarse voice of a ewe, the higher cry of a lamb.

It seemed a long time since she had paused on the bridge coming home. But she didn't have much longer to wait. The reaching fingers of headlights appeared, and the raucous sound of the venerable canvas-topped Land Rover Dougal had more or less rebuilt overtook the peaceful night noises. Tension rushed back, and uncertainty. What would he think of her for waiting about for him like this? What if he thought they'd moved on from there? What if he saw it as cheap, the sort of thing Jill might do, which made him so angry?

Cristi then did the silliest thing so far in all this silly dithering. She hid. She ran down the slope of the bridge, vaulted over the stone parapet of the approach and tried to find cover. Dew-laden sweet cecily, tall cranesbill and heavy-leaved comfrey instantly soaked her and made it hard to move forward. Her sandals were so wet her feet couldn't grip them. There were nettles too, and a trailing spray of dog rose caught at her shoulder.

She was too late in any case. The lights had caught her, and Dougal would never miss the slightest movement or detail out of place in the familiar scene. The Land Rover swung over the bridge and checked. Then, with both relief and disbelief, she heard it pick up speed again. But only for a moment. It had stopped, was backing up. The engine died, leaving a brief silence before the softer natural sounds made themselves heard again.

As Cristi shamefacedly picked a way back, her sandals

sliding about maddeningly, she heard the door slam, and Dougal's measured tread on the tarmac.

'Here.' He leaned down, reaching his hand to her just as he had done in that memory of the past.

Cristi put her cold wet hand in his, found a toehold and felt the smooth output of strength as he pulled her up beside him. She nearly lost a sandal and, curling her toes to hold on to it, gasped as cramp seized her instep.

'You all right?'

'Cramp.'

He held her arm as she bent and tried to pull against her icy toes. Wincing with pain, furiously impatient that this boring nuisance should take over the precious first moment of meeting, knowing it was her own fault and that she'd been a fool, Cristi wished with all her heart that she had had the sense to go home and go to bed.

This was all wrong, Dougal holding her arm in rock-like silence, waiting while she sorted herself out. With sudden passionate need she wanted things to be as they had always been. He should have dropped down on one knee, letting her steady herself with a hand on his shoulder as he took her freezing, agonisingly crimped foot in his strong warm hands and worked the pain out of it with his capable touch. That was how it should have been.

And when he came to haul her back onto the drive he should have said, 'What in God's name are you playing at down there?' so that she could have said, 'Hiding from you,' and they'd have laughed, and conversation would have rolled on, ordinary and effortless.

'OK now?'

'Yes, thanks.' A twinge in her calf as she put her foot to the cold tarmac warned Cristi it wasn't, but she was desperate to break the deadlock of silence and awkwardness. Surely after a whole term away there should be more than this, a greeting of some kind if not a hug or a friendly kiss. But it was a long time since there had been such contact, she had to admit. How lovely it had been, she thought forlornly, when touch had been part of the pleasure of being together again, normal life resumed, knowing that without discussion they would spend every moment possible in each other's company while she was home. Touch then had been Dougal's broad palm ruffling her hair, a mock punch thrown, a hand to help her over some obstacle, a casual whirl round in his arms, particularly when he had been teasing her and knew she was getting cross.

Now he withdrew his arm as soon as she put her foot to the ground, and actually took a step back, away from her, looking at her with an expression she found difficult to read in the half light.

'Want a lift up to the house?' he asked, after a pause that seemed to stretch for ever.

Protests, explanations, appeals, flurried up in Cristi and failed to shape themselves into words.

'Yes, please,' she said meekly.

In the Land Rover the past engulfed her. It felt comfortably warm, its air redolent with the mingled smells of diesel, canvas, tools, dogs, dust, straw and sacking. Without needing to see she could visualise the clutter in the compartments along the dash, the oily rags, the twist of wire, the tangle of string, the dirt-stiffened gloves, the odd spanner and the silt of washers, screws and rusty nuts and bolts under the rest. Back rushed the memories, of hours spent with Dougal in this vehicle on their way to do some job about the estate, to beat or ghillie, howk tatties, help at lambing or gathering, dipping or clipping, to clear ditches or mend dykes, to burn heather, plant trees or repair the ravages of storms. This battered old vehicle had also taken them to ceilidhs and parties, first-footing at Hogmanay, down to the pub in the village or over to the Cluny Arms, to the Kirkton Show and every other event in the glen calendar. And often they had simply sat here, sheltering from some bitter snow flurry or particularly heavy downpour, or because they had started to talk and everything else had been forgotten. Those hours and hours of talk . . . The memories, flooding back, brought an ache of helpless nostalgia to Cristi.

'I've been up at your mother's,' she said, seizing on anything to talk about which seemed normal and obvious, though her voice didn't sound quite normal, she found. 'I went up after having dinner at the barn.'

'Oh aye.'

'Then I was coming down and and I—'

Don't, don't, the voice of sense warned her. Leave it. How could she say she had longed to see him then had chickened out? Had it been obvious that she was trying to hide? Could he have thought she was simply walking along the river bank? She didn't think it very likely, and inwardly cursed that unlucky impulse to run. How she hated this second-guessing or anything less than straight-forward between them.

'I hoped I might see you,' she said.

Dougal said nothing. Were they going to arrive at the house without another word exchanged? This silence seemed to hold more than the constraint which had developed between them in the last year. It seemed to hold actual hostility, and that was unbearable. There was only one explanation that Cristi could think of. Jean's words came chillingly back. So you'll be getting too grand for us now.

Matters couldn't be left like this. They'd be at the house in another two seconds. She went for it.

'Did your mother tell you about — the letter I've had from Brazil?' She felt it was essential to choose the right words, yet hated having to do so.

Dougal turned his head briefly, then looked ahead again. 'She did,' he said after a pause.

'It's all a bit scary.' Cristi was conscious of her voice sounding almost apologetic, and was angry with herself. She really didn't know how to deal with this.

'Yes, you'll not have been expecting it,' Dougal said politely.

This isn't how we talk, she thought with despair. Where were the ready words, the laughter, the under-standing taken so carelessly for granted for so long? Dougal, don't you know it's tearing me apart to think of going? I'm terrified at the thought of meeting these people who've always loathed the very fact of my existence. It's so weird to imagine myself back there, in a country I barely remember. And I'm having a really hard time handling the bad vibes I get when I try to piece the memories together. Surely you can see that.

If she couldn't find a way to say this to him, how much harder it would be to try and explain the tug of fascination and challenge which made itself felt in spite of her fears and resistance, the feeling that mysteries buried for too long should be unravelled. And how could she find words for the instinct which told her this must be faced, whatever the consequences?

Already they were through the belt of trees, crossing the open space created by Archie when he first began the work of letting light into the sombre house, with its rules and repressions, its nursery nightmares and adult absence of love.

Round into the courtyard. The Land Rover pulling up.

'Dougal, please –' Cristi hardly knew what she wanted to say. She only knew she didn't want him to drive away. She made no move to get out. 'Could we talk?'

He lifted his arm and turned his watch towards the light over the door, and she felt herself blushing.

'I'm sorry. Of course it's late, and you've got to go to work in the morning.'

'I have.' Nevertheless he switched off his lights and the engine and, though he didn't turn towards her, waited for what she had to say without any sign of impatience.

'Would you like to come in?' Cristi suggested, though hesitantly. 'We could have—'

'No, I'll not come in.' She knew that tone of old. Any attempt at persuasion would be useless. Still, he was there. She must take her chance.

'Dougal, I feel so mixed up about this whole thing. It's hard to take in. College, Edinburgh, the flat, all wiped out overnight. Then being home again . . .'

She broke off. Being home. How could she put into words all that that meant, especially now? But in the past she wouldn't have had to.

A small silence, then Dougal said, 'Things have to move on, Cristi.' In spite of the bald words there was something in his voice which comforted her, a message that he had understood much that had not been said.

'Well, I just wish they wouldn't,' she muttered rebelliously. 'I hate change.'

'That's talking like a child.' No comfort there. Another pause. 'It seems to me,' Dougal went on, and now there was a real hint of feelings suppressed beneath his even tone, 'that plenty people would be glad to hear the kind of news you've just had.'

Again Cristi felt the colour rise to her cheeks. The last thing she had looked for was this measured but unmistakable rebuke. But of course this was how he would see it, and who could blame him? A startling inheritance falling into her lap, of the kind few people would dream of, and she was complaining.

How stark by comparison his own circumstances must appear, forced as he had been to abandon his plans for university and settle instead for a course at the local college; obliged to be at home and reluctantly taking a job as manager of an agricultural supplier's in Muirend; putting in as much time as he could helping out on Drumveyn during Donnie's illness — and now, still — as some repayment for Archie's generosity, and picking up any extra jobs he could to supplement the family income. He not only made himself responsible for Jean, since his elder brother Donald, always wild and uncontrollable, gave her more grief than support, but at the same time did his best to deal with the troubles Jill brought on them. Dougal, with his hunger for land, his longing to farm no matter what crisis farming was in, his fierce desire for an independence he had little hope of achieving, had every reason to be angered by her ingratitude for the good fortune which had come her way.

'I am glad,' she said guiltily. 'Grateful anyway. Of course I know how lucky I've been. It's just that it's so out of the blue, and all tied up with that business when I was a child, my parents shunting me off, my mother's family not wanting to know . . .'

Why was she saying this? Dougal knew the story as well as she did.

He turned his head away, though there was nothing to look at but the blank doors of the garages. He took his time to sift through the words he longed to spill out, letting himself be swept away by a rare anger he hardly understood himself. Anger at circumstances which couldn't be altered. Anger because Cristi had hidden from him tonight. Hidden from *him*. He had been right; the gulf between them had yawned too wide and was impassable. They lived in different worlds. He should be thankful that she was going, out of his life, so that the pain of departures and the almost equal pain when she returned, her nearness and inaccessibility, the chance glimpses he lived for, the aching difference between past and present, could no longer torment him.

But even as he thought this a wild resolve never to let anything or anyone take her from him banished reason and good sense. Jesus, she could put him through hoops.

All this he crushed down ruthlessly.

'I'd best be off,' he said, then winced at the harshness he had not intended her to hear. 'It's getting late,' he added more gently.

Wouldn't he even talk to her any more? Blind with tears, Cristi fumbled for the door handle.

'Hang on.' He was out and round at her side to offer his hand as she slid down.

'Thanks, Dougal.' He could barely catch the words, and bent his head to hers as he held onto her hand for one extra fraction of a second. Dougal wasn't tall, and had desperately minded this, and his stocky build, when he was in his teens, but Cristi was so small and finely built that with her he was never conscious of his lack of height.

'Good night, Dougal.'

Was that it? He didn't even say goodnight in return. But he stood to watch her go in.

'Cristi!' He hadn't known he was going to call.

She turned eagerly.

'Listen, we'll talk. Another time. OK?'

He saw the lift of her hand. '*Good!*' he heard her say, and the door was shut.

'Take care.' He said it aloud, watching her flit from one window to the next along the lighted corridor. Cliché, meaningless leave-taking. From him, for her, words spoken from the heart.

Chapter Five

Dougal, not forgetting for the sake of sleeping Napiers to make as little noise as possible as he drove off, headed for the farm. He imagined Cristi running noiselessly up through the big house he knew so well, to her own narrow, simple room.

In fact Cristi was leaning against the kitchen door, her head tilted back, her eyes screwed tight, doing her best to cope with the sort of wrenching sobs it would be fatal to give way to. She knew that if once she began to cry she would never stop. Tiredness after what felt like an endless day; the realisation that the student years were over for good and that she had left a host of friends behind, especially Torie and Isa and the hectic, happy life they had shared; anger at the distant family who cared nothing for her, yet expected her to jump at their summons; and dread at the thought of the long flight to a country where she was now a foreigner, crowded in on her till she felt she couldn't bear any of it.

Even so, she was aware that all this was peripheral to the central core of pain. To be with Dougal and find it impossible to talk, to have been so idiotic as to hide from him, and not even to have done it effectively, so that he was bound to be puzzled and hurt, to have this strange barrier rear between them — it was unendurable. It was some minutes before she could crush down the tears and shakily, her limbs hollow, creep up to the sanctuary of bed.

Jean, hearing the Land Rover coming up the hill, went to put the kettle on. Dougal was late. Either he'd run into Cristi or he'd missed her by a fair bit. Perhaps he wouldn't tell her either way. He'd not had much to say lately, her open, cheerful, easy-going lad, and she often felt guilty about all he'd had to take on his shoulders, and the way she'd got into the habit of relying on him for everything. That other pair, Donald and Jill. They'd inherited the bad blood that came from her own family. Shaking her head, her mouth tight, she reached down the old tea caddy, its once bright panels now rubbed bare.

But Dougal didn't come in.

He was still in the Land Rover, his arms folded across the steering wheel, his head down on them. After a few moments he got out and walked across the yard to the field gate between byre and tractor shed. No stock to see after tonight, that last-thing ritual which even in the worst of weather he never minded. Summer now, feeding at its best, in the brief weeks before ground frosts started again.

He leaned on the gate. The ponies would be down at the far end, by the burn and the big ash tree. Had Cristi had time to come and see them yet? The night paled as his eyes adjusted, the hills standing out clear and black against the soft grey of the sky. As Cristi had done earlier, he tried to let the quietness enter into him, but it didn't work. She was a million miles from him already. Never had he found it so difficult to talk to her, the words hard as stones in his throat. He hadn't even asked her how her exams had gone, or how she'd fared with that portfolio she'd been so taken up with when last she was home. The truth was, he hardly knew what to ask any more, didn't know the right words to use. Still, that had never stopped her having plenty to say about anything she was interested in. A grin lightened his face for a moment, and he shifted, putting a foot up on a bar of the gate, as though physically trying to throw off his sombre mood.

But then, all this that was happening to her. His thoughts couldn't keep off it. Going back to the country where she'd lived as a child, meeting these strangers who'd always refused to have anything to do with her yet were her only true relatives, it was a big thing. Who knew what their attitude to her would be after all this time? And getting herself out there, landing up in a city famous for its dangers, dealing with lawyers and business affairs in a language she hadn't used for years. Good thing Archie had always seen to it she kept it up. And that fuss about Brazilian Portuguese and not the other kind of Portuguese. Perhaps it had mattered after all.

He moved again, straightening his back. There were

things to be decided in his life too. He'd hoped to talk to Cristi about them this summer. She'd not have time for that now. How long would she be away? Had her life really changed for good?

Dougal gazed for a couple more minutes down the shadowy field. Best go in, his mother would never go to her bed until he did. But questions were the last thing he needed.

And where was Jill? Was she in? She could be anywhere, was the answer to that. His mouth grimmer than nature had ever intended it to be, he turned and went with his slow stride towards the house. The house the Galloways didn't own, and never could own; the house where he'd been born, and which nothing could ever make his.

Cristi, with Broy bundling along at her heels with a faint feeling that term-time sloth usually lasted longer than this, made at a round pace for the Achalder cottages. Delight in the beautiful day and the familiar scene lifted her spirits in spite of the fearful speed at which matters were racing forward. After an early ride up the hill track this morning — the views widening below her as she gained height, and the feel of the sweet morning air on her cheek, had been so magical that she had almost decided to forget the whole thing — she had nevertheless polished off a few more chores to do with the journey. The letter to the Rio lawyers was already on its way, saying that Cristi would come and meet the Fonseca family as requested.

She had wondered if she should phone or e-mail, but Archie had said shortly that a letter would be fine.

'I know they made it sound urgent, and quite possibly the family have some private agenda we know nothing about –' he couldn't imagine them not putting up a fight over Cristi's inheriting such a slice of her grandfather's estate '– but I think we should go at our own pace, and arrange things to suit you.'

If only he could go with her, he had thought worriedly. This could easily turn out to be too much for her to handle. But he was so tied up just now. Getting a new grieve was becoming more urgent every day, but with Donnie's replacement temporarily accommodated in the grieve's house . . . He must talk to Dougal.

In spite of Archie's insistence that she should move at her own pace, when Cristi had called BA a flight had been available much sooner than she had expected, and it had shaken her to realise how simple arrangements were going to be. Her passport was valid; she had only to give her Visa number and make the booking. It was too easy, making departure seem just round the corner. But it is only a visit, she reminded herself, abandoning the lazy swing of the track and dropping directly down the steep slope to the river. I'm only going to find out what it's all about. But if I own land there, that's not exactly being a tourist, is it? Own land! The very words still seemed outlandish in relation to herself.

She turned to wait for Broy, who was taking the slope with care, then crossed the wooden bridge, a pleasant smell of creosote coming off it in the warmth of the afternoon sun, and took the path across the rough ground in the curve of the river, fringed by alders and housing a busy spread of kennels and runs.

Cristi always enjoyed coming here. The pair of cottages with its couple of acres been purchased from the estate by the Quebells the year she had come to Drumveyn. One cottage had been intended for Joyce and Stephen Quebell, the other for Stephen's mother. Joyce, however, who found her tough old mother-in-law better company than she did her dreamy husband (or bone idle husband, according to the point of view), had chosen to move in with her, and together they had set up the breeding and boarding kennels which, in spite of the remote location, had done unexpectedly well.

Quite soon, however, in an agreeably understated manner, the pattern had changed. Old Mrs Q had died, and Lisa, the Napier daughter back at Drumveyn in search of refuge after the departure of Cristi's father, had drifted down to live with Stephen, taking Mrs Q's place in the business. Over time, without fuss, Joyce and Stephen had been divorced, and Lisa and Stephen had married.

However, to the rich amusement of family observers, as time went on it had become clear that Lisa preferred Joyce's company to her husband's and history repeated itself when she eventually moved in with Joyce. No earth-shaking emotional dramas brought this about; simply Stephen had a cold which lingered on in an annoying cough, Lisa had moved next door in order to get a decent night's sleep before a show, and had never moved back. Stephen hadn't appeared to mind.

Had Stephen noticed? Tom and Archie questioned.

'Was there ever a man like him for being steamrollered by one bossy woman after another?' Archie would ask in awe.

'Or with such a knack of getting rid of them,' Tom would add with what sounded more like admiration.

'Shouldn't think he's got many complaints though, would you?'

What, indeed, did Stephen have to complain about? By profession he was an illustrator of children's educational books, and it was assumed that he still produced work occasionally. What was certain was that he had as much time as ever to wander the glen by day or night, to stand for unmeasured hours on the river bank or in the shaggy garden which only the irregular and impatient assaults of Lisa kept under any kind of control, or to recline on the base of his spine in his old armchair in the studio, doing absolutely nothing.

He was fed and watered, as the dogs were. Nothing was asked of him in emotional terms; he was just there, serene, kind, unchanging. But no one could doubt Lisa's affection for him. To her he was wise, perceptive and totally to be trusted. Howard had moulded her to his requirements; Stephen loved her for what she was. It was all she asked.

Joyce maintained the same approach as she always had towards him, benevolent if distant, and no dissension ever interfered with the rigorous work ethic to which she and Lisa adhered.

The only problem was that Stephen tended to be

overlooked. Forgotten, to be blunt. Though a minimum of time was dissipated on social comings and goings between Achalder and the big house, such as dinner parties where Joyce and Lisa both tended to nod off, or lunches that ran away with half the afternoon, for major family events they did consent to appear. At one Christmas lunch, never to be forgotten, it wasn't noticed till an empty chair and an extra plate were discovered that Stephen had been left behind. Archie had gone down at top speed to collect him, but even as he joined a tableful of people who had already made serious inroads on the turkey, Stephen had seemed unaware that anything unusual had occurred.

The fact was that, peculiar as its menage might appear to an outsider, the essence of Achalder was one of adult people doing and being what it suited them best to do and be. There seemed to Cristi great good sense in this, and she had always felt at home here. Today, however, heedless of the volleys of barking which accompanied her — and kept Broy close to her heels, his eyes rolling — a small chill made itself felt as she went down the weedy path beside the fence, which still divided the two gardens because no one had ever found the time to pull it out.

Impossible today to ignore something which as a rule she never thought about — Lisa was, technically, Cristi's stepmother and guardian. For that reason if for no other it seemed important to talk to her about what was happening, yet for Lisa, of them all, these associations with the past would surely bring pain.

I always come to see them as soon as I'm back, Cristi

argued with herself, and knew that what she really wanted was to have everything the same as usual, her welcome no more effusive, interest in her affairs going no further than a couple of kindly questions, a little well-meant encouragement which revealed a total want of comprehension, followed by a right-then-back-to-work squaring of shoulders and the resumption of whatever task had been on hand.

Today it was all alarmingly different. After the bellows for silence, the reluctant dwindling of the cacophony, the automatic once-over for Broy's girth and the state of his coat, the bone-crushing hugs smelling of dog and All-in-One and Imperial Leather soap and hard work, Joyce said briskly, 'Great to see you, love, but I've got a pile of entry forms to sort out and I really ought to get on with them, damned things. I've put it off far too long, that's the trouble. Anyway, why don't you and Lisa sit out here, and I'll bring you some tea before I get stuck in.'

Sit down? In daylight? Have tea brought to them by Joyce? No, no, it was all wrong. Cristi wanted to be sent to make the tea herself, or given a job, saying whatever had to be said while she brushed a dog or got soaked holding one for shampooing, or filled a long row of feed bowls in accordance with a mind-blowing list of diets.

Lisa seemed as uneasy as she was. She dumped her well-padded backside (she and Joyce not only wore identical check shirts and green cords, moved and spoke alike, but seemed over the years to have become the same age and the same shape) on the weathered wood of the old bench, and planked her hands on her spread knees.

For a moment she watched Broy rolling with a couple of his near relations on the speedwell and daisies of the lawn. Then she looked at the straggle of bushes beyond and remarked, 'Don't think those blackcurrants are going to do much this year. Probably time to have them out.'

Such an anti-climax; so very Achalder. Cristi laughed, tension deflating, and with quick affection touched the well-muscled brown arm with its elbow so awkwardly stuck out.

'Oh, Lisa, I don't want anything to change,' she said, allowing herself a yearning tone she hadn't risked with anyone else. It wouldn't upset Lisa, and it was a comfort to be able to say what she felt.

'All that old business cropping up again.' Lisa lifted a flap of moss with her toe and kicked it aside, but perhaps feeling this didn't answer the case she gave Cristi's hand a little pat in return, not looking at her. 'You must be feeling a bit shaken up about it.'

'Just a bit,' Cristi assented temperately but, in spite of the seriousness of all they were trying to approach, she couldn't help smiling at the bald understatement.

Lisa responded with a little huff of laughter.

'Yes, well, I'm not very good at this kind of thing, am I? Anyway, how far have things got?'

Joyce appeared, holding high and ceremoniously before her, as though to emphasise that special efforts were being made, a round metal tray with a high rim, which looked as though she might have nicked it from a bar. She came to a halt in front of them, looking around as though expecting a table to be there.

'Shall I put it on the bench?' Cristi suggested.

Joyce handed over the tray as though she'd shot her bolt and was glad that was done with.

'Biscuits may be a bit soft,' she said. 'I think they must have got left behind when we started that craze for gingernuts,' she added aside to Lisa, as though this would excuse their shortcomings, and stumped off waving an earthy dismissive hand as they called their thanks.

Two mugs and a plate with four Rich Tea biscuits stood in a pool of dark tea on the tray, which did indeed have the Carlsberg logo flourished across it. The biscuit Cristi took folded as she bit it, then glued itself against her teeth.

'Definitely past it,' Lisa said, pressing her finger on another. 'Fusty too, bound to be. Chuck them into those Welsh poppies – gosh, they've fairly taken over, haven't they? – then she won't be hurt. No, *don't* give them to Broy. Though he'll get that extra fat run off him soon enough when Peta and Josie get home.'

And I won't be here. Cristi put down her mug.

What have I said, Lisa wondered in alarm, seeing the poised head droop, the dark lashes sweep down. And then, her attention for once fully caught, she thought, goodness, she's pretty. We take her for granted, but she really is the most gorgeous little thing.

'Cristi,' she began in awkward concern, 'I know there's all this business about your grandfather's ranch and so on, but I'm sure you don't have to go out there unless you want to. I mean, everything could be sold, couldn't it? They can't put any pressure on you, not by this stage, or make you do anything that doesn't feel right for you. Doesn't Archie say the same?'

'I know. I'm sure you're right. But you see, I do feel there's a kind of obligation to go,' Cristi said, her eyes abstractedly on Broy, who had hoped no one would notice his stealthy foraging in the yellow poppies. 'Maybe there is something else behind it, it's such a turn-around, but however they've behaved these people are my family. It would feel wrong, cowardly even, to turn down the contact when it's offered. And if this is a chance for reconciliation, well, I think I'd feel pretty guilty later on if I didn't take it.'

'But you wouldn't stay out there? I can see going out to meet them if that's what you want to do, getting the feud or whatever it was out of the way, now that the old man's died. But your home's here. That could never change, could it?'

The question which everyone, even Dougal, had been afraid to ask. The question which Cristi herself didn't have the courage to face yet.

'I can't look that far ahead,' she said. 'I just don't know. But I can't imagine life without Drumveyn and all of you there in the background. You know that.'

And yet, and yet, the ties of blood. That strange tug of need to know who she was, where she came from.

Lisa let a moment or two pass. 'But you're hoping too that you'll hear some news of your real mother, and of Howard.' Perhaps only Stephen would not have been surprised by the gentleness of her voice.

Cristi nodded mutely.

'Yes, I can see that you'd have to go, for that if nothing else.'

They sat for a few moments saying nothing, thinking many thoughts, in the quietness of their sunny corner, their eyes on the bright tangle of early summer flowers all fighting for space, and on the well-groomed corpulent bodies of the Dandie Dinmonts now slumbering on the grass.

'Cristi, look – maybe this isn't the right moment, but since emotions are running a bit high, there is something I'd like to—'

Lisa broke off, at a loss in the uncharted territory of personal revelations.

'What?' Cristi wasn't sure what was coming, but felt fairly certain it couldn't be any further reference to Justina. That was beyond both of them. 'Tell me.'

'Well, it's just that, I've sometimes wondered, you know, whether you ever felt I'd let you down. Over that business years ago.'

Catching the startled look which Cristi couldn't hide, Lisa gave another of her brusque little laughs, so much like Joyce's. 'Hard to believe I ever think at all, is it?' she asked sardonically. 'Oh, yes, occasionally things pass through my brain other than worming puppies and checking for ticks.'

'But Lisa – let me down, whatever do you mean? How could I think that?'

'Off-loading my responsibility is what I mean,' Lisa retorted, glad this was in the open at last. 'Howard sent you to me, and all I could think of was sending you straight back. Then I ran for home, without even trying to cope, and when I got here, what did I do? Handed you over to Mum. And when I moved down here, I took it for granted that Archie and Pauly would look after you.'

'But I don't think they mi—' Cristi began blankly, feeling the foundations of her world crumbling.

'Oh, God, I don't mean they didn't want you,' Lisa rushed in, horrified to realise what Cristi might read into this. 'Don't ever think that. Everyone wanted you, in fact. No, but what I've sometimes wondered is, have you ever felt *hurt* because I left you with Mum?'

At the time Madeleine, newly widowed, had been feeling her own way into a braver, less restricted life, shaking free of the constraints imposed by her selfish and domineering husband. Taking care of Cristi had been something she had both needed and passionately wanted to do, and in her view Cristi had given her quite as much as she had ever given the deserted child.

'Lisa, no, I've never thought such a thing.' Cristi found it hard to imagine Lisa worrying about it, but was moved to think she had cared enough to do so. 'I promise you, it never crossed my mind. Sometimes, as I got older, I did wonder what it must have been like for you, having me dumped on you like that. And I've wanted – only I knew you'd hate it – well, I've thought maybe one day we could talk about it, and I could hear your side of things.'

Her voice had grown more tentative as she went on. Lisa had had dumped on her doorstep her husband's child by another woman. She was surely the last person who would want to rake up this painful story. But to Cristi's surprise Lisa's strong hand gripped hers firmly.

'It would be such a relief to me. Not now, perhaps. You've got enough problems of your own to think about, but one day, we'll talk about it properly.'

She looked relieved already, as though merely touching on these past events had robbed them of their power to hurt, and it didn't seem odd to either of them when she accepted a hug from Cristi without protest.

When Cristi had gone, however, asking Lisa to give her love to Stephen, for the myth that his work mustn't be interrupted was always faithfully observed, Lisa went round to the other cottage and into the studio. Stephen was, at it happened, busy at the high desk he preferred for his meticulous and delicate work. Lisa went to stand beside him, not touching him. He laid down his brush and reached back his arm to draw her in. She leaned her forehead against his shoulder and he held her quietly. They didn't speak.

Chapter Six

In the crowded days before she left Cristi found herself torn between wanting to do exactly as she usually did when she came home – seeing estate people, neighbours and friends, renewing her acquaintance with every corner of this place she loved so much, letting the family scene close over her head – and a helpless feeling that everything had already altered, or at least that her own place in it had. As in the day of hurried packing before she left Edinburgh her existence there had slipped beyond her reach, so now there was a feeling of being already on her way, the past left behind. Yet much as she disliked the idea of things changing, she knew that if someone had told her now it had been a mistake, none of it was happening and life would go on as before, she would have had a sense of having ducked some important challenge.

It was impossible not to be swept forward by practical preparations, as well as by speculation about the future. The latter could produce apprehension but it also aroused both an irresistible excitement and the optimism which was characteristic of her.

She found a similar difficulty in reconciling a need to spend as much time as possible with the people she so missed when she was away – she was eagerly looking forward to the return of Nicholas and the little girls – with an equally urgent need for time alone, time to fix in her mind every precious detail of her surroundings. For she had a feeling that, no matter what happened, and even if she only spent a brief time in Brazil, nothing here would ever be the same again.

Apart from catching up with everyone, she wanted to ride, walk Broy, swim, take the boat out on the loch, get involved in whatever was going on about the estate. Inescapably, however, thoughts of Dougal haunted her whenever she found time for any of the activities they had always shared, and there were some very lost and lonely moments to get through.

It was some comfort to be with Pauly, helping her in the house and garden, for concerned as Pauly might be about what was in store for Cristi, and hating the thought of the family being split, she was always in too much of a rush to delve too deeply into these anxieties, and her natural cheerfulness never deserted her for long.

Cristi also went up to the barn when she could to see Madeleine, and to spend time with Tom. She had always had a special affection for him and it moved her to see the courage with which he faced his disablement.

The continued freedom to come and go in Jean's kitchen was something she was relieved to find still open to her. As well as being part of the past, she recognised that it was good for Jean to have someone to whom she could spill out her worries about Jill and her elder son Donald, that wild pair who had given their parents so much trouble over the years.

To chat with Jean also meant the chance to pick up precious crumbs about Dougal, and with departure looming there was every excuse to indulge in reminiscence, happily trotting out the well-worn favourite stories over endless cuppies. That helped a lot.

Something that perturbed her, by contrast, though she spoke of it to no one, was the way in which her own work failed her. She found herself not only unable to paint, but quite unable to derive pleasure from using her skills in any other medium. Usually, whatever else was going on in her life, the moment she applied herself to any of the crafts for which her studio was so well equipped, the simple pleasure of using her hands would absorb her, hours flowing by unnoticed. Now nothing held her attention. Her brain refused to switch off, and her hands were leaden and inept, refusing to translate images and thoughts into form and colour.

One pleasant surprise during this unsettling time was that Torie and Isa, not impressed to have her haled away so summarily, hired a van and turned up with several items from the flat which she had recklessly bestowed on them in the panic of packing up. Cristi confessed to being glad they'd done it, particularly pleased to see again one or two cherished pieces on which she had collaborated with Torie.

After being together in their first year, when all art and design students took the same course, Cristi had gone on to study textiles, Torie choosing fashion and performance costume, so it had been a great joy in the fourth year to work on their final project together. Isa, opting for the more mundane Environmental Studies, and within that discipline Housing and Planning, had endlessly complained that she must have been mad to share with two creative design nuts, and had fluently savaged ninety per cent of their efforts.

She had done plenty of grumbling on the domestic front too. While conceding that Cristi was unnaturally tidy for an art student, she had had trouble with the chaos created by indolent Torie. Although no one could be more easy-going and good-natured, she would grudgingly admit if pushed.

It was marvellous to see them again, Isa whip-thin and unsmiling, hair scraped back, the dark-framed specs and look of weary disdain firmly in place; Torie plump and smiling, with her tangle of light hair, her floaty clothes and air of all-encompassing calm. But Isa's oh-spare-me look concealed a lively personality and a dry wit which had much enlivened the years the three had lived together, and Torie too concealed much of her true self beneath the somnolent façade. Her fat, dimpled hands could work astonishing magic, and the final collection she and Cristi produced had been amongst the most successful of their year.

Torie professed to like coming to Drumveyn, but to Cristi's frustration when she did she rarely surfaced before noon, spent most of her time stretched on a sofa or in the sun on the terrace, and only came to life at dinner-time (for which she always nicely offered help just as everything was done), when she would down quantities of wine, do more than justice to Pauly's marvellous food, and seduce all males within her orbit with her lazy charm. She shuddered at proposals to ride, walk to the village, go on the hill.

'What hill?' she would ask, raising a languid hand to shade her eyes as she gazed into the far blue distance, before sinking back into torpor like a deflating air cushion. 'Another time perhaps.'

In fact she had been brought up with three brothers on an estate in Appin very like Drumveyn, knew its way of life inside out, and liked being somewhere where no unexpected or bothersome demands would be made on her.

Isa, on the other hand, was a town bird, and just as she used to moan about finding herself condemned to live with a couple of arty-farty weirdos, she would bitterly ask, every time she came to Drumveyn, what had possessed her to let herself be dragged yet again to this privileged slice of wilderness, where she had to wear ear plugs in bed to shut out the silence. She had been brought up in a thirties semi in Slough, divided by a strip of dead earth and a slip road from the A4, and she still found it hard to sleep without the sound of traffic or the comforting sense of urban sprawl around her. But she too liked coming to Drumveyn. Her interest in how people lived drove her to poke into every facet of the workings of the estate, and both Tom and Archie relished her pertinent questions and terrier-like pursuit of facts. Though Archie did once or twice ask Pauly if she thought Isa knew how abrasive her comments could be.

For Cristi, as the three of them carted the contents of the van into the studio, it was like being given back a slice of a life she had thought lost for ever. It was fun to squabble about the disposal of the various artefacts (or rubbish, in Isa's terminology), to sit gossiping for hours, first downing long vods then tidying up the odds and ends from the drinks store which Torie and Isa had self-sacrificingly kept back for shared disposal.

The only drawback to the visit, and for Cristi it was to prove a damaging one, was its timing. Pauly took one look at the pair who appeared in the kitchen to say goodbye, Isa convinced she was fully in control but with her eyes slightly crossed, Torie already on the brink of easy tears, and put her foot down.

'Forget it. No one's going anywhere tonight. I don't care how much black coffee you've swilled down, that van doesn't move an inch with either of you at the wheel.'

'But we've only hired it for today,' Torie pointed out, with a sort of owlish conviction that this would make their journey legal and justifiable.

'And we've things to do tomorrow,' Isa added, hoping Pauly wouldn't ask what they were because she couldn't remember offhand.

'Anyway, Cristi said we couldn't stay because—' Torie broke off with a squeak as Cristi dug her with a quick elbow. 'Didn't you say that?'

'It's OK, Pauly.' Cristi saw she would have to bite the bullet. 'They know they can't drive really. It'll be all right for them to stay, won't it?'

'You know I did my best to persuade them to in the first place,' Pauly reminded her, beaming at the prospect of two more for dinner at the last moment. She liked people round her table, and it was good for Cristi to forget for a while the concerns hanging over her.

Cristi was horribly torn. She'd have loved having Torie and Isa to stay on any other night. Parting from them would be harder than ever after today. But this was the evening when she'd arranged to see Dougal – the only evening he was free. But clearly they couldn't drive. The decision was out of her hands.

Dougal, keenly conscious that his two-year course at the local college had been no substitute for the degree he had hoped for, went to Muirend on two evenings a week, attending a course in business administration run by Perth College. Grimly aware that he would never have a chance of farming in the way he wanted to farm, on land of his own, he had decided to qualify for some kind of career on the business side of the agricultural industry.

Cristi knew better than to suggest him missing a single one of these lectures, for he followed the syllabus with unswerving dedication. His frustration at its content, and at the direction in which it was carrying him, he kept to himself.

On other evenings and at weekends he was so often busy, taking any chance to make a few extra pounds where he could, that Cristi had begun to despair of ever seeing him alone. She couldn't remember it being like this before, even during the last year when they had begun to drift apart. Somehow they had always been aware of each other's movements; there had never been this feeling of being so shut out.

But Jean had let slip the fact that tonight Dougal had promised to give her a hand with the garden. Nowadays it was all too liable to get away from her, as it had now, when a succession of warm days followed by rain had sent weeds as well as flowers and vegetables shooting up.

Cristi, reluctant to phone and have Jean answer and call Dougal, though nothing could have been more normal, and nervous in a way she had never imagined any encounter with him could make her feel, had caught him as he left for work this morning, and asked if she could come up to help him after dinner.

'It's just the odd bit of weeding,' he had told her gruffly, taken by surprise, and Cristi, rebuffed, unsure whether to pursue the idea, had had no clue to the lift his heart had given to think of them working together, companionable and easy, in the old way.

'I could still help,' she had made herself persist. As Dougal said nothing, instinct warning him in spite of this tempting image to find some way of putting her off, she had gone on awkwardly, 'It's only that, well, we hardly ever seem to find a chance to talk these days. I know you're busy, it's the busy time of year of course, but I just thought, time's racing on at such a horrible rate. I haven't quite taken it in myself, but I'll be gone in a few days.'

She had stopped, looking into his face in mute appeal,

afraid, as he very well understood, that she was pushing too hard for something he might not want. Then before he could reply she had rushed on quickly, 'I'm sorry, I'm holding you up. You're on your way to work. It was a silly idea—'

What's got into you, you bloody fool, Dougal had cursed himself. 'No,' he'd said hastily, 'you be there. Whenever you've had your dinner.'

Then he had cursed himself again for bringing up that thorny issue, which had dogged the years from childhood on. Tea-time for Dougal as a child had been when Donnie came in, five-thirty or thereabouts. In just the same way he had his tea now when he came in, more like the back of six. But for Cristi at the big house it had been dinner, from anywhere between seven-thirty and nine, or even later, and dinner took up a lot more time than tea. When they were younger it hadn't been too much of an issue. Cristi had times without number had tea with the Galloway children at Steading Cottage, or Pauly had given the three of them something at the big house. As the younger Napiers were growing up Cristi had often chosen to join them for supper so that the evening was free, but as the years went on it had become a problem she and Dougal were always trying to work around. It had been, in effect, the most obvious of the differences separating the two households; not just when they ate but what they ate, and what they wore to eat it, quite apart from the fact that at the big house dinner was part of social life and guests were frequently present as well.

Tonight, Dougal had thought as he drove on, Cristi

would be unlikely to turn up much before nine. Well, there'd be a good hour and a half of light left after that, more maybe after the fine day this promised to be. Putting his foot down as he reached the glen road, whose twists he could have driven in his sleep, he had felt more elated at the prospect than he had felt for months, and could hardly believe he'd risked losing this chance to be with her through his own daft pride.

And now Cristi wouldn't be able to go. She'd have to phone and explain that she was tied up. But the worst of it was, she wasn't free because of Isa and Torie, and in her heart of hearts she knew that the estrangement from Dougal had had a good deal to do with these two. Not that it was in any way their fault, and nothing had ever been openly said about it. She didn't even like thinking about it, or what it implied. Anyway, what she had to deal with now was telling Dougal.

It didn't take long, once she got past Jean, as ready to chat as ever.

'That you, Cristi? Aye, he's here, just finished his tea. Are you wanting a word? While you're there, though, will you tell Pauly I've found that recipe we were speaking about for the Berwick May Day tarts. I have them here, there and everywhere on wee scraps of paper, and I never can put my hand on the one I'm wanting. Tell Pauly I'll drop it by for her when next I'm passing. . . .'

Then you don't have to go on about it now. Dougal would be gone if Jean didn't shut up. But at last she was saying, 'Och, here's me blethering on, and it was Dougal you were wanting. Here he is for you now.'

'Dougal?' Cristi found her voice oddly wavery.

'Yes.'

'Look, about tonight. I'm really, really sorry, but I won't be able to come up after all because—'

'No matter.'

'Yes but you see, Torie and Isa have turned up, and they weren't supposed to stay the night, only now they'll have to because – well, never mind about that. But I'm afraid it means I'll have to be here . . .'

Cristi could feel the drop in temperature at the mere mention of their names. She was tempted to say it was Pauly who had insisted on Torie and Isa staying, but she was not good at prevarication. They were staying because the three of them had chosen to spend the afternoon polishing off their alcohol supply and had had a good time doing it.

'It's not as if it was anything that mattered.' Dougal sounded impatient to be gone. 'But if I'm not to be getting help, I'd best be getting on with it.'

He had intended this as a small joke but it didn't sound like that to Cristi. Emotions were very near the surface these days.

'But could we talk another—?'

She heard his voice riding over hers, 'Enjoy your evening.' The line was dead.

She did do her best to enjoy the evening, reminding herself that it was a bonus to have this time with the others. Who knew when they'd next be together? Already summer plans for her visit to Appin, for Torie coming here, and for all of them meeting up in Edinburgh for the Fringe performances they specially wanted to see, had had to be put on hold.

But behind all the cheerfulness of the evening, Pauly and Archie both putting themselves out to make the girls welcome, the thoughts of Dougal ran . . .

She imagined him working away methodically in the summer dusk, producing in Jean's shaggy garden the neat order he could so effortlessly create, thinning and transplanting, hoeing, edging, earthing up tatties; swifts and house martins slicing the air above him as he worked, bats hunting in silent flight.

That scene and this, the beautiful kitchen which Cecil, Archie's first wife, had designed, the splendid meal which had begun with croissants stuffed with scrambled egg and smoked salmon, and gone on to rack of lamb, new potatoes and what must be just about the last of the broccoli from the freezer. Pauly was now at the Aga, her shining hair roughly dragged back to free her for the frenzy of creation, producing lemon pancakes to order. Archie, after saying they'd had quite enough to drink already had relented, since all they had to do was fall upstairs, to the point of opening a couple of bottles of Australian Chardonnay which he felt might not do them too much harm, and was refilling glasses even now. There would be cheese and fruit to come for anyone who wanted it. Coffee. Brandy for Archie, and certainly by this stage he wouldn't neglect to offer anyone else whatever they chose.

Such different scenes, but both had their appeal for her, were part of who she was. Tonight they had proved mutually exclusive, and she hadn't liked that, and couldn't quite drag her mind away from the fact.

Chapter Seven

The even droning, the dimmed lights, the dislocation of place and time trapped in her slot among the rows of strangers, but above all resistance to being where she was, going where she was going, created in Cristi a sense of being cut off from reality. Her thoughts were the formless images of half-sleep, jolting her with sudden wild alarms, about her ticket, her passport, finding the person sent to meet her. More than once she thought she'd spoken aloud but the unfriendly man in the crumpled suit, who'd been so irritated when she'd had to climb out past him, was still snoring, mouth open.

She did her best to focus on facts to banish the muddled dreams. How lucky that both flights had been on time. Now all she had to do was to sit in this seat for a few hours more, and at breakfast time Brazilian time she'd be there and — then childhood associations made her check. She didn't feel brave enough to look ahead yet.

Her thoughts turned homewards again, though she

fixed on something safe to remember. Yesterday, wanting solitude, she had walked to the head of the glen. On Drumveyn there was always work going on, Archie somewhere about, the keen eyes of keeper or shepherd picking up any movement from miles away.

Below the ridges closing in the glen to the north, its small fields higher than the arable land of Drumveyn, lay the farm of Ellig. It was empty now. Its owner, Miss Hutchinson, hadn't lived there for years, and the main farmhouse was derelict, its roof off, willow-herb filling the empty shell, elder branches thrusting through the gaping windows. Last winter Miss Hutchinson had died, and Ellig was up for sale.

Jed Maclachlan, who had farmed it for her, had let the place fall into almost total disrepair. The father of a turbulent and notorious brood, ever on the increase as his daughters regularly produced offspring who, no matter who the fathers were, always ended up at Ellig, and with a wife who came and went in a sequence of violent rows and tearful reconciliations, Jed had begun to drink and, without supervision, had lacked the motivation to keep the place in order. Cristi, running into him in the village last Christmas, had been shocked to see the bent, shambling figure where once there had been a powerful, fit and flamboyantly handsome man.

They were gone now, the whole fighting, layabout crew, leaving behind them land in poor heart, tumble-down dykes, clogged ditches, buildings with leaking roofs and choked rones, and a grieve's house so battered it was unlikely anyone would buy even to renovate.

But somehow, yesterday, this sad place had suited Cristi's mood. Peesies had wheeled with their evocative cries over the ragged fields, swallows had arrowed from the shadows of the barn through the gap between the doors, both off their hinges. Nettles grew in the steading yard, ground elder had overtaken the vegetable patch. Peering through filthy windows she had winced at the squalor of the deserted rooms.

Archie was keen to add Ellig to Drumveyn. Apart from giving extra summer grazing, buying would mean that an eyesore on his doorstep could be tidied up (no more drifts of thistle seed floating down the glen every summer), and ensure that no new occupant could perpetuate Jed's sins of killing protected species, putting down poison, and leaving rabbits flailing in snares until it suited him to check them. But Archie had more than enough to look after at present, and until he had a new grieve it was hardly feasible to take in more land.

What would become of it, Cristi had wondered, going round to the front garden, where lupins and columbine struggled up through mats of saxifrage and snow-in-summer, and where the rowans planted to ward off evil spirits, originally meant to form an arch over the gate, now nearly obliterated it. In spite of everything, she had felt her spirits lift at the view before her.

To her right the burn spilled down its rocky falls towards the village a mile away. Down the glen the tawny patches of sprayed and direct-drilled fields looked, as always, oddly out of season against the summer greens of young foliage, foot-high barley and hay almost ready for cutting. As she'd traced the course of the river looping past Achalder and Drumveyn, her eye caught by the perfect frieze of dark conifers against the sunlit flank of the hill, she had made herself a promise. Whatever happened, all this should not be lost to her. Walking on through ragged grass thick with buttercups, heart's-ease and speedwell, in the bright solitude of that high open place, the vow had comforted her. It had been a private farewell, but not a final one.

Now, dozing again, she fell into panic. She was searching for Nicholas and the little girls. They were supposed to be meeting, but she was in a place she didn't know, crowds of people jostling her, their voices roaring in her ears. She tried to call to the others, but was certain they would never hear her.

Shaking herself awake, mouth dry, Cristi wished with all her heart that she had seen them before she left. It had been the wrong decision not to. It was discussed, of course, and though there had been no official leave-out before her flight date, Pauly had been sure something could be arranged. But in the end it had been decided that it would be better not to make too big a thing of this journey and what lay behind it.

'We don't know how things will turn out,' Pauly had said, and Cristi had felt a chill at the words. 'But whatever's decided,' Pauly had hurried on, perhaps guessing this, 'you'll be home again soon, then you can tell the others more about it. Especially Nicholas.'

Yes, Nicholas. In the event, it had proved impossible to gloss over the reasons for her sudden departure to him, and Cristi winced to recall the inadequacy, the uncertain pauses, of their conversation.

The moment Nicholas had said, his voice cracking up to a note she knew he would be furious about, 'You're going to see your real family?' she had known she should have managed somehow to go to see him and talk about this properly.

'Well, my mother's people,' she'd answered awkwardly. 'I don't think of them as my real family.'

'But they are, aren't they?'

'Technically, yes. But they're strangers to me.'

'But you will meet them.' She had been puzzled by the insistence, even hostility, in his voice.

'Yes.'

An aching pause.

'Nick?'

'Look, I've got to go, OK?'

'We'll talk some more before I—'

'Have a great time. See you.'

Cristi had been wretchedly aware that she had failed him, though even she didn't fully understand how. Ever since the day Archie had brought two-day-old Nicholas home to Drumveyn, to be looked after among them all, she had been especially close to him. His mother, Cecil, had rejected him from the moment of his birth, refusing even to come back to the house, and he had never seen her since. A sturdy, healthy, good-tempered baby, he had flourished, however, as Cristi had done, in the non-nuclear family group.

She could not have guessed at the helpless, inarticulate

sense of misery which had filled Nicholas after her call. Many doubts and questions had begun to stir recently, hardly capable of being put into words, and the news that Cristi was to make contact with her real mother's family, perhaps even with her mother herself, brought those questions pressing uncomfortably close.

For Archie was not Nicholas's biological father. Suffering from the problem of a low sperm count, he hadn't been able to give Cecil the child she'd wanted. Or believed she had wanted, since, having chosen the option of donor sperm, she had found herself utterly repelled by the whole process of giving birth. No matter what the circumstances, however, Archie regarded Nicholas as his son, without question, and always would.

After Archie and Pauly married they had hoped desperately for a child of their own. Archie in particular, who knew he made love a great deal more often to Pauly than he ever had to Cecil, had let himself believe it might happen. But, when Pauly failed to conceive, they had decided to go ahead with adoption before too big an age gap stretched between Nicholas and the next child, so first Peta then Josie had arrived to complete the family.

To Cristi in this lonely moment it seemed incredible that she had left without seeing the others. Talking was no substitute for the sight of them, and the hugs which the little girls at least would have returned with fervour. Down her spirits spiralled. It was the low point of the night, the extra hours taking their toll.

That clash with Jill too; how horrible it had been. How could things between them have reached such a point? Arriving at Drumveyn all those years ago, Cristi had been thrilled to find the Galloway children, not much older than herself, so close at hand. Though the Mowat girls, Alison the younger her own age, had lived at the Lettoch, a Drumveyn farm where their father was tenant, they had been just that bit too far away. Dougal, responsible and protective, had become her hero, but Jill had been a good companion too, and for a while they had been a tight-knit trio. Even when Cristi had gone away to school it had still been taken for granted that they would spend most of their time together in the holidays.

But as Jill moved into adolescence everything changed. To a bewildered Cristi it had seemed to happen in the space of half a term, though adult observers might have told her the trend had been clear long before. There had been endless trouble about smoking on the school bus, about truancy, wearing make-up or not wearing uniform, and then the more serious trouble of experimenting with drugs. There had been letters from the headmaster, Donnie had delivered angry lectures, and Dougal had refused to have anything to do with Jill or her friends.

For Cristi it had come out of a blue sky. All Jill's latent envy and resentment had come to the surface as she sneered at Cristi's accent, her clothes, her manners, and her willingness to stick to the rules. Jill, gravitating to the worst company she could have found, both at school and in the village, had had no mercy.

It had been Cristi's first encounter with overt class bitterness. As a child in Brazil she had been more or less brought up by servants, their presence accepted without thought. Once at Drumveyn she had naturally accepted things as they were. Though she had been allowed to go to the glen school with Jill and Dougal as she had longed to do, she had clearly understood that she wouldn't follow them to Muirend High.

Sent to Glenalmond, after some initial unhappiness when undue interest was taken in her foreign appearance (a problem she would face again at university), she had soon found her feet and made friends.

To come home and be called, by someone she regarded as a friend, a snob, a show-off and a wee sook, reminded that she was no more a Napier than Jill was and asked if her mother was a black, had been a terrible shock. Both families had done their best to smooth matters over but Jean, for one, had known in her heart that her daughter was set on a course from which there would be no turning back. Hadn't her elder son, Donald, been just the same, beyond even Donnie's power to control, wasting his time at school, drifting from one job to another when he left, spending every penny he had at the pub? He'd been forever in and out of trouble, and Jean had almost been glad when he had moved away from the glen for good.

Now in her mid-twenties, Jill had unnumbered affairs and two abortions behind her. Though married, she didn't live with her husband, whose mother was at present looking after their son in Glasgow. Jill had recently been on a drugs rehab programme, and was nominally living at Steading Cottage, but was hardly ever to be seen, sleeping through the day, picked up most evenings by unknown vehicles whose drivers tore up the hill blaring their horns, tipped out again at any hour of the night scarcely capable of finding her way indoors.

Jill was one of the reasons why Archie was reluctant to put pressure on Jean to vacate the cottage, much as he needed it, and much as he would have liked to see the last of Jill. Jean had her name down for a council house in the village. This might mean a wait, but the alternative was Muirend, which Archie knew she would hate.

Cristi had known her thoughts would circle back to the core of pain. This flight was far too long, that was the trouble. It gave her too much time to think.

Jill had been at home when Cristi, having established that Dougal had no plans as far as Jean knew, had gone up to Steading Cottage on her last evening at home to make one last attempt to talk to him.

Jill had been lolling in Donnie's old chair, her face pasty without make-up, breasts slack under a grubby T-shirt, legs in baggy jogging pants sprawled wide. Dougal, a newspaper spread on the table, had the toaster in pieces in front of him. Jean had been at the sink.

'Oh now, here's Cristi,' she had exclaimed in the placating tone she used when Jill was there. You never knew when she'd fly up at the least thing.

Dougal had come to his feet and Cristi, her perceptions over-acute where he was concerned, hadn't been sure whether this was prompted by the good manners instilled by Donnie, or a wish to be somewhere else now that she'd come.

'What's she doing here?' Jill had demanded, and Jean's mouth had pinched in distress and alarm.

'Here, Jill, that's no way to—' Dougal's fair skin had reddened beneath his tan.

'No way to what?' In a violent movement, startling them, Jill had heaved her shapeless body out of the chair. 'I can say what I bloody well like in my own home, can't I? Who does she think she is anyway, barging in without so much as a chap at the door? Oh, yes, Lady Muck, I've heard *your* news.' And she had thrust her face into Cristi's, menacing her with her height and bulk.

'Jill, mind your tongue,' Jean had gasped, but Jill had taken no notice.

'You with your money and your ranch and your dago family waiting to welcome you, what are you doing here? Do you think we want to know, do you think we fucking care? The truth is, you lot can't wait to chuck us out. My dad worked his guts out for this place, and was killed doing it, while you get more and more given you without ever getting off your backside – ach, you make me sick—'

'Jill, that's enough!'

Cristi, stunned by the ugly, illogical attack, had already turned to go, but had caught Dougal's movement towards Jill, and the anger in his face. They were fighting because of her. That was awful. Then she had been out in the sweet cool air, away from the heat and hostility of the small kitchen, and had begun to run.

✳   ✳   ✳

Cristi shifted in her seat, as though trying to shake off the memories. She was glad she was small; at least she had plenty of leg room. Five hours till they landed. How hot was it going to be? Winter, and early in the day. But Rio was in the tropics. Would she be able to find the lawyers' representative who was supposed to be meeting her? And what then? But it was all too vague to displace the other, insistent images. Better to confront them.

It was horrid to think the encounter with Jill would be her last memory of Steading Cottage. And, apart from a brief phone call before she left, her last contact with Jean, after all the years of closeness and kindness. Not her last contact with Dougal though. He had followed her. And he had known exactly where to find her.

She had jumped as the door of the studio opened, but she'd known it would be Dougal. He had stayed in the doorway, his expression unreadable.

'Cristi, you know better than to take notice of anything Jill says,' he had begun without preamble. 'She's out of her skull half the time, remember.'

Cristi, crouched in the corner of the old sofa, knees up to her chin, arms wrapped round them, had given a jerky little nod, acknowledging this, but she'd been unable to speak, and a taut silence, charged with feelings held in check, had seemed to pin them down.

'For God's sake, you know what she's like,' Dougal had tried again, more urgently, and now he had come across to her, his face frowning, eyes intent. 'She fights with everyone. She swears she's clean, but it's obvious she's still getting the stuff from somewhere, and that means she's not—'

'But what she said was true, wasn't it?' Pain had forced out the words. 'Under the jeering she was saying what she thinks. She's hated me, and what she thinks I represent, for years.'

'Cristi, you're reading too much into this.' Dougal's voice had been gentler, his whole body language sending the message that he wanted to comfort her.

But she hadn't let him go on, a terrible emptiness filling her. 'And Jean feels the same, deep down.' A crackling pause. 'You too, probably.' The words had hung between them. They had stared at each other in rigid stillness, and a flush had risen in Dougal's face.

'Do you believe that?' he'd asked quietly.

Cristi had gazed up at him in mute misery. He had looked very broad and powerful, standing over her like that. For all his quietness Dougal was a man of strong presence and authority, and Cristi had known that he wouldn't let this go. She had unwound her locked limbs and come to her feet the better to face him.

'Isn't it part of why we've grown so far from each other?' It hadn't been the way she would have chosen to talk about it but there was so little time left.

'Go on.' She winced to remember the level coldness of that.

'Well, like minding when I went to university, as though you thought I wouldn't want to be with you any more, and hating it when Isa and Torie came—'

She had broken off as he turned away slightly. She

knew him well enough to realise it was a moment of decision for him.

'OK, we'll talk.' With an authoritative gesture he had waved her back to the sofa, though he hadn't dropped down beside her as he would have done so naturally in the past, instead pulling forward the stool from below her big drawing board. I will come so far towards you and no further, the action had announced.

'In the first place I didn't mind you going to university,' he had said rapidly, as though this was a minor point to be got out of the way. 'But I minded like hell not going myself. It had nothing to do with you. But in broader terms, Cristi, looking at my life and yours, the facts are there. You can't change them. It does have to do, in a way, with what Jill flung at you tonight. No, hang on a minute,' as Cristi made a sharp sound of denial, 'no one else would have put it as she did, and there's no excuse for her. But you've got to accept it, things were different when we were kids.'

He made it sound so rational, so obvious, that it barely needed saying. I can't believe you're holding me at arm's-length like this, Cristi had thought blankly, as he had talked calmly on, like a stranger.

'But we can still be friends,' she had argued, and derived little comfort from his ready, 'Of course we can, don't be silly.' It was as if he'd chosen his stance and would not be moved from it; nor did he intend to let the conversation descend into pleas, accusations, or emotional exchanges of any kind.

How Cristi had longed to break through the barrier he

had seemed to be building brick by brick, and tell him how she really felt. How impossible he had made it for her to do so.

'We live in different worlds, that's all there is to it.' Such a cool and damning summing-up. But Cristi had caught his glance round the studio as he spoke, and she had seen for the first time that it was the perfect statement of what he meant, revealing what he saw as the gulf between them not only in material terms but in interests and goals. There was the old oven where Cristi had fired her ceramic tiles during the stencilling craze when no fabric, earthenware, glass or wood at Drumveyn had been safe from her attentions. And there, among the products of different dyeing and printing techniques, the water colours, pastels and oils, the needlework and leather work, stood the computer and big copier. Everything she needed provided.

Looking at these objects through Dougal's eyes, Cristi had had a disturbing new insight into how they must make him feel distanced from her. Why had it never struck her before?

'Listen, Cristi,' Dougal had said, cutting across these questions, 'put that ranting of Jill's out of your mind. You've sense enough to do that. This is a new beginning for you, a big, important one and—'

'A terrifying one, you mean,' she had interrupted with a shiver. 'Oh, Dougal, I feel so scared.'

'Hey, come on.' He had leaned towards her, concern in his eyes. 'What's so frightening?'

That had been better. At least he had no longer

sounded as though he were reading from some prepared script. She had said hesitantly, longing to talk freely, but still not sure he would welcome it, 'I feel so mixed up about it. I'm not going to Brazil because I want to "claim my heritage",' making the inverted commas on the air. 'You know that, don't you?'

'I know you've never expected anything of the sort.'

She had nodded. 'But I do have to go.' It had been hard to explain, even to him. 'For one thing, I'd feel a coward if I didn't. But also — I know this sounds a bit over the top — I'd feel I'd kind of closed down the lid on part of myself.' She had pulled a face at the phrase. 'Whatever I find in Rio, I must *know*. Growing up, I wouldn't give a thought to any of this for ages, then every so often I'd feel desperate to find out who I really was. I'd remember I wasn't connected with anyone here — as Jill so kindly pointed out. But it's more than curiosity. I'm not sure I can put it into words . . .'

'You're doing fine.' The quiet reassurance had been a poignant reminder of former ease and closeness. This was the Dougal who knew and understood her, who had always looked after her, the rock on which she leaned.

'Well, it's — I do feel this pull, this awareness of a link I can't ignore. A genetic link, I suppose I mean. Then there's the way I look. Sometimes I *hate* it.' She had brushed his involuntary protest aside. 'You know how mostly you look in the mirror to see if you're tidy or to put on make-up or whatever, but how every once in a while you *look*, really look? Well, I can get quite frightened when I do. It makes me realise I look totally bizarre beside Nicholas and Peta and Josie. Even though they're adopted or whatever, they look like family, like Archie and Pauly. Their ages fit too. I'm only ten years younger than Pauly. I couldn't be her daughter. I can't tell you how bad those moments are.'

Her voice had wavered, and she had drawn up her knees again, dropping her forehead on them. Not so long ago she could have counted on Dougal's arm coming round her in a bracing hug. But there had only been a beat of silence, and then his voice, rather husky, saying, 'I didn't know you felt that. That's rough on you. Yes, I think I do see that you have to make this journey, for these reasons as well as the rest. But we're going to miss you.'

We. Everybody. In general. Cristi had nodded, managing a smile but not words.

'And speaking of journeys, perhaps it might be an idea for you to get some sleep.'

'I know. I should go in.' It had been over. Unbearable. But she hadn't moved. To move was to begin the journey. No hug, no loving touch. No futher words. After a tiny silence she had heard, with an anguished emptiness, the sound of Dougal replacing the stool – so like him – and then his quiet steps as he went to the door.

Chapter Eight

Dazzle and glare, light beating back from pale concrete, from the shiny body of the aircraft, and pouring down from a cloudless sky. A forgotten quality of engulfing heat too, but it was the light which seemed to attack, as Cristi allowed herself to be carried in the drove of other passengers towards customs. She felt crushed and rumpled, her eyes dry and prickling, her skin tight and unclean. She felt as though she hadn't slept at all, yet if she hadn't where had those jostling, uneasy dreams come from?

She found herself overwhelmed by powerful and contradictory feelings. There was, in the first place, the excitement of being here, irrespective of anything that was about to happen. Anticipation had seized her in the final stages of the flight, when looking back had at last been overtaken by looking forward, and the spectacular sight of the great mountain-ringed bay as they came in to land had taken her breath away. It was as though she had scarcely realised till now what a huge adventure this was going to be, and her natural optimism soared as she looked around her.

She was startled by an almost atavistic sense of the heat and light, the very taste of the air, being deeply familiar. She hadn't been prepared for that. And because she was light-headed with tiredness her mind examined the word atavistic with detached interest — grandfathers, rather appropriate. Then a memory returned, amazingly clear after so many years, of being in this airport at a moment of her life so terrifying that it had engraved itself indelibly on her mind, though in self-protection she had rarely let herself think of it since. Here, weeping and resisting, she had been delivered into the hands of the stranger who was to take her to England; here, under-standing nothing except that she was being torn away from the only life she knew, she had hung back from that dragging adult arm and turned to see Isaura, the one dependable person in her life, standing bereft, in tears herself as she waved and waved. Isaura in her butcher-blue uniform with its white collar and cuffs. Isaura with her lovely smell of cleanness, her strong comfortable arms, her broad sandalled feet.

It was weird to have this picture flash into her mind with such vividness, yet on another level be merely the adult traveller arriving from abroad, knowing no more of her surroundings than any other passenger landing at Rio's international airport for the first time. Yet that wasn't quite so, for some vestige of long-ago condition-ing, surfacing in a scene to which she unconsciously related, was telling her there was probably only a fifty-fifty chance of someone being there to meet her as arranged. Well, there were bound to be other options for getting into the city.

Behind all these thoughts was something else, more disquieting than any of them, the slow, sick churning of apprehension at the prospect, now very close, of coming face to face at last with her family. Her mother's brothers. Her uncles, João and Joachim. She didn't know the names of their wives or their families. She knew nothing about where they lived, what they did, what sort of people they were, or what their motives might be in sending for her like this. Her hands sweaty, she changed her grip on the strap of her big leather tote bag.

In the hubbub of the terminal she had a moment's wild panic that she wouldn't be able to understand a word that was said. The clamour around her might as well have been in Swahili. Then suddenly it resolved itself into sounds so familiar, so distinct from the Portuguese of Europe, that she felt a surge of joyful recognition, and once more that fleeting, quite unforeseen feeling of homecoming.

She had been instructed to look for a middle-aged man carrying a card with the name of the legal firm. There was no such person to be seen. Fine, no big deal. Where did the bus go from?

But in spite of being ready to cope on her own if she had to, she was tired enough to see not being met as a first sign of rejection, a reminder that she had been summoned here because of the surprising revelations of a will, and not for her own sake.

'Maria-Cristina?'

No one had called her that for years. She herself had almost forgotten it was her name. Yet here it sounded so natural that she turned without hesitation, not even noticing that her surname hadn't been added. The man addressing her held no identifying card and hardly looked 'middle-aged'. He was above average height for a Brazilian, and had all the dark good looks of his race. He was smiling at her in a way she might not have expected from a lawyer's clerk, but she beamed back readily. Things were looking up. No bus.

'I am delighted to meet you.' Using English but sticking to the flowery formality of his own language, she supposed, as he shook her hand, inclining his head slightly as though he would more naturally have bowed over it. 'Shall I enquire if you had a pleasant flight? Perhaps not. Several hours of discomfort would probably be a better description. At least you have arrived almost on time, for which we may be grateful. Permit me to welcome you to Brazil.'

He spoke English with easy fluency, only a slight ceremoniousness of phrase sounding foreign, and even that held an ironic note, as though he found this job of being sent to fetch her somehow diverting. As he spoke he'd snapped his fingers to the porter at his heels, and Cristi's luggage was already on its way to the exit. Pleasure to find everything being taken care of after all made her ready to accept the slightly mocking manner.

'Thank you so much for coming to meet me,' she said. 'I'm really grateful.'

'It is of course my pleasure.' He gave her an amused look, and catching the flashing smile in the lean brown face, noting the shapely head and thick dark hair, Cristi was aware of something she had subconsciously absorbed since landing – not only were the majority of the people around her strikingly good-looking but, for the first time in fourteen years, she herself didn't stand out as unusual or incongruous.

'I think today will be hot for the time of year, but at least you will be thankful, coming from Scotland, not to be arriving in summer.'

It was the merest of small talk, expecting no reply. He was sweeping her out to the car, opening the boot for her single bag, tipping the porter, opening her door. He gave the impression of a man impatient over practical details who disliked being held up.

The car was long, low and luxurious. Cristi didn't recognise the make, but it did strike her that the law must be a profitable profession in Brazil if a minion who did airport trips owned such a vehicle.

Then for the next few minutes she had no attention to spare for anything beyond the series of rapid, combative manoeuvres which took them out of the carpark and onto the highway. It appeared that to switch on the engine was instantly to enter a competition – or a race, she amended, as the car arrowed towards the first of the links between the islands which would take them to the city.

'You don't recognise me?'

The question, once more amused, was accompanied by a longer and more searching look than Cristi thought his role warranted — certainly longer than was clever at the speed they were doing. What did he mean?

'No, of course not. How could you?' he went on before she could answer, shrugging but at least returning his eyes to the road.

'I'm afraid I don't . . .' Cristi did her best to marshal her weary brain to work this out. Had they sent a photo, so that she would be able to pick him out in the arrival hall, and it hadn't reached her? Suddenly dreadful anxiety seized her. She'd got into the wrong car. This man had nothing whatsoever to do with her. He hadn't given her his name, or mentioned that of his firm, and she, like an idiot, hadn't asked. This was Brazil, and she'd read and heard enough about its dangers to be seriously alarmed at what she'd done. And in the airport, she'd had her bag, its top yawning open, slung carelessly over her shoulder, in it her passport, money, traveller's cheques, and the addresses and phone numbers she would have needed if . . .

But this man had addressed her as Maria-Cristina, had referred to Scotland.

'Ah, what a shame to tease you. How horrified you look.' He was laughing at her. 'Of course I am not some dutiful and insignificant lawyer's clerk. I carry no little placard on a stick. But long, long ago you and I have met. When, if I am to be honest, little cousin, you looked very much as you do now, and that is — quite extraordinarily like my aunt Justina. I am, most sincerely, charmed to meet you again.'

In the whirl of surprise and adjustment, the recognition of details overlooked till now — how could she have been so blind; everything about him spoke wealth, his manner as well as what he wore — and thankfulness that the final stage of the journey had been so easily leapt over, it was the casual use of her mother's name which most jolted Cristi.

'Your cousin, Luis Francisco Ribeiro da Fonseca. I know, I know, I should have introduced myself at once. How unforgivable of me . . . I could have been anyone.' The glint of a sidelong smile, openly teasing now, told Cristi he wasn't going to let her forget this. He could indeed have been anyone, and she had got into his car without argument and let herself be driven away. But this dazzlingly attractive man was her *cousin?* Wow.

'The son of your mother's brother Joachim,' he said. 'You don't remember me at all?'

'We never met, did we?' Were never allowed to meet. Yet memories were struggling to form themselves. Blinks of memory. A shadowy, high-ceilinged room with towering dark furniture, shutters half-closed against the sun. Several children, older than she was. Recalling them stirred an associated memory of disdainful hostility on their part, anxious longing to be accepted on her own. Grown-ups talking in the background, grown-ups whose faces and shapes she couldn't recapture — except her mother's.

Her mother, her beautiful, elegant mother, that slim figure flitting through the childhood impressions still retained, always eluding her, never emerging clearly in precise scenes or any recollection of time spent together. And, as always, the image was connected with loneliness, expectancy, disappointment, waiting, endless waiting and, more enduring than all the rest, a baffled helplessness at promises broken.

'Yes, well, our meetings were not frequent,' Luis was saying lightly. 'These ancient quarrels. But they are not our quarrels, are they?' Then, in a different tone, as though speaking to himself, 'They are, in any event, ended now.'

Cristi turned to him in quick guilt. 'I'm so sorry. Your grandfather. I should have . . . You must be missing him.'

Luis's attention was for the moment concentrated on overtaking a high-sided, enormous lorry, with an equally enormous trailer, which seemed to Cristi to be racketing along almost out of control.

'Yes, of course we grieve for my grandfather,' Luis said, his eyes on his rear-view mirror as he cut in in front of the lorry, which blared its several horns at him. The words conveyed conventional courtesy in response to her words rather than any genuine feeling. 'However,' he shrugged again, lifting both hands from the wheel, 'he was very old, and had been ill for some time.' A pause. 'He was your grandfather too.'

'I know. I know he was.' Cristi floundered, for this opened the door to a multitude of complex issues which she knew she wasn't ready to face yet. 'It just seems so odd to think of it, after all this time.' The very name grandfather seemed to stir up secrets like old leaves, secrets inextricably linked with sadness and pain. Her mind slid tiredly away from these large questions, and suddenly she longed to be somewhere without movement, somewhere quiet and cool, not with the unnatural air-conditioned coldness of the car, defying the brilliant light and heat pressing upon it, but cool with shade and softness. She longed to be out of these clothes too. She tried to work out how long she'd been wearing them but failed to compute the time difference. She longed for a shower, for bed and a respite from emotional demands.

A scene she could have done without at this moment swam into her mind: Drumveyn in silvery morning light, the grass dew-drenched, birds singing, wisps of early mist drifting up from the loch. She wrenched her mind away. Don't go there.

Anyway, how could she be so ungrateful? Here she was in one of the most fabulous places in the entire world, her biggest dread already removed since she had been so generously met before she could feel lost or unwanted for a second. The whole big adventure was just beginning. What did she have to complain about?

'My dear Maria-Cristina,' Luis was saying, 'how could you have imagined we would allow a stranger to welcome you home to your native land?' Now that was flowery, if you like. The light, bantering note was back, Luis turning his head to give her another of his devastating smiles. 'However, until today it was quite impossible to say which of us would be free to do so. Things crop up, things change at the last minute, there are so many demands on one's time . . .'

Though he didn't shrug this time, the shrug was in every word, and the sense of familiarity stirred again. It was more than an acquired view, the accepted cliché of

Latin-American outlook and temperament; it felt to Cristi like something always known.

'It was good of you to come,' she said gratefully. 'Much nicer than being met by someone from the lawyer's office.' She meant it. To find one of the family cared enough to take the trouble, and to meet the others with Luis beside her, made all the difference.

'Undoubtedly,' Luis agreed. 'But now that you have recovered from the first shock, shall I prepare you a little for the encounters ahead?'

'I'd be glad if you would.' Apprehension hadn't gone far away after all.

'Yes, well, it shouldn't be too alarming. Because of – well, for various reasons – we have become a somewhat reduced family group. My father, as I said, is Joachim. My mother is called Sylvia, and they now live in the Fonseca family home here in Rio. The elder brother, João, moved to California some years ago, so for the present we need not concern ourselves with that branch of the family. There, you see, half a dozen names you can dispense with at once. How easy I am making it for you.'

'I can cope so far,' Cristi told him. What luck, and what fun, to have this incredibly good-looking man, with his ready smile and light-hearted fluency, take her under his wing. She hadn't expected anything like this.

'Then, of the immediate family whom you will meet later today,' Luis was continuing rapidly, 'there are my elder sisters, Gabriela and Catarina, both married, both with families – the names of whom we shall skip for the present, since they will not appear at the welcome dinner which my mother is giving for you this evening. Yes, yes, of course,' as Cristi turned to him in quick dismay, 'she will insist on that. Quite useless to try to stop her. But you needn't worry, it will be the simplest of affairs. A mere half-dozen . . .'

'I hope that's true.' Cristi didn't trust his innocent tone. What she longed to ask, and couldn't, was whether there would be any contact with her mother, any further reference than the passing comment on her own similarity to her. Had grandfather's death meant that Justina, too, could be accepted back into the fold? Had any of the family known where she was, kept in touch?

But none of this could be embarked upon now. It mattered too much, and was bound to be entangled with implications she couldn't hope to grasp at this stage. In any case, all Cristi felt capable of at present was facing the next step, arriving at the house, perhaps entering the very room whose image had been preserved in those uncertain shreds of memory, meeting her uncle Joachim. Thank goodness that Luis's thoughtfulness meant she wasn't facing it alone.

'Do you remember any of this?' Luis was swinging away from the expanse of Guanabara Bay, heading for the exclusive suburbs high above the city.

'Only broad-brush,' Cristi said. 'I can't remember anything about Rio itself. Maybe I never even went into the city. I know no more about it, or where we're headed now, than the greenest tourist. My memories are of home, the people there, being driven to school at the convent, driven home again.'

Yet there were odd wisps of memory, which she didn't share with Luis; impressions more than memories. She was surprised, for instance, to find her brain turn up a word which had been part of childhood, never thought of since. The *baixada*. To her the word had signified a dark and ominous place, lying somewhere below the safe, bright height where she lived. The flatlands round the river mouth with their giant slums. A scary place, out of sight but never quite forgotten, full of vague horrors.

And something else rushed vividly back, as the car turned in towards high gates in a blank wall, their fine wrought-iron work backed by metal sheets, and they swung open by remote control. Being shut in; trapped behind locks and bars, windows covered by grilles; rules, supervision, never allowed to get wet or dirty, never allowed to go out in rain or wind or too harsh sunlight; the endless, stifling over-attentive care. And she remembered, on the short journey to and from school, the ever-present awareness, which had both fascinated and repelled her, of a very different world outside.

She was shivering as the car rolled forward. There was an impression of an immaculately kept garden stretching out of sight, dotted by the stooping figures of gardeners. Then the house took her attention, with its rows of balconied windows, its elaborate traditional architecture. Solid, handsome and established, it spelled out the unshakable confidence of its owners.

Luis pulled up before heavy double doors and on the instant a servant appeared to look after the luggage, another to take away the car.

Luis turned to look at Cristi, an eyebrow lifting as he saw her expression.

'No one's going to eat you. Come along, be brave.' But his voice wasn't teasing now, and his smile was warm and encouraging. Gratitude that he was there filled Cristi again, as she went up the wide steps with his hand cupping her elbow.

Chapter Nine

'She'll have arrived by now, won't she?' Pauly asked, having spent a few serious moments while the coffee percolated in working out whether to add hours on or take them off.

'Soon should have. Hey, she'll be fine,' Archie urged, seeing her unhappy face.

'I know. Of course she will. It's idiotic to worry.' Pauly put the coffee pot on the table and went to open the French window before she sat down. 'Um, smell the roses after the rain. Heavenly.'

'Damned rain, with the last of the hay to get in. If only it had held off one more day.'

'We haven't done badly this year,' Pauly reminded him, putting her hand briefly on his brown arm below the rolled-up sleeve.

'I know.' He turned to smile at her, and perhaps because he knew how forlorn she was feeling, or perhaps because he had been more harrowed himself than he had cared to admit by Cristi's departure yesterday, he examined her more closely than usual, and the smile deepened into a look of love.

To him she was still very much the smooth-skinned, amply-endowed nineteen-year-old who, by bringing her casual cheerfulness and giving spirit into this house, had woken it to new life. And who had come into his own life at a time when, defeated in all attempts to rescue his marriage with Cecil, with her emotional hang-ups and her inability to form any kind of loving relationship, he had desperately needed warmth and generosity. Pauly today, her heavy toffee-coloured hair unbrushed, wearing a capacious safari shirt which Archie thought had once belonged (or perhaps still did belong) to Tom's son Rob, still looked so like the smiling girl his mother had found hitch-hiking up the glen road and brought home to cook for them, that he put down his cup and went to hug her.

At this tears welled in her eyes. 'Oh, Archie, it feels as though she's really gone,' she wailed, burrowing against him. 'Term-time was bad enough, but this is awful. She's always been such a marvellous person to have around. She enjoys life so much, she's so into everything. Now it feels as if she's gone for good and I can't bear it.'

'Oh, sweetheart, don't. Cristi could never stay away from Drumveyn for long. You know she'll come back. This will only be a visit. But she had to go, it was always a piece of unfinished business. That mystery about her parents vanishing, and who her father was really married to — if he'd taken the trouble to marry anyone.'

'Yes, I suppose I do know.' Pauly's voice was muffled

as she turned away from him, reaching for a cushion to apply to her face for want of anything better to mop up her tears. 'God, these covers need washing,' she added in an ordinary tone, pitching the cushion onto the floor in disgust. 'It was so weird, wasn't it, the way she arrived here? I suppose she has to find out what it was all about, anyone would. It's pretty amazing, inheriting the ranch and everything, if you think about it. But yesterday – was it yesterday, it feels like a week ago – when we were seeing her off, it was really odd. I suddenly noticed how foreign she looked, as though I'd never seemed to see it before. Not *as foreign*, I mean. She was just Cristi. Do you think we made her understand that this is her home, Archie, and that we'll always want her, no matter what?'

'Don't be silly, she knows that,' Archie said, pushing the soft mass of hair aside so that he could put his cheek against hers. 'Of course she knows it's her home. She loves you as much as you love her, and she loves Madeleine, Tom, the children, all of us.'

'Yes, well, I just wish the children would hurry up and get home,' Pauly said crossly, and Archie understood perfectly her need for their voices and laughter, their squabbles and dramas, in a house hollow with an emptiness oddly different from its normal term-time quiet. He knew she wanted to lavish hugs and warmth, fill the house with people and cook enormous meals. Smiling he pulled her close.

But as he went up to see what damage the overnight rain had done to the hayfields above the farm, always the last to be cut, the question Pauly had asked tugged at him too. Had they in truth lost Cristi? Not because she would want to go, but by force of circumstances? Pauly had touched a nerve when she had remarked on how foreign Cristi looked. She would re-establish ties which couldn't later be ignored, and she would be taking on new responsibilities too, a tie in themselves.

Dougal, starting on another stultifying day's work in the office, was doing his best to put the same questions out of his mind. Had Cristi really gone? Would she reappear at Drumveyn in future only for fleeting visits, every moment taken up by the family, the extensive circle of Napier friends, and the friendships she had made outside the glen?

After that bleak goodbye which had been no goodbye at all, he had been filled with a despair quite unlike his usual equable, pragmatic approach to things. All right, so he had been determined to keep things on a realistic footing between them, but he had known Cristi since she was eight years old, for God's sake. He could at the very least have given her a reassuring hug to send her on her way, letting her know beyond any doubt how much she would be missed.

But he couldn't have risked any such thing, he knew. To have once put his arms round her, or touched her at all, would have carried them, carried him, far beyond any ordinary, friendly farewell.

Each time he reached this point, then and in the empty days that followed, he told himself that he had been right. He couldn't have played it any other way. That was how it had to be. More than that, he now had to make a serious effort to put the whole thing out of his head. Cristi's future was no business of his. What he should be concentrating on was sorting out somewhere for his mother to live, trying yet again to get Jill back on the rails, and getting on with his own life. It would do him no good to go hankering for things he could never have.

The unsettling mix of the new and the hauntingly half-remembered assaulted Cristi once more as she was ushered by Luis into the large, and to her rather oppressively splendid room. There was first and foremost the muted light coming through cream linen blinds, bringing instantly back a perception of the sun as the enemy, to be excluded or avoided, against which valuable objects must be vigilantly protected. Out of nowhere came her mother's voice, '*Mas que calor!*' and she was shaken at hearing the petulant words so clearly.

But there was no time to think of this, for moving forward to welcome her were her mother's brother and his wife, Luis's parents. It was happening. She was being received, in the house where her mother had been born and had grown up, by members of her own real, biological family.

Such a thrilling, life-changing event, yet on the surface there were only the most correct of greetings, Joachim shaking her hand and bowing over it as Luis had not quite done, Sylvia wafting the most fleeting of scented kisses past each cheek in turn in the conventional *abraço*, murmuring half-heard phrases which to Cristi sounded as soothing as a long-ago learned nursery rhyme.

'Maria-Cristina, how enchanted we are to meet you at last. Such a great pleasure . . .'

Joachim Ribeiro da Fonseca, inches shorter than his tall son, presented an altogether more stereotypical figure. In his mid-fifties, he was solid in build, with a bullet head and broad shoulders. Immaculately groomed, wearing a grey suit of some light fabric, white shirt and dark tie, he carried his weight well. The hand he gave Cristi was smooth, plump and manicured.

Hand-made shoes, no question, Cristi summed him up.

Sylvia too, though it was still early in the day, was formally dressed and impeccably turned out. Her hair looked as if she had come straight from the hairdresser, which suggested that she used the services of a personal maid. Cristi, feeling she had stepped back a decade and a half in her own memory, but more like half a century in terms of lifestyle, guessed that her aunt wouldn't normally appear at all at this hour, and she was grateful for the courtesy shown to her.

But the perfect turn-out of the reception committee, the impressive room with its ornate ceiling, heavily framed paintings and dark, elaborately carved furniture, its display of treasures on every side, made her feel diminished, uncouth and juvenile. Her clothes, the skirt with the African bark-cloth pattern she had designed herself, the brief silky knitted top, had been chosen with this moment of arrival in mind. Following her own preference she would have worn her comfy yellow dungarees for the journey. She might as well have done. In this setting what she was wearing was pretty much on a par with them.

Below the smiles, the greetings, the enquiries about her journey (made in fluent and obviously well-practised English), and the clear intention of extending a warm welcome to her, random observations occupied a disconnected corner of Cristi's mind. These good-looking people, two of them related to her by birth, had an olive-tinted skin tone which she didn't share. Perhaps after all she had inherited something from her fair English father, though the creamy texture of her skin was very different from fine English pink-and-whiteness.

But those eyes, those smiling eyes. Cristi knew, with a pang of terrible home-sickness for Pauly's wide, happy grin or Madeleine's quiet glimmer of a smile, that she would never be sure what thoughts really lay behind them. Black, unreadable, calm with an absolute self-confidence. She wondered in sudden doubt if her own eyes, as dark as theirs, revealed as little. Had other people found that, smiling back at her? It was a dismaying thought.

The flow of polite nothings effortlessly continued, and Cristi was glad of the easy contributions Luis made, more relaxed than either of his parents. Coffee was served. *Cafezinhos*; the word slipped readily back. In her mother's house, Cristi recalled, coffee had been served in tiny straight cups, with sugar thick at the bottom, which by some strange convention was never stirred. In the kitchen, after Isaura had taken away the tray, Cristi had sometimes been allowed to spoon out this sweet sludge as a treat, though not officially allowed coffee.

She dragged her mind back to the present.

'But, my poor Maria-Cristina,' Sylvia was saying, 'we mustn't keep you any longer. Of course you are tired. These long flights are so exhausting, even if one manages to sleep. I wondered if perhaps you would like to have breakfast in your room and rest during the morning? If you prefer English breakfast you have only to say. Please ask for anything you wish for. Our house is yours . . .'

A mere form of words, as Cristi knew, yet it reminded her of why she was here, she, the interloper, the rejected member of the flock, who had so unexpectedly been left a slice of its wealth. Had such a thought crossed the minds of these urbane people at the phrase? If it had no hint of it would be evident. Such considerations were quite apart from this smooth, civilised rite of welcome.

So much still to be discovered and resolved. And fought over? Cristi shivered inwardly.

'Thank you, it would be lovely to sleep,' she said politely. And to be alone. 'If you're sure that's . . .'

'But of course,' Sylvia disposed of the question firmly. 'Joachim must go to the office this morning, but then we shall have family lunch. Luis, I believe you said you would be here? And this evening you shall meet our daughters and their husbands, who are naturally looking forward very much to knowing you. We shall only be a small gathering, no one outside the family. Now, let me take you to your room.'

The men stood, smiling.

'Thank you again for coming to meet me,' Cristi said quickly to Luis. 'It did make such a difference.'

'The pleasure was entirely mine,' Luis assured her, and made it sound as if he meant it. No Scotsman could have made it sound like that, Cristi decided.

In the pretty, high-ceilinged bedroom, when Sylvia had gone (and Cristi fully appreciated the signal run up by Sylvia taking her to her room personally), she stood letting the stillness and quietness flow through her, washing away the tensions of the flight. Here, on the shady side of the house, facing south, she reminded herself, the shutters of the two tall windows were folded back, and fine white inner curtains floated gently in the soft drift of air. Heavier brocade curtains were looped back with such exact care that they looked sculpted. Each window had a plump-breasted wrought-iron balcony overlooking the garden, which was backed by a dense line of trees. Nothing to be seen that wasn't beautiful. That would not be permitted.

Behind her, in the room, it was the same. The furniture was cream, gilded, with cabriole legs and delicate flower decoration. No stencils, Cristi thought with a spurt of amusement which turned before she could prevent it into a desperate longing for her studio, and the sprawling, happy, comfortable house across the courtyard, the loch below the lawn and the long views of moor and hill.

No, no looking back. She was here, and this was marvellous too. None of that was lost to her; it wouldn't go away. But for now it would be a good thing to avoid reminders. She crossed the room, where already, after so brief an interval since she had arrived, her belongings were unpacked and disposed of, and went into the bathroom. Here the maid, whom Sylvia had introduced as Diamantina – well, not introduced, told Cristi she was called would be more accurate – had run her bath, and every luxury awaited her. But here too, bringing the past leaping back even more clearly than the memory of such taken-for-granted service, was the faint, over-sweet, cloying smell of some bathroom product, and Cristi came to an abrupt halt, childhood a step away.

Nothing could have brought it sweeping more evocatively back. Closing her eyes she was once again in the small, exquisite house with its white marble floors, its gleaming order, its tiny, bright, enclosed patio. She felt as though she could reach out and touch Isaura's smooth strong arm; Isaura who had looked after her from the day she was born; Isaura who had slept in her room every night of her life until Cristi was sent away.

I'm not sure I've got the emotional stamina for this, Cristi thought, trying to pull herself together. Why had she not foreseen the knifelike stab of such reminders? How many more lay in wait to catch her unawares? But the question brought with it a lift of excitement too.

There was going to be so much to feel and see and learn. Because of the decision of a hostile old man whom she had never met – and who knew how arbitrary that decision might have been or what had driven him to make it? – she had been given the chance to come back to the country of her birth, a beautiful, immense and vibrant country where, in ways she could only guess at, she might discover new aspects of herself.

Miles to the south of here, in a place she had never seen, though as a child she had longed to go and had been passionately jealous of the cousins who she knew spent their summers there, lay several thousand hectares of ground which she owned.

The thought, still almost impossible to grasp, brought with it, tamping down her anticipation as soon as it awoke, thoughts of Dougal. How she longed to write to him, now, telling him all she was seeing, doing, thinking and feeling. But he had made it so clear they were no longer on that footing, and never could be, and her inheritance of land, though it had never been directly mentioned in this context, was part of that implacable distance he perceived as existing between them.

Don't think about that. Concentrate on the present.

After a cool bath, abandoning after one glance the arcane and antique controls of the shower, and with no intention of summoning Diamantina, Cristi padded to the windows to shut out the bright day and the high arch of empty blue. The bed had been turned down. As she stretched her tired limbs at last in its wide ungiving spaces, she wondered if she wasn't after all too exhausted to sleep. She'd forgotten how hard the pillows were here . . .

It was her last drifting thought before sleep overtook her, and she was sliding away, gone, the morning quietness of the great house, in spite of its many occupants and concerns, its more or less ceaseless flow of activity, enfolding her.

Chapter Ten

It was a busy time for Archie, and it took him a day or two to catch Dougal. He wanted their meeting to be private. He also knew that if he phoned Steading Cottage Jean was almost sure to answer, and in her present state of worry about the future she would read all kinds of things into the fact that he wanted to speak to Dougal. He had no wish to give her any more sleepless nights.

He found his chance a couple of evenings later, as he was on his way down from the barn where he'd been having a nightcap with Tom, and yet again chewing over – when did they talk about anything else these days? – the urgent need for management help on the estate. After tea Pauly had gone over to Grianan, on the other side of the glen, taking several pounds of raspberries for Sally Danaher. It had been such a good year for soft fruit as well as everything else that even Pauly had thrown in the towel at the thought of making still more jam. Since

Grianan was a thriving small hotel it was a useful place to dispose of such surpluses.

Another reason for going over whenever she could was that, sadly, Sally's husband Mike was less able to cope with life with each month that passed. He had suffered serious brain damage twelve years ago, and though he had recovered sufficiently to lead a contented and active life with Sally and his two children from a previous marriage, his brain could never be fully restored. Of late his vagueness and forgetfulness had been increasingly notice-able, and he succumbed more and more frequently to the depression and lack of motivation which had been a feature of the early stages of his recovery. Sally found this the hardest of all to bear.

Her many friends, and Pauly in particular, had been giving her as much company and support as they could, and Archie hadn't been surprised when Pauly had phoned to say she would be staying at Grianan for dinner. As this was the most hectic time of the day for Sally, he guessed that any talking would have to wait till dinner for the guests was over, so he didn't expect Pauly back very early.

He heard with satisfaction the unmistakable throaty voice of the old Land Rover coming up through the belt of trees round the house. He was eager to sound out the plan he and Tom had agreed upon. Whatever Dougal's reaction to it, or to its less orthodox alternative, it was essential to move forward in one way or another.

The Land Rover pulled up beside him in response to his lifted hand.

'Evening, Dougal, just the man I wanted to see.'

Dougal switched off the engine. 'Hello, Archie. What can I do for you?'

Was there news of Cristi? Could she possibly be coming back already? God, did that have to be the first thought? And how daft could you get, there was no way Archie would have stopped him to tell him that.

'I wondered if you could look in for a chat some time,' Archie said. 'There are a couple of things I'd like to talk over with you.'

Dougal stared in front of him, his face settling into grim lines. It had to come. No one could expect a cottage to be kept available indefinitely for a family making no input on the place. Well, if need be they could rent somewhere, till the right house for Jean came up. And to be fair, setting aside the fundamental iniquity of the system, which wasn't going to change in a hurry, Archie had been more than generous.

Dougal turned his head and gave a nod of agreement. 'Fine. Any evening would suit me.'

'Are you in a hurry to get home?'

'Just now? No, I'm in no particular hurry.'

'You've eaten?'

'Aye, I've eaten.' A few hours back.

'Want to come down right away?'

'Fine by me.'

But for all his outward calm Dougal noted that his heart was beating harder than usual as he followed Archie in via the gunroom door, across the wide hall and into what had once been the drawing-room.

Here Archie's grandmother, a grim authoritarian

figure who had terrified the life out of the Galloway children, had reigned with an unbending formality. Here Archie's mother, Madeleine, complying with the rules her mother-in-law had laid down, had spent many empty and lonely hours until, after her husband's death, she had found the courage to chase away the tight-lipped ghosts and create a new atmosphere in the gloomy house. Part of the revolution had been turning this room into the estate office. A contribution of Archie's had been to cut down the mature trees which had crowded close to its windows, and since it faced east and south it was now a spacious, light and pleasant place to work.

It was not particularly tidy but it was highly functional, with not only the traditional large-scale estate maps on the walls, some going back many years, mahogany Victorian filing cabinets and big director's desk with worn leather top, but also the full range of equipment essential to a modern office.

Dougal was at home in this room, in its present form, as he was, or had been while he was growing up, in the rest of the house. But tonight he felt far from relaxed as he accepted a dram from Archie and settled in one of the swivel chairs of dark buttoned hide.

'As a matter of fact, I've been wanting to get hold of you for some time,' Archie began, not sitting down himself for the moment, but prowling across the room to one of the long windows and looking out at the gathering dusk. Earlier already, he noted. The year had turned.

Dougal waited in silence. Since the day of his father's

first stroke the inevitability of having to leave had always lain somewhere at the back of his mind. Well, perhaps at the end of the day they'd be better off clear of the whole boiling, independent of Drumveyn and the Napiers, however things turned out. Not caught up in this outdated set-up, a relic of a past that ought to be buried for good and all.

'Look, Dougal,' Archie began, abruptly for him, turning and coming to sit at the desk, though swinging his chair away from it, as though to emphasise the informal and personal level of their talk. 'I know we've touched on this before, in a way, but perhaps your views have changed since then. I want to ask again if there's any chance that you'd be willing to work on Drumveyn. Not taking your father's place – though Tom and I very much appreciate all you did to fill in for him while he was ill, and the work you've put in since – but coming in on the management side. No, hang on, don't say anything yet,' as Dougal shifted in his seat, startled and frowning, 'hear me out first.'

Archie wanted this badly. He liked and respected Dougal, knew his capacity for hard work, his competence and his readiness to give one hundred per cent to anything he undertook, and he was also keenly aware of the difference it would make to work with someone who knew the estate so thoroughly. Some of this he urged on Dougal.

'It takes time to get the feel of a place this size. You know it like the back of your hand, and you know everyone who works here. You have your training behind you, though of course you'd be able to continue with the business management course you're doing at present – which, in fact, would be the ideal qualification for the job. Tom, as I'm sure you know, would like to ease out altogether, though he's willing to go on looking after the accounts side for as long as he's needed. That could be sorted out among the three of us. What do you say? Would you consider it?'

'But you'd need somebody with a proper degree for a job like that, wouldn't you?' was all Dougal could blurt out in his surprise at this opening. When Archie had spoken to him before about working on Drumveyn, he had not been talking about a job like this. Dougal knew he should make it clear that he was grateful for the compliment Archie was paying him in making such an offer, but that was all he could find to say.

'You're amply qualified for our needs,' Archie assured him, watching him carefully. 'Besides which, your knowledge of the estate would carry far more weight than any degree.' Dougal's unguarded response had reminded him of something he had almost forgotten: how much Dougal had minded having to forego the chance of university. So the sense of second best still nagged at him? Well, it had been bad luck, no question of that, and there was no question either that he would have done well had that been open to him.

'Yes, but—' Dougal floundered; too many things needed to be said. 'What I mean is, you're not just thinking this would be the best way to – give my mother a place to live and all the rest of it?' He had to get this straight before all else.

'No, I'm not,' Archie said quietly. 'Fair enough, when we first spoke of you working for the estate I suppose that aspect was in my mind. I saw you as taking over Donnie's job, maintaining the status quo. I knew you hated working in Muirend and thought you might like the chance of employment here. But you were right to turn me down. However, things have moved on. Tom, quite apart from the damage caused by the accident, though thankfully he's well on the mend now, is at retiring age anyway, something we tend to forget. If he'd been fit I don't suppose it would have been an issue. But as things are I'm being run into the ground. So many things come battering at one, EC regulations changing every week, right to roam, new game laws, and most of it churned out by people who never leave their nice warm city offices. There's no time left to do any damned work. Anyway, you know as much as I do about all that.'

Dougal wasn't sure that he did; he was also very sure that he could learn. But he didn't interrupt.

'On a more immediate level, having a new tenant up at the Lettoch as well as a new shepherd hasn't helped, and there have been a few problems, as I daresay you've heard. Management help is urgently needed, and you'd be the ideal person for the job. Plus, I can't think of anyone I'd rather work with.'

Dougal flushed beneath his tan, giving an embarrassed chuck of the head to acknowledge the emphatic words. For a moment temptation almost swept him away. To be back here, spending his days in the landscape he loved and understood, involved in the running of this place where he had grown up, putting his skills and knowledge to use at last . . . To work for Archie, fairest and most approachable of bosses. He thought of the long-standing links between the families, his father's loyalty to the estate. He thought of Jean safe in her own house, her fears removed.

And there was another thought, more potent and beguiling than all the rest put together. He would be here whenever Cristi was home. He would be able, naturally and as of right, to share with her the things they had always enjoyed together, the seasonal jobs, days on the hill mending butts or burning heather, the odd bit of fencing or dry-stane dyking, brashing plantations, clearing fallen trees, repairing a bridge, mending a ford.

No. He pulled himself up sharply. Though they might, on occasion, find themselves involved in such pursuits together, they wouldn't, and never could, share them on an equal footing again. He'd be paid to do them. Cristi would be playing at them, going back to the big house afterwards to dress for dinner. He knew the phrase was absurd, tossed up by his anger and frustration, nothing to do with the present-day style of Drumveyn, with its relaxed gatherings round the kitchen table, gatherings in which he himself had so often been included. And would be again? The farm manager invited in from time to time? His cheeks burned.

Then the other inducement which had tempted him, the thought of Jean secure in 'her own house', that was even more fatuous. Steading Cottage was 'her own' for no better reason than that she had come into it as a young bride, had reared her family there, gone through her trials with Donald and Jill there (and presumably hidden her disappointment at the way his own life had been forced to go), and had seen her man lose his robust health and cheerfulness and decline and die there. But it was not her own in any other way. She could be put out of it at any moment, as a matter of course. He knew he was being less than fair to Archie, but he pushed that aside. That was the principle.

To be at Drumveyn, yes, the idea had a compelling attraction, but to be there for ever as the employee? Dougal knew that if he committed himself to the plan his own sense of responsibility as well as circumstances would probably mean he was there for good. As his father had done, he would give his life to the place. There were worse ways to live, he knew, and the alternatives at his command were a lot less appealing, but they gave him his independence and that was the crucial factor.

Archie, observing him with a wry expression on his face, read more of this than Dougal guessed. But he said nothing, respecting Dougal's right to make his own decision.

'It's a great offer and I'm grateful for it.' Dougal hesitated, wanting to get this right. 'I know it's a chance most people in my position would give their eye teeth for. But – I'm sorry, Archie, I just don't think I can do it. It's not – it's not what I want out of life. I don't know that I can exactly explain.' He broke off, frowning, hunching forward in his chair, his hands balled into fists on his knees.

Part of Archie's mind, as he waited with patience and sympathy, noting the breadth of Dougal's shoulders and his big hard-working hands, reflected that the stocky lad who had been in and out of the house through the years, inextricably part of the scene as Cristi's bosom pal, had matured into one powerful and formidable young man.

'Talk to me,' he said abruptly. 'Don't worry, I'm not going to argue about whatever decision you make, but I'd like you to talk to me, if you can, about how you feel and what you do want.' The alternative proposal which he had up his sleeve was unusual, to say the least of it, and he needed to be sure of his ground before broaching it.

Dougal made a visible effort to unknot his muscles, sitting back in his chair with a determination to be relaxed which made its spindle protest audibly. Maybe it would be good to get some of this into the open, and it shouldn't be that hard to put it into words for Archie, who had always been something of a hero to him when he was a child. In more adult terms, Archie's direct, hands-on approach as laird had created a good rapport with everyone on Drumveyn in the years since his indolent, arrogant father had died, and Dougal respected that.

'In most ways there's nothing I'd like more than to grab this chance,' he said, as Archie refilled their glasses. 'I think you know that. I hate that damned office, and the job itself is totally dead-end. But even although I'm paid by somebody to do it, it's not like — well, it still lets me feel independent. It's my choice to be there. I can move on whenever I like. Though saying that, I come home to Steading Cottage every evening.'

He paused, shaking his head. This was harder than he'd expected. What difference was there, in truth?

'Listen, Dougal, I know what you mean.' Archie thought it was time to help him out. 'These damned tied houses, that's what it's all about, isn't it? In one way, they're a relic of the past, yet what workable alternative is there? The cottages can't be sold, lying as they mostly do in the heart of the estate. And if they weren't available we couldn't get people to work here because there's nowhere else for them to live. The very nature of the job usually means they have to be on hand. You couldn't have shepherds or gamekeepers or cattlemen doing nine to five, driving up from Muirend, especially in winter conditions.'

'Aye, I know. You don't have to tell me,' Dougal agreed. 'And the fewer families here, the sooner the school closes and the next thing is the village dies.'

'It's the same all over the Highlands.' Archie got up to walk restlessly across the room again. 'But the down-side is still iniquitous – man loses job loses home.' He rubbed a hand through his hair, his face tired. 'To be honest, I don't know what the answer is.'

'Don't think we're not grateful,' Dougal said hastily, smitten with compunction to see that look of tired frustration on Archie's normally cheerful face. 'There's not many places we'd have been let stay so long after Dad died. Or after the job got beyond him. You've been very good to us. I wouldn't want you to think because of what I've said that we don't appreciate—'

'I don't think so,' Archie cut him off. 'But I do

understand how it makes you feel. And I hate to think of Jean having to move, and being worried about it.'

'Well, fair's fair, she's always known she'd have to. It's part of the deal. If Dad had been alive they'd have ended up in a council house at the end of the day just the same. It's the way it's happened that's made it hard. And the problems with Jill on the top of it.'

'Yes, that's been difficult for you both.' But Archie didn't want to be deflected by that. 'So tell me what you'd want, truly want for yourself, Dougal, if the world were a more equitable place?'

'Ach, daft things.' Dougal looked down with a grimace at the glass he was twisting in his hands. 'Somewhere of my own is what it would come down to, I suppose. And how mad is that, when farming is a dying way of life, and farmers are selling up, going bankrupt or topping themselves every day?'

'But if you had the chance, that's what you'd want? Even with things as they are?'

'I'm not sure there's a lot of point talking about it,' Dougal said. 'But yes, since you ask. I do feel a need, not just for a few acres of my own, the feeling that I'm living under my own roof, but for beasts to tend, living creatures around me. I know it's a dream. Even with farming in such straits it's way beyond anything I could ever achieve. But as a way to live, even keeping the day job – well, you'd never get by without – I'd see that as pretty much the best anyone could ask for.'

Constraint was falling away now, the whisky doing its work, and Archie, satisfied, encouraged him to open up about thoughts which he knew were normally kept strictly under lock and key. He had had little real hope of capturing this prize for Drumveyn, and he and Tom would have to think again on that score, but he admired Dougal more than ever for his independent stance and for his honesty.

He let the talk flow on, touching on the effects the present crisis in agriculture was having on neighbouring landowners, discussing plans for new planting out towards the Lettoch, assessing the prospects for this year's entries for the Kirkton Games. And presently, when the moment seemed right, into the peaceful exchanges, the open and receptive mood, he floated the alternative proposal he and Tom had devised, with the enthusiastic approval of both Pauly and Madeleine.

Chapter Eleven

In the pause before he launched into his new subject Archie caught the faint sound of a car coming up the slope, blanketed as it went round the end of the house. Pauly coming home. She would have seen the light on in the estate room, would see the Land Rover in the courtyard, but he knew she wouldn't disturb them. Scatty and impulsive as Pauly might be, she understood the crucial and sensitive nature of this discussion. She'd be dying to know the answer, though. Archie's face was amused for a second, guessing the trouble she'd be having crushing down her curiosity, then it grew serious again. He must get this right. Dougal possessed a fierce and admirable pride, and it was vital that he had it clear from the outset that no one was trying to offer him charity or do him any favours.

'Dougal, look, there is another possibility I'd like to kick around if you're interested. Not strictly speaking to do with Drumveyn. At least not as it relates to you. Want to hear it?'

'Not to do with Drumveyn?' Dougal looked blank.

'It's to do with Ellig. Ellig farm, that is, not the village.'

'Ellig? How d'you mean?'

'Right, now listen, and don't interrupt.' It was Archie who sat forward this time, fired with enthusiasm for his plan, which until now he had scarcely believed might be a runner.

'OK.' Dougal's expression said he thought Archie was losing it, but now that he was settled in he was quite content to sit here chatting and downing malt whisky till the cows came home.

'Right.' Unconsciously Archie took a deep breath. 'You know the state Ellig is in, after years of being at the mercy of that feckless Maclachlan crew.'

'I know there's barely a dyke standing, and that you'd get a good crop of ragwort off it and not much else.' It angered Dougal so deeply to see such criminal neglect that he never went near the head of the glen these days if he could help it.

'And every building ready to collapse, the whole place silted with broken-down machinery and God knows what other rubbish.' Archie nodded. 'Yes, it's sad to see, and now that it's to go on the market I've been thinking it would be a good idea to take it into Drumveyn if that were feasible. It's too small a unit to be viable on its own, in today's conditions. As you say, it would be hard to make a living out of it, and it's not an attractive option anyway with the house in the state it's in. The Danahers won't want to add it to Grianan.

They've got enough to do keeping that huge garden of theirs under control, especially now that Mike's not well. And I certainly don't want a succession of wasters like Jed Maclachlan trying their hand for a year or two then giving up, harming the environment at every turn. There's some good summer grazing up there, and a nice little pocket of arable beside the river if it could be reclaimed.'

Archie paused, his eyes on the glass he rolled for a moment between his hands, as he decided how best to go on. Dougal waited, very still. What was coming?

'The thing is,' Archie resumed, feeling his way more cautiously, 'I wouldn't want to take on another man to get the place in shape, so I've no use for the house.'

Large questions were beginning to turn in Dougal's mind, but he kept all sign of them out of his face.

Archie looked directly at him now. 'I wouldn't want it sold separately either, if it's to have Drumveyn land around it. And if it wasn't sold the only answer would be to take the roof off, as was done with the original farmhouse. Or knock them both down.' The fate of many a dwelling in these high glens.

Dougal still couldn't see where this was going. Archie knew as well as he did that he was in no position to buy land, no matter how few acres or in what condition. And surely he had made it plain that he couldn't stomach being an estate employee, with all that that entailed. Yet there was obviously something here to do with him, and again he was conscious of the beat of his heart. His eyes never leaving Archie's face, he reached to put his glass on the desk, pushing it a little away from him.

Archie wondered if he was putting it out of harm's way, or thought he needed to keep a clear head, but guessed that more probably Dougal was unaware of the action.

'OK.' This was it. 'Here's my proposal. I buy the Ellig ground, but make over to you the house, the buildings, and a couple of acres surrounding them. You'd own those. The title deeds would be in your name. They'd be nothing to do with Drumveyn. In return you'd put in time to get the farm into shape, fences, gates, dykes, drainage, have a go at the bracken and the seedling trees on the low ground, whatever. In other words, instead of doing homers for other people as you do now in your spare time, you'd be doing them, in a sense, for yourself. The house needs a lot of work, so all in all it may look too much to take on. But the thing is, there'd be no hurry. I don't have any immediate need for the extra ground, but nor do I want it to degenerate into a complete wilderness on my doorstep.'

'I'd own the house?' Dougal sounded stunned, clutching at this as the simplest question to ask.

'Legally and without ties, except that I'd ask for the usual right of pre-emption clause to make sure Drumveyn had first refusal if ever you chose to sell.'

'Bloody hell.' Dougal stared at him, struggling to take it in. 'What can I say?'

Archie laughed. 'I know it's a bit unusual. You'll want to think it over, and questions or drawbacks may occur to you that we haven't considered. But broadly speaking I can't see why it shouldn't work. It would certainly be doing me a favour.'

Dougal sat very still. Visions of that high, light, windswept place rose before him; the small grey house with the hill at its back and its face four-square to the sun. There was nothing to stop him living in it as it was, while he worked on it. Summer still, hours of daylight. Good water supply up there, always had been. Clean it out, check the electrics . . . Jesus, Jesus.

Archie watched him, his face sympathetic. That blaze of incredulous, dazzled speculation would, he knew, give way to doubt as other aspects came flooding in.

The first to find voice was, 'But Archie, you can't go giving away a house. I can't accept that, no way.'

'How much do you honestly think anyone would give for it? Away up that awful track? What sort of buyer would be interested? It's too exposed a spot to attract the wealthy retired. And it's not the sort of place most glen people want nowadays either. Certainly not the ones your age. They prefer the so-called amenities of Muirend. I might get a few thousand for it if I was lucky, then what became of it would be out of my hands, and I'd still have to get the farm into good heart.'

Dougal shook his head. 'All the same, it seems to me I'd get by far the best of the bargain. I don't want any favours done me.' A warning note there.

'I knew that would worry you, so let's get it out of the way at the outset. I regard the advantages as being on my side. To be frank, this is hardly a proposition I could put to anyone else. I want to help you, that's true. I'd like nothing better than to see you take this chance – though it's not something many people would see in that light!

Also I see it as a way to repay a little of what your father put into this place over the years and—'

'That was my father, not me.'

'Come on, Dougal, don't turn grouchy on me. Why shouldn't I be grateful? And why shouldn't I see the unfairness of the tied cottage system as clearly as you do? Only I'm fortunate enough not to be at its mercy.'

Dougal allowed himself a reluctant grin, thinking of the extreme contrast between their situations. But there was no doubting Archie's sincerity.

'But that aside,' he was continuing forcefully, 'I want to help *you*. I've known you all your life and I think you're worth helping. No, shut up for a minute. You haven't been dealt a particularly fair hand to date. Not only did you have to miss out on university but you've had a tough time at home. You're the younger brother, but because of the way Donald behaves you've had to take on a lot of responsibilities which weren't strictly speaking yours. And while we're on the subject, may I indulge in a little frank speaking?'

Dougal grinned more broadly this time. 'That'll be different from what you've done so far, will it?' In spite of the doubts and objections, somewhere beneath them an intoxicating euphoria was rising, quite beyond him to subdue. A foothold of his own, as he had always dreamed of having, but knowing it could never be more than a dream. And here, in Glen Ellig. Not only where he had always wanted to live, but where Cristi lived, or at least where she would come and go, where her home was.

Or was it, now? Had events carried her in a different

direction? That possibility was never far from his mind. But no, he thought, angry with himself. Whatever he decided, he mustn't above all be influenced by this. He had already accepted, hadn't he, that, wherever she was, Cristi's life was separate from his.

Archie, grinning at Dougal's dry response, was conscious of surprised relief. He had feared being met by instant stiff-necked rejection, but they were safely past that point now. 'Here,' he said, 'what am I thinking of, more than time for a refill.'

As he poured the drams he said more seriously, 'You've hardly had time to think through the details yet, but obviously in its present state the grieve's house at Ellig isn't fit to take Jean to.'

He saw at once, from the way Dougal's face changed, that the vision had been of living alone, in a house of his own – freedom. He saw guilt awake as Dougal realised that he hadn't given a thought to Jean being there with him. But if he was to live in the glen, and Jean wanted to stay in the glen, keeping two households would be daft.

'What I wanted to say,' Archie cut in before Dougal could speak, 'though I'm quite aware it's none of my business, is that I don't believe you should even think along those lines. Jean has her name down for a single council house, doesn't she? So neither of you had envisaged, when she left Steading Cottage, that you'd be living with her?'

'I'd thought it would make more sense if I found somewhere in Muirend.' How he had dreaded it. 'Nearer the job. But if I was to be up here . . .'

'You'd be nearby, and Jean would be tucked up warm in a cosy little house, near the shop and near her friends, with the bus to take her down to Muirend once a week and the library van once a fortnight. I think she's earned that, don't you? Just think what she'd insist on taking on if she moved into that filthy little house up above.'

Dougal gave a resigned chuck of the head. 'Scrub it out from top to bottom the first day. Don't tell me.' Then his expression became more bleak. 'There's Jill, though, don't forget. She'll never stick in the glen for long. She just runs back now and again when she's nowhere else to go. I'd thought if I had some place in the town . . .' He didn't finish, his heart sinking to imagine the daily hassle and strife that would mean.

Archie was silent for a moment. Then, speaking carefully, he said, 'Dougal, it may be time to distance yourself a bit from that situation. Let Jean have her house in the village, where you'd be able to keep an eye on her, and take a stand, if you can bring yourself to, against Jill creating havoc as and when it suits her. I know it wouldn't be easy. Your instinct is to take care of her, but remember, you have given her chance after chance. Only she can turn her life around. As long as she knows she has somewhere to run to, where everything is laid on, she may never take the necessary pull.'

'Easy enough said.' Dougal's mouth settled into harsh lines. He looked, as he often did these days, older than his twenty-six years, and Archie felt they were talking very much as equals. It reinforced his conviction that he had been right to make his offer.

'I know,' he agreed. 'I can only guess at what it must be like to have to deal with such a problem. But this way you'd still have a roof to offer Jill if she needed it. All I'm saying is, maybe it's time to stop basing decisions about your own future on the needs or shortcomings of others.'

'So that's why you dreamed up this deal?' Dougal's face coloured, and his eyes met Archie's with an anger he rarely showed.

'It's part of it,' Archie replied, meeting his look steadily. 'But only part. The plan would benefit me, as you can't fail to see. I want to make sure Ellig doesn't slip through my fingers, and this is one way it could be done.'

Archie was wryly aware as he spoke that, while they could discuss at length the dire state of modern-day farming, it wouldn't have crossed Dougal's mind that with Tom retiring, and hence a manager's wage to find, Drumveyn would be stretched to take in extra acres and make them productive. He had been accustomed since childhood to the easy 'it's a broad shoulder' outlook of estate employees; the laird had a bottomless pit of money. That went without saying.

'But going back to Jill for a moment,' Archie said, aware that he was on delicate ground here, 'I know you've tried to get help for her in all the ways available, and I do understand that you'd never want to give up on her, but — I'm not sure that you can afford to go on letting her problems affect your own life.'

Dougal was silent, his mouth grimly set.

'She's an adult, Dougal,' Archie urged quietly. 'Other

people can only help her up to a point. After that it's up to her.'

'I know.'

'I just hate to see her closing doors and wrecking chances for you. She's given you and your parents a lot of grief over the years.'

'She has.' Dougal's voice was flat, his defensive anger under control. He knew Archie had his interests at heart. 'But you know yourself, you can't get anywhere near her. If you do succeed in getting her to talk to you, you can't get any sense out of her. On the one hand she's too lazy to get herself as far as Glasgow to see the baby, yet on the other she rants on about getting him back, saying he's the only thing that matters to her. It's not a question of getting him back anyway. No one took him. She left him with his grandmother herself.'

His nephew. Dougal had never seen him. He seemed to belong completely to that shifting, shadowy, destructive world which had sucked Jill in.

Archie winced to think of Dougal taking responsibility for the child on his shoulders too. He knew the power of his conscience.

'Well, you know my view, for what it's worth. As to Ellig,' he deliberately let the tone lighten, 'what's on offer is little more than a lot of damned hard work. I can't think of anyone else who wouldn't laugh in my face at the mere suggestion of taking it on. But it may suit you. We could go up and have a look around some time, and you could get a clearer idea of what could go with the house. About ten acres or so,

I had in mind, to give you room for some livestock. How would that be?'

Dougal stared at him, dumbfounded. He had supposed, hardly daring to imagine it, that the sale might include one or two acres at most. Ten acres! Then, taking him entirely by surprise, he found the muscles of his face out of his control. He ducked his head, putting up a hand to cover his eyes, furiously ashamed of himself. After a second he was grateful to feel a hand on his shoulder in a brief firm grip.

'That's what we'll do then,' Archie said, his own voice husky.

This was going to happen. He couldn't wait to tell Pauly, knowing how thrilled she'd be, and needing too to share his relief and pleasure. Just as well she wasn't here though; she'd have disgraced herself for sure.

Cristi sat alone in the shade of the deep verandah, beside her on a glass-topped table a tall glass of freshly squeezed orange juice. A maid in a grey dress with white collar, cuffs and belt, starched and trim, had brought it for her. She had been smiling and friendly, making sure the table was within Cristi's reach from her cushioned lounger, asking if there was anything else she needed.

The servants, one and all, had taken to Cristi, who was not only young and pretty, but whose reappearance in the family home was intriguing, since her parentage and her story were well known to kitchen gossip. She also smiled, and thanked them when they did things for her, something to which they were not accustomed. One or two of the older ones, in fact, would murmur, 'There is no need to thank,' feeling it was not appropriate.

But, the moment of smiling contact over, Cristi knew she could ignore no longer the creeping chill of loneliness, or the more disturbing sensation, so strongly associated with the past, of being trapped in some luxurious but inexorable prison.

She had been trying not to face this thought. How could she be so ungrateful? Who in the world could be more fortunate, who could ask for more? Cristi was by nature positive, and she hated to feel so on edge in this house, missing the affection, laughter and straightforward values of home. Without Luis she knew she would have been lonely indeed.

She looked around her. There was not a single object in sight which was not designed to please, from the elegant furnishings of the verandah to the magnificence of the garden. It was the same in the house. On every side there was evidence of cultured taste backed by the solid wealth of generations. With her artist's eye she could delight in it, and she had spent many enthralled hours since she had arrived examining these treasures.

But the self which she thought of as her real self sometimes wanted passionately to see muddy boots by the back door at Drumveyn, Broy curled up on one of the children's beds, the ponies pacing up the field to greet her as the dawn light warmed with sunrise. She wanted to see the kitchen table a chaos of eggshells, slabs of yellow butter with the stag pattern made by the old wooden pats, the jar of vanilla pods, the bottle of rum, chocolate taking on a rich dark gleam as it melted in the double bank, Pauly chatting to some passing caller who sat, lightly dusted with flour, a glass of wine in front of her, enjoying the bravura performance as Pauly lashed up one of her stupendous puddings.

She wanted to see Archie come in in his check shirt with the ragged collar, his faded moleskins worn to smoothness, his brown face creasing into a smile at the sight of Pauly. She wanted her own retreat of the studio, and the robust comfort of the old barn, planned to suit Tom's masculine taste, and accepted exactly as it was by Madeleine. She wanted to see Madeleine herself thigh deep in the burn on a summer evening, her face absorbed, time forgotten, the smooth practised casts of her line, the trout on the bank, the dancing maze of insects over the water. She wanted the hurly-burly and arguments of the others, at home now – Nicholas always with some project on hand, trying to shake off the pursuit of the younger ones; Josie's laid-back cheerfulness; even Peta's wild alarms over nothing.

Behind this web of fleeting images, behind all she did or thought, there ached the longing for Dougal. Dougal who had decided that things between them could never again be on the happy footing of understanding and trust which had been a cornerstone of her life.

Don't think of that, don't think of any of it. Concentrate on the good things here. There were plenty of them. Her stunning surroundings for one; no childhood memories had prepared her for the fabulous variety of natural beauty that Rio had to offer. Then, she had been cordially welcomed by everyone she had met, and in view of the long estrangement that was pretty impressive. From Luis there had been real, instant friendliness. Thank goodness he'd taken the trouble to be here when she arrived, for Cristi knew by now that he lived in Porto Alegre, in the southern state of Rio Grande do Sul.

The fact that she had briefly given way to homesickness was partly due, she was aware, to Luis's absence. He had gone to São Paulo for a few days on business (unspecified), and without his lively presence, his flow of conversation, his jokes and teasing, the formal atmosphere of the house had begun to weigh upon her. There had also begun to grow in her a strange sense almost of foreboding.

Cristi shivered as her mind went back to her first evening here. Though she had not been aware of it at the time, it had set the tone for all that followed.

Chapter Twelve

Cristi knew that what she saw, looking back, was a distorted vignette of herself on that evening of arrival – a small, overwhelmed figure, outlandishly dressed, among a throng of other figures self-confident and assured, their movements calm and measured, their substantial flesh firmly contained and their faces, though kind, revealing a readiness to patronise if not actually disparage.

The Fonsecas were without exception well-dressed and well-groomed. On that evening Cristi had felt the words *haute couture* and designer label hovering in the air. For a simple family gathering the women had sported some pretty over-the-top jewellery, she had decided, but the attempt to be mildly amused by it had withered as she remembered her mother had dressed exactly like this.

This was how they lived, in their guarded enclaves behind the security cameras and electric fencing, the high walls and locked gates, in an exclusive paradise of wealth, assurance and luxury, refusing any contact, even in their minds, with the poverty, unemployment, homelessness and crime which were rife in the city below. It was in many ways a lifestyle long out-dated, yet the gulf between the tiny nucleus of the very rich and the mass of the very poor was as wide as ever.

Luis's elder sisters, Gabriela and Catarina, though still in their thirties, seemed to Cristi to belong to the same generation as their mother. Impossible to imagine them in casual clothes, their hair untidy, their manicured hands dirty. Pauly was only few years younger than these elegant matrons. A vision had warmed Cristi, as this occurred to her, of Pauly with her cheeks scarlet, hair all over the place, wearing khaki shorts and one of Archie's shirts, yelling her head off in a game of family football on the lawn.

The introductions had been made according to strict protocol by Sylvia, and as the scented *abraços* were offered, Cristi had caught cooing murmurs of, 'We are so delighted . . .' 'It is such a great pleasure . . .'

She had known these expressions were the usual form. Ceremony, it had been clear, still ruled. But it had meant that her own eagerness to meet her cousins was reduced to a similar formality. She had been obliged to accept that spontaneous hugs would not have done.

Before and during dinner, which had gone on for ever, smoothly served by two white-jacketed servants who might have been automata for all the notice anyone took of them, serene exchanges ran along oiled lines. Each of the group made a point of welcoming Cristi to Brazil; each asked the kind of social questions intended to convey a courteous interest without intrusive curiosity.

Cristi knew her memory of the scene was exaggerated, but all the same there had been, apart from Luis's lively and what she thought of as 'normal' conversation, a baffled feeling of talking to everyone else through a glass wall. It had not been difficult to play her part, there were no awkward silences, no topic was introduced which produced constraint, but the possibility of ever making natural, affectionate contact with these people had seemed depressingly remote.

It had probably been her own fault as much as theirs. She had still been jet-lagged, in spite of having slept that morning and enjoyed a lazy siesta after lunch. The scene had been new to her, the occasional strange flash of recognition only adding to her sense of disorientation. And she knew she had minded more than she should have the discovery that they all, even Luis, took it for granted that she must be thankful to escape the horrors of Scotland to return to a more civilised country.

It had not occurred to her, when they asked about Drumveyn, that this would be their starting point. She had answered readily, missing home already and happy to talk about it, and had been startled by their dismissive comments and patronising smiles.

'Ah, yes, Scotland. So beautiful. The mountains and the locks. Lockses? Losh? But then the weather, how terrible the mist, the cold, the greyness must be . . .' 'And you do not mind living *no interior* – so far from any cultural centre, from contact with people?'

So much for Scotland.

Afonso, one of the sons-in-law – and how suitable for the part both appeared to be, younger clones of Joachim, already hung about with the discreet aura of affluence and success – asked about hunting deer, saying he had thought of trying the sport some time. (The look of resolve that he should do no such thing which appeared on Gabriela's face had told Cristi, who was having trouble sorting out the couples, which sister he belonged to.) When, however, Afonso had discovered that no army of beaters would be deployed to assist him, that he would not be taken by vehicle to within shot of the quarry, and might expect to return with one trophy per day at best, he soon lost interest.

English had been spoken throughout. Cristi had suspected that this was not only offered as a civility to her, the guest, but because it had been assumed that her Portuguese would be inadequate and no one had wanted to wait while she struggled with it. It would hardly have been polite not to accept this courtesy, and it was true that her Portuguese had been far from fluent at that stage, but it had added yet another element of restraint to the already formal atmosphere.

Nothing had been said, at this first gathering to greet her, about the reason for her presence. No reference had been made to grandfather, other than when Cristi herself had offered her condolences on his death. Yet behind the smiling welcome, the obligatory compliments on her appearance offered with barely a quiver of the eyelids, the warm invitations from Gabriela and Catarina to visit their homes and meet their families, the inference that she had at last done the right thing, by returning to the place where she belonged, had always been there. In view of the years of silence from these very people it had been hard to accept it without some comment, but Cristi had known it had not been the time for that.

Less understandably, and it was beginning to bother her, the reason behind her return had continued to be ignored. Since she had been summoned with some urgency this had been puzzling, but in the end it had become rather intriguing to see just how many days would be allowed to pass without the subject being raised. Did they think she wouldn't notice?

Joachim had informed her the day after she arrived that a meeting with the lawyers was being arranged. He had also told her that a startling sum of money had been made available for her immediate needs. Luis would take her to the bank to provide the necessary signatures. Joachim had then remained invisible for several days, leaving for the office before Cristi appeared in the mornings, never appearing for lunch, and busy elsewhere each evening.

Sylvia, when approached, had been vague.

'Forgive me, *querida*, I have little to do with such matters. Joachim will explain everything, I am sure, but at present he is so occupied. Then there must be a meeting, and it's so difficult to find a time when everyone is free. Perhaps João will wish to come back from the States for it after all, though at first I believe he thought it not necessary. *Vamos ver.*'

We shall see. Well-remembered phrase; and well-remembered too the shrug that went with it, though in Sylvia's case it was merely elegantly sketched.

'Meanwhile,' Sylvia had dismissed difficult questions with a charming smile, 'we must make sure that you feel properly at home. Everyone longs to meet you, and there is so much for you to see. How fortunate that Luis is on hand to look after you. He spends very little time in Rio as a rule . . .'

Between them they had thoroughly spoiled her and, Cristi had to admit, it had been wonderful. The days had slipped by, filled with the kind of pampered pursuit of pleasure she had never indulged in before and which, to be honest, she wouldn't have thought would have appealed to her. The whole scene, the superb climate, tropical but close enough to the subtropics to be perfect all year round, the mountains and forests, lagoons and beaches, woke a vivid response in her. There *was* a sense of belonging, of returning, which she couldn't deny.

Her own appearance was part of it. The family, now that they were all on a more familiar footing, teased her about her slight build, her look of being a young girl, but they were also very ready to tell her that this look charmed them and that she was beautiful. She wasn't used to such outspoken compliments, and for the first time since she could recall being aware of her appearance Cristi felt no need to be self-conscious about it. She wasn't different; she wasn't fending off the attentions of crass males drawn by her 'foreign' looks. Among these handsome relatives she felt at ease with her appearance, accepting it for the first time.

'You cannot imagine how delighted I was when I saw you at the airport,' Luis would say. 'I'd been quite prepared to slip away if you proved unsatisfactory. I would have abandoned you without a qualm. What a strange word, qualm. I'm not sure I've ever said it before. Is that how one pronounces it? Yes? How clever of me. But of course, I promise you, I should have phoned the lawyers, said I'd been unavoidably detained, and told them to send someone to retrieve you. But there you were, so wide-eyed and naive, so entirely delightful. Naturally I did my duty.'

Despite the gleam in his eye, the flattery which was as natural to him as breathing and meant absolutely nothing, it was fun to hear all this. As it was fun to go with the flow, and let this new way of life, of which she was legitimately part, sweep her along.

For the first time in her life she plunged into the pleasures of shopping, which had never attracted her in the past. When at home she resisted anything that took her out of the glen. In Edinburgh, though she had enjoyed what the city had to offer, she had had better things to do with her student allowance, and in any case enjoyed using her creative ideas and newly acquired skills to design and make things for herself.

Here, in one of the great fashion centres of the world, the shops were a wonder and a delight. Even the less expensive displayed their wares with a flair and style not often found in Scotland's capital. Though able to mock herself for being seduced by this new experience, Cristi could still hugely enjoy it.

Each evening was occupied. There was a dinner party at home, she was swept away to some other splendid house belonging to a family member or friends, there was a concert or a visit to the theatre or ballet, or she was taken to dine and dance by Luis. In theory, with no occupation of any kind before evening, the days should have held stretches of empty time. But, in a way which brought back memories of her mother, a great part of them was taken up with the strenuous effort underpinning this endless social activity.

Dining late, and more heavily than she was accustomed to, Cristi found herself sleeping later too. Breakfast was brought to her room, and after a leisurely shower it was time to go out with Sylvia, who never seemed to spend a morning at home.

Down they would be carried in the big car to the boutiques and galleries of Ipanema, more sophisticated (and expensive) than the thronged shops of Copacabana, or to visit Sylvia's beautician, dressmaker or hairdresser. Much as Cristi had liked the clothes she'd made for herself, she couldn't resist the beautifully-cut little dresses in the vibrant colours which the sun, the tropical vegetation and the light from the immense blue bay called for. These colours were part of her heritage, and she indulged in wearing them with frank pleasure. It was enjoyable, in short, to play little rich girl for a while, to succumb to manicures and face massages, have her hair cut with superb skill, trawl the scented shops for mouth-watering scarves, bags and belts, for fun jewellery and elegant sandals.

Gabriela and Catarina both lived in luxurious mansions overlooking the Rodrigo do Freitas lagoon, and Cristi was made free of their houses in the traditional manner, met their children and their cosmopolitan circle of friends, and swam in their tempting swimming pools.

Only during the sacrosanct period of siesta, for which Sylvia made a point of being home, did the feeling of being bowled along by events let up a little. The afternoons were not too hot at this time of year, and Cristi rarely felt like sleeping. This was the time when she could be alone, often reading but usually busy with endless letters home, and to Torie and Isa, describing all she was doing and seeing, needing the contact with everyone she loved and missed.

To Dougal she wrote all the time, in her head. Much as she longed to write in fact – talking freely about her doubts, her feeling of living in some temporary, fragile bubble of unreality, her attacks of homesickness, her mixed feelings towards the family, and in trying to express these things to him find comfort or maybe reach some clearer understanding of herself – she dreaded him being surprised to hear from her, or even annoyed. She sent him instead a postcard of the Corcovado, and cried after she had posted it. No hope that he would reply to such a banal communication, as she so desperately longed for him to do.

The best part of any day was being driven by Luis away from the well-run fortress of her uncle's house, away from Sylvia's oppressive correctness, away from the slow turning of its unstoppable routines. Her spirits would soar with elation and relief.

Though she was never clear about what precisely occupied him when he was elsewhere, Luis liked to give the impression that his business interests, like his father's, were extensive, varied, high-powered and not up for discussion. Even so, he seemed to have plenty of time to spare to show her this most beautiful of cities, though he disdained the more obvious tourist haunts.

'You may read about it,' he would say. 'You will only catch something appalling if you insist on going there.' Or, 'Let me assure you, *O Redemptor* is perfectly hideous at close quarters. Its only excuse for existing, if it has one, is to be seen from a great distance.'

'The view must be worth it,' Cristi suggested.

'The view? If you can't survive without seeing the view then I shall take you up to fly over it.'

The flight had not materialised, but Cristi had got her views when Luis swept her up the stunning road to Petrópolis, the small town high in the mountains where the Brazilian Imperial family had built their summer palace. True, he had been more interested in a carefully chosen gourmet lunch than in giving her time to examine the documents, jewels and works of art of the present-day museum, but Cristi had loved the day.

Though Luis declined absolutely to show her 'the sights', he was perfectly happy to take her to fashionable restaurants, exclusive country clubs and the houses of his friends, and particularly to the nightclubs favoured by the rich and famous. Cristi was fascinated by these glimpses of glamour, but what really thrilled her was being shown them by Luis.

He was enormously attractive; there was no denying it. In fact she found him, since he was setting himself to please and entertain her, pretty well irresistible. He was a fluent talker, had a sharp sense of humour, was gregarious and, when he was interested, had a great capacity for enjoyment. For Cristi the days soon revolved around time spent with him.

She took the chance to visit places like the Museum of Primitive Art, or the artists' haunt of Apothecary Square, when he was occupied with his own affairs, but these expeditions lost much of their charm without him – and also when Sylvia insisted on sending her in the car, which waited for her and firmly brought her back.

Drumveyn began to seem far away. Sometimes Cristi would feel it spinning so far out of reach that she would deliberately summon up contrasting images to bring it close again. Lazing on the veranda, the elegant, well-dressed, indolent Brazilian *senhorita*, she would close her eyes and imagine the waxed texture, the rubbed folds and tattered cuffs of her favourite old Barbour. She would think herself back into a winter's day on the hill with the wind like a knife on her cheekbones, the hair on her forehead clinking icicles. She would think of filling potholes in the drive with Archie, seeing the ancient tarring machine and the appalling clothes kept for the job. How horrified Luis would be. Would he renounce her as his cousin if he saw her like that? Amusement at the thought was a timely reminder of other ways, other values.

For behind her light-hearted willingness to go along for the moment with the luxury so extravangantly on offer, there nagged the awareness of being shut away from so much more. She missed the personal freedom she had always taken for granted. She wanted to do ordinary things, on her own — explore downtown Rio, stroll with the crowds, ride the scenic tramline over the Carioca Arches, eat spicy snacks and drink *guaraná* at a corner bar, join in the weekend *feijoadas*, literally beanfeasts, on the beach. She wanted contact with people of her own age, people who didn't inhabit the rarefied Fonseca world.

Such simple pleasures were literally inaccessible. She had found, with a sense almost of outrage, that it was impossible to leave the house at will. The big gates operated only for vehicles. The door by which the servants came and went was kept locked, and when she asked one afternoon for it to be opened she had only succeeded in embarrassing the apologetic gardener who had to refuse her.

'But my dear Maria-Cristina,' Sylvia had cried in horror when she heard about this, 'you cannot walk out into the *avenida*, unaccompanied. Why should you want to? Where would you go? If you want to walk you can be driven to the Botanical Garden or to the Tijuca Forest. They are both very beautiful. You can be taken anywhere you wish, at any time, you have only to ask.'

Not wanting Sylvia to think her care and thought for her guest had been found lacking, Cristi had tried diffidently to explain that sometimes she just felt like going off exploring on her own.

'On your own? *Mas, querida*, don't you realise the dangers? Don't you understand that any member of a household such as ours is at risk? We haven't spoken of it as we didn't wish to alarm you, but there have been many cases of kidnapping, of hostages being held, of threats. Anyone in a position such as Joachim's is a target, and as one of his family, you can see for yourself . . .'

There had been no argument against this, but it had made Cristi see in a new light her protected childhood, to which the freedom of Drumveyn had seemed such a magical and exciting contrast. But it had also made her feel, with instinctive resistance, that she was being permitted to see one side only of this multi-faceted country. There was so much, she knew, to shock and appal beneath the glittering surface, and it seemed wrong simply to shut it out.

Even more urgently, as the beguiling days succeeded each other, she wanted to find out about her inheritance, something the Fonseca family seemed conveniently to have forgotten. It was hard to believe sometimes that she had let so much time go by without pushing for the long-promised meeting with the lawyers. How reminiscent this smiling procrastination was. In just this way her mother had allowed promises to evaporate and come to nothing.

The difficulty of broaching the subject brought home to Cristi how superficial her acceptance into the family had been. Everyone had been generous and kind, more than fulfilling the requirements of hospitality but, apart from Luis, whose company she enjoyed more and more, she was no closer to a single one of them than she had been on the day she arrived.

This was her life they were putting on hold, she told herself. She had a right to know the truth.

Chapter Thirteen

'Might Cristi come home before we go back to school?'

'Oh, darling, you keep asking me that. I only wish I knew.' Madeleine turned her head to send a quick rueful smile to Josie, in the back of the Range Rover. 'But it doesn't seem likely. Everything in Brazil is taking for ever. From her last letter it sounded as though she didn't know much more than when she left.'

'It's not a bit the same without her. I hate it.' Peta always took things harder than outgoing Josie. 'And she didn't even say goodbye to us.'

'Yes, she did. She phoned.' Nicholas, in the front beside Madeleine, rounded on her. Peta was an idiot the way she got so worked up. His face pinched as he remembered his own conversation with Cristi.

'She might never come back.'

'Don't be stupid.'

'She will, won't she, Grannie?' That was Josie getting upset now.

'Of course she will. It's just that arranging things is going to take longer than we thought.'

'But she *could* live in Brazil, couldn't she?'

Madeleine knew Peta was persisting more for the sake of argument than anything else, but nevertheless the question reawoke her own lurking doubts.

She was aware of Nicholas turning his head to look at her, and smiled at him.

'You miss her too, don't you?' she asked quietly.

Nicholas lifted a shoulder, half nodding. After a moment he said gruffly, as if almost against his will, 'It's her real family she's with now though, isn't it?'

Such simple words, but Madeleine was conscious of a sharp dismay. When the three younger ones had come home from school there had been great excitement about Cristi being an heiress, and the jokes had ranged from her having to lasso and brand her own steers to finding a huge impoverished family waiting to have their debts paid off. There had been trouble all round when it came to converting acres into hectares. But it had not crossed Madeleine's mind, and she doubted if anyone else had thought of it either, to imagine that the sudden re-emergence of Cristi's relations would disturb Nicholas by any comparison with his own circumstances.

As far as Archie was concerned, Nicholas was his son. He had never seen him in any other light and never would. But Nicholas knew this wasn't technically so, for when Peta and Josie had been adopted Archie and Pauly had made a decision to tell all the children the facts about their origins. As they grew older this had been done, in terms that were acceptable and comprehensible to them.

When Cecil, Nicholas's mother, had elected to be inseminated by donor sperm rather than to adopt, seeking, in her exaggerated way, 'the total experience of giving birth', Archie had not found it easy to reconcile himself to her decision. During the early stages of her pregnancy it had been hard not to mind the changes taking place in her sleek and elegant body, and he had fought a tough private battle in order to come to terms with them. But he was a man of generous spirit, and as the months passed he had not only dealt with that resistance, but had come whole-heartedly to want the child. When Nicholas had been born and Cecil had so violently rejected him, repelled by all contact, there had been no question in Archie's mind that the child was his to love and care for.

Madeleine had had her own problems over accepting Cecil's plan, which at first she had found distasteful in the extreme, but on that momentous day when Archie had come home from the hospital with Nicholas in his arms, saying, 'I should think, among the lot of us, we should be able to cope,' the beautiful fair-haired baby had been accepted by her on the instant as a Napier – Archie's son, and her grandchild.

When Peta and Josie joined the family, though she loved them dearly, there had remained a subtle distinction in her mind between them and Nicholas, just as Cristi was different again, and had her own unique place in Madeleine's heart. These distinctions had never mattered, and would have been almost impossible to put into words, even to herself, but they existed.

Now Nicholas's words reminded her, with shock, that in genetic terms he belonged to the family no more than Cristi did. And, as they struck her with a new significance, she found herself wondering, something she hadn't done for years, who his father was. A donor of life. Would there be any record still in existence of who he had been? Madeleine found she definitely didn't want to know. But Cecil herself, strange, exotic, sad Cecil, with her crippling inability to form relationships, damaged for ever by a childhood of being passed like a parcel from one set of unstable adults to another — where was she, what was she doing now?

A wild sense of inadequacy billowed up in Madeleine, then subsided. Not a fraction of this could be going through Nicholas's mind. He was thirteen, fourteen very soon. Mature as he had always been for his age, the two-year gap between him and Peta always appearing much bigger than it was, his remark could surely only mean that he felt there might be more behind Cristi's departure than he had been told.

'I suppose there are different ways of having a "real" family,' Madeleine said, hastily gathering her wits. 'Certainly the Fonsecas are Cristi's relatives, but even when she lived in Brazil as a child there was hardly any contact. They thought her mother had behaved badly, so she was more or less banished from the family.'

'Cristi has a mother and father somewhere, though, doesn't she?'

Madeleine had to lean towards him to catch the mumbled words.

'Well, yes, that's true.' Assuming they were still alive, and there was no reason to suppose they wouldn't be. It was an odd, unsettling thought, and Madeleine knew it had been very much in Cristi's mind before she left. 'It didn't suit them to have Cristi with them, as you know, and no one's heard of them since they disappeared. So Drumveyn became her home, and we became her family. Nothing will change that.' Again that stir of apprehension, the uneasy awareness of large forces in the background which could influence Cristi's life, carrying her beyond the reach of their loving protection.

Nicholas hesitated, his face tight with the reluctance of his age to get into this deep stuff. Then, needing answers of some kind, though barely knowing what, he blurted out, 'She's different from the rest of us, though, isn't she? I mean, she looks different.'

It was obvious that something was worrying him, and Madeleine was ready to do all she could to help, but it did strike her that he could have chosen a better time to broach it. Not when she was driving up the glen road, clogged with summer drivers, and had Peta and Josie racketing in the back.

'Well, Cristi's looks aren't exactly Scottish,' she agreed. 'No one could argue about that.'

'She hates it,' Nicholas said unexpectedly.

'Hates what?'

'Looking like that.'

'She said so?' Madeleine was startled.

'Well, once. She said she wished she looked like the rest of us.' Nicholas gazed away from Madeleine out of the window. He had launched into this almost against his will, driven by a need he hardly understood. Cristi's departure, with all its uncertainty and half-guessed-at implications, had made him restless and suddenly unsure of his own position. He felt obscurely that he had to know more, but now he scarcely knew what to ask, and was beginning to be afraid of digging any deeper.

'Yes, I can see that looking more like the rest of you might have made things easier for Cristi at times,' Madeleine said carefully, after a moment of panicky dread that she would say the wrong thing. She wished Tom were there. He always knew what to say. 'You three are so fair.' And look so right as a family for Archie and Pauly.

Nicholas nodded, but seemed to have nothing more to say. Afraid that she had failed him, but not wishing to pursue the subject if he wasn't ready to do so, for Madeleine had a deep reticence of her own and respected it in other people, she left the matter there.

'Maybe I should have tried harder,' she said worriedly to Tom as she unpacked her shopping. 'Maybe there was lots more he wanted to say, or to ask. I know it wasn't the best of times to choose, but perhaps I should have given him another chance when we got back.'

'Wouldn't that make rather a big thing of it?' Tom suggested. 'We don't know that he's thinking of anything beyond what's happening in Cristi's life. And we all feel a bit unsettled about that.'

'We certainly do,' Madeleine agreed with sudden wrath. 'What can they be thinking of, dragging her out there post-haste and then fobbing her off at every turn? Wretched people, they've no right to behave like that. But about Nicholas, Tom, it would be so awful if he was worrying or needing to talk to someone and we didn't seem to be listening. Yet I hate to intrude—'

She broke off, memories returning of her own children's obdurate teenage silence and her ineptness in dealing with it. Archie had been uncommunicative because he saw it as the most sensible option. Hating the repressive regime his father imposed, he had filled his life with other interests, leaving home as soon as he could. Lisa's silences, on the other hand, had been the silences of sulking and resentment and, recalling the pain of that period of her life and her own ineffectiveness, Madeleine winced to think she might fail the next generation too.

'Should I get Archie to talk to him, do you think?' she fretted.

'I shouldn't think Nicholas would be too happy about that,' Tom commented, raising his eyebrows. 'Didn't you hate it when you found the grown-ups had unhesitatingly kicked around something you thought you'd told one of them in confidence? Nothing makes a youngster feel more betrayed, or more helpless.'

'Yes, I know you're right when you put it like that.' Though Tom never to her knowledge had long soul-searching conversations with Rob and Ian, his two sons now in their thirties, and indeed they were capable of spending hours together in untroubled silence, he had an excellent relationship with them both, which was worth remembering.

'Nor do I think Nicholas would like being directly questioned about it, do you?' Tom added.

'No, you're right. And it would be difficult for Archie too, I can see that,' Madeleine conceded. 'But goodness, how unsettling it is to have these old troubles raked up again. There was a lot of hurting. We're an oddly put-together family when all's said and done.'

'Loosely ravelled,' Tom suggested, taking her hand in a comforting clasp. 'But don't worry about it. If these things have begun to turn over in Nicholas's mind then the right moment will come to talk about them. He's pretty articulate for his age, and he's on very good terms with Archie. With Pauly too.'

Madeleine laughed at this, as he had hoped she might. 'Can you imagine anyone not being on good terms with dear Pauly?'

'We'd better wait and see how things go with Peta,' Tom warned with a grin.

'Oh, don't. Poor Peta, she takes everything so hard. What will she be like as a teenager? At present they're missing Cristi, that's what's bothering them.'

'You are, you mean.' Tom drew her close in a quick hug. 'For you, nobody will ever quite take her place – isn't that the truth?'

Madeleine, remembering vividly the response aroused in her by Cristi's courage after the long, bewildering journey which had brought her to Drumveyn, her spark-ling pleasure in all she found there, her instant trust in

Madeleine herself, her zest and resilience, nodded mute acknowledgement. It distressed her to think that Cristi, meeting her mother's family at last, might face unkindness or even overt hostility, and that none of them was on hand to help.

Cristi, facing Joachim in the sombre library, where so many treasures and relics of family history were collected, felt her heart begin to beat uncomfortably.

She knew she had pushed harder than good manners allowed for this interview − or this confrontation, for such, she realised with trepidation, it was going to be. But she had finally seen, amazed at her compliance till now, that Joachim was capable of delaying and making promises for ever, always reasonable, always convincing, but always deftly evading action. The family must have some hidden agenda of their own, she was beginning to suspect, but she couldn't think what. Why had they insisted on her coming if they were prepared to let time slip through their fingers like this once she was here? It was beyond her, but it meant she must force the issue herself. She had chosen tonight because, although with guests present it wasn't ideal, at least Joachim was dining at home.

'My dear Maria-Cristina,' he had protested in good-humoured surprise when she asked to talk to him, 'how can I leave my guests? What can be so very urgent?'

She hadn't been rash enough to say, merely repeating her request and promising it wouldn't take long.

'What can we discuss tonight that can't wait till

morning?' His tone had still been benign, but a hint of avuncular 'what a silly child' had crept in, which had only increased her determination not to be fobbed off.

'I really should like to talk now, if you don't mind.'

In the morning, Cristi knew, the familiar scenario would repeat itself. Joachim would be gone, Sylvia would have no idea when he would be back, and in the evening they were going to the theatre. Then it would be the weekend and, with people coming and going the whole time, it would be impossible to have a serious talk about anything.

'If you will permit me to point out, this is hardly a convenient moment.' Joachim's manner had become less affable. He was not used to being pushed into a corner. But he had given in, though clearly annoyed, and recovering his usual urbane poise had gestured Cristi to a chair. He watched her now with an unreadable expression.

Two things were perturbing Cristi, though the first was relatively minor. The chair Joachim had waved her into dwarfed her. If she tried to sit back in the hope of looking relaxed her legs would stick straight out in front of her like a child's. Had he done it deliberately? Surely not. Yet the question was part of the larger concern, the one that was making her heart bump.

She had been reminded again, looking into Joachim's face as she sat down, that she had no clue as to what truly lay behind the welcome she had received here. The dark eyes could be concealing anger, contempt or dislike. She would never know. But she suddenly felt chillingly sure of one thing: these people had not sent for her because they wanted her here for her own sake.

For the first time the smiling affection with which they treated her seemed actually sinister, and she felt terribly alone and vulnerable. Why hadn't she waited to do this when Luis was on hand?

Pulling herself together she said quickly, 'I apologise for taking you away from your guests, Tio Joachim. I hope you will forgive me.' Although they were speaking English, as they often did even now, it came naturally to use the polite form of the Fonseca world.

Joachim inclined his head, his eyes unchanging.

'It's just that—' Cristi hesitated. She should have prepared her words more carefully. An off-the-cuff cosy chat with an uncle was not what this was about. 'Well, when you made contact with me via the lawyers, and I agreed to come to meet you all, I had the impression that there was some urgency about it, about grandfather's will being finalised and so on,' did the watchful eyes narrow? 'but time seems to be slipping by, there's been no meeting or anything, and I feel I don't know much more than when I first arrived.'

Cristi stopped, looking at him with appeal. This was reasonable, surely? But Joachim made no attempt to help her out. The over-elaborate splendours of the room seemed to close in upon her. She screwed up her resolution.

'I wondered if perhaps I should meet the lawyers on my own,' she said. To her relief, her voice betrayed none of her nervousness, nor did it sound too challenging. With difficulty she suppressed propitiatory riders.

This gained a reaction. Joachim's expression sharpened, his mouth tightening to a grim line. He appeared to be choosing his reply with care.

In this Cristi surmised correctly. Though the family might treat her like some pretty little doll who had suddenly appeared among them, to be spoiled and pampered and given glimpses of the wonderful life which could be hers, Joachim was shrewd enough to realise that Cristi's upbringing would have given her an independence of spirit which no brief lotus eating would undermine.

In his estimation, in spite of the practical difficulties, he didn't think it beyond her to arrange such a meeting. Nevertheless, stalling tactics and a disinclination to relinquish control were so much part of his make-up that his first response was no more than the usual suave prevarication.

'Of course that can be arranged if you wish,' he assured her. 'There would be no difficulty over that. However, I cannot believe it would achieve a great deal. As I'm sure you understand, it would still be necessary to bring together everyone concerned, whether you had talked to the lawyers separately or not. It's not yet certain whether João will wish to be present or not. We are still waiting to hear from him. And I myself have so many demands on my—'

'I do appreciate the difficulties,' Cristi broke in, unable to bear another run-through of the well-worn excuses. 'But at least then I should have some idea of my position, shouldn't I?'

Joachim allowed himself faint surprise at such regrettable manners. The delicately conveyed reaction wasn't lost on Cristi but she refused to be deterred.

'It just seems strange,' she went on, as smooth as he, 'that as a beneficiary I haven't seen a copy of the will.' Had she really said that? Courage seemed to be meeting demand. She hadn't been sure it would.

Joachim recognised it too.

'But my dear child,' he began, then saw in her face that she wasn't prepared to be patronised, and moved swiftly on. 'There is naturally no problem there. How remiss of us not to give you the opportunity to read the conditions of the will long before this. You must forgive us, but at such a sad time . . . You will, understandably, be anxious to know more about the ranch. I believe you never went there as a child?'

You know damn well I didn't. But Cristi felt a lift of excitement. The ranch had been mentioned at last. She had thought about it so often, but it had hardly seemed a topic she could introduce herself. Nobody could be exactly thrilled at the idea of it coming to her.

'I shall see that arrangements are put in train at once. But now, if you will forgive me . . .' Joachim was glancing at his watch, rising to his feet. The interview was over.

Even with a date for a meeting agreed upon — he would get the lawyers to write to her — they could spin things out for a little longer. During these weeks already gained they had been able to establish the essential fact: Cristi was in almost every respect a suitable candidate for their long-term plan. And, angered though he had been to find himself cornered into this dialogue tonight, there had been an element of pleasure in it which he had not expected. This charming little niece, in spite of her origins, had faced up to him with admirable courage.

Also, assessing her dispassionately, he applauded the changes which her time here had produced. Sylvia had done well. This evening, in a slim coral-coloured dress of perfect simplicity, Cristi looked infinitely more acceptable than she had in the outré art-student garb of her arrival. He also found her fine-boned, pliant body an appealing contrast to the more solid lines of his wife and daughters.

Apart from her delightful appearance and – generally – better manners than he could have hoped for from a member of the British student population, it occurred to Joachim with some irony, as he ushered her to the door, that her barbarous upbringing in Scotland had endowed her with a greater strength of character than she could have hoped to inherit from his sister Justina.

His mouth twisted down in a bitter expression at the thought, as he followed Cristi along the wide softly-carpeted corridor to rejoin his guests.

Chapter Fourteen

'Oh, my, you'll get blown away, living in a place like this.'

Jean, clambering down from the Range Rover with Archie's assistance, looked round her with a satisfaction her words did not suggest. Her face was beaming, her eyes moist. That they should do this for her lad. His own wee place, after all the disappointments he'd had to put up with. How proud his dad would have been. And how she wished he could have been with them this evening, for as much as anything she saw this as Donnie's reward for his years of hard and loyal work.

Dougal, who had brought Nicholas with him in the Land Rover, was startled to find his legs oddly trembly as they joined the others. Afterwards he found he couldn't remember anything of the drive up the bone-shaking track, or a word he and Nicholas had exchanged. Now he felt an odd sensation, as he walked forward, that his feet weren't quite making contact with the ground. Who would have thought such a moment could ever have come, and come in the end so swiftly and effortlessly?

It was typical of Archie and Pauly to want to make this a special event, entering into the excitement of Ellig, or these few acres of Ellig, being his, and making sure Jean shared in it too. Yet grateful as he was, grateful beyond words, part of him wanted this moment to be his alone, to be tucked away in memory as one of the great turning points of his life. Beneath these conflicting feelings he ached, helplessly and inevitably, for Cristi to be there. Without her, the essential element was missing. How could this have any meaning without her there?

Grinning at Jean's words, he knew that she was as thrilled as anyone could be about what Archie had done for him, but he understood that, with her superstitious native reluctance to get too excited about anything in case it wasn't all it seemed, she had to find fault somehow. His grin broadened. She'd find plenty to go on about once she got inside. He felt a rare impulse to crush her in a big hug, but he knew she wouldn't like that much either.

The Napiers had no inhibitions about expressing either feelings or opinions.

'My God, it is in a state! You weren't joking, were you?' That was Pauly. 'But what an incredible spot.'

'You can see the whole village,' Josie shouted, climbing on the highly unsafe dyke to see better.

'You can see the whole glen,' Peta added, though she was being much more cautious about the dyke.

'You can see the whole of Muirend!'

'No, you can't,' said Nicholas. 'And get off there. You're going to bring Dougal's dyke down.'

'It's ages since I've walked or ridden up this way.' Pauly too was looking at the wide view with delight.

'Yes well, with all those mad Maclachlans running loose it wasn't the first place anyone would choose for a quiet outing,' Archie remarked, standing back to take a look at the house roof, where slates were missing below the chimney stack, others skewed at crazy angles. 'You know, Dougal, I'm not sure I did you any favours by persuading you to take this lot off my hands.'

'Oh, but he's that grateful to you,' Jean rushed in anxiously. 'Aren't you, Dougal? It's a grand chance for him. He never thought of having such a start, and I don't know how we'll ever be able to thank—'

'Whist, Jean,' Archie saw Dougal's embarrassment. 'I'm getting the best of the bargain. I mean it.'

There had been no difficulty about the purchase of Ellig land by Drumveyn, or the making over of the grieve's house and the acres around it to Dougal. Archie had been in contact with Miss Hutchinson's lawyers from the outset and the place had never gone on the market.

Ungrateful as it was, Dougal had not been able to stifle a pang of resentment that for someone like Archie things could always be managed this simply. But it was how things were; they wouldn't change. And if he disapproved so much why was he prepared to benefit? He wasn't going to turn the opening down, so that dealt with that.

Now it was unbelievable to be walking among this little gaggle of friendly people towards his own door. He almost had to remember how to breathe. Here was Archie, handing him the keys with a flourish, Pauly behind him, her arm in Jean's, the children crowding round ready to dive in the instant the door was open. They were turning it into a ceremony, making the moment significant for him. He had a vision of Cristi's bright face and sparkling smile – she should be here, she should be here – then he was pushing the big old key into the lock, angry with himself to find his hand shaking. The little girls raised a shrill cheer as the door opened.

'Well!' Jean's shocked eyes and down-turned mouth told her opinion of the Maclachlans and all their works. But it wasn't her place to criticise, she had to remember that. 'You'll have plenty to do here, right enough,' she said, doing her best, and this time Dougal did put an arm round her and pull her close, laughing at her.

'It can be sorted,' he said.

'Yes, well, we can do without this daft carry-on for a start,' she protested, struggling free but unable to hide her pleasure. 'It seems to me I'd best be up here first thing with my scrubbing brush and pail.'

They all laughed now, affectionately, knowing this was as big a moment for her as it was for Dougal.

'You'd have your work cut out,' he told her dryly. 'Wait and see what the rest's like.'

'Yes, there's a bit to do before the scrubbing brush stage is reached, Jean,' Archie warned.

'My foot went through the floor,' they heard Josie

yelling from the back bedroom as they went upstairs. 'Sorry, Dougal.' She didn't sound very repentant.

'You watch what you're doing,' Dougal called back. 'Never mind the floor, we don't want any broken bones.' And in those words the reality of ownership hit him, a moment deeply, privately satisfying.

'We'll be careful,' Josie promised glibly, but the words were drowned by a scream from Peta.

Dougal, so newly aware that he was responsible for what went on here, was about to leap to the rescue when Archie caught his arm and made him listen instead.

Down came an indignant wail. 'Yuk, horrible spooky spiders! I hate spiders!'

'See?' said Archie.

As they trooped thunderously down the wooden stairs after inspecting the bedrooms, where, if one wished to find polite things to say, the best thing to do was go straight to the window and look out, Nicholas, who had vanished at a word from Pauly, reappeared staggering under a large cardboard box. Archie, taking it from him and putting it on the noisome draining board, lifted out a handsome cake on a board which he gave to Pauly to deal with, then, spreading out a couple of tea-towels, began to set forth glasses, champagne and bottles of Coke.

Dougal, taken by surprise, felt the colour rise in his face and for a moment was afraid he was going to make a fool of himself.

'Oh, here, you shouldn't have bothered with all this,' he began helplessly.

'To celebrate a very special occasion. Grab this.' Pauly leaned to plant a kiss on his cheek as she handed him a mammoth slice of cake on a buckling paper plate.

Archie, smiling, handed him a glass. He and Pauly had had trouble deciding between champagne or whisky.

'They prefer whisky.'

'But I'm making a gooey cake.'

'They don't seem to mind having it with cake.'

'It's not about what they like, it's about making an occasion of it. Jean will love telling everyone we had champagne, even if it does go up her nose and she thinks it tastes of nothing. And I bet Dougal won't even notice. It'll be like getting married, you don't have a clue what you're eating or drinking.'

Archie had thought this was putting it a bit high, but had let Pauly have her way.

'Peta, Josie, where are you? Cake time! Jean, I'll put yours here.'

Dougal saw Jean's mouth prim. Even on a plate she'd be horrified to think of food being put down anywhere in this midden. He smiled to himself, happiness washing through him.

'Can't we have champagne?' Peta and Josie came racing in. 'We had some at Ian's wedding.'

'Well, you weren't supposed to,' Archie said. 'All right, a sip each, then it's Coke.'

'And be quiet,' Pauly added.

'Well, Dougal.' Archie turned to him, his face serious, but satisfaction in his eyes to have brought this about, confident that Dougal would make something worthwhile of it. 'Here's to you and to your future in this house. May it be a long and happy one.'

They raised their glasses, even the children solemn. Jean thought of Donnie again and, caught by a bleak despair she rarely allowed herself, wished things with Donald and Jill could have been different, and that they hadn't gone so far from her. She sniffed back a tear and at the same time took an incautious gulp of champagne. This resulted in a disintegrating coughing fit which, though she hardly knew where to put herself for embarrassment, carried her past the dangerous moment.

'Who thinks the place could do with a new name?' Archie tossed out the idea casually, after Pauly had whipped the inevitable kitchen roll from the box and Jean had been put to rights. 'To mark the new start.'

'But it's always been Ellig.' Dougal, caught off guard, resisted the suggestion instinctively. Realising that he had given himself away, he reflected with ironic humour that it hadn't taken him long to get used to the idea of ownership.

'Oh, keeping the name in some form, of course. But it might be nice if your new demesne was distinguished from the old one. Just a thought.'

'Something specially for Dougal.' Pauly was seized by the idea. 'Ellig House, as distinct from the farm? Or House of Ellig, that has a ring to it.'

'Is that no' a bit grand?' Jean's voice sounded more than doubtful. She didn't want folk thinking Dougal was getting too big for his boots. There'd be enough said as it was. 'No' that it's for me to say, of course' she added hastily.

'Do you think something with a ring to it is exactly

what's wanted?' Dougal questioned, looking round the kitchen with its filthy windows and cracked and bulging plaster, the slew of rubbish on the floor.

'Ellig Hill.'

'Ellig Castle.'

'Ellig Palace!'

'Shut up, you lot. Go and finish your cake outside if you're going to be silly.'

'Mustn't get Dougal's nice floor dirty,' Josie shrieked as they went. 'The floor of Ellig Mansion.'

'And don't break anything out there, unless it's your necks,' Archie shouted after them.

'I know what,' Jean said, and Pauly wasn't sure whether the patches of red had appeared in her cheeks because of the amount of champagne she had drunk to suppress her coughing, or because of nervousness to find herself so boldly putting forward a suggestion.

'Come on, then,' Archie said, reaching to refill her glass as encouragement. But catching a look from Pauly, and remembering that Tom and his mother were waiting for them at the barn, he added a mere few drops.

'Let's have it.' Dougal found himself hoping the name would be a good one. It mattered to him that Jean should have some share in his new life. Feeling guilty, more like, because he'd been firm about not bringing her up here to live with him. But he knew the decision had been right.

Jean looked at him, her eyes bright. 'Croft of Ellig,' she said triumphantly, then rushed on at once, confidence failing her, 'I know it's not a proper croft by rights, you don't have to tell me that, but—'

'That's perfect,' Pauly exclaimed. 'Exactly right. At least,' at a resigned shake of the head from Archie, '*I* think so. But it's up to Dougal.'

'Quite,' said Archie.

For Dougal, there and then, that was what the place became in his mind – this parcel of land, too small to be called a farm, which had so miraculously fallen into his hands, turning dream into reality. The old word, so linked with Scotland's history and traditions, rang true. Jean was right; technically this wasn't a croft, but there could be no better choice of name.

'That'll do me,' was all he said, but his face showed what he felt, and they drank a second toast, spirits soaring, chorusing the new name with a will. Then a silence fell, and they found themselves looking at each other with a moved awareness of all this meant.

Pauly broke the mood by wailing, 'Oh, God, too much emotion, I can't stand it,' turning to hide her face against Archie's shoulder.

As they laughed and relaxed, and she and Jean began to tidy up, Archie took the chance to say to Dougal, 'Look, Nicholas can come with us, there's plenty of room. You hang on here for a bit if you want to. Get the feel of the place on your own.'

Dougal looked at him gratefully. How like Archie to understand that was exactly what he was hankering for. 'But the drinks at the barn,' he said.

He had been surprised and gratified when Tom and Madeleine had issued the invitation, but reluctant to let them take so much trouble. Then he had realised how much they must mind being excluded from such occasions by Tom's disability. Having everyone back to the barn — even Lisa had said she would look in, though Dougal doubted Stephen would stir himself — was their means of sharing in the celebration. He had accepted warmly.

'No hurry,' Archie assured him. 'Take as long as you want to. This is your day.'

Dougal nodded, unable to find words. It was so exactly what he needed, a few minutes alone to take in what had happened. How good of Archie to see that, and give him the space to do it. As he had given him so much more.

'Archie, hang on a minute.' Dougal barely knew what he wanted to say. 'About this — and everything else — I mean, keeping my dad on when he wasn't fit, and Mum staying on in the cottage. I am grateful, you know.'

He was shaken by a need, surging up out of nowhere, to articulate long-buried, scarcely formulated feelings about much more besides, about what it felt like growing up as the son of an estate worker, part of a paternalistic micro-society like Drumveyn, recognising the benefits, yet coming to hate the pernicious imbalance of the system. He felt as though, in this moment of heightened feeling, he could make Archie understand it all, and at the same time free himself from the ambivalence of his own attitudes. None of it could be said, of course. Apart from this not being the time, he wasn't sure he had the words at his command.

Archie had taken his arm in a quick friendly grip. 'No need for that,' he said.

'No, but—' Dougal rejected the vast unsayable, and concentrated on facts. If he didn't do this now he never would. 'It's more than that. It's all through the years, your mother first, then you and Pauly, letting us have the run of the big house, including us in everything. You didn't have to do that, and it meant a lot to us. I'm only sorry that Jill—' It seemed strange to find he wanted to say, 'let you down', but that was how it felt.

'I appreciate what you're saying, Dougal.' Archie could guess the effort it had cost. 'And for my part, I'm delighted you'll be staying in the glen. I mean it. I'd hate you to move away, and I'm more than satisfied that the Croft of Ellig will be in your hands.'

He gave the new name due emphasis, and was pleased to see a smile lighten Dougal's serious face. Archie was glad not only that Dougal would put the ramshackle little place in order, as he undoubtedly would, but that he would remain in contact with the estate. Neither he nor Tom had quite given up their hopes with regard to that. 'Right,' he went on more briskly. 'We'll be off. See you at the barn. Don't think you've got to come racing after us. You'll never have this particular experience again.'

Archie was right, Dougal thought, as the sound of the Range Rover faded down the hill and he found himself alone. Nothing could ever again be quite like this, a moment intense and vivid, tentative and incredulous, with a thrill to it which nothing in his life before had ever given him.

'Mine.' He said the word aloud, then stood letting the silence draw him in. Though it was a mild, almost muggy, early autumn day, the sun struggling to break through cloud, a breath of wind stirred here, cooling his cheeks. High above, a faint mewing pierced the quiet and he tilted his head back to watch the buzzard lazily circle. Behind its thin cry he became aware of background sounds ignored till now, the perpetual sounds of this high place, the movement of air in the firs which gave shelter to the steading yard, the voice of the burn tumbling down its scoured-out rocky course towards the village below. His landscape.

He turned, his eye passing over the dereliction of the yard to rest on the house. In his mind he welcomed every second of the labour he must put into it. And his mother could think what she liked, but she wasn't coming up here with her scrubbing brushes and her cleaning rags. This house was his.

He went inside again, into each room in turn, claiming them. Then he locked the back door behind him and went round the house to the ragged garden. Noting the colour of the berries on the guardian rowans, signalling how far on autumn was already, he let himself, at last, think of Cristi, picturing her here beside him.

His throat constricted. For him she was indivisibly part of this scene; she knew, loved and understood it all. Letting his mind range back he saw her entwined with every aspect of it. She understood too, as no one else did, his hopes and ambitions. She had heard them all, in the days when everything was still shared between them. But his intention in summoning her image was not to indulge in nostalgia or unattainable dreams. There was something he must sort out, here and now, for good.

So, he owned a place of his own. No matter that it consisted of a few acres of thin, wind-scoured soil and a clutch of knock-kneed buildings. He would make something of it, he had no doubt of that. At one step he had left behind the trap of living one's working life in a house one could never own. The doors were open.

But this change in his circumstances, a quantum leap for him, changed nothing with regard to Cristi. Between them lay much more than material differences. The problem was not that she was suddenly rich and owned unknown tracts of land in South America. The truth was that in a dozen more subtle ways she belonged to another world, to another breed. He had only to picture the graceful fine-boned body, the beauty which could catch at him over and over again, as though he'd never seen it before, to know his dreams were absurd. Yes, but how many times had he seen her muddy and windblown, getting stuck into some nasty job, indifferent to anything the elements could throw at them? She was as tough as a bit of bent wire, he thought, smiling in spite of himself. It was all part of her.

But he refused to let this deflect him.

A woman like Cristi was not for him, with his ordinary looks and plodding ways. The Croft of Ellig, and an office job in Muirend, that was his life, and Cristi was an artist through and through. She was far away from him, in spirit as well as in miles, and it was time to face the fact.

He thought of the postcards she had sent, and his face tightened. Postcards, densely filled as they might be with her tiny, exquisite writing, were a far cry from the letters he used to get, especially those written during her first term at university, when he had been the one person to whom she could pour out her troubles. How the impersonal messages of those cards had hurt him, and how impossible he had found it to reply. No question, it was time to put the thoughts of her behind him. She had no part in this new beginning. He must get that firmly into his head and keep it there.

Unconsciously Dougal squared his shoulders. He couldn't hope for the impossible, but he had been given so much in other ways. He wasn't going to throw it away. He turned, stepping over the wind-battered crocosmia and golden rod which had encroached over the path, and went to the Land Rover. Keep the facts before him, and start right now building a life which could never include her.

Or, right now, go to the party.

Chapter Fifteen

Cristi drew a long breath of satisfaction and relief, pressing back in her seat as the Rio Sul flight lifted into the air. She had begun to think this moment would never come. In a couple of hours they would actually be landing at Campo Novo. She turned her head to look at Luis, and found him smiling at her, his eyes gleaming.

'You shouldn't look quite so much as if you have escaped the lions' den,' he reproached her.

She hadn't realised it would be so obvious. 'That's awful,' she said guiltily, 'after your parents have been so good to me.' Then, taking another look at him, 'Though I have to say you look pretty cheerful yourself.'

In this upbeat mood she felt free to make such a comment. She was talking about her own uncle and aunt, to her cousin; wasn't she allowed a little family freedom of speech by this time? But to be truthful, the labels meant little. The relationship explained the welcome extended to her, and the trouble taken to entertain her while she was in Rio, but now, with the doors at last opening on so much that had seemed deliberately kept from her, she saw how little real contact there had been.

She knew she wasn't wrong in believing that Luis shared her feeling of release. Their mood as they drove to the airport had definitely been one of leaving the grown-ups behind. And even in that short time she had been aware of a subtler change, as though, law unto himself as he always appeared to be, he had become his real self now that they were on their way south, and on their own.

No one was better company than Luis when he was relaxed and doing what he wanted to do, and Cristi felt happy anticipation fizzing up as Rio was left behind. She enjoyed being with him whatever his mood, but today he seemed ready for once to abandon his teasing manner. Far too often he treated her as the naive little cousin, rescued from an uncouth existence among the uncivilised tribes of the north, charming in her way as he had not failed to make clear, but to be groomed and moulded as much as spoiled and indulged.

He had, with an indolent forebearance which could swiftly turn to boredom and the quest for a more stimulating scene, shown her what he wished her to see of the abundant riches of her native land, but never for a second had he allowed her to look below its surface. No one was more adept than he at letting questions he didn't care for slide past him. No one was more apt to become impatient when serious topics, not of his choosing, were raised.

Time spent with him had been fast-paced and pleasure-seeking, and Cristi had soon learned that she must accept its pleasures on his terms. But the stimulus of his company, the exciting sense of being at the heart of the action which he could so effortlessly produce, had more than made up for this.

Today, however, Luis was ready to talk. They seemed to have reached a new and agreeable footing of two adults on equal terms who knew and understood each other. This pleased Cristi very much, particularly today, when such thrilling, but also daunting, discoveries lay ahead.

'I know it's been hard for you, this waiting,' Luis began abruptly, when *cafezinhos* had been served and they were left alone. 'You must have wondered sometimes if matters would ever be resolved.'

Cristi looked at him in surprise. She was used to him shrugging off references to her reason for being here. He had been adamant from the first that he wouldn't petition on her behalf with his father to get things moving, insisting it was nothing to do with him.

'Well, it has been frustrating at times, I must admit.' Cristi found it hard to believe now that she'd let so many weeks slip by in promises and evasions, without putting up more of a fight. 'I did begin to wonder why I was here.'

'My sweet, you must have realised by this time, it is how things are done.' Luis couldn't abandon irony for long. 'There has to be this delay and that change of plan, urgent affairs dealt with before anything else can be begun, saints' days intervening, holidays taken, a major player unaccountably indisposed. Without all this how could anyone believe the matter had any weight? What importance could be attached to a meeting organised with a mere couple of telephone calls?'

'It can work,' Cristi assured him.

Luis snapped his fingers in derision. 'Trifling, amateur. No, but seriously, this whole business has been somewhat distressing for the family, as I think you will readily comprehend.' Somewhat distressing. His mind went back to the fury and hysteria of the days after the will had been read, the full-scale family conclaves, the disbelieving anger as it became clear that its terms could not be overturned. This little innocent beside him had no idea.

'Of course I understand,' Cristi said. 'It's one of the reasons it was so impossible for me to approach the subject myself. I was the last person to do that.'

Luis offered no comment.

'About what grandfather left to me – you must realise that I've wanted desperately to find out how you all felt about it, and to say I realise how unfair it must seem. In fact, when I first heard about it, I thought of not coming at all, relinquishing my claim, or whatever one does.'

She missed the sharp turn of Luis's head.

'It must have been a shock,' she went on. 'Or had you had some idea of what grandfather was planning?'

'Our grandfather, my sweet, was not a man to communicate his intentions to anyone about anything if he could help it.' Luis took some trouble to keep the bitterness out of his voice.

'I had to remember you'd be grieving for him, in a way that I couldn't. Even now, it seems something private to you, the real family, nothing to do with me.'

Her sincerity penetrated Luis's darker thoughts.

'Ah, *querida*, it must have been strange for you at times,' he exclaimed with unforced sympathy. 'Returning in these circumstances, the first contact after growing up so far away, meeting so many unknown relatives.'

'It wasn't that so much.' Cristi, free to say what she felt at last, spoke with eager gratefulness. 'It was more not being able to talk about anything that mattered, forever coming up against a wall of silence. The worst thing was wanting to ask about my mother, and knowing I couldn't. If I could have heard the story from the family's side . . . For me, it was the most important thing, to find out more about her if I could, where she went, what happened to her. I didn't let myself hope that I might see her.'

'But you have accepted, haven't you, that no one knows where she is?' Luis realised he sounded less than sympathetic, and modified his tone. 'I can imagine how you must have longed to find out more, but alas, nothing has ever been heard from her.'

Cristi nodded. She had had plenty of time to deal with this in the past few weeks. She dragged her mind away from the ache of loss it brought, and picked up the thread of what she had been saying.

'I did feel, whenever I thought about this matter of the ranch, that I needed to know what grandfather was like, as a person, and what made him act as he did. On the one hand I was being told I belong to the family and my place is here, but on the other hand not a word was being said about anything important.'

Luis nodded, understanding what she was saying, but shrugging at the same time.

'I see that it was perhaps baffling for you,' he said, 'but that is how things are done. In families such as ours reticence and good manners come first – or perhaps, more cynically, consideration for appearances.'

There hadn't been much reticence in private. His mouth turned down at the memory.

'I respect that,' Cristi said, 'of course I do. But it did feel odd sometimes,' chilling and lonely, she might have said, 'to realise how many weeks had gone by, and I seemed to be no closer to anyone than when I arrived. At home—' she checked, fierce longing storming up at the word 'if something like this happened we'd talk about it. Certainly if it concerned someone in the family.'

She broke off. She wasn't related to anyone at Drumveyn, and in that sense wasn't one of the family at all. Unbearable thought.

'Cristi.' Unlike the rest of the family, Luis kept to the diminutive even when they were speaking Portuguese. 'There's a lot of feeling about this, as I am sure you appreciate. No one had received a hint of what grandfather was planning. Also,' another shrug, 'many things occurred in the past which are not easy to talk about. Besides, excuse my saying this, we have known you for a very short time.'

'I know.' Long as those weeks had seemed, in relative terms Luis was right, it hadn't been long. 'But what things happened in the past? I can ask that, can't I? There seems so much mystery about everything. I'm used to things being out in the open.'

'Well now, where to begin . . .' Though Luis's face and tone were considering, and he was obviously deciding what could and could not be said, at least he hadn't brushed the question aside.

'Everything comes back to grandfather,' he said after a moment. 'You will have grasped that much. He was an overbearing, harsh, unforgiving man, and by the end of his life he had quarrelled with every friend he had ever had, and with every member of the family besides. For years he refused to leave Campo Novo, living virtually as a recluse there.'

'He quarrelled with Tio João?'

'He did, years ago, which is why João decided to make a new life in North America.'

'And decided not to come to the meetings about the will?' Hardly admitted to herself, Cristi had had a dim idea that, since her elder uncle had chosen to distance himself from the family, he might just possibly have kept in touch with Justina. It had been a blow to hear that after changing his mind several times he wasn't coming after all.

How true was that, she wondered suddenly. Could these changes of heart have been invented to suit Joachim's own purposes? Not a comfortable thought.

'I imagine João feels life can be supported without concerning himself over such trifles.' The mocking tone had an edge to it this time which made Cristi frown. But she knew what Luis meant. No one appeared likely to suffer materially from any games her grandfather had played and, as she now knew, there had been considerable assets distributed around the family quite apart from the ranch and the money left to her.

'But quarrels with grandfather,' Luis went on, 'didn't drive only our uncle away. They were the reason behind your mother leaving as she did, and one supposes the reason she never attempted to make contact again.'

'I thought she left because of me.'

It was a child's fear, never uttered before, swimming up out of nowhere, unadorned. Luis, arrested by the bald words, guessed this, and his face revealed more than he usually allowed as he turned towards her in quick compassion.

'Cristi, that wasn't so. There were many things to drive her away. Fights long before you were born. I gather that your mother, of all the family, was the most like grandfather, and they fought over everything. I've heard she was a passionate and wilful girl, constantly defying him, especially over her faith.' Safer to focus on that than on the other stories.

'I didn't know that,' Cristi said. 'I was sent to a convent school, but I don't remember anything ever being said about religion at home. I haven't been brought up as a Catholic, of course. I wondered if it would matter, when I came back, but it hasn't seemed to. At least, no one's mentioned it.'

Sylvia went to mass on Sundays, Gabriela more often, but as far as Cristi had observed no one else seemed to practise their faith in any way.

'Ah, well, different days, different ways.' Luis found it politic not to enlarge on the point. 'But while on the subject of grandfather, and since we are on our way to the ranch, perhaps I should give you some idea of what you'll find there? I should hate you to arrive with too many false hopes.'

The sardonic glint was back, but Cristi didn't care. On the way, to the Estancia dos Tres Pinheiros. The ranch of the Three Pines. Estancia rather than *fazenda*, as had been explained to her, because this was gaucho country and the ranch bred horses as well as cattle. And now was *hers*. She still hadn't taken it in. In fact, it had begun to seem increasingly remote and improbable during the weeks of waiting. Now it was close at last.

Cristi drew an uneven breath which didn't seem to reach her lungs.

'I was warned by the lawyers,' she reminded Luis, concentrating on the practical to calm herself down. 'They told me how run-down it is, and how little it produces.'

The first meeting, when finally it took place, had gone on for hours and had cost her a sleepless night. She had been awed by the scale of her inheritance and the responsibilities it brought with it, flurried by the sheaves of documents put before her, most of them in a Portuguese so grandiose and archaic that it was like an entirely new language. Although she had known from the start – Joachim had told her as much to silence further questions – that the ranch was being managed on her behalf, bills being met and employees paid, it had been impossible to feel it had anything to do with her. But at that formal and long-winded meeting, as the reality unfolded before her, she had felt very young, vulnerable and scared, wishing fervently that Archie or Tom could be there to put their experience and wisdom behind her. She hadn't dared to phone either of them afterwards, knowing she would never be able to hide her alarm.

'Yes, I'm afraid the land has suffered from what is known as predatory farming,' Luis was saying, no amusement in his voice now. 'Nothing put back into it. But the problem goes deeper than that. It's part of what we were talking about just now – our revered grandfather's extreme bull-headedness. He had his own views, his own way of doing things, and he could never see beyond them.' Conscious of the anger his voice revealed, he took a grip on himself before going on. 'The fact was, he had an obsession with the past, the past of the *gaúcho*. He wanted to preserve it and all its traditions, its history, music, poetry, dance, dress, customs. He wanted not only to preserve it, but to live it, outdated as it is. What's more, he wanted to force everyone around him to do the same. He was fanatical about it, and it meant that he resisted progress in every shape and form, so that the land, the methods he employed to farm it, the buildings, every damned thing on the place, has been caught in this web of the past, losing money year after—'

Luis stopped brusquely, looking away from Cristi. She would see for herself soon enough.

Cristi, fascinated, glad to hear about things kept till now tantalisingly out of reach, didn't realise the depth of his anger.

'I suppose lots of old people hate to modernise,' she said tolerantly. 'It was the same at Drumveyn, when Archie's father was alive.'

Deus, but she had a naive view of life. 'True, but even the oldest will scarcely have made their starting point somewhere in the last quarter of the nineteenth century,' Luis retorted with heavy sarcasm.

'The nineteenth?'

He spelt it out for her. 'Then, you see, the gaucho was a heroic figure, not a relic of some superseded way of life as he is today. He was a man of pride, skill and courage, but above all a man of simple values. He wanted nothing more in life than his horse, his gun and his freedom. Oh, and a woman, maybe, but only after the rest. His food was of the most basic, he wore no colour in his dress except perhaps to indicate some political affiliation, and he was immune to the temptations of progress.'

'It sounds idealistic, but not all that unreasonable,' Cristi hazarded, not liking the contempt which had overtaken humour as Luis went on.

For he had been unable to hide the frustration which his grandfather's chosen style of living sparked every time he thought of it. And he was angry with himself for letting it show. It wasn't part of the plan.

Forcing a lighter tone, he wound up, '*Então, vamos ver.* We shall be there very soon, and you will see for yourself.'

Cristi was content to find the topic dismissed. She needed an interval to gather her thoughts – and to look out at the scale and emptiness of this vast land over which they flew, its endless forests patterned by vivid gashes of red earth.

Close now could be a moment she had spoken of to no

one, the realisation of a hope she had hugged close ever
since she had known she would come here. Her longing
to uncover any shred of news about her mother had been
associated in her mind with pain and rejection, further
complicated by finding it a taboo subject for the Fonsecas. Someone else, however, had been part of those early
years, someone who had never betrayed her trust. Isaura,
who had looked after her since the day she was born, had
been the daughter of the head peon at Tres Pinheiros.
And Isaura, as far as Cristi knew, had come back to
Campo Novo when Justina and Howard packed up the
house, dispatched Cristi to Lisa, and disappeared.

It seemed amazing that Isaura might be close at hand
and able to tell her some of the things she longed to
know. Cristi had said nothing of this to Luis. No matter
how approachable he seemed today, she knew this was an
area where she must tread carefully.

Unconsciously seeking comfort, she found as she
relaxed that thoughts of home at once overtook the
present. Her mind went first, as it often did here, to
Madeleine, perhaps because when Cristi first appeared at
Drumveyn it had been Madeleine who comforted and
cared for her. Then other beloved faces jostled, and
closing her eyes she gave herself up to the memories.

What if she hadn't come, the thought occurred to her?
What would her life be now, if she had followed her
original plan of taking up that attractive offer to work
with Maggie in the studio on the Royal Mile, getting
hands-on design experience? Hunger to be doing just that
swept her, in control of her own life, using her hands in

satisfying creativity, putting her acquired skills to use. Though neither Isa nor Torie was in Edinburgh there would have been plenty of other friends on hand, and she longed for their easy company, the laughter, the freedom they took for granted as they went from one favourite haunt in the old city to another.

Perhaps calling up images of home hadn't been a good idea, for in spite of her best efforts her attention went straight to the aching tooth — the piece of news which had been somewhere at the back of her mind ever since Pauly's last letter. Dougal now owned the grieve's house at Ellig. They had had a ceremonial door-opening and a party at the barn, and she had not been there to share in either. And, deeper even than the pang of missing such an event, was the ache of knowing that Dougal's life had taken such a colossal step forward, changing everything for him, and she had had no part in it.

She had been torn by conflicting reactions when she had read the letter. The knowledge that Dougal was established in the glen and she need no longer dread his leaving was a relief. Yet it was all wrong that she should be shut out from the new scenario by the whims of the arrogant Fonsecas.

She caught herself up, ashamed. To have had so much poured into her hands and still to hanker for more — that was outrageous. But, in spite of her earlier excitement, in that moment as their approach to Campo Novo was announced, her new possessions seemed, more than anything, an alarming burden.

Chapter Sixteen

Cristi's first impression of the town of Campo Novo was that it was planked down in the middle of miles and miles of nowhere. This was the great plateau of the southern highlands of Brazil, where the forests of the north merge into the grasslands of Rio Grande do Sul. As they emerged from the aircraft she was conscious of a sweep of air infinitely more bracing than the tropical heat of Rio. A huddle of white airport buildings, a handful of people and, taking her slightly by surprise, a personal welcome for Luis, smiling greetings for herself.

A hefty four-wheel-drive vehicle was waiting for them. As Cristi drew in a breath of that marvellous air, catching for the first time the acrid tang of the red dust in her nostrils, she was vividly aware of being in a different country from the Brazil she already knew.

A grizzled old man of Negro origins was hopping nimbly about dealing with their luggage. Wearing faded grey-striped *bombachas*, the baggy gaucho trousers, and the fraying remnants of rope-soled sandals, he didn't look much like a porter.

Cristi wanted, as Luis accepted the jeep keys from the old man, to ask if they could go straight to the ranch. But this was Brazil. No one went straight anywhere. In any case it was lunch-time, and since according to Luis the house at the ranch was shut up, nothing could be provided for them there. She would have to be patient for a little longer.

As Luis drove rapidly through the town, she observed that the clutch of modern high-rise buildings in the centre looked shabby and down-at-heel. There was a church too grandiose for its surroundings, then an irregular spread of humbler dwellings rayed out on roads which soon dwindled into dirt tracks. The width of the main street struck her, the dusty pick-ups and cars parked nose in to the pavements leaving a broad space.

'Why is it so wide?' she asked.

Luis raised his eyebrows. 'Come on, Cristi, sharpen your wits. Now you are here, you must think cattle. Cattle first, last and always. Well, to be fair, you can think mule herds too if you wish. This was a main drove road from the south for them. I'll show you pictures of it, unpaved and lined with wooden board walks, just like a Western. But nowadays we are anxious to be up to date, as you see.'

He looked disparagingly at the plate-glass windows, the unchecked clutter of advertising signs, the scruffy supermarket. Cristi looked too, and didn't think it looked as up to date as all that.

'At least this part hasn't changed much,' Luis remarked, turning into a tree-lined road of colonial-style houses with white stucco ornamentation and pretty colour washes, set in shady gardens.

'This is lovely,' Cristi exclaimed.

'Hm,' said Luis, thinking his own thoughts.

This house, where their grandfather had lived when he wasn't at the ranch, had come to Cristi as an intrinsic part of Tres Pinheiros.

The jeep had to be parked in the street, and they walked up a path overhung by orange trees to the square pink house, and up dazzlingly white steps to a door already being opened by a smiling elderly maid. Cristi found it odd to think that once Archie had come here, years ago, to try to persuade grandfather to accept her back into the family.

Inside, the house was hideous. Small dark rooms were crowded with heavy furniture, the sombre velvet curtains at their windows looped back to reveal thick lace curtains and half-closed shutters. There was a smell of trapped air, old fabrics and old age. The bedroom to which Cristi was shown appeared to have layer after layer of drapes and covers, and made her feel as though she'd been shut in a trunk in someone's attic. The bed felt as hard as a board, and she preferred not to speculate about the bodies which had lain in it.

Though everything was scrupulously clean, the fittings of the tiny bathroom were decidedly antiquated, and functioned with noisy ill-will. A whiff of something best not identified was not quite cloaked by the sickly-sweet scent of verbena. The bidet wasn't attached to the plumbing at all. Different.

Weird to think this house was hers. The concept had no reality, in fact was rather repellent, and Cristi shivered as she hurriedly washed, the temperature reminding her that here they were more than three thousand feet up, with spring barely begun.

Luis was waiting in the gloomy dining-room, and there began a creakingly slow ritual as two maids served a simple lunch. In spite of elaborate silver and fine glasses, in spite of finger bowls and napkins of coarse cream linen, there was only mineral water to drink, and the food was nothing more elaborate than mounds of rice, perfectly cooked, and a stew of purple-black beans.

Luis watched Cristi's face as she sampled it, his eyes gleaming.

'I hope you enjoy it, my sweet, because unless you take drastic steps, probably losing every servant you have in the process, this is what you will be given on a daily basis. *Feijão*, the staple food of the gaucho. If it's any comfort to you, it's said to be an excellent source of protein.'

'Thank you,' Cristi retorted composedly. 'As it happens I rather like it.' Well, she didn't absolutely dislike it.

Resigned to waiting while Luis took the mandatory siesta, and finding her unpacking already done, she tried to settle down to a letter to Torie, but she was too conscious of exciting discoveries close at hand, and the question which threaded all the rest made it hard to concentrate. Here, in this house, there could be someone who had known her mother, who perhaps knew Isaura.

But the Fonseca aura was still strong. Cristi knew she would ask no questions as long as Luis was there.

Startled by a tap on her door, she was delighted to find him ready to go.

'Great,' she exclaimed. 'I was beginning to think I'd go mad if I had to wait much longer.'

It was good of him. He'd hardly taken any siesta. It was good of him too to come here with her – and to have given up so much of his time to her in Rio. How different her arrival in Brazil and the weeks of delay would have been without him. Grateful, she beamed at him, feeling closer to him than ever before, wrapping both hands round his arm. 'Oh, Luis, I can't tell you how much I'm looking forward to seeing Tres Pinheiros at last.'

'Now that does come as news to me.' But he smiled back at her happy face, returning her touch by drawing his fingertips lightly down her cheek. What an ardent little creature she was, with her transparent honesty and goodwill. And more beautiful, because of that warmth, than his aunt Justina had ever been.

'I had a horrible feeling you might make me wait till tomorrow,' Cristi said as they went down the path.

'You think I have that kind of courage? And besides, you would no doubt have ordered a taxi, hired a car or found a horse. Anything to get out there.'

As he put her into her seat and went round the front of the jeep Cristi took another look at him. His appearance when he came to knock on her door had startled her. Gone was the city look. He was wearing black trousers, with some silver emblem on his belt buckle, and a shirt of heavy-textured white cotton, open at the neck. In his hand he carried a black hat with a flat brim. He looked lean, trim, filled with a new energy, and quite stunning.

He caught her look, and smiled a secret smile. 'You hadn't realised that in this place I breathe my native air?' he teased as he got in. 'You surely didn't think I was a *carioca*?'

A native of Rio. Well, yes, in spite of knowing he now lived in the south, Cristi had supposed he was.

Luis's smile widened as they swung out of the sleepy road. 'Let me assure you, I was born and bred a gaucho, which is why I choose to live in Porto Alegre, the gaucho capital. As a boy I spent every moment I could at Tres Pinheiros.' In spite of himself, his face darkened.

'I used to envy all you cousins so much,' Cristi sighed. 'I'd hear tales of you riding and going to rodeos and eating *churrasco*, and I couldn't bear to miss it.'

Tales told by Isaura. How strange it was to think she might be somewhere close by.

Luis glanced at her, frowning. Had she heard nothing of the other stories; didn't she understand even now how completely the family had cast Justina out? There had never been the remotest chance of Cristi coming here as a child. It might be wiser today, however, to leave the shadows of the past undisturbed.

'You know our roots are here,' was all he said. 'Though the Rio house has been in the family for some generations, and grandfather — as well as my father and uncle — were educated at the British School there, the south is our true home. Wasn't that what you were taught?' No one had loved Tres Pinheiros more than Justina.

'My mother never talked to me about her childhood.' Or about anything.

'She spent more time here than her brothers did when they were growing up, and by all accounts was a wonderful horsewoman. So, yes, your roots are here, and since you were not permitted to visit as a child, I consider it an honour to be the one to bring you here at last.'

The words were a mere flourish of formal courtesy, and the expression in his eyes scarcely matched them, but Cristi accepted them at face value, and the thrill they gave her was evident in the smile she flashed at him. Not for the first time, Luis was confounded by her candour. In the normal course of things, it wasn't a quality which greatly impressed him. Being so ready to see the best in everything struck him as childish and naive. But it made her very easy to be with – and that smile of hers was warm and lovely. He really didn't want to hurt her.

The last shacks of town, with their roughly fenced patches of ground which would grow squash and sweet potatoes and perhaps a row of Indian corn, were left behind. The road crossed a covered bridge of weathered wood which made Cristi long for her sketchbook, and, beyond the deep-gouged gorge it spanned, climbed a steep escarpment. The banks were furrowed by erosion, and rocky channels scoured on either side made the turns hazardous.

'Is this a public road?' Cristi enquired, holding onto the dashboard.

Luis laughed. 'It serves three ranches. It used to be the route for cattle coming through from more distant ones.'

But Cristi wasn't listening. The sharp ascent had opened before them a view dramatic enough to seize anyone's attention. The red road, no longer metalled, led away across a great stretch of rolling grassland, patterned by patches of pine forest and rocky outcrops, cut by deep ravines. Against the deep blue of a wider sky than Cristi had ever seen, two or three large birds lazily wheeled.

'Oh, Luis, stop for a moment, please stop. This is stunning, fabulous!'

Resignedly, he stopped. Much as he hated being held up when he was set on doing something, who could have refused that plea?

'Those enormous black and white birds——?'

'Gaucho eagles. As you see, they observe the purist rule, disdaining colour.'

'Is that their proper name?'

Shrug. 'Perhaps.'

Cristi laughed, turning to him with her face alight with eagerness. 'Luis, it really is fantastic. I hadn't imagined anything like this.'

What had she imagined, she asked herself, when Luis, soon getting bored with views, drove on. Not much, with any clarity, was the answer to that. Her ignorance of her sprawling and complex native land was shameful. Then, her attention momentarily distracted, she realised how naturally she had used the term. Was that how she was beginning to feel about it?

'This is all Tres Pinheiros land,' Luis said, and Cristi, gazing at the distant hills he indicated, assured herself that he couldn't mean it.

After five miles they came to a high gate; carved on its cross-bar was the ranch brand of the Three in Flower. Of course, that was the emblem she'd noticed on Luis's belt buckle but hadn't registered, it dawned on Cristi as, refusing her offer of help, he went to open the gate. How slow of her.

'As you see, grandfather regarded cattle grids as unnecessary luxuries,' Luis remarked acidly as he drove through. 'But then, he had a peon to run ahead when he was leaving the house. And coming home, if he was feeling lazy he fired a shot for one to come running out again while he sat here waiting.'

'That I don't believe. But this is really where the ranch begins, isn't it?' Cristi asked, as they left the gate behind them. The track ahead curved round the base of a grassy hill crowned by flat-topped Paraná pines, and vanished. 'You were teasing before?'

'No, I promise you.' Luis appeared to be gratified as well as amused by the question. 'We've been on the ranch almost since leaving town. You'll just have to get used to it, my pet.'

Yes, well, no need to be too patronising, mate; Drumveyn runs to an acre or two as well. But there was no time for comparisons now. They were entering an avenue of eucalyptus trees, the tracery of their narrow leaves a delicately moving pattern on the red earth. Ahead a second high-arched gate of silvery wood was set in a stone wall — another fleeting reminder of home. Luis blasted the horn, and a shabby figure in a poncho appeared on the run and dragged the gate a couple of feet back.

'Damn thing's falling down,' Luis grumbled, pulling up outside it. 'Like everything else. *Olá, Enrico, tudo bem?*'

'*Bem, bem, obrigado, Don Luis. Boa tarde, senhorita, boa tarde.*'

Enrico was skinny and swarthy, bowing and beaming at Cristi, anxiously assuring Luis that the house was prepared and everything ready. What had the ranch employees been told, it occurred to Cristi to wonder. Here, one never quite knew. Another question shook her. Would Enrico have known her mother? Revelations likely to be fraught with pain seemed suddenly too close.

Something about the old man caught at her, reminding her of the grey-haired Negro who had dealt with their luggage at the airport. But it must wait; there were too many other things to think about just now.

'Come.' Luis led her up a path of stone flags laid across the coarse grass of a small lawn, and she had a brief impression of a single-storey house with faded blue-grey shutters, and a roof of soft apricot-coloured pantiles which swooped forward over a verandah whose posts were smothered in climbing roses. Then Luis was waving her forward through narrow double doors already folded back.

The square hall was the simplest of rooms, but in that first second Cristi fell in love with every inch of it. The floor of wide honey-coloured boards glowed with polish. There was a cavernous fireplace with a great plastered chimney breast, a basket of pine cones on the hearth, and on either side of it a handsome rocking chair. A cane-backed sofa stood against the opposite wall, and there were various pieces of dark, carved Brazilian furniture. But what charmed Cristi was the functional unity of the room, its instantly felt sense of period, the feeling that everything in it had been made by hand, probably here, and lovingly cared for down the years.

'Luis, how perfect!'

'You think so?' Luis seemed to find her enthusiasm somewhat overdone. 'Just as well you do, however, since it's the only sitting-room there is. As you see, not only does the front door lead into it, under which the *pampeiro* – the wind from the south – can scream with sufficient force to overturn lamps and lift pictures off walls, but two bedrooms open from it, as well as the corridor to the rest of the house.'

'May I look?' Most of what he was saying went straight past Cristi.

Luis stood with a strange expression on his face, an angry contempt he couldn't quite suppress fighting with reluctant sympathy for her eagerness, as she went to look into the bedroom on the left. Its door too was divided down the middle, and felt flimsy to her hand. It had glazed panes, but patterned paper, giving the impression from a distance of stained glass, had been pasted over them.

It was a dismal room, its light cut off by the verandah

roof and its sagging swags of rose branches, most of the space taken up by a forbidding, high-ended bed. Grandfather's? The room opposite, however, had a second window in the side wall, looking out onto a strip of garden with magnolia and camellia trees thick with buds. It was light and fresh, with white loose-weave curtains floating at the windows, white painted furniture and blue rugs.

'These amazing golden floors,' Cristi said to Luis, who had followed her, still with that air of not wanting to be part of this.

'Jacaranda wood,' he said tersely. Things were not going according to plan.

This room, Cristi knew at once, she could sleep in. But she said nothing of that as yet, letting Luis show her the study with its old-fashioned rolltop desk, and its shelves crammed with manuals and reference books. Glancing at the titles, she was taken aback to find Haldane's *Drove Roads of Scotland* and *The Great Glen Cattle Ranch* by J.W. Hobbs, as well as such offerings as *Beef Cattle Husbandry* by Allan Fraser and *Animal Breeding* by A.L. Hagedoorn. Suddenly it seemed unbearably sad that she would never know the man who had collected, read and turned to these books again and again. Her grandfather, who had handed down the genes that were part of her. Had she really imagined that by coming here she would somehow find him; in some fanciful way be accepted by him?

Luis had crossed to the window. 'Grandfather used to make the men, even the head peon and the foreman at the farm, come round to this window if they wanted to speak to him. They had to tap then wait till he felt like answering. I've seen them stand there for minutes at a time, the rain sluicing off their hats, and grandfather in here calmly writing or reading. If it was cold, which believe me it can be at this height, he didn't open the window at all but made them bawl through it.'

Cristi decided she felt less sad about not knowing him.

A long bare room ran across the back of the house, a plain wooden table flanked by benches at one end.

'Your dining-room,' Luis announced with a mocking flourish. 'Where, it may or may not interest you to know, a chapter of the Bible was read before every meal, going straight through Old Testament and New and beginning at the beginning again, while the food grew cold under our noses.'

The big Bible still lay to hand, on a lace mat on its own shelf, and again Cristi felt the powerful presence of the old man who had daily handled it.

Tacked on to the rear of the building was the kitchen, a mere earthen-floored shack boasting, however, a splendid pot-bellied wood-burning stove with polished knobs and decorative hinges.

'What a beauty,' Cristi said reverently.

'My sweet, you have the strangest tastes.' Luis sounded exasperated. 'This archaic object represents your sole means of heating your water. With a struggle it could just about provide one hot bath, as I recall – grandfather's.'

Behind the kitchen was a further lean-to, the traces of a fire in the centre of the floor.

'What's this used for?'

'I told you we were back in the dark ages,' Luis said, clearly more irritated by every sign of interest on Cristi's part. 'This is where the peons congregated in the evenings, brewing coffee, gossiping. Sometimes they would tell stories or sing. Great poets and story-tellers, the gauchos. As a child I used to like coming out here to listen when I was supposed to be in bed.'

For a moment there he sounded almost human, Cristi thought. 'The entire place is fascinating and beautiful,' she announced firmly, as they left the shade of the lean-to and went down the slope of orange orchard to the stream below. To the right an ancient sway-backed barn, roofed with the same warm terracotta tiles as the house, over-looked corrals, chutes and handling pens, fenced in wood pale and smooth with age.

'Cristi, it's a primitive, ramshackle little place, which the next gale will probably reduce to matchsticks,' Luis snapped, the moment of nostalgia over. 'You did observe, I suppose, that there is no electricity, no telephone, no modern amenities of any kind. Ah, we omitted the bathroom. Come along.'

But the bathroom, as far as Cristi could see, wasn't so very different from the one in town. She turned on the cold tap. After a choke and a gurgle it produced water of much the colour she was used to at Drumveyn. The hot tap said nothing. Well, who needed it?

'I thought the house was shut up,' she said, as they went back to the hall. 'But the beds are made up and the windows open and everywhere is spotless.'

'Naturally. I sent a message to say we were coming.'
Luis was looking at his watch.

'But no one's living here?'

'Enrico lives at the farm, on the other side of the road,
a mile away. His wife will have done the cleaning. And if
you want to see the farm today we should go. I have
things to do in town this evening.'

How like Luis. Wherever he was, Cristi guessed, he
would have people to see, business to transact – business
which, however vague, he would regard as a clear priority.
As she knew by now, there were males in Brazil, as
elsewhere, who were prepared to accept that in the
modern world their needs and interests were not necessarily paramount. Luis was not one of them. He was
fortunate – or perhaps disadvantaged – to be a survival of
that vanishing breed of men who are never in their lives
required to put anyone else first, and on whom no tedious
domestic demands are ever made.

'I'd like to see the farm today if possible,' was all Cristi
said. She had ideas of her own for the evening.

Chapter Seventeen

Luis headed back towards the road. 'The farm's just out of sight down that slope.'

'What are the buildings round the house then?'

'To do with the *gado* – the cattle. The farm is about the crops, planting and so on.'

'I thought grandfather was only interested in cattle and horse breeding and refused to diversify?'

She caught the turn of his head. Had it occurred to him at last that, growing up on a Scottish highland estate, she might know a little of such matters?

'When he was younger he did experiment a bit,' Luis said dismissively. 'Growing alfalfa and trefoils for winter feed, for instance, instead of letting the herd nearly starve to death out on the range each year, as used to be the case.'

On the range. Cristi tucked away the term with relish, but wasn't impressed by the practice he outlined. 'That sounds a bit brutal.'

Luis shrugged.

'It was how it was done. I remember seeing the steers in the spring – mostly zebus, brahmin cattle, though grandfather had Herefords and shorthorns as well by that time – and they looked like skeletons. They produced some appalling beef, I do have to admit, following that system. They weren't fat enough to sell till they were five or six, and by that time they weren't good for much except *charque, carne seca* – meat dried in the sun. I remember it. Boot leather.'

'Sounds like shark. But grandfather did start to grow feed crops?'

'I suppose the market demanded better quality and he was forced to do something. Somewhere in the sixties, I think. My father has told me about it. The Point Four programme was the big thing in those days, US aid to developing countries. Grandfather had American agronomers out to advise him, and it seems got briefly excited about contour ploughing and planting belts of eucalyptus to minimise erosion, that kind of thing. He stuck in a groove forever after, however.'

Luis's voice had grown contemptuous as he went on, and he seemed to welcome the interruption of opening the road gates. Watching him, Cristi was once more reminded of something that had nagged at her.

'When we landed at Campo Novo,' she asked as they drove on, 'the old man who carried our bags – he wasn't part of the airport staff, was he?'

'Alfeo? Of course not,' Luis's eyebrows went up. 'He didn't look much like it, did he? He's the gardener at the town house. He brought the jeep out for me.'

'And then walked back?'

Luis frowned, not seeing what this had to do with anything. 'Walked, yes. It's not far into town.'

Two miles to the house, Cristi would have thought. Or more. But it had clearly been unthinkable that Alfeo should be given a lift. Luis had joked about grandfather summoning a peon to open the gate by firing his pistol. She couldn't see much difference.

The farm came into sight, an unsightly cluster of basic wooden houses and sheds, around them a spread of newly planted fields, patches of young oats already a thin but brilliant green.

Again Luis sounded his horn, and again people materialised, gathering a few yards from where the jeep pulled up on an open patch of dusty earth. Luis made no attempt at general introductions, and Cristi had to content herself with smiles and nods, which were willingly returned. One fact struck her immediately. Everyone here was elderly; one or two really old. This, presumably, was the human face of grandfather's resistance to progress. No young man would work for him without modern machinery and decent housing; there were no young families growing up here to provide the work force of the future. The old had clung to the place and ways they knew, perhaps because they preferred to, or perhaps because, as Cristi had learned enough to suspect, the terms under which they had lived and worked left them no alternative, no matter what the conditions.

Had Isaura grown up in one of these bare little houses? Did some of these people remember her? It was strange to think news of her could be so close, but Cristi knew she couldn't make any enquiries with Luis there.

In any case, she had more than enough to think about. She was beginning to glimpse the scale of what had been so arbitrarily put into her hands, and something very like panic filled her for a moment. It was she who now employed these people. The conditions under which they lived were down to her. And she knew nothing about them, this country or this way of life.

I'm an art student, she thought wildly. None of this has anything to do with me. She felt very nervous and uncertain as she responded to the greeting of the man whom Luis was introducing as Leopoldo, the farm manager.

A well-built man with a kindly face, perhaps in his late fifties, he welcomed her with smiling courtesy to Tres Pinheiros, but didn't attempt to bring anyone else forward to meet her. Cristi, conscious of the watching group, not all of whom were dark-haired and dark-eyed, for many people in the southern states of Santa Catarina and Rio Grande do Sul are of German origin, could imagine the interest this new development would arouse. The old *patrão* who had ruled their lives dying, and the land going not to his sons or his grandsons, but to the daughter of Justina, the beautiful daughter who had vanished so long ago. Cristi wanted to make some contact with them, be invited into one of their houses, but knew that for today it was important to observe customary form.

She was thankful that the weeks in Rio had improved

her Portuguese sufficiently to cope with the sing-song speed of Leopoldo's speech, made unfamiliar by the soft consonants of the south.

They didn't stay long – Luis's impatience to be gone must have been evident to everyone – but the essential thing had been to put in an appearance, and to meet Leopoldo. Tomorrow he would be present at the meeting in town which had been arranged with the factor, as Cristi would have called him, who administered Tres Pinheiros affairs.

As the jeep approached the road she braced herself for confrontation.

'Luis, I think I'll stay here tonight.'

She had almost said, 'Would it be all right if I stayed?' but as she opened her mouth to speak had remembered that here she didn't have to ask. She was no longer a guest in someone else's house. Come to that – her spirits rose at the thought – she had a couple of houses of her own to choose from. She no longer had to behave according to stifling Fonseca rules. A heady moment.

'Stay here?' Luis was visibly taken aback. 'Of course you can't stay. It's out of the question.'

'But it's what I'm going to do.'

She had taken the precaution of firing her opening shot – shades of grandfather – while they were still on the farm track. If they'd been out on the road she knew Luis would simply have driven off to town.

He tried every argument. He couldn't think of leaving her here alone; as he had commitments this evening he couldn't stay with her; there was no food in the house;

she had nothing with her; tomorrow's meeting in town was scheduled to start early. For Brazil, Cristi supposed he meant. But by now she knew enough of life here, or of life as lived by the Fonsecas, to be certain that any practical difficulty could be overcome. For once she had no compunction about manipulating the system. A much-used verb here was *aproveitar*. Right, it was her turn to profit.

Luis became angry, in a way he had never let her see before, and it wasn't pleasant. The truth was he had been ruffled by the way the day had gone, and he needed time to reassess his strategy. Cristi had shown none of the expected dismay at the isolation, the primitive level and marked dilapidation of her property. On the contrary, she'd been rapturous about it, and the reaction had thrown him.

Now she was behaving like one of those brash foreign women he so abominated, not only being unreasonable and stubborn, but threatening to jeopardise his plans. Until now she had seemed so amenable. What had gone wrong?

Cristi was not a quarreller by nature, but two things made her stick to her resolve – an image of the dark town house which had held such bad vibes for her, in contrast to the shabby charm of the ranch to which she had instantly responded; and something else she could hardly have put into words – an instinct which told her she was on the brink of something significant and that making a stand at this point mattered.

'I know you'll think it strange,' she said to Luis, careful

to keep her voice level in spite of the anger in his, 'but this is something I really want to do. I expect it can be arranged without too much trouble. The house is ready, even the beds are—'

Luis released a Portuguese oath with which she was unfamiliar. 'It has nothing to do with cleaning or beds! It's simply that it would be unthinkable for you to stay here alone, a young girl—'

That sounded pretty dated, but Cristi knew it wasn't the ground on which to fight him.

'It is my house,' she said quietly.

For a moment, seeing the leap of rage in his eyes, she wished she could have recalled the words. Then, as she had seen his father do, without perceptible effort Luis emptied his face of all expression. He was thinking, though Cristi couldn't guess it, that there was still a long way to go.

'Then all I have to say is that you will inconvenience a great many people,' he said stiffly.

Cristi managed not to smile. When had that ever been a consideration for a Fonseca?

'I'm sorry,' she said.

The very lack of elaboration or attempt to justify herself told Luis she meant to do this. Sweet-natured she might fundamentally be, but it had to be remembered that she had received the worst kind of upbringing. And would it serve any purpose to fight over this?

'Well, if you're set on this absurd plan,' he said curtly, 'I suppose someone will have to bring out your things. You won't need much for one night.'

'I shall need everything,' Cristi said. 'Everything I brought with me to Campo Novo.' She would have preferred, in truth, to have left nothing behind in the Fonseca house in Rio, but for various reasons had decided it would be diplomatic to do so.

They stared at each other, defiance crackling in the air. Then an unwilling smile touched Luis's lips. 'So, my sweet little cousin, it seems you are not quite so malleable as you would have us believe.'

It was a word Cristi would remember him using. For now, his smile didn't linger, and his eyes were cold. Cristi couldn't tell what he was thinking, and had an idea it might be better not to know.

The memory of that first evening alone at Tres Pinheiros would stay with her all her life. Alone, that is, in the Fonseca sense of the word, for before he left Luis ordained that Enrico and his wife Selma should install themselves in one of the servants' rooms, behind the flimsy wooden stables tacked on to one side of the house. Cristi didn't argue. She had won the vital point.

The moments as the sound of the jeep, driven fast, faded away down the avenue (Enrico dispatched ahead to open the gate and then fetch Selma from the farm), and the silence flowed back, were filled with mixed sensations. Had she really pulled this off? She had hardly dared to hope she could. Her senses felt acutely alive, her heartbeat quickening.

She was alone in this vast, exhilarating, unknown landscape. At her back, the empty house waited for her, with its air of being barely disturbed from its sleep, the little house with its lack of pretension, its glowing golden floors, behind it the deserted yards and corrals, the ancient barn, the neat rows of the orange orchard. For the brief period before Enrico returned she truly was on her own here, something she guessed she would be unlikely to achieve again.

She walked almost stiffly, tentative and excited at the same time, across the coarse grass to the flat-topped stone wall enclosing the garden to the south; the *taipa*, its dry-stone construction not so very different from the style she knew at home.

Unaccountably finding tears close, she gazed out across the meadow, with the blue-grey line of the eucalyptus avenue to the west, a low ridge sheltering it to the east, to the long fall of open country beyond the road, beyond the farm, which gave the impression that nothing would interrupt its limitless waves until the very southernmost tip of the continent was reached.

The impact of this scene, new impressions of every kind, tumbled in her brain. And how many discoveries and experiences were still to come? It was huge, this whole adventure, huge and challenging. She urgently needed these quiet moments to put it into the context of 'real' life.

Leaning on the *taipa*, as a vivid sunset faded and a dusk considerably colder than she had bargained for descended with the abruptness of the sub-tropics, she turned her thoughts homewards. Emotions running high after the thronged events of the day, she found herself missing

Drumveyn with a passionate longing. She needed desperately to talk to people who loved and understood her, putting this place, with its potent mix of beauty, scale, undercurrents and as yet unfaced demands, into perspective by 'telling' as she was accustomed to do. She didn't want to search for words, be tactful, respect different views. Above all she ached for shared humour, ready laughter. She had been homesick before but this evening the longing had a keener edge. For there had been a moment today, when first she laid eyes on this enchanting, abandoned house, of feeling that she was back where she belonged.

She had resisted the response at the time, but it had been real, adding a new dimension to the need to discover her inheritance. Could it mean, she wondered, shivering in the gathering darkness, that this place would one day matter more to her than Drumveyn?

The idea rocked her, and for several moments, blind to everything around her, she let the memories come, calling up a hundred pictures, listening with head bent and eyes closed to the voices of home.

And finally, cold now, her arms wrapped round her, but not ready to go in and, by entering the house, embark as it were on this new phase of her life, she let herself think about Dougal.

She hadn't heard a word from him about Ellig. The Croft of Ellig. She liked the name. She hadn't heard a word from him about anything that counted, or how he felt at this crucial point of his life. That hurt. Surely it showed her something though. She had no alternative but to accept that childhood closeness could never be more than adult friendship. Even as she told herself this, she realised how much she still wanted to share with him every detail of what was happening to her. It hardly seemed valid without that sharing. She ached to remember that once it would have seemed unbelievable that this ease of communication between them could ever fade away.

But it was time to believe it. Time to move on. For another truth she had been evading must be faced. In recent weeks, weeks passed in exotic, fascinating scenes, when over and over again had come the almost physical tug of recognition, Luis had been the focal point. There was no use trying to deny that her pleasure in it had depended largely on being with him.

Her thoughts were broken into by the arrival of Enrico and Selma, padding quietly up the avenue bearing what they needed bundled up in cloths. Greetings, smiles, assurances that to be summoned in this way without notice, to be expected to produce a meal out of thin air, was nothing, nothing . . . Alfeo arrived from town soon afterwards with Cristi's belongings. This too was nothing, a pleasure . . .

Dinner, of delicious savoury doughnuts and a steak twice the size Cristi could handle, with a tiny blob of very sweet caramel pudding to follow, was prepared and served without any apparent difficulty. When Cristi came back to the hall, where Selma had taken the coffee, she found not only the lamps lit, with their faint agreeable smell of oil, but a fire of pine knots in the big fireplace, and on the hearth a jar of eucalyptus branches, placed there so that the warmth could draw out the aroma of their leaves.

The simple room looked perfect in the soft glow of lamplight and flames, but Cristi found herself too restless to sit for long, too conscious of the unexplored landscape outside, now hidden under velvety darkness. She had noticed a row of hooks along the corridor wall. From one she took down a big poncho of soft grey wool, and wrapping herself in its comforting folds went down again to her post by the *taipa*.

It was as though, by eating her first meal in this house, her house, the present had displaced the past. She had almost known it would. As she leant on the stone slabs, her face turned up to the mellow brilliance of the stars, she acknowledged the truth she had come close to earlier. She thought a great deal more about Luis by this time than she did about Dougal. And, even more honestly, though she had fought to be alone at the ranch, right now she wanted nothing more than to see lights coming up the avenue, telling her Luis was on his way back.

She had grown used to his company, to his flashing smile and teasing eyes, his quick tongue and restless energy – even to his Fonseca assurance that everything he wanted would materialise at a snap of his fingers.

Where was he at this moment? What was he doing? Still involved in his urgent business? He probably hadn't even had dinner yet. He was unlikely to dine alone, she knew that much. Not in a hurry, probably, to return to the old-fashioned, airless and colourless town house.

Going in at last, hooking the latch across the doors, Cristi breathed in with pleasure the warm mingled scents of the hall. Selma had heard her, and came whispering along the corridor in her slippers with the trodden-down backs to make sure she had everything she needed for the night. Her dark face was kind and smiling, and if someone had to be there to look after her Cristi was happy for it to be Selma.

In her bedroom she looked round her with grateful pleasure. Her belongings were already put away in the plain white wardrobe and chest of drawers. The shutters were closed and the squat silver lamp beside the bed was turned low, its light throwing a faint peachy glow on the snowy sheets so immaculately turned down.

Turned down to reveal a monogram, Cristi saw, looking more closely. Embroidered in blue was the Three in Flower, the ranch brand. Her brand. It was repeated on the pillowslips, and on the towels folded over a wooden rail. It had doubtless been on the napkin she had flicked onto her lap at dinner without looking. How over the top – but rather nice too.

Not so nice, as she got into bed, was the meagreness of the single blanket and blue cotton cover. Had anyone ever slept here before, in what tonight felt more like the tail end of winter than the beginning of spring? As she got out to fetch the big poncho, Cristi grinned to think that the first purchase she intended to make in Campo Novo would be a hot-water bottle.

As she settled once more in the narrow bed, not sure that she would sleep with so many images thronging, she became conscious of a background sound she had been vaguely aware of for some time – the throaty but not unmusical chorus of frogs. Varied in tone, but as steady in volume as the rushing of a hill burn, it had a wonderfully lulling quality. She barely had time to register the astonishing fact that she was going to sleep for the first time in a house she owned, when oblivion overtook her.

Luis, whose evening had not been satisfactory, ended a long telephone conversation with his father and sat for a while unmoving on the rusty red plush of the hard sofa. His face was dark with ill-temper, his thoughts far from agreeable. Presently, with an angry exclamation, he got to his feet. He might as well go to bed as sit here. Damned place. Barely past eleven and everything was shut down already. Not a night club for two hundred miles.

This was not the way it was supposed to be. The sooner he got Cristi to Porto Alegre the better. She had out-manoeuvred him here in a way he hadn't imagined her capable of. She wouldn't be able to do the same there.

Chapter Eighteen

Lines of light round the ill-fitting shutters made the small white-walled room bright, and brought Cristi fully awake the moment she opened her eyes. The excitement of remembering where she was and what lay ahead was the excitement of childhood, a burning impatience to be up and out, exploring and discovering. Shivering in the cold air, she hurried into her clothes. She was tempted to take the big poncho, but it was too long to walk in easily. Once she was out in the sun she'd be warm enough.

In the hall, she found a bar in place across the doors, which were bolted top and bottom and also locked, the key removed. No point in wasting time on that lot. Going back to her room she went out via the window.

That first morning prowl round the ranch was pure delight. The keen air was wonderful after the heat of Rio. Mist still clung to the long descent of ground below, turning it into a pale mysterious sea without horizons, and as Cristi went down the lawn she saw a sight which made her catch her breath. Crossing the bottom of the field, in silhouette against the sunlit mist, rode a gaucho. His back was straight, his hat brim level, and his poncho made an exact triangle as it spread over his mount's hind quarters. The horse moved with a floating gait Cristi had never seen before, the rider unmoving in the saddle. It was a sight so perfect, and so perfectly timed, that she longed to share it with someone, wishing after all that Luis had stayed. She could hardly wait to see him.

The horseman gone, nothing else moved except the birds, whose unfamiliar songs filled the air. Cristi went out by the high-barred gate and along the field, working her way through the corral fences to peer into the shadowy barn with its lingering smells of feed and animals. Going down to the stream, she came to a stretch of marshy ground which was no doubt the source of last night's strenuous frog chorus. In the orchard she watched a busy brown bird making a mud nest on the trunk of a walnut tree, and caught a glimpse of a slimmer bird like a flash of pure scarlet against the dark foliage of the orange trees.

The stables were empty, but their familiar redolence made her sharply homesick for a second, as she ran her palm over wood polished smooth by years of hands and hides. There was still tack there, though it wasn't light enough to examine it. There must be riding horses. Where? Out on the range? The Americanism Luis had used didn't seem outlandish. Could one be brought in for her? Who'd do that? She imagined heading off across these enticing open miles.

Well, this morning she was to be driven to the meeting in town by Leopoldo. She'd be able to ask these questions, and maybe others which mattered more.

Taking the path between stables and house, she saw smoke rising from the kitchen chimney, and startled Selma, busy feeding wood into the stove, by appearing at the open door. Selma's main concern seemed to be that she hadn't been up in time to provide hot water, tea or whatever Cristi required when she woke. At Tres Pinheiros working hours were not geared to the clock but to the needs of the *patrão*. And now the *patroa*.

But Cristi couldn't deal with that yet. Cutting short Selma's apologies, she asked her what the birds she had seen were called, and was charmed to be given country names like *João de Barro*, John-of-the-mud, and ox's-blood for the scarlet one, and to learn that the lilies below the *taipa* were known as cups-of-milk. These details brought a feeling of intimacy, of touching, in however small a way, the reality of this place, which the weeks in Rio had never given her.

Breakfast was a thin porridge called *mingão*. Cristi didn't think it would have gone down too well in Glen Ellig. It was followed by solid bread with apple jelly so over-boiled that it stuck first to the cold knife, then to Cristi's teeth. The coffee, on which she had pinned her hopes, appeared in morning guise – some cheap powdered brand, by the taste of it. Perhaps domestic arrangements could be improved upon. But there was no hurry.

Hesitantly, sure Luis would be angry if he knew, for

the Fonsecas had made it clear that anything connected with Justina was a taboo subject, Cristi took the chance on the way to Campo Novo to ask Leopoldo if he had known Isaura's family. It was strange to pronounce the name, bringing the past disturbingly back.

Leopoldo was happy to talk, and though his accent occasionally made him difficult to follow, it wasn't hard to sort out the essential facts. Years ago Isaura had been sent home from Rio in disgrace. As a result her father had lost his job, and no one else in the area would give him work. The family had been forced to leave, and had never been heard of since.

Did no one have any idea where they might have gone?

Far away, Leopoldo thought. Perhaps Curitíba. It sounded to Cristi as though he'd plucked the name out of the air to oblige her.

She thought of the vast scale of this country. Isaura could be anywhere. And of course no one at the ranch would want to keep in touch with a family who had left under a cloud. Grandfather's uncompromising authority would see to that.

My mother was responsible for this, Cristi thought, dismay at the idea of lives being so ruthlessly destroyed mingling with sick emptiness to find that the last fragile link no longer existed. She had known this hope was slight. But it was hard to learn in a few brief phrases that it must be relinquished for good. The past would hold onto its secrets. She would never be reconciled with her mother, never know the truth about her parents and why they had left her as they did.

She almost wished, so much did this hurt, that she hadn't questioned Leopoldo, and it wasn't easy to greet Luis normally when he appeared, or apply her mind to the business in hand. But she had to do it, and she resolutely pushed away her aching sense of being newly bereft.

The meeting was satisfactory as far as it went. Because of the sheer size of the ranch she had seen it as an operation even more complex to manage than Drumveyn, but its day-to-day running seemed relatively straightforward. The herd had been steadily improved over the years and now had an established reputation. Apart from feed no other crops were grown. Jobs such as vaccinating, tagging, culling and cutting the calves, were handled by men who had done them all their lives. Outgoings on maintenance were low – no surprise. A point which bothered her was that the older workers, whom she would have thought should have been pensioned off by now, were allowed to stay on in their houses in return for work at reduced rates. This seemed all wrong, but Cristi knew she had no basis for questioning it. She had no idea of the regulations; it might even be regarded as a valued bonus. But the question brought sharply home to her the fact that her ownership of Tres Pinheiros was the merest technicality, nothing more than words on paper.

She left the office of the ranch-manager – a suave, corpulent, middle-aged man in a tight black suit, who called himself Dr Elisario on the grounds of an engineering degree – feeling much as she had after her encounters with the Rio lawyers. She had been fed as much information as the men thought fit. Behind the smiling greetings and elaborate courtesy, she had been patronised because she was female, young and half-foreign into the bargain. It was accepted that as legatee she would wish to be seen to take an interest, but any such interest could only be nominal.

And they were right. Until she knew more, or had some idea of what she wanted to do, the ranch had no more to do with her than it had when she was still in Scotland. Its operation would go on as before. In real terms, Cristi knew that in her mind, as well as theirs, it remained Fonseca property.

As they left the office building, Cristi ruefully conscious of all she had not been told or shown, but knowing she could expect nothing else, she heard Luis tell Leopoldo to take her luggage to the town house.

Leopoldo avoided her eye.

She leapt in quickly. 'Nothing to take, Luis. I haven't brought my things.'

'What do you mean, not brought them?' Luis snapped out the question in English, and it was clear from his tone that he realised the decision was significant.

Leopoldo, without appearing to move, effaced himself from the exchange.

'That was silly,' Luis went on angrily, as Cristi didn't reply. 'Now someone will have to fetch them.'

'There's no need.' Cristi eyes met his squarely. 'I'm staying at the ranch for a bit longer.'

'Staying? But you've seen it. That was the object, wasn't it. There's no—'

'I'd like to spend more time there.'

'But you've just heard that, archaic as its methods may be, it functions quite adequately. Surely you're not thinking of interfering in—'

She saw the effort he made to stop himself there.

'I don't want to interfere in anything. But I wouldn't mind learning a little more.' There was so much to rethink now that she had seen it. Huge questions, affecting her whole life. Questions about who she was.

'You know perfectly well our flights to Porto Alegre are booked for tomorrow. What difference can it make to spend one more night at Tres Pinheiros?'

'I want to stay longer than that.' And when had Luis ever let anything he wanted to do be affected by a detail like a flight booking? 'I'll come on to Porto Alegre soon.' She was looking forward to it, grateful for the opportunity to see another bit of this enormous and diverse country – and to be shown it by Luis.

'Cristi, it's out of the question, you must see that. I can't leave you alone at the ranch. And I have things to do in PA which can't wait. If you want to see more we can arrange something later on when—'

'I'd rather stay now.' Cristi had been in Brazil long enough to know how much trust to put in vague promises. 'I can easily postpone my onward flight. I can get whatever I need here in town – boots for one thing – and go back with Leopoldo. Nothing could be simpler.'

Luis looked at her, his face tight with annoyance but also with calculation. Disconcerted as he had been to find

how enraptured she was with everything at Tres Pinheiros, even so he had underestimated its appeal for her.
He hadn't made sufficient allowance for this damned
British independence. No right-minded Brazilian girl
would consider such a plan for an instant. And here
was Cristi planning to buy boots. How long, in God's
name, did she intend to stay?

But, looking into the determined face turned up to his,
he recognised, with reluctant admiration, that she wasn't
about to let go. She looked so fragile and lightweight, but
her steady look told him a great deal. Her expression
wasn't challenging. On the contrary, it conveyed a simple
confidence which impressed him. To her this proposal
seemed both obvious and feasible.

Luis saw that a different strategy was called for, and
without further debate came round full circle.

'Though I expect you to repent of your madness, so be
it.' The teasing smile was back. 'However, with your
permission of course, perhaps I may revise your plans
somewhat. Why don't we have lunch in town, where we
are expected, then I shall take you out to the ranch
myself, and also stay for a day or two.' It flashed through
his mind as he spoke that in effect he should be invited,
and he suppressed swift anger at the thought. He went on
smoothly before Cristi could speak, 'So, that's settled. I
shall give myself the pleasure of instructing you on our
family's dubious past.'

Cristi's face was alight with pleasure.

'Luis, would you really stay? There's nothing I'd like
more.' Magical as that solitary hour this morning had

been, exploring in the dew-drenched stillness, there had been a need too to share its beauty. To share it with Luis . . . What more could she ask? She wasn't tactless enough to remind him of the business in Porto Alegre which couldn't wait.

With this decision made, Luis's attitude radically altered. Now he wanted nothing more than to introduce Cristi to this part of her heritage, as previously, from different motives, he had wanted to show her the very different delights of Rio.

He began even before they left town by taking her to the boot factory. Here, she learned, boots had been made for every male Fonseca from great-grandfather down. In the past everything was made to order; nowadays there was also a shop with ready-made goods. Here, as her welcoming present to Tres Pinheiros, as Luis said with a flourish, he bought her a beautiful pair of riding boots.

She peacocked in them rapturously. 'They're gorgeous! Soft as slippers. I've never seen such leather. Oh, Luis, thank you, they're totally fabulous!'

'They should have been made for you,' he objected, his mouth turning down disparagingly. 'And of course,' he added more lightly, 'had the Three in Flower tooled on them. You'll somehow have to get along without that.'

As Cristi laughed, turning her foot from side to side in happy admiration, his mind went back to last night's conversation with his father. Perhaps, after all, this decision to stay at the ranch for a day or two would prove advantageous. If he could stand the boredom of rural life. He'd enjoyed the ranch in the past, but his interest in it took a different form now.

With Luis there, everything moved up a gear. Whatever was needed materialised with ease and promptness. Two saddle horses were brought in, and Cristi was excited to find they were Palominos. They were welcomed by Enrico with satisfaction, and he set to work at once to brush out their flowing cream manes and tails and burnish their amber coats, just coming into condition with the new grass. They were both mares, and Cristi asked Luis if he had chosen them particularly.

'This is, after all, the spring,' he said, looking amused. 'I wouldn't wish you to be carried away to the furthest corners of the estancia against your will.'

His presence brought other changes. Now they had drinks before dinner, and to go with them Selma made appalling little squares of hard-baked toast. Luis threw them into the fire. Dinner was a more elaborate affair. Extra lamps were lit, extra blankets produced, and by some miracle piping hot water issued from the bathroom taps. A second elderly woman appeared to help Selma, and warmth and bustle brought the little house to life.

But what was most magical for Cristi in the days that followed were the rides she and Luis shared, over miles of this wide cattle country which she still couldn't begin to think of as hers. The first time they went out she was charmed to find that whereas Enrico had saddled Luis's mare with the *pelego*, the traditional gaucho saddle of sheepskins covered by a square of soft tanned hide, hers had a splendid Mexican saddle with silver ornamentation, its stirrups protected by leather shields, its pommel so high that she felt as if she was sitting in a bucket.

'Not that we have a great deal of cactus here,' Luis commented drily, when he saw her examining the stirrups. 'This was your grandmother's saddle. The *pelego*, being rather wide, wasn't considered suitable for ladies. Your mother used this saddle too.'

Her mother. That seemed so real and close, yet only yesterday she had had to accept that she would never establish contact with her. Tentatively, Cristi asked, 'Did you ever see her ride?'

Catching the tremor in her voice, looking at her quickly, Luis wished he'd kept his mouth shut. They were so used to damning Justina out of hand that it was hard to remember that Cristi must still feel something for her. Yet in the same moment, the softened look of her eyes and mouth tugging at him, he was glad that he had produced that expression. She could be as light-hearted as a teenager, and with that undeveloped body looked like one, but in other ways, in outlook and perceptions, she was very much a woman. A sexually unawakened one, he was fairly sure. Against all expectation.

Apart from the drawback of Cristi not having been brought up as a Catholic, the image of her as a British university student had been the most worrying factor for the family. They had been pleasantly surprised. Her clothes, of course, had been terrible, but that had soon been dealt with. In other respects, she had turned out to be very far from the image they had dreaded. Apart from her innate elegance, inherited from her mother, she was articulate and well-read, and had manners, attitudes and tastes which had proved surprisingly acceptable. Perhaps the barbarians hadn't done such a bad job after all.

They paced down the avenue, to let Cristi get the feel of the unaccustomed saddle and bit, but once out of it Luis took his mare into a faster pace, and Cristi's went with it. Both settled into the run she had noted before with such pleasure, and she found all she had to do was to sit well down and be carried smoothly forward.

'Luis, this is brilliant!'

He laughed at her. 'They cover seven miles an hour at this pace, and can keep it up all day. Horses trained to an extra smooth gait for ladies were called "hammock horses".'

'Good name. I feel I could go for hours too.'

The Mexican saddle, however, though virtually impossible to fall out of, was hard, and Cristi soon persuaded Enrico, in spite of his protests, to strap a fleece over it, thus gaining the best of both worlds.

It paid off, for sometimes she and Luis rode for most of the day, as she gradually formed a picture of the extent of the ranch, what stock it held, and where the cattle ranged in different seasons and conditions. From high rocky outcrops they gained wider views, or by contrast plunged into the clefts of deep-gouged water courses where light filtered down green and eerie.

Having made the decision to stay, Luis found himself enjoying the ranch more than he had for years. Though he still found it necessary to disappear to town at least once a day, Cristi's enthusiasm, her readiness to learn, the way she rode (and the way she looked when she rode), added to the fact that she made no secret of enjoying his company, made a seductive combination.

For Cristi did enjoy being with him. Dismissive and critical as he could be, his mood was usually buoyant when they rode. Also, he was unexpectedly at home in this setting, and that added to her pleasure. He was an expert horseman, and with his lean build and dark good looks Cristi found him even more attractive than she had in Rio. Though he often teased her, the patronising tone had gone, their conversation tended to range more widely, and Luis was even willing, occasionally, to ask about Cristi's world.

Chapter Nineteen

'You don't think we've lost her, do you? For good, I mean.' Pauly blurted out the question awkwardly, no longer able to keep her fears to herself.

Madeleine looked up from the closely written pages to find Pauly standing over her with the coffee tray, her eyes full of appeal, looking very like the impulsive, disorganised but tender-hearted nineteen-year-old she had first known.

'Pauly, I'm sure we haven't. Don't say such a thing!' she protested, adding more practically, 'Though I think you should put that tray down if you want to get emotional about it.' She had lost too many precious and fragile objects in the lively days of Pauly's reign in her household to want to risk those rather pretty cups, paltry as the consideration might be at such a moment.

'I don't *want* to get emotional.' It was an indignant wail as Pauly slapped down the tray so heedlessly that Madeleine barely had time to rescue her other glasses.

'I hate getting emotional, I'm hopeless at all that stuff. Heavy stuff, I mean.'

Madeleine perfectly understood the distinction. Tears could spring to Pauly's eyes more readily than to anyone else's she knew, over a puppy whose tail had been trodden on, over images of global disaster, Judy dying in *Seven Little Australians*, a present the children had made for her themselves, or pretty well any demonstration of human kindness. But to 'get heavy', as she called it, to put anxious feelings into words, was another matter. Pauly liked being so busy looking after people that there was no time for whys and wherefores. She liked the family around her, the house full, plenty of friends on hand and plenty of jobs clamouring to be done.

That was her security blanket. For her, doing and giving said all she needed to say about her affections. Archie understood that, and she luxuriated in the perfect confidence that he asked for nothing more. She knew, however, that for other people it wasn't always that simple, and she humbly did her best, when it seemed called for, to take her part in 'deep' conversations. But she wasn't good at it, and, in the rare moments when she looked so far ahead, she would quail to think of the rocks lying in wait for the children. With Peta especially, for pale, skinny Peta, with her over-active conscience and her desperate anxieties, was going to find the going hard as she grew older. Thank goodness for Archie and his calm good sense, Pauly would think philosophically, and plunge into whatever task lay nearest to hand.

Madeleine would have liked to remind her that she

was being a rock of support for Sally Danaher now that Mike was visibly failing, and Sally was trying to take care of him without letting him see that she no longer trusted him alone, at the same time looking after her hotel guests, and providing a loving, stable home for Mike's son and daughter from his first marriage. But Madeleine knew Pauly would have stared at her blankly, not even beginning to understand how much she was doing for Sally. As she would see it, she only nipped across to Grianan with the odd pint of cream or few pounds of surplus fruit. But Madeleine knew how much these visits meant to Sally, and how many other people up and down the glen also welcomed and depended upon Pauly's breezy support.

Today, however, something was bothering her enough to make her talk, and with a little chill Madeleine recognised the fears behind that need. They were fears which had been riding her too, even before she had hastily skimmed the letter Pauly had brought with her.

Archie had taken Tom down for his physio session today, and as soon as they'd driven away Pauly had phoned to ask if she could come, offering as her excuse news from Cristi. This in itself had alerted Madeleine. All coming and going between the households was very relaxed, and letters from Cristi were shared as a matter of course, as she intended them to be.

Madeleine wished she had had time to read this one more thoroughly while Pauly was making the coffee. Though she was reluctant to admit it, there was a note in it which seemed new, but it was hard to pin down, and she would have liked more time to absorb and consider it.

'Honestly, who would have thought things could drag on like this?' Pauly demanded, scowling at the letter Madeleine was putting aside, as though it were to blame.

'I know, it seems such ages since she went. Though to be fair, I think we were all somewhat naive about it.'

'How d'you mean?' Pauly looked mutinous. She wanted to have a good go about these wretched people who seemed to think they had the right to run Cristi's life.

'Well, what exactly did we think would happen? That Cristi would go out to Brazil, be welcomed back into the family, have the details of her inheritance made clear, and then – what?'

'I thought she'd find the Fonsecas were so ghastly that she'd come straight home! No, I suppose what I really expected, though I didn't think it out very carefully, was that Cristi would turn out to have inherited a share of her grandfather's money, but that the ranch would somehow stay in the family. That part just didn't seem real. I don't think I ever imagined Cristi actually *owning* it. Not personally. Oh, I don't *know!*' Pauly shoved at her heavy hair with an impatient hand. 'I'm useless at saying what I mean.'

'I think you've put it rather well,' Madeleine remarked ruefully. 'I felt much the same. It was lovely for Cristi to think her grandfather had remembered her, and right that the family should acknowledge her at last. It even seemed right that she should – how did she put it? – rediscover that part of her. But I realise now that I still saw her, quite definitely, as belonging here. I was sure, in my heart, that

Drumveyn would always be her home. Perhaps she'd go out to Brazil from time to time, but with this as her – her starting point, her base. No, I hadn't thought about it properly either.'

She had forgotten that she was supposed to be supplying comfort. She needed to talk this out as badly as Pauly did.

Pauly stared at her miserably, her coffee untouched. 'You felt it too, in the letter? As though this time she wasn't just giving an account of what she's been seeing and doing, visiting a new country, but more as if she – oh God, what *do* I mean?'

'There was a different response to what she's found on the ranch?' Madeleine suggested slowly. 'Almost a – well, a sort of feeling that she'd arrived home?'

'That's it exactly!' Then at the awfulness of having her groping fears so precisely defined, instead of being dismissed out of hand as she had hoped for them to be, Pauly looked more than ever ready to burst into tears. 'It's even this writing paper,' she exclaimed, grabbing up the flimsy pages with a vengeful hand. 'Even it's sort of exciting, I can see that. Horrible stuff.'

Madeleine, smiling in spite of a strong desire to share the release of tears, said, 'It is exciting though, isn't it? I have to agree with you there.'

Cristi's letter had begun: 'Just look at what I've found. I came into the office – yes, at last, at last, I'm at Tres Pinheiros, hard as you'll find it to believe, and as you can imagine there are a million things to tell you – to look for any old paper to start a letter, and I found piles of this. At first I thought I shouldn't pinch it, then I realised it's mine. That's so odd, and keeps taking me by surprise. Anyway, we now know how long the Fonsecas have been around, and you can see the fantastic brand of the Three ending in flowery twirls. It appears on just about everything you touch here.'

The letter was written on sheets of the finest onion-skin paper, their letterhead announcing *Estancia dos Tres Pinheiros, fundada em* 1663.

'Up till now,' Pauly said, frowning at this as she groped for the words, 'I've felt she was still with us. That we were the people she still needed to talk to and describe things to because she was in a strange place among strangers. We were her home people. It felt as though she was marking time, making the best of things, and even though the Fonsecas were her mother's family she was still only visiting. But now,' Pauly's generous smiling mouth pursed unattractively as she struggled with difficult concepts, 'she sounds as though she's come alive again.'

Madeleine's face tightened, but she nodded. 'It reminds me a little of when she went up to Edinburgh,' she said thoughtfully. 'Those letters we received at first, descriptive, always careful to be positive, but telling us nothing of what she was really going through. Then when she found her feet and became happier their whole tone changed. She spoke to us.'

'She'd always spoken to Dougal, though,' Pauly observed. 'Through that bad time.'

They looked at each other.

'She hasn't written to him this time.'

'Maybe now?'

'I think I'd be surprised,' Madeleine said carefully, after a tiny pause.

'Me too. It makes me feel so sad. You'd think nothing could spoil a friendship like that.'

Madeleine could think of something which might, but wasn't ready to discuss it. 'I hope Archie doesn't let him do too much up at Ellig,' she said, a different concern surfacing. 'He seems to be working every hour of the day and night at present. In fact, if you think about it, in one way Dougal was the worst possible person for such a deal. He's far too conscientious, forever worrying about putting in as much as he takes out, or more.'

'And half killing himself in the process. But isn't it good about Jean getting her house? What a relief when old Maisie Mack agreed to go into the nursing home. She should have gone ages ago.'

'I'm even more pleased on Dougal's account. One worry less for him. And I was impressed that he was so firm about not having Jean at the Croft of Ellig. It would *not* have been the launch into independence he deserves.'

Pauly laughed. 'It would not. Thank goodness he's put his foot down about Jill as well. I was so relieved when she went off to Glasgow, and so was Archie. I don't know how she could have stayed away from her baby for so long, though. Can you imagine it? Surely it will help her to be with him again.'

'Who knows?' Madeleine wasn't so sanguine. Could the problem of Jill so neatly disappear? 'Still, as you say, her departure couldn't have come at a better time for Dougal.'

If only he would be as tough about the issue that really mattered; but an awful lot was stacked against him, she had to admit.

'We're dodging about Cristi, aren't we?' Pauly met Madeleine's eyes with a wry look.

Madeleine read it with affectionate sympathy. She knew Pauly had come here today determined to face her fears, and didn't intend to let herself off.

'You're thinking Cristi may have discovered she's a Brazilian at heart?' She spoke very gently.

'That's it exactly!' Pauly looked relieved to have it so succinctly put. 'I keep thinking about how she looks, about how pretty and elegant she is, and – oh, you know, feminine, sort of dainty, though that's a dreadful word and I don't think it's ever passed my lips before. But anyway, different from us.'

Madeleine, a small-boned and elegant woman in her own right, let this pass without comment, but saved it up with pleasure to relate to Tom.

'And then I think,' Pauly plunged on, pushing her hair about in her determination to get this into the open at last, 'how she was nearly nine when she came to Drumveyn, not a baby. There'd been those years of childhood in Brazil, and they have to count. I imagine her now surrounded by a load of handsome Brazilians, and it seems sort of right. Yet when she was in Rio I didn't get this feeling of her slipping away from us. It's now, now she's at this place.' A brown, work-worn, housekeeping, gardening finger jabbed down on the flowering three. 'Do you know what Archie said?'

'What did Archie say?' Madeleine was interested to hear, for her son was blessed with a perceptive and generous humanity which even Tom couldn't match.

'Well, I hadn't thought of it,' Pauly said, 'only you know how Cristi's always been mad keen on the estate, ever since she first arrived, and how she likes to get stuck into the work, and how much she's learned about it from Donnie, and from Archie and Tom too of course . . .'

Madeleine waited patiently. Pauly would get there in the end.

'Well, in a back to front way,' Madeleine scarcely imagined these had been Archie's words, 'he thinks being keen on Drumveyn makes her keener on the ranch. Rio was fun, play-time, glitz and glamour, but it was more like a holiday, indulging herself for a while.'

Pauly wasn't explaining things too badly, Madeleine thought. 'So the ranch, which I must say sounds glorious, is a sort of Brazilian Drumveyn to her?' How appealing if so; how understandable if Cristi were carried away by the astonishing fact of owning it.

'He said something about – I'm not sure I'll get this right, but anyway – about how amazing it would be for anyone to discover their roots in a place which could give them the best of both their worlds.'

The truth of this struck cold at Madeleine's heart. We've brought this about, she found herself protesting absurdly. Why did we give her the one thing which would take her away from us? But how could we have known?

Then, getting a grip on her thoughts, she reminded herself, Cristi's not a child any more, not even an adolescent; she's a young woman. There's no reason for her to cling to her adopted world. Perhaps the role Drumveyn had played in her life was over. It had been crucial once, rescuing her from the saddest plight a child could be in, but what was there to hold her there now? Madeleine's mind turned again to Dougal, and the contained and resolute look he wore these days rose vividly before her eyes. Had he already accepted that Cristi was gone?

But Pauly's need for reassurance was the one immediately to hand. Madeleine pushed the image aside.

'I told Archie,' Pauly was pursuing, 'that Cristi couldn't possibly run a place like that. She's only a girl, barely out of university. But he said it didn't sound as though her grandfather had been much involved recently, so some system must be in place to keep it going. He actually seemed to think it was quite feasible. I got so cross with him.'

'I suppose he was trying to be realistic. I can see what he means, in practical terms.' Tom, Madeleine knew, had his own views about the Fonseca family, and was convinced they were following some agenda of their own which had not yet been made clear. There was no point, however, in putting more worries into Pauly's mind. 'But, imagining for a moment that such a thing should come about, you can't believe that Cristi would ever stop caring about us? She's part of the family.' She meant to add, 'That could never change,' but to her dismay the words refused to come.

'I know that. Of course I do,' Pauly said restlessly, 'and it seems dreadful of me to think otherwise even for a second. But sometimes, when I remember that I'm only a few years older than Cristi, that there's no way I could be her mother and that she can't see me in any such light — well, I don't want her to but you know what I mean — I feel terribly unsure about everything. And a bit stupid too, to tell you the truth. Cristi's so mature for her age, not like a student at all, and she's so creative and talented, while all I can do is fling the odd pudding together—'

'Pauly!' Laughing in spite of her own racked feelings at this saga of woe, now gathering ominous volume, Madeleine got to her feet and went to hug her. 'I've never heard such rubbish in my life. You're the perfect mother, for all four of them. All right,' as Pauly opened her mouth to remind her that she wasn't anybody's mother, 'then the perfect central female figure in the household, the perfect source of stability, love, comfort, security, whatever you like to call it. But perfect anyway. I mean it. And you know Archie would say the same.'

And of all women in the world, Pauly should have had children of her own. That thought could still tug at Madeleine.

'Well, yes, I do believe Archie still thinks I'm OK,' Pauly admitted, a smile beaming momentarily through the tears which dampened the wild straggles of hair, and sparkled against the warm peach brought to her cheeks by the effort of voicing such tricky sentiments. 'Only,' self-doubt returning, 'sometimes I feel so *young!*'

'Oh, Pauly darling.' Madeleine gathered her close. 'Don't complain about that, whatever you do.'

Pauly sniffed and laughed at herself, returned the hug vigorously, then freed herself to sit up and swipe at her eyes with her sweater sleeve.

'I don't usually. I just race along doing whatever I have to do. But I suppose this business with Cristi has made me realise a few things.' She hesitated, then made up her mind to go on. 'I thought Nicholas seemed a bit quiet, for one, on his last leave-out. Did you notice? It's probably a bit far-fetched but I did wonder if the Fonsecas making contact with Cristi after all this time has made him think about Cecil.'

Madeleine remembered her conversation with him in the summer, and guilt returned that she hadn't followed it up. She also recalled Tom's view that what Nicholas had said had been in confidence.

Before she could speak Pauly went on, 'It would be only natural. Then I remember that he's in his teens and has all sorts of pressures to cope with, puberty, bloke's stuff, you know, and I feel quite terrified.'

'But Archie's there to look after that.'

'Um.' Pauly didn't seem reassured. 'As a matter of fact, I know Archie wants to talk to him soon about not being his real father. Well, Nicholas knows that, just as they all know that Peta and Josie are adopted, because Archie dreaded him ever feeling he'd been misled about it. But now he thinks Nicholas is old enough to hear more of the story, and he knows it's going to be tough to deal with.'

'It certainly will be.' Tom had been right. This would

sort itself out without her input. But Madeleine's face was grave as her mind went back to the shock she herself had felt at the news that Cecil had chosen to have a baby by donor sperm. She could still feel shame to recall that much of her shock had been blind, unthinking disgust. She was sure that Nicholas, at fourteen, would be better informed than she had been on such topics, and theoretically more broad-minded, but such a discussion would still be hard to deal with. Thank goodness Archie had had the forethought to safeguard against hurtful chance discoveries by making it plain that he was not the natural father of any of the children.

'I think Archie will talk to him next holidays,' Pauly said. 'He wants to give Nicholas time to take it in while he's on hand to talk, if that's what Nick wants. It won't be ideal, with Christmas and Hogmanay and so on, but he doesn't want to leave it any longer.'

Madeleine thought this was wise.

'Anyway, no time would be ideal for something like that,' Pauly wound up ruefully. 'I can't bear to think of Nicholas feeling for a moment unwanted or uncertain. He's such a — such a *staunch* sort of person.'

She had had to hunt for the word, but Madeleine didn't think she could have found a better one. How much, she realised, they expected and took for granted from Pauly. She had come swinging into this oddly composed family group, very young, very inexperienced, never raising a second's protest about the responsibilities she'd had to take on. Instead she had poured out warmth, laughter and her own robust brand of care on them all.

We don't value her nearly enough, Madeleine thought, looking at her with love.

'Archie will do it well,' she said consolingly. 'You know that. And Cristi is bound to come home soon, whatever may be decided for her future.'

'I just wish they were *all* here, *all* the time,' Pauly declared ferociously, catching a couple of large tears on the back of her hand.

Chapter Twenty

Luis, bending low on his mare's neck, pushed a way through the screen of trees along the lip of the ravine, and began the steep descent.

'But haven't we been to this gorge before?' Cristi asked. He had promised her a special treat on their ride today, though in fact she didn't much mind where they went so long as she was with him.

'Wait,' was all he said, as he turned to make sure she was following.

This had been one of his most secret boyhood haunts, though he hadn't been here for years. Cristi's pleasure in all she found at Tres Pinheiros had tempted him to share it with her, but he hadn't been quite prepared for the feelings it awoke in him to return.

Down, down he led her. The shadows pressed in upon them. Mosses and ferns grew everywhere and the dank air left a taste on the tongue, a flavour of wet earth and vegetation never touched by the sun. Then abruptly, just as Cristi was beginning to feel slightly spooked by the green gloom, the absence of birds, of sound or of any movement of air, light began to strengthen ahead. They came out onto a rock shelf overhanging a pool, beyond which the stream cascaded down the cliff-face, its lacy falls dazzling in a shaft of sunlight, which also made the depths of the pool glow green. The great rock slab, in full sun, looked warm and inviting.

Luis swung down and came to help Cristi dismount. 'I've never brought anyone here before. Never in my life,' he said softly, and Cristi knew that he was not only telling the truth, but speaking with an openness rare for him.

'It's magical,' she said in the same quiet tone, as she slipped to the ground. 'Magical in both senses — beautiful, but strange and mysterious too.'

Luis nodded, keeping his arm round her. 'You have to come at the right time of day. Without the sun it's very different. Sometimes when I was a boy I used to let myself believe I'd never find the way out again. I'd get quite scared even though I knew I was making the whole thing up.'

'I can imagine it. I don't think I'd like to be here on a sunless day.' Cristi shivered to picture it. Or on her own, she thought, as she watched Luis lead the horses to the water and wait while they drank, then loop their bridles over the branch of a spindly pine which struggled upwards in search of light. She was struck by his willingness to make such a confession. He was a different man here from the worldly Rio playboy, used to the best of everything, forever seeking the stimulus of new scenes, showing his little cousin around as long as it suited him, but never letting her forget his kindness in doing so.

He brought the ponchos they carried behind their saddles and unrolled them on the rock, where waterworn hollows provided comfortable seats.

'Think of the years it took to do this,' Cristi commented, tracing the smooth scoops and whorls with her fingertips. 'And to cut these deep ravines. Looking across the plateau you hardly realise they're there.'

'Probably hardly anyone in the world has ever found this place,' Luis said. 'Strange thought, isn't it? It was grandfather who brought me here. He'd been brought here by his father when he was a child.'

It was the first time Cristi had heard such a note in his voice, as though nostalgia for something which had once mattered to him had overtaken his usual glib irreverence almost against his will.

'Did you get on well with grandfather then, when you were a boy?'

Luis's face closed, as though questioning him about it went too far, and Cristi thought he wasn't going to answer. Then with a grimace he replied, 'In those days he was my hero, believe it or not. I always imagined that eventually – well, never mind about that.'

He leaned back to prop himself on his elbows, hat brim hiding his eyes, and Cristi thought that was all she would hear, but after a moment he said harshly, 'He wanted so much from everyone close to him. Subjection, principally. He couldn't be satisfied unless he felt he owned you. That's why Tio João left, as you know, and why my father, though he lives in the Rio house, made sure he was financially independent of the old man's whims. That's what they were. Whims, violent and destructive. It was impossible to please him, whatever one did.'

So he had tried and failed, and he minded. But his tone warned that he had said all he intended to say on that point, and a small silence fell.

'None of you knows where my mother is, do you?' Cristi hadn't known she was going to ask, but the route by which she had arrived at the question was clear enough.

Luis, hearing the bald appeal in her voice, tipped his head back to look at her, then sat up. He moved closer so that his shoulder was against hers and took her hand — even then not failing to note the pleasing feel of the slender fingers in his. His tone as he answered had a tender intimacy which Cristi wouldn't have imagined him capable of, and she was grateful for it.

'No, *querida*, we truly do not know. Justina left no trace behind her and in all the years there has never been a shred of news. I'm sorry. It's hard for you. It must have been so much in your mind when you came here.'

Extraordinary that this was the first time that had been acknowledged.

'I asked Leopoldo,' Cristi said abruptly. 'About Isaura.' She hadn't liked the feeling of having done so behind Luis's back.

'Isaura?' Luis looked baffled, but also instantly alert and suspicious.

So her instinct had been right, Cristi thought. How these Fonsecas liked to be in control.

'My mother's maid,' she explained. My maid. How outlandish the phrase seemed, part of a long-ago life. 'She was brought up on the ranch. Her father was head peon. I don't know his name. I'd wondered if she'd still be here and might know – or someone might know—'

'Oh, Cristi.' Luis's arm came round her, pulling her close, and she was grateful for its comfort. But even as her forlorn tone touched him Luis was planning, in the best Fonseca style, to have a few words with Leopoldo.

'They left years ago, apparently. When it all happened,' Cristi explained. When I was sent away. 'A man put out of his job, a family put out of their home, just because of the connection with my mother.'

'Yes, that's how it would be.' Luis's voice was flat, though since his arm was round her he refrained from shrugging. 'Grandfather would strike out at anyone or anything associated with her. As he did at you.'

'But now?' She twisted to look at him. 'What can have made him change his mind? Did he forgive her? Did he talk about her before he died?' Did he talk about me? But that was too hard to ask. 'What really made him leave the ranch to me? It seems such a weird thing to do.'

Hatred made him do it. Sheer anger and spite because there wasn't a single blood relation left, except this unknown granddaughter, with whom he hadn't picked a quarrel. But on that point Luis intended to keep his feelings to himself.

'Remember he adored your mother as a girl.' He saw

from Cristi's face that he had chosen the right thing to say. Keeping irony out of his voice he added, 'And it mattered to him that the land stayed in the family.'

'Of course.' This seemed obvious to Cristi. She had been surprised when no offer, predicted by both Archie and Tom, had been made to buy her out during the time in Rio. For the family, she could only suppose, as for her, any such possibility had been put on hold until she had seen the ranch.

Her mind reverted to something closer to her heart. 'I must admit I've wondered, once or twice,' she said hesitantly, 'whether, if grandfather had lived longer, after making this will I mean, he'd have wanted to see me. To get to know me a bit.'

Luis glanced at her averted face, compassion forgotten in sardonic wonder. She really believed that such decisions were made on sentimental impulse? Where was her Fonseca blood? But he belonged to a culture where telling people what they want to hear is part of good manners, and he only said, 'I'm sure he'd have wished it. He was making a gesture of forgiveness, you may be certain. A gesture which places you in something of a difficulty, however, does it not?' Joachim was pressing him to find out what she meant to do. 'It brings responsibilities which must be alarming at your age, my sweet, if you don't mind my mentioning your charming but extreme youth.'

Though the tone was light, he gave her a little hug for good measure to take the sting out of the words.

'Well, it certainly didn't occur to me at first that I

could keep the ranch, if that's what you mean. Let alone run it.' Cristi tucked herself against him in response to the hug, glad they were talking about this at last. 'I only looked as far as meeting you all and finding out how we got on, if possible discovering what grandfather truly intended and coming to see Tres Pinheiros.'

'And now?' Luis took some trouble to keep his voice neutral.

'Oh, Luis, it's so hard to say, or even to think about it as a reality. I get swept away by how lovely it is, and there are moments when I feel as though I belong here, and it all seems – familiar almost, in an odd way. But of course I know it's crazy to think of looking after such a place. Me, at twenty-three, not a clue about anything except art, in a country I know nothing about. Then I think about Drumveyn and the glen, and everyone there, and I know I could never exist without them. That's home.'

On that word, though she didn't move, it was as though she left him.

Autumn now – the grass stark with frost at dawn, mist rolling up from the loch to shred against a milky blue sky; wild winds and beating rain leaving the garden ragged, the lawn dredged with leaves; the beeches turning their glorious bronze, stags roaring nightly challenges, the first line of snow cresting the hill, the river running full and high. *That* was her world. And apart from the response which its landscape never failed to stir in her, it was where she was safe, loved, *known*. There she didn't have to choose her words, and words spoken to her didn't have to be decoded or second-guessed.

'Ah, my poor Cristi, you have been more homesick than you have let us see.' Luis's voice was warm and sympathetic. 'You have been so good, saying little about this Drumveyn you love, thinking it would bore us.'

'Bore you, you mean,' Cristi retorted, with a return to cheerful directness which made him laugh. Though in recent days he had asked her more about her life, she hadn't felt her answers had exactly grabbed him.

'Tell me more now,' he persisted. It was not disagreeable to sit in this hidden spot, the sun full on them, the spray from the falls cooling the air, knowing that he could play as he chose on the responses of this transparent little creature, who fitted so neatly against the curve of his body. Not that she awoke any but the mildest sexual desire in him, which was fortunate since for the moment he had other priorities. There were certain points, however, on which he wouldn't mind being clearer.

'You'd be yawning in two minutes,' Cristi said. What could she offer that would interest him? He wouldn't think much of the shabby old house, for a start. Though under Pauly's hand it was full of warmth, comfort and good food, and Cristi couldn't imagine a nicer place to live, it could hardly be described as either orderly or elegant, qualities rated by Luis. And seen through his eyes, how prosaic Archie would seem, immersed in farming and estate concerns, with his even temperament and lack of ambition. Tom and Madeleine would be nothing more than a quiet elderly couple content in each other's company and the small world of village, glen and estate. Nor would Luis want to hear about Nicholas, Peta or Josie. Cristi had seen him shrug off the attentions of his nephews and nieces with unconcealed impatience.

She couldn't deceive herself, however. The first person who had come to mind, as she felt this conviction that Luis would find tedious whatever aspect of home she talked about, had been Dougal. The discovery produced an uncomfortable flurry of shame, defensiveness and anger at her own disloyalty. She blushed in distress, having glimpsed, fatally, the two of them side by side, Luis handsome, urbane, articulate, lazily smiling, supremely self-confident, and Dougal – as he had been before she left, anyway – reserved and unapproachable, going his own quiet way, sticking to what he perceived to be right, unmoved by anyone else's views.

Well, that showed self-confidence too, Cristi found herself arguing, but in that unwilling comparison she knew he had appeared obstinate and dour, and a different, hurtful anger took over as she recalled the way he had distanced himself from her.

'Tell me more about your studies,' Luis suggested. If the mention of Drumveyn sent her off into wordless reverie he must find something else to move things along. 'You haven't talked much about them.'

Because you didn't want to listen. But Cristi let it go. This was a more bearable opening, and she grasped at it, not only because it might have more chance of holding Luis's attention, but because it related to a part of her life she was beginning to miss rather badly. She missed using her hands, having the tools of her trade within reach, missed above all the absorption of creative activity, the elation and sense almost of liberation which came as the intense, focused hours flowed by.

Luis, however, was more concerned with her university experience as a whole. He led her on to describe the Old Town, the campus, the flat in Warrender Park Crescent, and presently, of all the unexpected places and moments in the world to lay bare such memories, Cristi found herself telling him things which up till now only Dougal had heard about.

'It shouldn't have been such a shock, I know. I'd been away at school. But I suppose I'd been terribly sheltered.' How to put into words for someone like Luis the rocklike stability of honesty, trust and kindness which life at Drumveyn had brought her up to see as the norm. 'I mean, even at school there must have been loads of things going on, but I never had a clue about any of them. Looking back, it seems to me I was as much a child when I left at eighteen as when I went there.'

'So what was different at university?'

'Well, everything's sort of in your face there.' Luis didn't particularly relish the momentary – though he assumed unconscious – descent into student language. 'It was all pretty much a steep learning curve. But what was hardest to take was, well, this thing about how I look. Up till then, except for when I went to boarding school, people hadn't made me feel completely one-off and weird.'

'Weird?' Luis didn't care for this.

'Well, of course I looked bizarre. Foreign.'

Cristi's voice was impatient. She still hated to think of that time. She missed Luis's surprised look at a tone he'd not heard from her before. 'But suddenly it was an issue. With the men especially — or not men, grubby-minded little boys. They chased after me as though I was some sort of prize they were competing for, not a person at all. They just wanted to score. I couldn't begin to handle it. In fact I got quite paranoid. I felt as though I couldn't go anywhere without being stared at, and if anyone showed any interest I was sure he only wanted to—' She rejected one or two expressions which Luis would certainly not approve of. 'Then I got the reputation of being frigid and a — well, you can guess.'

'But, my sweet, you must have expected male attention. You're a very lovely girl.' Luis spoke automatically. He might not like what he would hear if he pursued this, but it was important to know.

'Exotic. That was the word that kept coming up. All that hot Latin blood, etc. They were convinced I'd be incredibly passionate, amoral and in some way different. It was a nightmare.'

'Not just part of student life?' For which Luis felt unmixed disdain. Education was something different.

'Oh, perhaps. I have to admit there was lots which shocked me at first. I was such a little prig. I had trouble with quite ordinary things, like the way people lived in mess and squalor and were happy to eat ghastly food, and the way lots of them had no intention of working, not caring what they were costing their parents, or the taxpayer, and taking out loans they had no intention of repaying. But that was more the normal culture shock, like the drinking and drugs.'

'You didn't take drugs?' Such things had to be established. Luis didn't bother to wrap it up.

'Oh, I tried the odd puff, as one does.'

'You aren't ashamed of this?'

Cristi raised her eyebrows. She couldn't imagine Luis's worldly lifestyle leaving him entirely uncorrupted, but of course that would be different.

'It was what went on. At parties and so on. If you don't try you don't know what it's about, do you? I shouldn't think there's a student alive who hasn't experimented. I did it feeling ninety per cent repelled to start with, then didn't happen to enjoy the sensation anyway.'

Cristi broke off, looking round her with a wry smile. 'It's definitely peculiar to be talking about it here though. Another life.'

'But things improved?' Luis hadn't been deflected. He needed to know whether any of those crass young males had scored, as she had put it.

'Oh, yes. It was only during my first term that I was lonely. There didn't seem to be anyone I could *talk* to.' She had considered dropping out, in spite of her growing interest in her course. 'But of course there were loads of great people about. I just hadn't been looking.'

A memory of lonely weekends, November days when the dank cold of the streets seemed to push her back as she walked, when the world seemed encompassed by dour rain-streaked stone and the only solace had been writing endless letters to Dougal. What blessed comfort it had been to get his equally long replies, full of the details of home she yearned for, but also dealing faithfully with her troubles and anxieties. And what blunt good sense he had dealt out during the Christmas holidays, refusing to let her contemplate not going back.

On his advice she had sought out activities which took her into new circles, and in a reading group had found Torie who, ironically enough, had been in first year art school with her all the time. From then on she had never looked back. Although Torie and Isa had already been friends, there had been no sense of Cristi intruding. As a threesome they had worked even better, though any pairing within it had been good too.

'So you adjusted and integrated and all the rest of it, but I hope you are not telling me you became an idle, ungrateful, unwashed – what would you say?'

'Slob.'

'Thank you. I think I prefer not to add such a word to my vocabulary. Though I have to confess it is the image we have of the British student. You cannot imagine how relieved we were to find you charmingly free of such defects. No, no,' as she turned on him indignantly, 'let us proceed with the story. When you began at last to enjoy student life did you also find the lusting males less repulsive?'

Cristi shrugged. 'One or two were all right.' She had never found anyone she wanted to be with as much as Dougal, and the blatantly sexual approaches of that first term had done their damage.

'You're not going to tell me that in the entire three

years – ah, four – you didn't do some leaping into bed? In this day and age? My sweet, I should hardly believe you.'

'Then you're just going to have to make your own mind up about it,' Cristi told him placidly. Cousinly authority could go only so far.

On balance, Justina's daughter or not, Luis thought his original opinion had probably been confirmed. Amazingly, considering the freedom she had been given, and the notorious carelessness of foreigners, even foreigners of good class, in such matters, he believed she might be a virgin. At any rate, he had done all he reasonably could to ascertain the point.

Things might have been a great deal worse, that was certain. How fortunate that Cristi looked as she did. But surely she couldn't still believe that that blond scraped pig of an Englishman with whom Justina had finally disappeared had had anything to do with her conception? She was Brazilian through and through.

Chapter Twenty-one

Dougal sat with his elbows planted on the old table he'd brought up to the kitchen at the Croft of Ellig, and scowled at the colour charts spread before him. He could feel his resistance to this chore building before he'd even begun. He'd been putting it off for days, not admitting the real reasons behind his reluctance.

He just hadn't got round to it because he preferred to get his hands on more active, down-to-earth jobs, he'd told himself. This wasn't in his line, he was useless at the fancy stuff. He flipped over the glossy sheets, irritated by the absurd names, the almost invisible gradation of shades, and even more by the way different sheets folded in different ways so that you always had the damn things inside out or upside down.

However, there wasn't much sense going about the job in this frame of mind. Why not, just for once, take a couple of minutes to slow down, put everything else on the back burner, and do a little honest thinking? There had been mixed feelings all along, or at least feelings he hadn't dared to examine, about this life-altering step he'd taken, but he had been refusing to admit it.

Deep below the amazed gratitude that such a chance should have come to him, there gnawed an unappeasable, aching loneliness. Hard as he had worked, filling every moment so that when he finally fell into bed he was exhausted enough to go out like a light, whatever was on his mind, he had been unable to banish the images that haunted him. Time and time again, as he worked on the house itself, tackled some heavy job outside, or spent the shortening hours of evening light working on the part of Ellig which was now Drumveyn, he had been tormented by pictures which no amount of resolution could erase from his brain.

Pictures of Cristi, here, beside him, part of this. Everything reminded him of her. Whatever he did, he related it to her. It was as though without her his hopes and plans had no focus, and he couldn't rid himself of the habit of talking to her in his head, needing her response to everything he thought and did.

Odd, how this single chore he didn't want to be bothered with had brought him bang up against the truth. Perhaps not so odd, he conceded, resisting the temptation to dodge the whole issue by binning the despised charts and turning in relief to some strenuous physical job, less loaded with overtones.

God knows, there's enough waiting to be done, he thought ruefully. Maybe he shouldn't have risked stopping, but just forged ahead, keeping his mind off the danger areas. Decorating the house was another ball game altogether, no longer to do with putting to rights spongy plaster, woodworm, or floors that sagged away in the corners of rooms. Decorating was past the stage of straightforward tasks like slating, plastering, tiling and grouting, plumbing and wiring. Those he could deal with; what he didn't know he could learn, and friendly hands were always there to give him a lift when he needed it. It hadn't been so different from the homers he used to pick up about the glen.

But the job facing him wasn't like that. It had a new, personal element in it. It was about creating his own environment, making a statement about himself by what he chose to do with this place which had so incredibly fallen into his hands. He found himself uncertain, reluctant, almost resentful at having to do it.

'All right then, why?' he asked aloud in the empty room, where the smells of new wood and cleaning products, breathed air, coffee and warmth from the gas radiator had long ago overtaken the dead odours of cement, dirt, rotting lino and damp plaster.

Because, the answer was, he hadn't the first idea of how to create a home. He didn't even know for sure what he liked, though he knew, with a spurt of distaste, that he wanted nothing like the look his mother would have chosen. She went for strong colours, heavy patterns and a load of useless rubbish crammed into small spaces. Any room she touched became more self-conscious than comfortable. She wasn't the only one either. He could think of a score of houses that looked exactly like the one she'd moved into in the village. Where he came from, that was the norm, the desirable goal. He thought, knowing he'd do better to think of something else, of the ornaments on Jean's mantelpiece, forever set out in their unshakeable order, always shining and dusted – and all basically junk. A china poodle wearing a Glengarry, a Princess Diana mug at one end, the Queen Mother at the other, a fluted stem vase which never held a flower, a pair of EPNS candlesticks which never held candles, a gappy-toothed primary school photo of Jill and himself in a tartan frame, and in the centre, the cheap brass of their heads and shoulders pale with rubbing, huddled the three wise monkeys. Household gods. Brass monkeys.

Because the doors of the big house had always been open to him as he grew up, he was nearly as familiar with its different style. Though no one could call Drumveyn exactly grand, it contained a good many beautiful things, disregarded as they might be in the pressures of everyday family life. Even those objects which no one would call beautiful had the stamp of quality, crafted in their day from good materials by expert hands.

In more recent times, the big kitchen created by Cecil, Archie's first wife, had added light and colour and a beauty of its own. Dougal had been twelve when the work was done and he had never given a thought to what it might have cost, beyond taking for granted that everything done by the Napiers would be at a level forever beyond the reach of people like his own family. Now he entertained himself by making a rough estimate, and gave a little half-resigned, half-angry chuck of his head at the figure he arrived at.

This wasn't about cost, though, he reminded himself. The price of a coat of paint was pretty much the same whatever colour you chose. This was about the dread word 'taste'. Not in the sense of good or bad taste, but his taste, his expression of himself. He had no intention of cloning Steading Cottage here at the croft, yet would he end up doing so more or less by default? What did he like? He didn't *know*. With an exclamation he grabbed up the charts, ready to pitch them across the room, then checked himself disgustedly. They were only one tiny part of the larger issue. All they had done was bring him face to face with something he didn't like.

Leaning back in his chair, he tried to conjure up images of how this room could look, not worrying about whether they were within his means or not. He found himself barren of ideas, unable to get beyond the basic constraints of what was already there.

He made himself think of kitchens he'd seen, and found that the old barn at Drumveyn was the one his mind fixed on most readily. Tom had made it simple, yet it was satisfying and all of a piece. Dougal, who had always liked it, let his mind rove about the long, handsome room. But at once he felt frustrated. He could never achieve anything even remotely like that. The very structure of the room, its generous proportions, its great window filling one end wall, the rich colour of the Paraná pine floor — all this was as far beyond his reach as the casually handled treasures of the big house. But the image persisted. How was it achieved? Good light, that came first. Then plain, strong lines, warm but subtle colour, an absence of meaningless objects.

Pushing the charts roughly aside Dougal came swearing to his feet. Did he have to copy someone else? Had he no identity of his own? But that, he knew, was what this was all about. That was the question he had been doing anything rather than ask.

His face grim, he crossed to the sink and mechanically filled the kettle, swilled out the mug that was standing on the draining-board, dropped in a teabag. Through the busy weeks there had been little time to dwell on it – he'd done his best not to dwell on it – but he was ready to admit tonight that by taking this step away from the life he was used to he had in a way stepped into space.

He had broken through the bonds which had kept his father, and presumably every forebear he had, trapped in the status of paid employee. In doing so he had left behind, in ways too nebulous to put into words, the whole mind-set of that situation. Who was he now? The way in which he had acquired this toehold of his own was so irregular that sometimes, still, he hardly dared to trust in it. That very irregularity brought its own problems. He had no capital for one thing, and no prospect of ever acquiring any. Sometimes that could make him feel almost as if he shouldn't be here.

Then he swore at himself again, as the kettle boiled and he filled the mug, added milk, and took it back to the table. This was just giving himself grief. What was wrong with him? If he had scraped and saved and somehow managed to get hold of some other place, he'd be in exactly the same boat. He didn't need capital. He could work. In a year or two he wouldn't need every penny merely to keep afloat. He could augment his pay by keeping a pig, a few chickens. He had enough room for a couple of goats as well. It was all and more than he'd had ever wanted. What was he whingeing about?

But the rows of little coloured squares still mocked him, and with a groan he dropped his head into his hands, accepting the fact they had so innocently forced him to face. This wasn't all he had ever wanted. He wanted Cristi, wanted her here, giving this new life meaning. He needed her. That was why he had put off this damned job for so long. The two of them should have been sitting shoulder to shoulder at the rough old table, discussing, arguing, caring about what they chose. He wanted this house to have her touch upon it. Without her, to have realised the dream of ownership was nothing.

No, not nothing. That was criminal ingratitude. But it had an emptiness to it he could no longer ignore. He could work day and night, and would do so, but all he was creating was a place to live in alone. He felt as though he'd left his roots far behind, but didn't know how to put down new ones. A bleak foretaste of a terrible and lasting loneliness, deep in his being, made him shiver.

She had gone. He had to face it. When she left there had been no intention of her staying away half this long. No one in the family, as he knew from things Pauly had said to Jean, and from comments Archie had made to him, had expected her to stay in Brazil all these months.

She had gone because it was necessary to sort out the matter of her unexpected inheritance. That was all. It hadn't ever been on the cards, surely, that she wouldn't come back. But now, it seemed, she was loving every minute of it, over the moon about this damned ranch, over the moon about the whole damned country.

He couldn't fool himself any longer. He could sense how she must feel about discovering the side of herself that had been, as it were, put on hold during the years at Drumveyn. Cristi was Brazilian by birth; her kinfolk were Brazilian. Everything she had loved or learned or become here had been superimposed on that. And another thing, how could anyone expect her to turn her back on owning land, when it was the very thing life at Drumveyn had equipped her for? She was rich, she had choices, she could come and go as she wished. From now on, she would be living there, paying visits here.

She would come to the croft, perhaps, on the first of these visits, and look at what he'd done, be warm and enthusiastic, full of pleasure and praise. She would keep in touch; there would always be news of her to be gleaned. But Dougal's mouth tightened at the thought of what that news might be, as she shaped a new life for herself, buttressed by wealth, possessions and a powerful family, in her own country.

So don't, you pathetic idiot, choose a colour for your walls that you think might please her. Don't devalue yourself to that extent. This is your life. You've got what you wanted. But Dougal knew, with an ache in his heart, that in his dream he'd never seen himself alone. There had hovered a golden vision, somewhere far ahead, unspecific, barely glimpsed, of the dream being shared. Not of being alone for ever.

Cristi was on her way to Porto Alegre alone. She was happy with that. Happy all round in fact. As the aircraft climbed for the south she tried to locate the ranch, looking at the scene with very different eyes from when she'd first arrived. An unexpected sense of being part of it took her unawares. The farewells this morning, Selma in tears, Leopoldo waiting to see her off, stiffly at attention, hat held against his heart, had moved her. All of it, the friendly airport officials, the smiles of the other passengers, made her feel as much at home as if she'd been buzzing down on the London shuttle. She felt a Brazilian among Brazilians, and that was special.

The days at the ranch had put several things into perspective. How remote the weeks in Rio now seemed. Then she had been the outsider eager for contact but subtly kept at arm's length. Here, she had been living in her own house, free of watchful Fonseca eyes.

It had not been easy to persuade Luis to go on without her but, magical as the days with him had been, she had wanted time alone at Tres Pinheiros. Fortunately, it appeared that by this time the demands of 'business' were real. Cristi had seen him off from Campo Novo, done a little shopping, then called on Dr Elisario.

As she was driven home by Leopoldo afterwards, many things had seemed simpler. With no Luis present, concerns over running the ranch had fallen sensibly into place. Antiquated as its ways might be, it ticked along. Even if she ultimately decided to stay here (a thought still too large to absorb), it didn't mean she would have to take on the running of it single-handed. With this clearer in her mind she had settled down to enjoy herself, though she couldn't have said, hand on heart, that she hadn't missed Luis a good deal.

It had been satisfying to get to know the people at Tres Pinheiros, to sit peacefully, with no one to drag her away, through gentle-paced conversations with someone who had spent his entire life there, never seeing a town other than Campo Novo, remaining untouched by the creation of a new capital, revolution, military dictatorship, the goal of globalisation or its failure, his work, food, what he wore and the way he passed his days altered little since the changes of the sixties.

Cristi's greatest pleasure, however, had been riding out with the gauchos who tended the herd. Apart from the leisurely conversations over the midday fire as they brewed their coffee, when they were ready to tell her anything she wanted to know about the ranch, they also persuaded her to try her hand at throwing a lasso. They had been amused by her readiness to learn, then impressed by her determination to get it right.

Cristi had also taken the chance, persuading Leopoldo to drive her, to visit the neighbouring ranches, an idea Luis had brusquely vetoed. She had been kindly welcomed, though she suspected that the warmth might have had more to do with traditional gaucho hospitality, and the joke of finding a naive young *patroa* in the place of her arrogant, warring grandfather, than any real wish for social contact with a Fonseca. But she had taken the welcome at its face value and much enjoyed her visits.

She had been interested by what she learned, however. Santa Catarina, it seemed, led the way in a new move towards agro-ecology, and prided itself on being the first state to turn its back on industrialised farming and the use of chemicals. So, though modern technology had definitely arrived, perhaps Luis shouldn't be so contemptuous of grandfather's style of operating; or angry, as if what he saw as a refusal to exploit the ranch's potential was a source of personal grievance.

One other thing she had had to accept; no clues would be unearthed which would lead her to her mother, or Isaura. No links remained here. There were memories of Justina, that was clear, but even the friendliest peon had proved reluctant to talk of her, having lived too long under the embargo of never mentioning her name. There would be no reunion, no laying of ghosts. If it had happened it would, Cristi could admit now, have been an encounter fraught with pain and accusation. Instead she must learn to live with the different pain of not knowing.

Her mind went back to the evening when she had finally relinquished her dreams. On the pine-crowned hill near the house lay the family burial ground. Luis had taken her there, his mood half mocking, half serious, as though he wanted to make it clear that he saw the absurdity of such self-aggrandisement, yet couldn't quite shed the respect for it taught him as a child.

There had been an amazing sunset the evening when

she had gone there alone, and from that high place the sense of limitless distance, of a land empty and untouched, had been very real. Above a band of clear sky on the western horizon the underbelly of a bank of ragged cumulus had glowed crimson, its light turning the spring grass a weird orange, patterned by lines of mist wherever water lay, the tips of trees etched against them. A group of steers had moved below her, their backs rimmed in gold. There had been an awareness, produced perhaps by the flamboyant drama of the scene, of silent presences coming close, of the place having some meaning for her. Would any Fonseca of the future choose to be buried here? Her mother would never know that, now, if she wished for such a thing, it would be possible.

But this wasn't the time to let the ache surface. This flight was about what she, Cristi, wanted. Duty was done. She had come to Brazil as bidden, met the family, played by their rules, moved at their pace. Now she was about to see a different Brazil again, and see it, she fully intended, on her terms.

There would still be Luis, of course. It would be marvellous to see him, no use pretending otherwise, but she didn't think he was going to be very happy about what she was planning.

Chapter Twenty-two

'It is totally and absolutely out of the question. I shall not permit it.'

Sorry, could you make yourself clearer. But Cristi didn't say it. The anger in Luis's face warned her this was not the moment for frivolity. Nor, however, was it the moment for giving in.

'It's really kind of you to invite me to stay with you, and I know it's what we planned, but I'd—'

'It's not a question of inviting you,' Luis cut in sharply. 'You're one of the family. It's inconceivable that you should stay anywhere alone when my house is there for you. And especially not in the sort of tourist accommodation you propose to use. I don't understand why you want to do this but I assure you it is *not* acceptable.'

'But it is what I want to do,' Cristi said, as calmly as she could. Broadly speaking, it was, but she knew that the prospect of staying with Luis, free of the watchful eyes of the family as they had been during that magical interlude at the ranch, could easily sway her unless she carried her point at once. Or if he tried persuasion instead of direct commands.

'Cristi, you're being absurd. Get in the car. We can't stand arguing here. Everything's arranged. You're coming home with me. If you want to think about something else later on, we can discuss the matter then.'

But Cristi didn't budge. She was well aware that the moment she was in the car — something else low and fast — Luis would ignore all pleas and arguments and take her wherever he chose. She hadn't wanted to start off with a fight. When she'd caught her first glimpse of him waiting for her, immediately distinguishable among the little crowd, her heart had done something unsettling and violent. It made her wonder how she would ever stick to her plan, or indeed why she wanted to.

But this was important. Not only did she want the freedom to explore this new place on her own terms, with no arbitrary barriers hedging her in, but she had no illusions about the dangers of embarking on shared domestic intimacy with Luis on his own territory. The cousinly relationship might satisfy the conventions, and no doubt there would be someone on hand to run the house — impossible to imagine Luis so much as knowing how to use a microwave — but Cristi knew she would find such proximity hard to handle. Luis, she was fairly sure, would have no problem in dealing with it. Attentive as he had been, making no secret of his pleasure in her company, during those days at the ranch when he had abandoned teasing and allowed her to see something of his private, more serious self, he'd never made anything that could be called a move. He would be astonished, or pretend to be, if she hinted that such an obvious arrangement as staying in his house might be unwise.

But Cristi didn't underrate the power of his attraction for her. To put herself in his hands, spending all her time within his orbit, would send her spinning helplessly in a direction she wasn't ready to take. God, it was tempting though.

She felt distinctly nervous as she repeated, 'Honestly, Luis, this is what I want to do. I'm sure the place I've found will be fine —' it had been useful to have had what was virtually her own office in Campo Novo to help her lay her plans '— and if you don't feel like taking me there I can get a taxi.'

'You are being ridiculous—'

'Please, I don't want to fight about it. And wherever I'm living I shall want to see you often. If you want to, that is.'

She looked at him with a sudden uncertain appeal which didn't move him in the slightest.

That, my precious, was the whole idea. But Luis took a grip on his temper. He had already learned that this charming little innocent, usually so amenable and willing to please, could be as resolute as the next person in a notoriously headstrong family. Cristi was, after all, Justina's daughter. And fighting this out in the airport carpark was neither appropriate nor productive. Capitulation now, guile and persuasion later. Luis had unshaken confidence in his power to charm.

He must at least, however, make sure that the accommodation she had found was appropriate.

In his eyes it wasn't, but nothing he could say, no turning down of his mouth or dismissive clicking of his fingers, could change Cristi's mind. She loved at first sight the shabby gentility of the tree-shaded *pensão* in a quiet street off the Avenida Independencia.

'It's perfect,' she declared, looking around with the delight her first sight of the ranch had given her, as they were shown the room allocated to her. It was large, square and high-ceilinged, its floor, bare of covering, ornately tiled in cream, terracotta and green. It had one tall window, flakes of dark-green paint clinging to its folded-back shutters, and close against the tiny balcony the delicate limbs of a cinnamon tree gave feathery shade. Already conscious of the heat of the city after the keener air of the high plateau, this cool dim room, with its agreeable aura of decayed splendour, though furnished with no more than a low bed, a painted cupboard, a table and a single chair, satisfied her thoroughly. She responded, as she always did, to the simplicity of life pared down to essentials. Though she knew her pleasure in having found this place had as much to do with relief at freeing herself from the Fonseca way of life, as with her own preference.

Excited anticipation seized her. With an urge even the ranch had not woken, she wanted to paint in this room, wanted to record the texture of the weathered shutters, the light filtering through the tenuous foliage of the tree.

She wanted to record it in words as well, describing it

without delay to everyone at home, to Dougal above all, placing herself for them in this new scene. She wanted to sit down now, straight away, spilling out what she was feeling to people who would understand.

So much was waiting. Beyond this tranquil street, with its dignified old houses sleeping half hidden behind their overgrown gardens, lay the city and, at last, the freedom to make contact in her own style with what she found there.

'I can only hope you will soon come to your senses.' Luis was intensely angry still, but recognised the need to play this with care. 'I trust, however, in spite of this temporary aberration, that you will have dinner with me as arranged. May I expect that much?'

He became more formal when he was cross, as Cristi had observed before. Or should that be pompous? Of course she wanted to see where he lived, and wanted to spend time with him, a good deal more than he knew. All the same, she had been right. It was vital to establish her own base. With that behind her, she would be able to meet him on a more equal footing.

From her very first walk, on that very first day, the brief distance from the *pensão* to the bustling heart of the city above the docks, Cristi knew that this was a place with a mood and tempo completely different from that of Rio. Perhaps it had something to do with being on foot, stepping out into the sunshine dressed only in sandals and one of the cheap cotton dresses (as basic as could be but every one in marvellous colours), which she had picked up in Campo Novo, a straw bag bought for next to nothing in the market slung over her shoulder.

There was a feeling of at last being at ground level and, as she came out onto the busy thoroughfare of the Avenida Borges de Medeiros and turned towards the river, of being part of the drifting, casual throng, indistinguishable from it. There came again the odd, agreeable feeling of security she had been aware of on the flight down.

She felt no undercurrent of danger and hostility here. Major city and gaucho capital as Porto Alegre was, it had an atmosphere all its own which was at once apparent. In Rio there had always lurked, below the surface glamour, the uneasy awareness of danger, of theft and muggings, gang warfare and daily shootings, of disease and poverty side by side with extravagant luxury. Living within the Fonseca orbit it had been impossible to forget that the wealth of the entire country was in the hands of a tiny proportion of the population. Their whole style of living was designed to protect and distance them from the distasteful problems created by this imbalance. For Cristi, too, the fear of horrors waiting to pounce had been deeply instilled in childhood.

Doubtless some or all of these problems existed here, but the initial impression was of laid-back, friendly welcome. It was good to wander as she liked, from smart, expensive shops to the nineteenth-century splendours of the covered market, selling local produce in colourful profusion, and down past the fish restaurants to the waterfront.

If she tipped back her head there were skyscrapers towering above the survivors of ornate, white-trimmed and colour-washed colonial buildings, but they seemed to have little to do with the peaceful swirl of life below, where old and new, simple and ostentatious, flourished in harmony.

It was fun to do ordinary things: lean on a railing above the river and watch the activity on the wide waterway of the Guaíba, slip into the incense-smelling shadows of a richly decorated church, and settle with a chokingly strong *cafezinho* before her in a workmen's café on the lively Praça 15 de Novembro.

Everywhere she was greeted with smiles and friendly words. She felt she could have embarked on a conversation with anyone. Had winning the battle to stay on alone at Tres Pinheiros, and the contacts she had made there, given her more confidence? Was the change in her? But in fact the opposite was true. Here she was herself again. It was when she was under the Fonseca sway that she was different, inhibited, too willing to be turned into something she was not, crushed by the sheer weight of their arrogance and authority.

It was hot in here. The table was covered in grubby green and white check American cloth, scored and torn. The air was thick with the smell of over-stewed coffee and sweet cakes. Local radio music jangled from a speaker over the counter. At the adjacent tables the thick accents of the men were almost unintelligible. Luis wouldn't have set foot in such a place; would have been appalled to see her there. Satisfaction filled her to have achieved this freedom.

Perhaps she shouldn't beam around her quite so fatuously, though. It might be misunderstood. She took another sip of the noxious brew from the tiny, straight-sided cup, pushed it aside and unfolded the street map she had bought.

It showed her a shorter way home than the one she had come by, but didn't hint at the social pitfalls of the route. The narrow street was pedestrianised, and had a character all its own. Shoe-shine boys were busy, children with trays of sweets, toys and plastic trinkets touted their wares, men selling lottery tickets and every kind of stamp and bond did a brisk trade, while political speakers pounding out their rhetoric seemed mainly to be talking to themselves.

The system appeared to be that the girls sauntered on the pavements, while the men gossiped and idled in the centre of the street, or pretended to read newspapers folded small so as not to impede the view. Cristi, never a saunterer, soon tired of struggling through the slow tide of females, ambling in twos and threes with linked arms. She dived into the street, where it was easier to carve a path. This produced whistles and calls, which she was happy not to understand. She was clearly transgressing the code, but what was equally clear was that the amusement she caused held no ill-will. It was rather pleasing to emerge unscathed at the other end with nothing but laughter to worry about. Oh, Luis, you'd never understand, not in a million years.

It was a contrast she couldn't resist, however, when he came to collect her that evening, and swept her up the

jacaranda-lined dual carriageway to the fashionable suburb where he lived. Fashionable it might be, but even here
the imaginatively designed houses of the rich were apt to
be flanked by a humbler bungalow or shack dwelling, and
that seemed to Cristi very much in keeping with the
impression she had already formed. This place accepted
people as they were.

Luis's house charmed her, a compact and elegant
gem of white stucco with pantile roof, deep verandahs
and wide windows, perched on a shelf of hillside
which gave a magnificent view over the city to the
Lagoa dos Patos, a hundred kilometres long, which
carried the trade of Porto Alegre's busy freshwater
port out to the Atlantic.

Inside, the house was modern, ingeniously planned
and luxuriously equipped and furnished. The paintings
on its white walls drew Cristi instantly.

'Now can I persuade you to forsake your seedy
downtown quarters?' Luis demanded as she prowled in
delight, examining the treasures he had collected, and
feeling that at last she was being given some clue as to his
individual identity, as distinct from that of his family and
heritage. But the answer was definitely no.

They dined on the minute terrace, and though Cristi
knew Luis would insist on the best under any circumstances, she guessed that he had taken some trouble over
this meal. The result was almost too perfect. There was a
film-set feel to the whole scene – in the skilful lighting,
the delicious food, the carefully chosen wine, the silent
comings and goings of two maids, the glittering pattern

of the strung lights of the city far below; even in the soft
light from the candles on the table, floating among
magnolia blossoms, which enhanced Luis's already dramatic good looks.

In one way, Cristi was tempted to go with the flow,
yielding with sensuous abandonment to all that was being
offered. That was the sort of language such a scene
provoked. But a more stubborn and more realistic part of
her refused the triteness of the clichés. Her mind went
with secret joy to the bare room to which she would
return, lit by a single bulb in the centre of the cracked
ceiling, with several ominous gaps in the elegant cornice,
and those of her belongings which wouldn't fit in the
narrow cupboard neatly set out on the floor. In spite of
the sybaritic lure of the evening, the stealing effect of the
wine, even the sexual desire which Luis could so effortlessly arouse in her, the appeal of that spartan refuge
could not be shaken.

Maybe it would have been different if Luis had made a
move, she was honest enough to acknowledge as, hours
later, she writhed and wriggled in search of a comfortable
groove in the lumpy mattress. In a way, in the care he had
taken to make sure everything was so perfect, he had
made the moves and sent the signals. Yet in physical
terms he had never once crossed the line of cousinly
affection. It was puzzling. Frustrating too, for there was
no question that he could and did set her senses singing.
Was he punishing her for defying him by staying here?
Or would it be, according to his code, unethical to
behave otherwise to a cousin under his protection, in his

own house? Too complicated. She'd have to think about it in the morning.

A stimulating sense of living two lives established itself during the days that followed. Time spent with Luis was a replay of the self-indulgent idleness of the Rio weeks. He showed her the Porto Alegre of expensive restaurants and night clubs, of luxurious mansions in the suburbs, country clubs on their fringes, and a smart sailing club on the shore of the lagoon. He introduced her to his friends, and they were generous in their hospitality and made much of her.

Yet Porto Alegre refused even this privileged élite an exclusive privacy. Security-conscious though Brazilians were, in a country where burglary is a way of life and a Christmas wreath will be whipped off a door as readily as washing off a line, there was none of the air of living behind barricades which had been so oppressive in Rio. Beside the expensive sailing club which Luis frequented, for instance, was a much more democratic affair where working men and their families spent Sundays in huge happy feasting parties among the trees, or took out battered old dinghies with patched sails to fish and sail alongside their richer neighbours.

Cristi liked that. This mood of sturdy independence which made the thronging city so accessible and un-threatening, made it easier for her to slip into her other self, diving eagerly into the warren of the streets to explore and discover. Though she didn't tell Luis, she found it the easiest thing in the world to meet people. As an ex-student (though by now that existence seemed a life-time away), it was an obvious choice to turn first to that scene. She had only to sit on a bench in the university park at lunch-time and a conversation would be struck up.

That was how she met Anita; and Anita led her to Jude.

Chapter Twenty-three

Anita was a striking and voluptuous twenty-two-year-old, fair as so many Brazilians of German extraction in the south are, and overflowing with enthusiasm which mostly turned out to be short-lived. She seized upon Cristi's company as she was eager to practise her English.

'To speak British English is so sweesh, so much more aristocrat of Norz Americano drowl, even in today,' she assured Cristi in her atrocious accent. The truth was she had recently been pursuing a young Englishman – 'I was on the beach and I met me a handsome,' as she put it – who was at present back-packing in Chile, and she wanted help in continuing the pursuit by letter.

Anita, with her glowing smile and careless goodwill, had droves of friends, and through her Cristi was drawn into a lively, easygoing group, in whose company she discovered a face of the city she could never have found for herself. She quickly became at home in the haunts they preferred for the endless *cafezinhos*, beers and gossip of the daylight hours, and occasionally was persuaded to join them in the heaving, noisy clubs they favoured at night. But though she enjoyed the music and the vibrant atmosphere, she found herself, ironically, once more targeted by the males as a 'foreign girl', which in their minds equated to easy sexual prey, and that she didn't like.

Luis, not surprisingly, deplored these contacts, and would question her closely about where she had been and with whom, more than once close to losing his temper when her airy answers showed how independent of him she had become. He responded by making arrangements at short notice, or even accepting invitations, on her behalf, needing to prove, perhaps, that she would drop everything to fit in with his plans.

Sometimes she let him get away with it, sometimes not. Much as she enjoyed the student crowd, she missed Luis when she was away from him for too long. He had become central to her life in Brazil. With his teasing affection, his energy and good looks, his quick tongue and sardonic humour – and the trouble he was prepared to take to entertain her – he was hard to resist. Through him she met interesting and dynamic people, whose more cosmopolitan outlook balanced the views she heard thrashed out in university circles. Also, however much she cherished the freedom she had won, Luis still provided a secure background behind it.

Improbably, it was the frivolous Anita who gave Cristi the opening she had, though hardly knowing what questions to ask, been seeking. One of Anita's recent enthusiasms, based on little more than the fact that her English boyfriend had been involved there, had been helping at a small voluntary centre which offered daytime care to the street children who swarmed here as they did in every other Brazilian city.

It was run by Jude Porter, a wiry, elderly, sharp-tongued Englishwoman, with a shock of rough grey hair, a jutting chin, and piercing eyes which clearly announced she had little time for half-baked good intentions.

'Getting fed up, eh, Anita?' she greeted them.

'Jude, *boa tarde*, I bring to meet you—'

Jude flicked a glance over Cristi, who though wearing the sort of cotton dress to be found on every market rail, had an air of elegance about her which cut no ice here. Then her eyes went back to Anita. 'He's gone, you know. He won't be back. Don't kid yourself. So that'll be the last we'll see of you, no doubt.'

'But now Cristi helps you,' Anita said quickly.

'Oh yes?' The accent was flat Midlands, the tone unimpressed. 'Listen, love,' Jude addressed Cristi, with another of those up-and-down glances, 'no offence, but I can't be doing with a trail of flibbertigibbets who come waltzing in here eager to save mankind, turn up three times, are all over the kids then have to clean up a knife-wound or find they've got fleas and suddenly can't seem to find the time to come any more. I need help, Christ knows I do, but I need it from someone who's prepared to get their hands dirty, and turn up when they say they will.'

She allowed herself one damning glance at Anita, and

went on in sudden anger, 'And I haven't got all day to stand here talking about it either, not with this lot to sort out.' She gestured at the littered room where a few basic teaching materials were scattered, a first-aid box was open on a table, and a pail stood beside a spreading damp patch on the floor.

Cristi said quietly, 'I shan't be in Porto Alegre for very long, and I don't have any special skills to offer. But I do have time.'

Jude looked at her shrewdly. Anita looked at her watch. In the silence Cristi became aware of a pungent mixture of smells – sun on dusty wood, some chemical from a door at the further end of the hut, disinfectant and, from the open doorway, the odours of silt and decay, oil and tar. For this primitive building, like the shacks surrounding it, stood on the marshy ground where several waterways fed into the Guaíba. Cleared from time to time by the authorities, the flimsy dwellings were always raised again, for this unclaimed land was very near the city and its rich pickings.

'Humph,' said Jude. 'Well, don't ask me what we do. We're here, that's all. A place for the kids to come. Kids left alone for the day, kids left alone for life. We feed them, tie up their wounds if the wounds are within our scope, and if there's time, and if they care, we teach them to write their names. Or count to ten.'

She sounded angrier as she went on, repacking the first-aid box, slamming down its lid. 'Don't ask what we achieve either, for after a lifetime grubbing about here and in places a damn sight worse, I couldn't say.'

Cristi waited in silence. She could feel Anita's longing to be away, freed by Jude's caustic words to abandon a project that now bored her rigid anyway.

'So, what do you think, then?' Jude demanded, swinging round on Cristi, thrusting a brown, seamed, belligerent face into hers. They were much of a height. Anita might as well not have been there. 'You up for a bit of do-gooding?'

No use jibbing at the phrase. Cristi knew her ideas were fully as naive as Jude perceived them to be.

'I'd like to try. I'm not sure how much use I'll be.'

'Nor am I.' To Jude's cynical eye Cristi didn't look as if she'd done a hand's turn in her life. Yet she had a directness that Jude liked. There might be more to her than first appeared. 'You're not a God-botherer?'

'No.'

'Good, can't be doing with that. Can you come tomorrow?'

'Yes.'

That rasping, creaking sound, Cristi realised, was a laugh. 'Good. Eight'll do for the first day.'

For Cristi, life more than ever fell into distinct parts. Much curtailed was what she called her 'own' life, free to flit about the city, spend time as she wished with whomever she chose, ride the one-line metro known as the Trensurb, eat in street cafés or *pizzarías*. Still precious was time spent in Luis's world, which she was honest enough to admit was her own world too in many respects. And then there was the *casa aberta*, the open house. This, with its new intensity of experience, its stripping away of inessentials and preconceived ideas, often seemed more real than the 'normal' existence to which she would return, dirty and exhausted, and often shocked or disturbed, from the hut on the river.

On these evenings she would be deeply grateful for her bare room with its cool austerity. She didn't think she could have coped with returning straight from the level of stark poverty she glimpsed by day to the luxury of a house like Luis's. It was hard enough to deal with the contrasts as it was.

She couldn't discuss any of this with Luis. When he'd found out where Cristi was spending so much of her time, he had finally lost his temper. It was a scene she didn't like to remember, and she certainly didn't want to provoke a repeat performance.

The first days at the centre had been hard. Jude, far from appearing grateful for her presence, had been sceptical and offhand. Justifiably, Cristi decided, when she learned more about the short-lived interest of other volunteer helpers in the past. Sticking to unpleasant tasks wasn't high on the agenda for most Brazilians.

There were two main points for Cristi to take aboard: the minuscule scale of what they did in the general scheme of things, and the fact that whatever they did, however hard they worked, there would never be any measurable long-term result.

'We're just here,' Jude would repeat, and that was the sum of it. 'Doing about as much good as chucking a water purification tablet into the river.'

Cristi, looking at the dark slow tide so close to them, carrying its quota of untreated human waste to add to the pollution of the world's oceans, thought she'd try to keep the analogy in mind. What she was learning about this country, even here, was only the tiniest fragment of its multi-faceted life.

Children would appear regularly for a while, seem glad to be there, respond to what was offered, then vanish, never to be seen again. Others would come in after long gaps, dirty, hungry, wary and hostile, their eyes often blank with glue-sniffing, milk the place of all it could give them, perhaps wanting to have treated the scabies-like skin disease so many of them suffered from, perhaps with some wound, but never permitting anything approaching personal contact. Some came to steal and vandalise, and occasionally gangs would swoop down, high on drugs, to terrorise the smaller children and drag them off to work for them on the streets.

'But we're never seriously attacked, you know,' Jude said after one of these terrifying episodes, as she moved about righting any bits of battered furniture which could do duty again.

'No?' said Cristi, too shaken to do much to help her. 'What happened just now, then?'

Jude philosophically toed aside a splintered table. 'That was just for kicks, to pass a pleasant hour or two. Porto Alegre isn't dangerous. Neither the poverty nor the violence come close to what you find in Rio or São Paulo. Anyway, there's a certain safety, I've found, in operating on this basic level – and in being old.' She gave one of her creaky laughs.

'How do you mean?' No children would come back today. This might be the moment to find out more about Jude's life, which had obviously been colourful and fascinating, but which she was never very ready to talk about except in oblique passing references.

Jude shrugged. 'I'm harmless, aren't I? Seventy next year. Just a potty old foreign biddy with rice and beans and a few bits of sticking plaster to offer. Not tied in with any organisation, not even the church. No connection with the *prefeitura* or the *Conselho Tutelar* – the branch of the local council supposed to protect the rights of children. I'm not a threat. And there's nothing worth stealing. They know I'm nearly as poor as they are. It's not worth the hassle of knocking me on the head.'

'They must see as well that you want to help.'

Jude's mouth twisted into an expression between amusement and scorn. 'Listen, my girl, one of the lessons worth learning in life is that offering help can be a deeply offensive thing to do. It says you're better than the next person. But there you go, I can't change my ways now. Anyway, what else would I do? And where the heck would I go? Back where I came from, to some bed-sit in Wolverhampton, huddling over a one-bar electric fire I could hardly afford to have on, doing my bit by flogging other people's cast-offs in a charity shop? No, I'm best off here. At least the sun can warm my bones.'

It was the first of many such conversations, which usually took place as they cleared up at the end of the day when the last child had gone.

'Never get too involved with an individual child,' was

the rule which Jude dinned into Cristi over and over again. 'You'll only break your heart if you do, and you won't do the child any good either.'

Sometimes, angry and contemptuous, as though such facts shouldn't need to be spelled out, she would throw statistics at Cristi. 'I suppose you know that half the population of a city like São Paulo lives in the slums, that's *seventeen million* human beings. Many of them use condemned tower blocks, a hundred families to one tap. Two thirds, *two thirds*, of the young men die in violent incidents, shootings, gang fights. You spent time in Rio, didn't you? You'll know, then, that there are five hundred *favelas* there, with forty thousand people in the largest one. You didn't know? No, of course you didn't. Why am I even mentioning it?'

Cristi would say nothing, understanding very well where this rage was coming from. Jude had a lifetime behind her of struggling with vast problems, knowing they were incapable of solution, and now she was conscious every day of her age, her weariness, and the bleakness of a future where everything she had ever done amounted to nothing.

Then Jude would get her anger in hand, and gruffly apologise. 'Here, what am I banging on at you for? At least you've stuck to it, and you've got more sense than most of the people who've swanned in up here saying they wanted to help. You're not afraid of a bit of muck either, I'll say that much.'

'You know I won't be here long,' Cristi took the chance to remind her, expecting to bring fresh wrath down on her head, but not wanting Jude to feel let down when the day came.

'I know, I know. Just when I find someone handy. But at least you said so from the start. It's the airy-fairy promises I can't take. I'll miss you for the begging, though,' she added, a gleam in her eye.

Jude had bludgeoned, by methods of her own, a few shops, businesses, pharmacies and surgeries to pledge money or goods to the centre, but these contributions were rarely forthcoming without persistent nagging and reminders. Jude had sent Cristi on the rounds.

'That pretty face and those lah-di-dah manners have to come in useful for something,' she had said grouchily, but she'd been dourly gratified at their effectiveness. She also had to admit that, posh background or not, Cristi had balked at nothing. She carried the big jerrycans from the standpipe two hundred yards away without any apparent difficulty; she cleaned suppurating cuts and minor wounds, dealt with fleas and head lice, scrubbed the walls and floor with disinfectant; and she took into her arms without hesitation ragged silent children whose only other contact with humanity appeared to be violence and blows.

Soon Cristi would move on. That was how it was. Jude wasn't sure how long she could hang on here, dependent for survival on what she could wheedle and scrounge. And with these aches and pains. She had been pretty badly knocked about, that last time in the Borel *favela*. Not that she intended to tell Cristi about it. But her nerve had gone that day, and she knew it. This was all she could handle now. Well, she'd go on as long as she could. As long as they let her. One day at a time.

Cristi, dispatched to charm funds and goods from reluctant donors, had had a decision of her own to make. Although it still had little reality for her, she had money in this country. Money, however, which seemed to her to be indivisibly tied up with the ranch. Every penny of it would be needed if the place were to be effectively modernised, and until a decision was made about the future of Tres Pinheiros, that capital couldn't be touched.

Apart from her own funds, Cristi was regularly in contact with people who could have met a year's expenses for the *casa aberta* without even noticing the money had gone, yet it seemed an unacceptable infringement of Luis's territory to ask them to contribute in any way.

Again, there had been Jude's comments about doing favours. There was the matter, too, though Cristi wasn't sure her thinking was clear on this, of respecting Jude's way of doing things. She compromised by slipping in small practical contributions of her own among the rest, and would often take with her, saying nothing about them, such basics as cleaning materials, coffee, pencils and felt pens.

But it was an anomaly which disturbingly highlighted the contrast between her separate lives.

Chapter Twenty-four

'Hey, sweetheart, it's not like you to be so down.'

Archie, who after a weekend of gales had been resecuring to their supports some young willows he'd planted in a small triangle between drive and river, had climbed the bank to have a word with Pauly as she passed. She'd been taking the girls back to school after half-term, and though she smiled to see him, for even after fourteen years of marriage every glimpse of him was still a pleasure, her misery was plain to see.

At his concerned tone tears welled in her eyes and, frowning, Archie went round to get in beside her.

'Come on, what is all this?' As he put his arms round her she startled him by bursting into tears. Pauly was nothing if not wholesale in her emotions, but her tears were usually reserved for sentimental films watched with the children, the plight of maltreated animals, or the sight of elderly men with straight backs and chestfuls of medals marching with a steady swing past the Cenotaph. She rarely cried for herself, being, as she said, far too busy.

Gathering her close, Archie looked out of the tail of his eye for the nearest supply of tissues. When Pauly let go mopping up could be a serious business.

'You're not feeling ill or anything, are you?' he asked as the first wave subsided a little. He sensed a weariness in her, a willingness to give in, which was so unlike her that he felt more alarmed than he was ready to let her see.

'I'm not sure I'm not,' she said dolefully, an admission unusual enough to make Archie lift her away from him (no easy task) and brush aside enough damp hair to let him look into her swimming eyes.

'What is it? Tell me.'

'Oh, nothing really. I've been feeling a bit under the weather for the last few days, that's all. Nothing in particular. I'm probably imagining it. This awful rain doesn't help. But Archie, hasn't it been horrid, this half-term?' she burst out, with a fresh gush of tears. 'Haven't you hated it?'

He presumed she didn't mean the weather. 'Because they weren't all here?' He hadn't minded, to be honest. He loved all the children, and whatever permutations or combinations they turned up in he was always delighted to have them at home.

'*Yes!*' Pauly exclaimed with something like her normal vigour. 'Do you realise it's the first time ever that Cristi hasn't been back for half-term? She never, never missed, all the time she was in Edinburgh, and you know how devastated Josie and Peta were not to find her here. They seemed to think I'd promised she would be, and in a way I suppose I did. I was so sure she'd be back by now. And then Nicholas not coming home either—'

'But, love, he's gone to stay with chums before. It's good for him to be with his own friends, we've always agreed on that. He's had a great time at Lagganmore, going out with the keeper on his own after hinds, having a gun in the Flemings' shoot on Saturday—'

'But that's it,' Pauly interrupted in a desolate wail. 'He's growing away from us. He doesn't want to be bothered with the others any more.'

'Pauly, that's rubbish. Sure, he doesn't want to spend all his time with them, but that's natural. It doesn't mean he's growing away from us, or home. I'd be more worried if he could think of nothing better to do than hang around here with Peta and Josie. He's mature for his age, and everything's opening up for him just now. He needs to meet people and go about a bit. Living in a glen like this doesn't offer nearly enough variety and stimulation, you know that.'

'No I don't.' Pauly said mutinously, her face buried against him, absorbing the comfortable smell of the beaten-up Barbour he wore for working.

He grinned, hugging her. 'Idiot. But this isn't really about Nicholas, is it? It's about Cristi.'

'Oh, Archie.' She heaved herself upright, puffing strands of hair away from her mouth, driving both hands into its tangles to push it back from her face. 'I have such an awful dread that she's never going to come back at all, except for polite duty visits when nothing will be real and it will all flash by in a second. I couldn't bear that.'

No tears now. She was voicing a serious anxiety here, threaded with a fear she felt too upset today to risk putting into words – that in some way she had let Cristi down, and not proved an adequate proxy parent.

Archie, his face looking suddenly older, didn't answer for a moment. In the warm shelter of the car, they faced this fear together.

'A couple of weeks ago I'd have said you were talking nonsense,' Archie said at last, breaking the silence with an effort. 'I wouldn't have thought it possible that she might decide to stay where she is. But there's a new dimension now, isn't there?' Pauly could hear in his voice how difficult he was finding this. 'She's broken free of that family set-up she found stifling, and she's trying to dig beneath the surface and learn something of the country for herself. I admire her for doing it, but you're right, it's bound to affect her outlook, even her decisions about the future.'

'Sometimes I wish she hadn't found a way to do all this e-mailing,' Pauly said illogically.

'Come on, you know you love the direct contact,' Archie urged.

'I suppose I do. But these children she talks about. These children will come to mean too much to her.'

Archie, his face grim, couldn't argue about that. Although Pauly had focused on one element in the wider picture, he knew it was a significant one. 'And this woman Jude,' he said. 'By the sound of it there's a genuine meeting of minds there, in spite of the difference in age – not forgetting the sharp tongue, the slave-driving and the amount of work she expects Cristi to do.'

For Cristi had conveyed a vivid picture of a trenchant, lively and battle-hardened personality, for whom she evidently felt a real affection.

'It's part of wanting to be independent of the Fonsecas,' Pauly said. 'Like finding that room of her own she likes so much. It's the down-to-earth side of her, the side that doesn't mind tackling any job, no matter how strenuous or filthy, the side that likes – oh, I don't know – real things, being out in a storm, white-washed walls, those clothes she used to make for herself, her plain little room. Damn, I'm hopeless at saying what I mean when it comes to this sort of thing.'

'No, I know what you mean exactly.' Archie gave her hand a loving squeeze. 'But the thing is, as far as I can see, she's beginning to feel involved. She's not an onlooker any more. There are different strands drawing her in. This new interest goes deeper even than the response to the culture which, after all, is part of her make-up. Deeper even than the landscape at the ranch which so swept her away. Sweetheart, we can hardly wonder at the way she's reacting. She's always been so wholehearted about things. That amazing country, with its contrasts and extremes, is enough to stir the most jaded traveller, let alone someone as eager to discover it as Cristi. You can see it must be pretty overwhelming.'

'So you really think she won't come back?'

It hurt Archie to hear the desolate note in her voice. His warm, generous, loving Pauly, to have to face this aching loss. He found himself wishing, with an ache in his own heart he had thought long ago put behind him, that they had been luckier about having a child of their own, over whom such questions could never tug and hurt. For then the tie of blood would have been there, undeniable and unassailable. Much as he had minded in the past his failure to father a child, it was a long time since he had felt quite this deep frustration.

While he did his best to comfort Pauly, abandoning his work and going with her when she drove on to the house, his thoughts remained on Nicholas. As he had said, he didn't believe Nicholas's decision to stay with a friend this half-term had meant anything special. All the same, it was very much on his mind at present that soon he must talk more openly to Nicholas about the circumstances surrounding his birth and, still dealing with the emotions Pauly's unexpected tears had stirred, the last thing he wanted to be reminded of was that Nicholas wasn't his true son.

Until Cristi had been summoned by her Brazilian family, an unwelcome reminder that other people had claims upon her outside the close circle of Drumveyn, it had been easy to forget this. Now Archie couldn't help looking ahead with new uncertainty. And another long-buried thought surfaced, adding to his sense of vulnerability – that somewhere existed the man who was Nicholas's biological father, whether he had any knowledge of his part in the process or not.

But Archie, in comforting Pauly, had been too sanguine, and he would have been shaken to know what had lain behind Nicholas's decision not to spend half-term at home. It had been a dread of change; a reluctance he barely understood and felt deeply guilty about, to hear that Cristi had found her mother, and had had answered all the disturbing questions about who she really was. Cristi had written to him from Brazil, as she had done from school and Edinburgh, chatty, lively, unchanged letters, but there had grown in him an uneasy conviction that she wasn't telling him the whole truth because he was too young to hear about serious matters.

All this had been muddled and troubling, and he had hated not trusting Cristi, always till now trusted without question. There had also been a dismaying feeling of having destroyed, by his own doubts, the absolute security of Archie and Pauly's love for him, and that made him feel horribly adrift.

He hardly knew what he thought by the time half-term came round. All that seemed clear was that he couldn't face home with everything concerning Cristi still so up in the air, and no way of talking about it to anyone.

Yet more than once during the days at Lagganmore, where he had stayed several times before and was readily welcomed, he had longed to phone Pauly to ask her to fetch him. But of course he couldn't; it would mess people about; there'd be all the questions. How could he explain? So he had stayed, and tortured himself observing the 'ordinary' family interacting around him, father, mother, three children, all related, all knowing exactly who they were, safe, confident, undisturbed by doubt. No vague enormous questions dogged Stuart and his sisters about where they belonged, why people who were nothing to do with them should love them, or what would happen when they grew up.

Nicholas, Archie and Pauly were not the only ones to feel that Cristi had taken a crucial step into her new life and away from them. Though she had imagined her letters and e-mails to be merely factual and descriptive, they had unmistakably revealed what Archie had pinpointed, a new sense of involvement.

Madeleine, meeting Lisa for once on her own in Muirend, seized the opportunity for a talk, persuading her to take half an hour off and come and have coffee. Inevitably the conversation turned to Cristi, and Lisa later reported to Joyce that Cristi seemed to be getting pretty well dug in where she was.

'Helping out with kids in some first-aid post or nursery school or something. Making loads of friends too. To be honest, I never thought she'd want to live anywhere but Scotland, did you? Can't imagine her settling down in the tropics somehow. It'll seem funny without her.'

'Well, there aren't many jobs round here,' Joyce said practically. 'She was bound to go off one day.' Then, seeing that Lisa seemed so down in the dumps about it, she added, 'She'll pop back to see us though. She won't stay away from the glen for ever, you soft lump. Now come and help me with that Schnauzer, you know he went for me yesterday and I don't trust him.'

That should cheer the old thing up. Neither of them

noticed Stephen slip away, looking as though he had lost something precious to him.

In the strange way that imprecise hints have of turning into facts, and disseminating themselves without anyone concerned feeling they've told anybody anything, word filtered round the village and glen that Cristi had a new job and was staying in Brazil.

Dougal, who had had a letter of his own telling him slightly more than he wished to hear about Jude and the day centre, had not received that impression. Hearing this news as definite from Jean, he reread the letter, aching again at its cheerful, impersonal tone. Was that what she'd been telling him? Certainty grew in him. He hadn't got the message the first time because he hadn't wanted to. Now he could ignore his fears no longer.

As he worked on the house in the dark evenings, or, needing to get stuck into something more physically demanding, on the dilapidated steading buildings, taking a perverse pleasure in being out there in the icy winds or sharp frosts of approaching winter, he forced himself to accept the truth. Not the truth that Cristi would make her home in Brazil. That had become almost immaterial. But the truth he still hadn't accepted that Cristi, no matter where she lived, was not for him.

Sometimes he missed her so much that he felt no differences of background could possibly matter. They were irrelevant, minor details which could be overcome or swept away, counting for nothing when set against what they had once had together – the ease and happiness in each other's company, the sense of completeness and peace. But now Cristi herself had moved away; other interests, other people, had become more important to her than he was. He couldn't sweep that away.

He made himself look ahead to when the work of renovation on the croft was completed. What would he do with himself then? How did he see his life in the long term? He couldn't let himself turn into a dour recluse stuck away up here on his own. Self-sufficient as he might be in many ways, he was not a natural loner. He must keep in touch with friends, get out and about, take part in local events. Cristi had gone, and he must make the best of it.

No one could dance like Luis when he abandoned his affectation of disdain and gave himself to the music. Cristi was not naïve enough to imagine that he had forgotten his anger over her involvement with the *casa aberta*, but he had at least concealed it in recent days. In other ways too, their relationship had moved on to another level, and Luis had been more openly affectionate towards her than at any time since their days at the ranch.

Not that he had to expend much effort to make Cristi forgive him. Images of him, and the longing to be with him, ran as a tantalising undercurrent to everything she did. Hard as it could be sometimes to make the switch from the destitution she daily witnessed to the kind of lifestyle he took for granted, the pleasures shared with him still had their attraction. It would have been dishonest to pretend otherwise.

Now, held firmly against his side in the correct

manner, she was conscious of the muscular hardness of his thigh, the support of his hand and the iron rigidity of his arm, as they swept and checked in the insistent Latin rhythm. His eyes were on her face, and there was something in his smile, a certainty, a private satisfaction as well as the approval he usually cloaked in teasing, which sent some highly pleasurable sensations up and down her spine.

During the last few days, when he had been so attentive and light-hearted, it had been impossible not to wonder whether he was ready to forget she was his younger cousin to be looked after, and to tell her at last how he really felt. Make love to her, in short. She knew she was being charmed, and knew Luis would be fully in control of what he was doing, but even so she found herself increasingly at the mercy of a physical longing she had hardly known she was capable of feeling. She'd done her best to resist it, but there was an undeniable excitement about it.

Luis had more to tempt her with.

'Cristi, what would you think about going back to Tres Pinheiros, together?' he whispered into her ear as the music released them. Keeping an arm round her, as though he knew she hadn't come back to earth yet, he led her back to their table in the discreet alcove. 'You'd like that, wouldn't you? Away on our own for a while? And if I promised you a splendid, wonderful surprise there, something you would love. . . ?'

As he tempted her, blatantly wheedling, his eyes gleamed with amusement at her resistless state. Did he guess what she hoped the surprise would be?

She could only smile back, abandoned to happiness. With Luis so close, in these seductive surroundings, at this hour of the morning – and not forgetting the wine she had consumed – Jude, the children, the shack on the mud bank and the struggles of the day seemed far away.

'What sort of surprise?' She must put up some show of resistance.

'A glorious treat which only Tres Pinheiros could offer.'

'You'll have to tell me more than that.'

Vain stalling. With his eyes on hers, his smiling face so close, her pulses still beating to the beat of the music, what hope did she have?

'And spoil it all? No, my sweet, I'm afraid you're going to have to trust me.'

Tempting enough to think of being back with him in that high immensity of light and space which at the same time offered a most intimate solitude. If there was to be some mysterious extra pleasure besides . . .

Nevertheless, Cristi had enough sense to recognise that by giving way to Luis's blandishments and returning to the ranch on his terms, she would be seen by him as agreeing to return to his world. So much of her longed to go. Perhaps there she would find some answer to the conflicting feelings which these days seemed to tug her in all directions. Sometimes it seemed incredible that she and Luis had come so close and yet there had been no more between them than the most conventional touch, the occasional embrace.

Then she would find herself wondering why it was so impossible simply to ask him what he felt. With anyone else she knew she would have done it without a second thought. But Luis wasn't that kind of man.

Chapter Twenty-five

Under a dawn sky flushed to the softest flamingo pink, the ribbon of road winding across the endless grassland looked almost scarlet. Even here on the high plateau summer had arrived, and this exquisite beginning promised yet another day of brilliant sunshine and pure blue skies.

At a huddle of houses, a single dusty street of shuttered shops, other waiting vehicles joined them and they wound on in procession, dust rolling behind them in a tawny-gold cloud lit by the rising sun. Ahead, distant buildings appeared among trees cresting a low ridge, and as they drove under the high gateway riders broke from the trees and came racing down to meet them, firing pistols into the air, while behind them rockets soared up in a welcoming display. The grinning riders surrounded the vehicles, and were greeted with shouts and laughter.

This rodeo to which Cristi was so keenly looking

forward was a legacy, she knew, handed directly down by her grandfather, preserving a tradition which had died out in many places. It was he who had not only formed his own roping team in the sixties, but had persuaded other ranchers to do the same, organising an annual season of competitions which had become a feature of the area.

'We are lucky that the final roping takes place so late this year,' Luis had said smoothly, when he had finally told her what his surprise was to be.

As was inescapable in anything to do with Luis, Cristi wondered if he'd had anything to do with the delay. He was as capable as grandfather had been of achieving his ends by whatever means suited him. But she would never know, and was too happy to let the question worry her.

It was wonderful to be back at the ranch, and good to be involved, in however slight a way, with the work of early summer. Everywhere now the grass was brilliant green, a host of new birds had arrived, and the air was sweet with the last of the orange blossom, a scent which ever afterwards would bring back the memory of these days of busy activity and intense emotional awareness.

And today another new experience lay ahead.

Peons brought the horses of the visiting teams, which had been sent ahead yesterday. As the men mounted, Cristi saw for the first time the Tres Pinheiros banner on its silver-tipped staff, the familiar emblem of the Three in Flower spreading out as it found the early breeze. Her brand. She was not a spectator; what was happening here really did have something to do with her.

The long line of horses began to wind up the hill, a small band playing the first of the signature tunes which would be heard many times before the day was done.

After Mass in the shade of a eucalyptus grove, for the women there was a move towards the house. Here the shutters were drawn against the threat of the day's heat, and coffee and little sweet cakes were on offer. Cristi thought it rather early in the day for such sticky goodies. She also, friendly though the women were, had no intention of holing up with them in this shady room for the rest of the day. As the conversation turned to children and schools, washing machines and catalogue shopping, she slipped discreetly away.

Outside she found herself not only in a different scene, but in a different century. Dust, horses, dogs, in the distance the raucous protests of penned cattle, and men sporting all the finery such an occasion allowed them, though apart from their distinctive team bandannas they adhered to the traditional absence of colour. The sheep being driven by at this very moment were lunch; the pit over which their limbs would be barbecued had been alight since yesterday and was red hot.

The early coolness of the day had already burned off, and Cristi was glad of the flat-brimmed gaucho hat which Luis had bought for her. His eyes had held a new light when he saw her in it, and his voice murmuring, not altogether jokingly, '*Olá, bem gaúcha!*' was a memory to which her mind returned with pleasure.

Luis, already mounted, appeared beside her.

'My precious cousin, what can you be thinking of?' he

demanded in mock horror, his eyes taking in with pleasure the slim figure which looked so much at home in this scene. 'Today is all about tradition. The women stay indoors and complain about the heat, the cost of living and their livers. Always, always, the *figado*. They fight for the mirror, the bathroom and little treats served up in a steady stream . . .'

'Really? Wonderful views from here,' Cristi remarked composedly, her booted foot up on the corral rail, her hat shading her eyes.

'Don't forget you have an image to preserve. You are, remember, the *patroa* of Tres Pinheiros.'

She flashed a smile up at him. 'Luckily I'm also the ignorant foreigner, of whom little can be expected. I think I'll make the most of that, thanks.'

He laughed. 'I can't say I blame you.'

'Anyway, I'm not the only female out here.'

A group of girls were talking to some of the riders. As their laughter rose Luis glanced at them with disdain, though Cristi, talking to them later, learned several were competent ropers in their own right, excluded on this day of strict tradition. She thought it politic to change the subject.

'What time does the roping start?'

'What time? When the men are ready, the horses are ready and the peons get round to releasing the first steer. Don't overdo the foreign absurdity, please.'

It was not a rodeo in the North American sense. No bronco-busting took place. This was roping, not the neck of the steers, but the horns only, and it was an impressive skill to watch. By the end of the morning bout Tres Pinheiros were in the lead, and Cristi was amused to note the satisfaction this gave her.

Lunch was uncompromisingly orthodox. The women sat on benches at long tables in which holes had been drilled. The men brought the meat from the barbecue impaled on big skewers which they stuck in the holes, then, with the razor-sharp knives they all wore, carved some selected delicacy and offered it to the girl of their choice. Surplus blood was soaked up by dipping the meat into some kind of meal, or with hunks of excellent home-made bread. There were quantities of Brazilian beer and red wine. The meat, though freshly killed, had been well grilled on the outside, was deliciously pink inside, and delicately flavoured by eucalyptus clippings added to the fire.

Cristi was swept away by the entire scene – not least by the fact that it was Luis at her shoulder, Luis deftly slicing the choicest titbits for her, Luis smiling as he tendered them with a mocking flourish, while at the same time his eyes sent intimate private messages which seemed to Cristi full of promise.

For the warm hours of siesta the men lazed in the shade, talking quietly or dozing undisturbed with their hats over their faces. Someone plucked softly at a guitar, then drifted into silence. The horses stood head down, resting a hoof; the birds slumbered, and even the waiting steers had ceased their bawling.

Cristi would never forget the evening – the golden light over the miles of open country as the heat died from the day and the second phase of the roping began; the cheers and laughter as a steer virtually without horns was released to try the skill of some expert; the roars of delight as the rope was laid over the tiny knobs.

With the competition over, not won by Tres Pinheiros, the serious business of the day relaxed into light-hearted challenges. Luis and the fat jovial rancher who was their host were persuaded into a head-to-head, and while there were howls of delight at the latter's panting efforts, for these days the *patrão* was rarely to be found astride a horse, Cristi hugged to herself a new glimpse of Luis, urbanity cast aside, throwing himself keenly into the contest. It was obvious that these skills came naturally to him – and equally obvious that he didn't like to be beaten.

Cristi was still absorbing this new side of him, when she heard her own name being called. Word had gone round that in her time on the ranch the gauchos had shown her how to use a rope, and with a friendly wish to include her, and acknowledge her as at least the titular head of Tres Pinheiros, a laughing group of riders had surrounded her, calling persuasion and encouragement.

Luis was at her side. 'I think you're going to have to do something about this,' he said, grinning at her dismay as he leant from his saddle to speak to her.

'Take part? Rope one of those creatures?' Cristi was horrified. 'I'm not sure I'd even want to ride in this mob of experts. Please tell them, Luis. They must be joking anyway, they can't mean it.'

'Look, it doesn't matter how well or badly you perform. They're being polite. It would offend them horribly if you refused. Ill-mannered foreigners, you know. Anyway, the more of a fiasco you make of it the more they'll enjoy it. I don't think you have a choice.'

It wasn't his final sentence which decided Cristi; it was the one before it. After all, she had ridden since she was nine. She could probably stay on, even if her steer hightailed it into the wild blue yonder. Serve them right if it did and they had to get it back. Suddenly she was eager to rise to the challenge.

Enrico, who'd come yesterday with the horses, was already leading one up for her. Enthusiasm for the novelty was spreading; even the house was emptying. No one wanted to miss this.

'Right,' said Cristi, 'I can only make a fool of myself, I suppose.'

Now that she had agreed to take part, which he hadn't actually believed she would, Luis became coolly professional, his innate competitiveness extending at once to her. Her performance would reflect on him, on the Fonsecas. He knew she could ride. His object now was for her to make as little of an exhibition of herself as he could contrive.

Committed by this time, whatever mess she made of it, Cristi forced herself to concentrate. The members of the Tres Pinheiros team had gathered round her and, hearing their comments as she mounted, she realised that although this was a piece of spontaneous fun, they were putting themselves heart and soul behind her. Merely by accepting the challenge she had won their approval.

It seems I'm about to attempt to rope a steer in public, she sent an amused message home. She could imagine the laughter of Archie and Tom. But they too, she knew, as Luis adjusted the leather apron worn by the gauchos to protect the thigh in roping, and someone else checked the girth, would like the fact that she was prepared to have a go. She rammed her hat down, and was up in the saddle in an easy swing – the *pelego* this time, not the bucket-like security of the Mexican saddle.

The crowd opened to let her through, sending her on her way with friendly cheers. As Luis rode beside her to the start point, Cristi wished she'd paid closer attention to what went on. A lot of eyes were watching. The burden of carrying the honour of Tres Pinheiros on her shoulders began to seem distinctly nerve-racking.

Out here, the distances seemed enormous, and the ground was by no means as level as it appeared from where the spectators stood. The pen where the steers were held was out of sight down a slope. A long delay strung Cristi's nerves tight. She didn't realise that a portly animal with nicely curving horns, successfully roped in both morning and evening bouts – and who felt he'd done quite enough for one day – was being brought hastily back on their host's orders to be released again.

'They'll shout when they open the chute,' Luis was saying. 'He'll appear *there*. That's your line. Come in on an angle, and run him off against the rise of the ground. Don't rush it, there's more time than you'd think.'

He sounded terse, his face concentrated under the shadowing hat-brim, his eyes gauging distances and the low light from the west, appraising her seat in the unfamiliar saddle, her grip on the reins and the coiled *laço*. 'Flat remember. It must go out flat.'

Cristi sent her mind back to her hours of practice at Tres Pinheiros. Then her only aim had been to master the arm action which sent the lasso out in the classic shape, more to please the friendly peons who instructed her than with any idea of putting it round anything. They were here today, in the team. She mustn't let them down.

A shout from the corral was echoed, it seemed, by every man, woman and child assembled to watch. The reluctant steer came puffing up the rise, and Cristi had time to be grateful for that generous spread of horns. Then, without waiting to be told, the experienced mare swept forward at the exact moment, carrying her in at the perfect angle. Trying to remember what she'd been taught, Cristi released the rope in the correct shape, but too soon and too high. A groan, mixed with friendly laughter and a few ironic cheers, went up. She had failed.

But before she'd even slowed, there was Luis alongside, and the leader of the Tres Pinheiros team, breaking all the rules, had appeared at her other side and was recoiling her rope, shouting commands to his men.

'Keep going,' Luis called imperatively. 'Keep the mare moving. There may be time to try again.'

Oh, God, and I thought it was all over. If there was one thing Cristi was certain of after watching the day's events, it was that there had been no second chances. But enthusiastic applause indicated that she was getting one. Right then, if that was what they wanted. She felt the adrenalin surge up, and put everything out of her mind but the job in hand – flurrying haste, hoofs pounding, the recoiled rope thrust into her hands, the mare leaping forward. But the steer, realising the chase was on again, set off faster than Luis had bargained for.

'Cristi, it's no use! There isn't time.'

But Cristi wasn't aware of the stone wall looming ahead of her, or of anything but the curving horns, and the stretching body of the mare closing the gap. She didn't notice Luis sweeping in to ride the mare off, or the three or four horsemen galloping hard to put themselves between her and the wall.

Nothing now but the lasso in her hand, the moving steer, the distance between them. Her riding was instinctive, as was her recognition that the clever mare was giving her every chance. Totally focused, face set, Cristi chose her moment, and once more the rope snaked out, to fall sweetly in the exact shape on the exact spot. She had forgotten all about the shock and jerk which would follow, and was nearly wrenched out of her saddle as the steer's head went down. She was also oblivious of how close she was to the barrier of stone, and afterwards could never quite sort out the hectic moments as the gauchos surrounded them in a mêlée of thundering hoofs, dust, shouts and laughter, the weight came off the rope, the mare swerved violently at the last second, and a steel-strong arm whipped Cristi herself to safety.

'For God's sake, didn't you see the *taipa*?' Luis sounded thoroughly shaken, though consternation at her recklessness was mixed with boisterous relief and admiration. 'What did you think you were doing?'

'I don't think I saw anything.' He was letting her slip to the ground, and Cristi was thankful that his horse, even after such a mad race, was standing like a rock, for everything else seemed to be whirling round her, the laughing faces, the hands reaching to pat her, voices calling congratulations on her feat. Then Luis was beside her, a hand under her elbow, and still shaking she leaned gratefully against him.

It had been the merest fluke, no one had any doubt of that, every part of it unorthodox and rigged, but what delighted everyone was that Cristi had been willing to try her hand. That this unknown Fonseca granddaughter, Justina's daughter, had been ready to enter into this sport with its roots so firmly in their past – the gaucho past. Helped as she had been on every side, it had been Cristi's hand which had put the rope round the horns. They couldn't make enough of her.

That evening held for ever a dreamlike quality in Cristi's memory. It had a splendour and colour so vivid that even as it was happening she found herself thinking, 'I must store away every detail. It's amazing and special and I may never see anything like it again.' She felt elated to have been part of the day's action, even if her contribution only went down in history as a good joke.

As this was the final competition of the season, prizes were awarded, the inevitable flowery speeches wound their course, signature tunes once more blared out, flags were paraded and rockets let off. Then followed an interval of inactivity, and Cristi supposed everything was over. But no one made a move, and presently huge cauldrons of rice and beans and chicken were carried out, plus mounds of the savoury *pasteis* she liked so much, and everyone gathered round a big fire to eat.

The food done with, gradually, in an almost casual way, the central part of the evening began. Darkness had fallen, but beyond the reach of the firelight a thousand stars lit the velvet arch of sky.

Music, singing – Cristi was prepared for these, but not for the lengthy poems which were recited, with a passion and drama evidently wholly acceptable to the intent audience. This was her first experience of the cherished oral tradition which recounted the origins and history of these proud people. She didn't need Luis's quiet input to guess that their grandfather had been instrumental in preserving this part of their heritage too.

There were more surprises to come. As impassioned recitation gave way to more frivolous offerings, cries rose for something else, a word Cristi couldn't catch.

'The *sapateiro*,' Luis said. 'You'll like this.'

On a patch of beaten earth someone was laying out a lightweight dress poncho folded lengthwise into a narrow strip. With much persuasion, insults and rallying, two men stepped forward and took their places facing each other at either end of it. The band, their faces smiling in the firelight, began to mark an insistent rhythm. One of the men executed a brief step across the line of cloth. The second did the same, using a different step.

'They mustn't repeat themselves, or copy the other

dancer,' Luis explained, speaking against Cristi's ear to make himself heard above the clapping being taken up round the circle. 'Neither of these two will get far.'

He was right. Inventiveness soon failed, and the first challenger retired to jeers, while another came forward to face the victor. Clearly lesser lights went first, taking their defeat in good part. Presently, however, matters grew more serious. There was no delay as a new contender leapt forward. The compelling tempo of the music never stopped, and the steps became so intricate that to Cristi it seemed impossible for any new ones to be devised. She couldn't have said either whether any had been repeated, but the keenly watching experts would have known without hesitation.

Then, taking her by surprise, Luis's name was being called. Although he had taken his turn at the roping, she wouldn't have imagined him ready to enter into this sort of public display. Yet presumably, since he'd been left in peace till now, he had skills of his own. For a moment it seemed he wasn't about to show them off, then with a fluid movement he was on his feet and walking into the ring of light, where he held his own for some minutes, his performance greeted with acclaim.

For Cristi it was a strange experience, to watch him almost as an unknown person, his good looks striking even in this handsome company, back straight, head up, his feet flashing in the complex steps. A swagger had crept in as the more accomplished dancers took their turn, and Luis proved quite capable of adding his share. The repeated refrain had a hypnotic effect, and the whole scene, the circle of watching faces, the leaping flames, the brilliant arch of stars, and the sense of empty land stretching away on every side, added up for Cristi to something barbarically splendid and unforgettable.

Then came the long miles home, traversing the dark seas of the plateau, enclosed in the jeep's dim solitude. For some way Luis drove in silence, and Cristi was content merely to be with him, close to him, fragmentary impressions of the day revolving in her mind. Presently, however, Luis reached across and took her hand. The movement was decisive, his grip firm, in fact for a startled moment Cristi found it quite painful, but she didn't mind, so much had she been longing for contact, any contact, for days now.

Luis rarely made such gestures. Holding hands was to him an adolescents' pastime. You either cut to the chase or you saved your energy. But with this odd little cousin of his he saw that the rules might have to be different. Anyway, whatever his personal inclinations, matters must be moved forward from their present stalemate.

Even so, it wasn't too convenient to drive on this kind of road with one hand, and after a couple of minutes he compromised by drawing Cristi's hand to his thigh, ordering it with a little pat to stay there.

Cristi, taken by surprise and uncertain how to react, was acutely conscious of the iron-hard horseman's muscles under her palm. Man about town as Luis professed to be, he kept himself ruthlessly in condition, and his capacity to perform as he had done in the roping today — and the dancing later — told its own tale.

Still he said nothing, apparently intent on his driving, but once in a while his hand would come down over hers, pressing it to his thigh, and Cristi sat in a daze of sensation. His lean, fit body was very near. The magic of music and firelight, wine and laughter, was still potent; prosaic everyday reality seemed far away. Her nerve-ends were jumping, her whole body seeking and hungry in a way quite new to her. There had been many weeks now during which physical feelings for Luis had been whipped up and left suspended. Tonight, surely, would be different.

Luis was pulling up the big vehicle. Almost before Cristi realised what was happening he had turned and was pulling her towards him. She made one small startled sound, though it was not a sound of protest, before his mouth came down on hers. In the whirl of surprise and leaping response, and above all thankfulness that this was happening at last, Cristi had time to be disconcerted that his grip was so fierce, his mouth so demanding, before all such thoughts were swept away.

Of course Luis wasn't the sort of man to think of making love, if that was his intention, in a parked jeep in the middle of nowhere. So Cristi reasoned, scrabbling back common sense with an effort as they drove on. But she felt a desperate need of words from him to help her to deal with the fact that he'd released her almost as abruptly as he'd grabbed her. It was hard to drag herself back to earth again, shaken by forces she scarcely recognised. She wanted to beg him to pull up, to hold her for a moment, to let her say something of this.

How tedious he would find the mere idea. What an idiot he'd think her. For what, in reality, had happened? He'd kissed her. Yes, but kissed her with a concentrated urgency he'd never come close to before. He had moved his hands with a questing authority over her body; had cupped her breasts and undone her shirt and let his lips travel across her skin, his fingertips caressing the hardened nipples till the sensation had been almost unbearable.

That was all. After the weeks of growing intimacy, of hope and doubt, that was all. It was nothing. She thought of the people she knew who would leap cheerfully into bed with someone met that evening at a party. To them this would be routine, enjoyable perhaps, but nothing out of the ordinary.

Yet for her – she shivered as she made herself face the fact – these first explicit sexual advances from Luis, so long awaited, had been hugely significant, wildly exciting. But, forcing herself to honesty, they had aroused in her something else as well as the clamour of need, something close to apprehension. Wasn't it cause for worry, too, if none of this could be said to him and, when he finally made a move, her main concern was to react as he would like her to?

But she pushed these questions away. Soon they'd be at the ranch. Surely, after this, matters would move on to their natural conclusion? Luis was no child to titillate his senses, and hers, in this way, and not want more. Cristi longed for the release and giving and tenderness of sex. Then apprehension coiled again. Would tenderness be part of sex for a man like Luis?

But surely he, mature, no doubt experienced and used to getting what he wanted, wouldn't draw back now. Hadn't they already committed themselves? It wasn't the moment to worry about where love-making might carry them. Think of nothing but the starry night, the lights of the solitary vehicle moving through it, Luis's arm warm against her shoulder, his profile harsh-etched in the dim light from the dashboard, her hand on his thigh feeling the pulse of his blood – and the empty ranch house waiting.

Chapter Twenty-six

Cristi came awake yet again to the memory that everything had gone horribly wrong. The after-effects of red wine weren't helping the damage done to her self-confidence, or her confused shame and uncertainty. She had slept little, her body restless and unsatisfied, her mind going over and over the details of the drive home, their brief halt, the thrill of Luis's touch and kisses, the dizzy delight of finding he felt as she did, then the disillusionment of that cool goodnight when they came in.

Luis had given no hint of wanting anything different. He had brushed her cheeks with a quick double kiss, and though his hands on her shoulders had not exactly held her away from him, he had definitely not drawn her towards him.

What had gone wrong? What had she done wrong? What had changed between the whirling moments of explicit sexual intimacy, and that almost formal parting? Luis had turned her towards her room with a little pat of dismissal which, hiding her hurt surprise, she had accepted without protest at the time, but which it made her hotly indignant to remember now.

Then, turning restlessly in the narrow bed, she told herself he hadn't meant to hurt her – he'd just been acting responsibly, making sure things didn't get out of hand. Or, shaming thought, he'd been shocked to find her ready to – to go the whole way. She winced at the fudging phrase. Should she have stopped him? Of course she should; he must have taken it for granted that she would. How awful to have let him go so far the first time he really kissed her. But she was twenty-three, for God's sake. This was the twenty-first century.

Or perhaps her response had disappointed him, and he'd wanted and expected something quite different?

On the other hand, perhaps taking her to bed had never crossed his mind. How surprised – and amused – he'd be to know that after a couple of kisses she'd seen it as inevitable. Memories of the trouble she'd had dealing with men at university, her sense of being out of step with her contemporaries, came wretchedly back.

A cold thought struck her. She was Justina's daughter, the product of a relationship that was either bigamous or adulterous. Had Luis assumed she was as amoral as her mother? Had he thought it would be all right to behave towards her in a way he would never have behaved to someone he respected?

Giving up all pretence of sleeping she sat cross-legged on the rumpled bed, her head aching, her hair in spikes, face tear-streaked, longing for Torie's smiling calm and soothing good sense. Even Isa's blunt tongue would have helped, reminding her this was no big deal.

When, pale and fragile, Cristi came nervously into the dining-room for breakfast, dreading facing Luis, she was relieved to be told by Selma that he'd already left for town. But as she hunched over her cup of (now excellent) coffee, a sense of anticlimax dragged at her. This only meant postponing something which had to be faced.

In any case, why had Luis gone into town this early? What could he be doing there at this hour? Did he want to avoid her? What clue, really, did she have to his reactions? He was a separate, adult person with his own agenda and, she reminded herself disgustedly, it was unlikely that she was the only thing on his mind this morning, as he was on hers.

She answered Selma's questions about the roping abstractedly, saying nothing about her own part in it. It looked nothing more than a silly piece of showing off this morning, a travesty of the real thing. She escaped from the house as soon as she could and, not feeling like riding (be honest, you don't want to go far in case Luis comes back), went past the stable and took the path up the hill. She needed to think, and on its isolated crown she would get the benefit of any breeze there was.

It wasn't a good choice. The Fonsecas interred in their iron-railed plot refused to leave her in peace. The whole weight of family opinion, ideals and expectations seemed to press upon her, as she sat with her arms wrapped round her knees in the shade of the pines, and looked out

over the wide acres her forebears had so long ago
acquired. She began to wish she had chosen any spot
but this, with its blatant statement of power, wealth and
status, but she felt too listless to move.

And terribly alone. Among all these people — well, the
living ones — this family she'd been so keen to meet, not
one felt close. Except Luis, and now, with him, everything
was in this horrible mess. Tears were close, but tears
would solve nothing. She fixed her eyes on the lazy
wheeling of one of the great black and white gaucho
eagles she always loved to watch. Following its slow
circling, her attention was caught by a reddish tail of dust
on the road from town. Could it be? Too far away to see.
But yes, the farm jeep, coming fast. It was stopping at the
gate. Luis was back.

How to face him, what to say? And what would his
mood be? Would he pretend nothing had happened?
Well, nothing did happen, Cristi told herself. Most of it
went on in your own head. As far as Luis is concerned, he
kissed you on the way home, and touched you up a bit
(she used the term deliberately, putting the incident into
the casual perspective of her peer group), as part of the
day's entertainment. He'll have forgotten about it by
now.

Still, better go and meet him, get it over with, and have
things back on an ordinary footing. Indifferent to the
mid-morning sun and the solid bodies of the grass-
hoppers which flew up to thump against her legs, Cristi
took the steep path at a run.

Luis was in unexpectedly high spirits, greeting her as if

nothing unusual had passed between them, shouting to Selma to bring cool drinks, dropping into the old-fashioned steamer chair under the camellia tree and fanning his face with his hat, putting out an arm, though without touching her, to gesture Cristi into the chair beside him.

'My God, it was hot in town,' he complained. 'They had a power cut last night, so although the electricity's back on hardly anything's working, or it's developed some glitch or the time clocks are wrong. *Deus*, no storms, no wind, no rain, and they manage to have a power failure. What a country.'

Cristi didn't ask why he'd gone to town. The answer would be Fonseca-speak. But how good it was to have him back. The day felt quite different.

'Do you know what I'd like?' Luis was saying. 'A nice cool swim. How do you like the sound of that? It's too hot to ride, but we could take the jeep, have a picnic somewhere. What do you say?'

Though he was smiling as he spoke, urging her to fall in with his plan, Cristi had a sudden impression that something had happened in town which, in spite of his upbeat mood, he hadn't altogether liked. A picnic would be lovely. An image beguiled her of the green depths of the hidden ravine, sun on green-gold water. In that place he loved Luis would surely shed this brittle edginess she couldn't quite pin down.

But somehow nothing worked out as it should. Taking the jeep, into which the dust of the road had filtered in a fine film which rose to prick the nostrils and catch the throat at every movement, was very different from taking the horses. The sense of riding free into expanses of space and light, so precious to Cristi, was lost. Also, the jeep held recent associations it wasn't comfortable to remember. The need to refer to them, not have them hang unresolved, was becoming urgent for her. But Luis at the wheel, concentrating on negotiating the rough track while the jeep ground and rocked, was hardly in a position to talk to her as he did when they rode knee to knee in sunshine and silence.

To her disappointment, though she said nothing, he didn't take her to his secret place today, halting instead at a spot near the track where a group of umbrella pines offered shade, and the river slid over a section of rock slabs which formed a series of deep pools. It was already too hot to be in the sun, and they swam at once, plunging with relief into the cool water. But somehow, for her mood today, this place felt too open and exposed for Cristi. It had no special character. The sun was oppressive the moment they were out of the water, the rocks too hot for bare feet.

They ate the lunch Selma had hastily put together – Luis grumbled at its dullness, grumbled again when the wine wasn't cold – then stretched out side by side in the shade. It all appeared normal, but it wasn't.

This, to Cristi, was the time to talk, or at least to acknowledge that things had moved on between them. Obviously they hadn't. In moments Luis was asleep. She, in spite of her broken night, remained awake, frustrated and dismayed. She was angry with him for ignoring what had happened, then angry with herself for letting him ignore it. Why shouldn't she be the one to take the initiative and get things out into the open? If she wanted to talk, why not talk? Why did it have to be down to him? But Luis had always been in control. That had seemed natural. Anyway, what could she say? Why did you grope me last night then drop me like a hot potato?

Not her language, not her style. Her soul shrivelled at the thought of challenging him so crassly. The whole incident, which she knew she was blowing up out of all proportion, had been no more than a moment's idle dalliance for Luis. Of course he would think the civilised course of action, sparing embarrassment all round, would be to act as if nothing had happened.

The blanketing heat, the glaring arch of sky, the burning rock beyond their patch of shade, the prospect of the dusty jolting journey home, made Cristi feel trapped. There was no way of escape except to go back with Luis. She could hear Isa's voice telling her she was being a wimp, and she knew she was.

It wasn't a satisfactory expedition on any count. They didn't swim again, but without discussion packed up and went back to the house, to doze away the rest of the afternoon in the warm, sun-ribbed half-light of their shuttered, separate rooms.

Only when they met on the verandah for drinks before dinner, in the hour before the sun dived out of sight, did Luis say what he had found it impossible to bring himself to say all day.

He waited while Selma brought drinks, a dish of

lemon slices, a plate of *tostados*, and hung the lamps on their hooks at either end of the verandah, where when dark came they would draw the moths and other flying insects. He waited a few moments more, then turned to Cristi with a purposeful movement which, minimal as it was, caught her attention at once. His voice, however, was smooth, light, as though he didn't want to make too much of this.

'Well, Maria-Cristina, it seems to me that you and I have some talking to do.'

Cristi, who had had enough of undercurrents and uncertainty, felt first eager relief, then something very like apprehension. Why? Luis using her full name was unusual, but there shouldn't be anything in that, or in his serious tone, to alarm her.

'I think by this time we both recognise,' he continued, when she said nothing, 'that our feelings for each other go a little further than cousinly affection. Isn't that so?'

He spoke matter-of-factly, as though stating a premise already taken for granted and not necessarily important in itself. Creating a situation, however, which demanded some response.

His hand reached for Cristi's, his lean fingers lacing with hers, and, though his expression was barely discernible in the shadowy light, she knew his eyes were on hers with that same intentness. As before, she was conscious of the strength of his twining fingers.

'It seems to me, *querida*,' Luis went on softly, leaning so that his head was closer to hers, 'that feeling as we do, and in all the circumstances, matters cannot go on in quite this way.'

What did he mean? This seemed such a strange approach. How could she reply? Cristi felt her heart begin to bump.

'Do you not think, my sweet, that the wisest thing for us to do would be to marry each other?'

The bus sped on, the bus which had been such an agreeable surprise to Cristi. Modern, clean, air-conditioned and punctual, its comfort soothed her to a degree she knew to be absurd. When she hadn't been able to get a flight to Porto Alegre at once, it was Dr Elisario's secretary who had suggested the bus, vowing that the Brazilian long-distance service was second to none. Cristi had grabbed at the idea not so much because she believed this, but because, apart from being instantly available, this means of returning south represented for her something independent, practical and ordinary. It was the room in the *pensão* all over again, to do with down-to-earth values; her decision, her choice.

She needed time to think, and surroundings where no Fonseca would ever be found were a good place to start. How unreal that whole scene with Luis still seemed. As its astonishing opening words came back to her, she felt again the blaze of amazed, uncomplicated joy they had produced. He did feel as she felt! It had been breathtaking, amazing — then there had been the check, the hurried tamping down of that thrilled reaction. She had come to her feet, ready to leap into his arms; he had come to his feet and taken her hands, but had held them down, easily and not, as it had seemed, deliberately, at their sides. Looking back now, Cristi knew it had been deliberate. He had wanted to warn her that heedless passion wasn't about to sweep them away.

She smiled wanly, remembering how he'd gone on from there. Pulling her chair closer to his, drawing her to sit down again and keeping hold of her hand, he had made it clear, speaking softly and tenderly, why they mustn't leap into rash embraces.

'My sweet Cristi,' he had said, sounding almost rueful, 'the romantic love in which you British have such faith will hardly be enough in our case. You must see that there are many obstacles in our path, and many issues to be discussed.'

Cristi had known he would think her absurd if she cried, But do you love me? And for heaven's sake, she had told herself, he's talking about marrying you. Never in your wildest dreams have you seriously thought that could happen. Shut up and listen.

It had been exciting all the same to sit there on the verandah with its soft pools of light, the evening frog chorus beginning to hit its stride, a whirl of dazzled speculation distracting her from what Luis was saying. Marry him. Live in this fabulous country. Share beautiful Tres Pinheiros with him. Settle for ever the conflict between the two parts of her. How thrilled Pauly and Archie would be for her, even though they'd miss her. How wonderful it was going to be to take Luis to meet them, to meet everyone.

One image had checked that excited whirl of half-formed thoughts, an image she would have avoided if she could. With arresting clarity she had seen Dougal, Dougal out on the hill in his battered old jacket, collar up, hair ruffled by the wind; seen his square powerful build, his steady stride covering the rough ground with ease, looking, as he always did, entirely at home in his environment. It had been a vivid, heart-stopping picture but one, she had at once reminded herself, which belonged in the past. It had vanished almost as it took shape, leaving a bleak ache of loss.

'There is, in the first place, the question of our being cousins,' Luis's voice had brought her back to the present. 'Would that be something to worry you?'

'But cousins do marry, don't they?' Cristi had felt tentative here, the irreligious barbarian to whom such questions have never been important.

'Certainly there is no history in our family to suggest there would be any genetic problem.' Luis had sounded a trifle impatient. 'And as you haven't been raised as a Catholic we don't have to worry about the rulings of the church, fortunately.'

'But the family? What will they say about it?'

Hard to believe today that until then she hadn't given a thought to the omnipotent Fonseca hierarchy in the background.

Luis had shrugged, mouth turning down. 'They have always known you were non-Catholic.'

'But—' the idea had seemed outrageous, 'you haven't discussed this with them, have you?'

She had caught Luis's quick glance, and heard in his voice that he had realised too late that this would not be acceptable to her. 'My sweet, it can hardly come as a surprise to them,' he had prevaricated hastily. 'They know how utterly you charmed me from the moment I set eyes on you. It's been no secret, has it?'

'You've never mentioned it to me.' Cristi had been only half joking. She had needed some reassurance, some heartfelt words of love. But Luis had only laughed, calling to Selma to refill their glasses, to turn up the lamps.

The small bustle, breaking across the focused intimacy of the scene, had given Cristi time to think. When Selma had gone she had mustered her courage to say, 'Luis, I have to ask, doesn't it bother you that I'm Justina's daughter? I mean, she was so much the black sheep of the family, and—'

'*Querida*,' he had interrupted her, laughing again, 'how can you ask such a thing? You may look like your beautiful mother, and indeed when I first caught sight of you the resemblance was startling, but in other respects – in other respects you couldn't be more different. In fact, I think you must be the best behaved and most delightful Fonseca who ever lived.'

That had been nice to hear, in its way, but Cristi had known she couldn't leave it there. 'But what about the fact that I'm almost certainly illegitimate? We don't know for sure that my parents were married. My father, Howard, was supposed to be Lisa Napier's husband too. Nobody knows which marriage came first or—'

Again Luis had cut in, though he hadn't been laughing

this time. 'Old history. Regrettable but, as you say, never to be cleared up now. However, this question of Howard Armitage. Surely you accept, now that you're grown up, that with your looks it's extremely improbable that he can have been your father. And since we shall never know the truth, it would be foolish, in my opinion, to let that affect us at this point.'

Luis was right. While she had been living in Brazil it had become harder and harder to believe she was half English. It had jolted her to learn that the Fonsecas had never thought so, but the most disquieting factor was that she would never have any idea who her Brazilian father was. Yet it had, in spite of its bleakness, subtly reinforced the sense of her rightful place, in genetic terms, being here.

Dinner had been strange. Cristi had felt she was functioning on several different levels at once: eating, drinking, maintaining a flow of superficial exchanges while Selma was present; resuming practical discussion with Luis when Selma was in the kitchen; and at the same time feeling as stunned as any girl who's just received a proposal, as she began to take in the implications of the prospect opening before her.

But after dinner she had come to earth with a bump. Confident that when they were finally on their own she and Luis would fall into each other arms, it had been a shock when he had said, apparently assuming that she would see this as obvious, that it was time he was off to town.

'To town? Now?' Cristi could still hear the hurt disbelief in her voice.

'But of course. I shall sleep there. With matters between us as they now stand, it would be out of the question to be here together. You see that, surely?'

Had he intended to put her in the wrong? Cristi, blushing, unconvinced by the logic but too abashed to try to persuade him to change his mind, had compromised by asking, 'But you don't have to go right away?'

He had looked at her oddly, then asked, 'Cristi, do you think it's easy to be here with you, alone like this, knowing we must behave ourselves? Have pity on me.'

She had had an odd feeling that it hadn't been the answer he had intended to make. She had also not wanted to be teased, needing, quite fiercely, to know where they stood. 'Luis, last night when we—'

He had stopped her, his finger to her lips. 'For that I can only apologise. But of course it's the very reason I can't stay. In any case, it would be most indiscreet. But you know, my sweet,' he had gone on swiftly, 'I think it would be wise to have some time apart, to think over all we've said, to make sure of how we feel.'

'I know how I feel.'

'Feel about me, yes, I understand that.' His expression relaxing, he had pulled her close for a moment, kissed her, then held at her at arm's-length. 'But how do you feel about the rest? You have seen enough to know what I mean. You must think too about Scotland, your home there, and all the people you care about. No, time on our own is essential. I am going to Rio tomorrow, so you will be on your own here and—'

'You're going to *Rio*?' Leaving her alone, when the

most important thing in the world was to be together, when there was this whole new life to talk about? 'But – you mean – tomorrow? Weren't you going to tell me?'

'I have told you. Don't be silly.'

'But Luis, I want to be with you. I need so much to . . .' Her voice had trailed away as she tried to see this through his eyes.

'I know, but listen for a moment, Cristi. I think it better at this stage to agree that no formal decision has been reached. No engagement, that is to say. A great deal is involved. It would be foolish to take such a step lightly. So, a few days apart and we talk again, yes?'

It had all happened so rapidly. He had gathered up a few things he needed and been on his way, leaving her as it were with her mouth open to speak.

It had given her another virtually sleepless night, but this morning she had been sure of one thing. She was not going to sit waiting for him at Tres Pinheiros. Yes, she would think; yes, she would do her very best to consider all aspects of this proposal (was she allowed to think of it as a proposal?) but she would get on with her life at the same time.

It would be good to talk to Jude. If I can find the courage, she amended, with a fleeting grin.

Chapter Twenty-seven

'You want my advice?'

'Well, I'd like to hear what you think,' Cristi said cautiously.

'Humph.' Jude grinned briefly at the distinction, her look of dry disapproval lightening. Though Cristi had been talking about emotions and experiences which had never come her way, it wasn't hard to see how a combination of things, this Sleeping Beauty ranch offered her on a plate, the appeal of its setting, the excitements of the rodeo, and the evident attractions of the posh cousin, had added up to something any girl would find it hard to resist.

Jude remembered too the doors that had been slammed in Cristi's face since she'd arrived in Brazil. She'd had to take on board the fact that no reconciliation with her mother was on the cards, that she wasn't going to able to track down this precious maid of hers, who seemed to have mattered even more in some ways, and that, something she'd most likely been ducking for a while, she didn't have a clue who her father was. All she had to set against these major disillusionments was the biological link with the Fonseca family. No matter how she felt about them, they were welcoming her, sort of anyway, back into the fold, and that was bound to sway her.

Cristi was such a mixture, responsible and mature in ways most kids of her age these days never came near, yet in other ways, compared to them, so naive and polite and innocent it wasn't true. She was good company though. They'd had a lot of laughs in among the other stuff, and Jude knew, with an unaccustomed sag of her spirits, that she would miss her. She'd let Cristi come closer than any other well-intentioned young hopeful who'd turned up at the *casa aberta* – closer, to be honest, than almost anyone she'd worked with through the tough years in Rio and São Paulo. Well, she should have known better, that was all there was to it.

'Go home for Christmas,' she said.

Cristi gave her a long look. 'Yes,' she said. 'I'm going to.'

It was Archie who met her, Archie who, with a smile, wrapped her not in her own Barbour against the dank December chill, but in a wonderful garment long treasured by his mother – an ankle-length coat of dark-brown velvet, its lining soft dense golden fur, and a label, which Cristi had liked reading as a child, saying, 'Hudson's Bay Company'. There was no sense in worrying now about any creature who had died to make it, and to have this particular garment around her made Cristi feel the family reaching out to her even before she was home. Reaching out not just with loving care, but with a joke they knew she'd enjoy. And that mattered; to be back in a world where the cherishing of such a battered but splendid relic needed no apology.

She could hear the voices.

'Coming from the middle of summer, she'll be frozen, poor love.'

'You'll have to take something really warm for her, Archie.'

'I know, why not Madeleine's old fur thing?'

'Brilliant, she'd love that . . .'

Tears stung Cristi's eyes, and it was good to bury her face against Archie's broad chest and dry them on the tweed of his old jacket.

He pulled the fur-lined coat close round her.

'Darling little Cristi, how we've missed you.' She was like a collection of bird bones, he thought with protective concern. He was hugging more coat than Cristi. His throat ached to think of her beyond his care, dealing alone with so many momentous new experiences.

'Come on, let's get you home.'

They didn't talk much, and that suited them both. Archie was more than content simply to have Cristi beside him, making the family complete again. Though he didn't say so, he was especially delighted that she had come just now. It was good to have this quiet time together, before the whirling welcome at home. Archie had never felt it necessary to attach any label to his relationship with Cristi. She wasn't his daughter, and he didn't think of her as such, but she was part of his life, with her own place in the family, and she was very dear to him.

Cristi too was glad of this time to adjust. She had known, without needing Jude to tell her, that it was time to come home. But things had happened so fast since she'd left the ranch that there had been little time to get past that basic certainty. She had hoped the flight would give her the chance to sort out her thoughts, but in spite of its endless hours her thinking had been little more than jumbled flashbacks of her time in Brazil, a longing to be home with the journey behind her, and dreamlike glimpses of a future with Luis mixed with pangs of missing him, which, the further away he got, began to seem more and more unreal. In fact, the journey home, though she might not have been ready to admit it, had been almost as restless and troubled as the outward one six months ago had been.

But there was no doubt about her feelings now. Excitement took over as the A9 was left behind and they began the swoop up the well-known curves of the glen road, almost empty of traffic. There was colour here, unlike the featureless grey of the landscape further south, and a wintry beauty, the beeches clinging to their last leaves, wet bracken a dark tan under late afternoon sunlight, barley stubble silver-beige, fields of eaten-off kale pale green. Ahead, outlining the familiar shapes of the higher hills, where dusk was already gathering in the corries, was the stark blue-white of snow.

With a little exclamation of pleasure to see it, in such contrast to what she had left behind yesterday, Cristi wriggled deeper into the soft coat.

Archie turned his head, smiling, and put out a hand for hers. 'Good to be back?'

'Oh, Archie.' The feel of his broad, hard-working hand clasping hers was so reassuring. How could she begin to tell him how she felt? Or deal with it, Cristi wondered, relief to be back swelling like a great bubble inside her. How could she have stayed away so long?

In a way, she was almost glad that Nicholas, Peta and Josie wouldn't be there till next week, much as she longed to see them. It was so good to have Pauly come running along the kitchen corridor to seize her in a huge hug, to be dragged into the kitchen, to be hugged and patted again while stout Broy, beside himself with delight, did his best to jump up but never quite achieved lift-off.

Exactly as when she used to come home at the end of term, there was so much to say that for the first couple of hours her bags got no further than the kitchen. Scarcely a sentence was finished, let alone any story. *This* was what she had missed, this effortless, eager, happy talk, this feeling of being loved without question, of having a place absolutely hers in this scene. Just for now, it was a comfort she sorely needed to be made much of in this way, to be the focus of attention. It seemed no time, with tea still on the table, before they were exclaiming at the time and leaping to take Cristi's luggage up and get dinner started before Tom and Madeleine appeared.

Cristi was only just down again, having barely had the

chance to appreciate her little room, with its lamps lit and curtains closed against the winter darkness, the radiator full on and an extra heater blazing away, when Lisa phoned to say hello and pass on greetings from Stephen and Joyce. Did Stephen know she was back, Cristi queried, amused.

'Oh, that reminds me, there's a card from Jean,' Pauly exclaimed. 'Sorry, it went straight out of my head.' Two kittens holding a ribboned basket from which a card stuck out saying 'Welcome Home'.

'I feel as though I've come out of hospital.' But Cristi was touched.

'And Sally phoned. She says you're to go over as soon as you can, she's dying to see you.'

'I'll phone and—'

But then Tom and Madeleine arrived, and though Cristi had been told that Tom no longer needed his wheelchair it was a huge thrill to see him out of it for good, and walking with two sticks. As Cristi hugged them happiness broke over her like a tide. These dear, dear people. How *could* she have stayed away so long?

One of Pauly's talents was that she could let wonderful and even elaborate meals unroll without apparent effort. She never panicked about timing, which created a relaxed atmosphere and allowed conversation to flow unhindered. She had made sure tonight that nothing would distract her, producing first cornets of smoked salmon filled with cream cheese, the savoury butter of their short-crust bases a secret of her own, then a pheasant casserole, and last of all Cristi's favourite, bramble summer pudding.

'Oh, Pauly, you are a dear to go to so much trouble,' Cristi cried as this final perfect tribute appeared.

'Yes well, lucky it didn't collapse,' Pauly remarked, giving it a shake as though suspecting it might even now let her down, then setting about it with a cooking spoon. 'Everybody, yes?'

'How can we resist?' sighed Madeleine, who tried to be careful about her waistline these days.

'Who wants to?' Tom had always been on the square side and considered that nowadays he had every excuse.

'But what's so lovely,' Cristi said, as she tempted Madeleine to thick Jersey cream, 'is that just about everything we've eaten was from Drumveyn. It's all home food.'

They laughed at her, but none of them risked answering, for her tone had told them so much.

In the surge of conversation, the enlarging on news already exchanged by letters and e-mail, the laughter and willingness to be interested in any traveller's tales she chose to tell them, Cristi realised, shaken by the discovery, that she wasn't ready to tell them about Luis. Or rather about the strange, open-ended situation with Luis, which already, at this distance and in the context of home, was beginning to seem hard to believe in.

She made herself admit, reluctant to face this truth, that if she had intended to tell it would have been the first piece of news to share. An odd, more disturbing thought came. How would it have been if Luis had come home with her, if he were here now, sitting among them at the kitchen table? For a telling instant, she was aware of resisting the image, as though she needed notice of such a question.

It was Pauly who went upstairs with her, their arms round each other, when the happy evening was over. Archie had gone to see Tom and his mother safely in.

'Pauly, that was such a perfect welcome home. I can't thank you enough.'

'You don't have to thank me,' Pauly protested. 'It's wonderful to have you back. Do you have any idea of how much we miss you?' She stopped, making Cristi turn to face her, speaking with a gravity not usual for her. 'To me, you're part of Drumveyn. You've been part of it since the day I came, before I ever met Archie or had the faintest idea it would be my home. You leave a dreadful gap when you're away, and no one else could ever fill it.'

'Pauly.' But Cristi could say no more, leaning into Pauly's ready arms, much moved.

'I know you had to go. I do know that,' Pauly repeated earnestly, with some muddled idea that even now she mustn't try to influence Cristi in any way. 'And I know you still have decisions to make and everything. But I want you to be *sure*,' drawing back to turn the hug into a fierce little shake, 'that this is your home *always*.'

Cristi did her best to smile. 'I think I needed to hear that,' she admitted.

'You shouldn't have to hear it,' Pauly retorted vigorously. 'You should know. Anyway, come on, let's get you into bed, or we'll all be limp rags tomorrow.'

'You're right, I suddenly feel wiped out.'

'And, believe it or not, there are one or two things we still haven't told you,' Pauly said as they went on up the stairs. 'We'll save them for now, though. I want you to sleep for hours and hours in the morning.'

'In my own bed. What bliss.' Cristi could hardly get the words out for yawns. 'Maddening as it is to have more gossip waved temptingly under my nose, I'm not sure I could take it in even if you told me.'

'Good, because I'm not going to.'

When Pauly had gone Cristi stood for a moment letting the stillness of the big, solidly built house seep into her, breathing in its smell, letting the excitement and emotions of the evening fold down into quietness. Then she went to the window, pulled the thickly lined, floor-length curtains open a little, and curling her fingers into the brass handles, pulled the sash up a couple of inches. The sound of the burn flowed in, the whisper of air in the firs. At once a perception of this house in its setting of hill and moor and loch was vividly before her eyes. But that flow of air was petrifying. Had she really had her window open all year round in the past? She was going to have to get used to this temperature. Pushing down the window, drawing the curtains closed, she turned back into the room, looking, touching things, taking in the reality of being here.

And admitting at last the secret, empty ache. In other homecomings almost the first thing had been finding the chance to race up to Steading Cottage, or at least to phone Dougal. Well, she could still phone. But she knew she wouldn't. All kinds of things made that simple action impossible.

Soundly as Cristi slept, she didn't sleep late. It was still dark when she woke, and for a blank moment she couldn't remember where she was. Then thankfulness filled her as realisation came and, as in every first day of every holidays, eagerness to be up and out. There was pleasure in everything, in hurrying into warm clothes, in running silently down through the sleeping house, in reassuring an owlish Broy, who didn't even pretend he wanted to get up at this hour, and hastily making coffee she hardly paused to drink. She had no plan, only this urgent need to be out in the wintry morning, back in the landscape that meant so much to her.

It was well after seven, and as soon as she was outside darkness dissolved into greyness, thinning every moment as the light grew. As she left the shadows of the plantation above the house, a red dawn was spreading over the eastern hills, and across the glen a band of light turned the heather-clad slopes above Grianan a fiery orange. There had been a frost, and as the light grew the thick white tussocks of grass took on this colour too, and the yellow of larches made a glowing contrast to the blue-green of spruce. White mist lay along the course of the river, patterned by the skeletal shapes of trees.

The cold bit into Cristi's bones, but she didn't care. She relished the mild discomfort, the sense of toughing it out. That too was part of home.

Then she checked. Without thought, her feet had brought her in the inevitable direction. In front of her was Steading Cottage, a plume of pale smoke rising against the brightening light of dawn. But not the smoke of Jean's fire. Someone else lived here now.

As she stared at the silent cottage, its curtains still closed, a swarm of memories assailed Cristi. Dougal, Jill and herself spilling shouting out of that doorway, charged with energy, off to look at new puppies, to catch the ponies, to sledge, race their bikes down the hill, go to their favourite pool to swim or take the boat out on the loch. She saw Jean in her floral cross-over pinny, in a familiar pose with one hand up to the mantelpiece, steadying herself as she swung the heavy kettle onto the fire. She saw the pulley laden with washing, the red chenille tablecloth, the rack of fresh baking, the big old teapot. She saw Dougal's room with its models, its collections of stones and animal skulls and other treasure which drove Jean mad; Jill's room with its squalor and cheap frippery.

What had become of those children? What had happened to the bond between them?

All right, the past couldn't be retrieved. Dougal was no longer here, close at hand, but she must see him just the same, without delay. Whatever estrangement had grown between them, however their relationship had altered, she must see him.

The Croft of Ellig. If she crossed by the bridge at Achalder she could cut round above the village. Luckily this was Saturday, so there was a good chance that Dougal would be there.

Not giving herself more time to think, she set off resolutely along the track.

Chapter Twenty-eight

Going via the old wooden bridge meant that Cristi passed very close to Achalder, where both Joyce and Lisa tended to be early risers. The other early risers were of course the dogs, and the kennels with their runs lay between the river and the cottages. But at this time of day the dogs' minds were unanimously focused on breakfast, their noses pointing in the direction from which it would come. Cristi, screened by a line of alders and hazels, leafless though they were, was able to slip by unseen. She wanted no distractions, friendly or otherwise, to delay her at present.

She crossed the single-track road leading to Glen Maraich, and began to loop round above the village. She derived a secret pleasure from taking a route which gave the handiest way over a high fence, took her across a stretch of bog by means of the almost invisible remains of an old dyke, and landed her beside the burn, running high at this time of year, at the exact place where a jut of rock provided a good place to jump across.

She told herself she was an idiot to find these small things so satisfying. She'd been away for six months, not six years. But it was all part of the pleasure of being home, and nothing could mar it.

She caught a flash of vivid colour as a squirrel flashed up a fir tree, and waited without moving for the moment when his face would appear higher up the trunk for a quick check on her. Blue-tits and great-tits were about in force. As she approached the burn a heron rose with the stately soundless flight she had always loved, and she paused to watch the elegant grey shape against darker grey rock and white frosted grass. These glimpses, and the thin mewing of buzzards, familiar background sound of Drumveyn, seemed especially precious today. So did the bite of cold air on her cheek, the view opening below, the colours the rising sun drew from bracken and heather, the gleam of snow above.

Leaving the burn behind, heading across the white fields, she was gripped by tense excitement. This, now, was Dougal's landscape, this high open place so silent in the grip of the frost. In a couple of minutes she'd be with him, seeing him for the first time in his new setting, his new life. How would they meet? How did matters between them stand? In the euphoria of being back, longing to see him, it was tempting to let herself believe this was just the same as any other arrival of the past, before anything had changed. Then back rushed the constraint of their last meeting, and the limping, banal exchanges since, which had gradually dwindled into silence.

What could she say to him? What would he think of her turning up like this, on her first morning home, as though confident that it was what he'd want?

But her brain slid away from these questions, and her feet continued to carry her forward.

Would he be there? Yes, she could see the tail-end of the Land Rover in the steading yard as she crossed the last field. The same old Land Rover.

How weird it was, to be approaching this place which in the past she would have taken care to avoid, the one-time stronghold of the brawling, chancy Maclachlan clan; but to be walking up to it with nervousness just the same, not sure of her welcome, not even sure which door she should go to.

'Are you mad?' she demanded aloud, angry with herself for being so ridiculous. When had she ever gone to the front door at Steading Cottage? What was she thinking about? But why was she finding it so difficult to breathe evenly, and why was her hand trembling so much that her first knock on the back door made about as much noise as a visiting gerbil would have produced. Calm down, calm down. She knocked more firmly, and heard Dougal's voice call, 'Come in.'

A small lobby, its inner door open to the kitchen. Through it, the table in the middle of the room, and Dougal, still at his breakfast, facing the door, a look of friendly enquiry on his face as he started to get up to greet whoever was coming in. The image that ever afterwards remained for Cristi was of the width of his shoulders in heavy sweater and green gilet, the broad brown hand putting down his mug, the healthy outdoor look about him as though he'd already been out and about this morning, and the total, unmistakable blaze of startled joy in his face at the sight of her.

'Cristi.'

He could barely get the word out. She was the last person he had expected to see at this hour, on her first day home. Though he hadn't heard a vehicle as he'd only just turned off the radio after catching the weather forecast, plenty of people looked in at the croft for this and that at the weekend. To see her there, hesitating in the doorway, her eyes huge with uncertainty, to see her slender beauty again, her skin tanned to gold by the Brazilian sun, and yet to find her exactly the Cristi he remembered in her old Barbour and boots, a red cashmere scarf at her neck, swept him with an adrenalin rush of pure delight and physical response.

But in the same instant cold facts swept back. He felt the blaze of delight die down as though the blood itself was draining from his limbs as, automatically, he reached a hand behind him to steady the chair which had rocked when he came to his feet in shock. And he caught it before it fell. That was all the time it had taken; that smallest part of a second as the chair rocked.

For Cristi too there was an identical soaring certainty, questions forgotten. Everything that mattered was here. Then she saw the joy wiped out of his face, and felt a painful lump form in her throat as dismay took over. For a glorious flash of time she had been ready to leap forward, into his arms, sure and happy. How dreadful if she had. Fighting down an impulse to turn and run, she managed instead a couple of shaky steps forward.

'Hi, Dougal. Hope it's OK to come barging in without warning. I know it's a bit early, but I couldn't sleep, and then couldn't bear to stay in bed. It's so fabulous to be home again, I just had to come out. So then I thought I'd walk up this way and . . .'

Suddenly it didn't seem the obvious thing to have done any more. She heard herself babbling like an idiot and made herself stop.

'Of course it's all right, you know that.' Dougal had pushed the chair out of his way, and he too had taken a step forward. Then he had checked. How could he greet her? How did they usually greet each other? Why think of that; everything was different now. 'It's great to see you.' How bald that sounded. This was Cristi, for God's sake. He tried again, gesturing to the table. 'I was just at my breakfast—'

'I'm sorry. I didn't mean to disturb you.'

'Don't be daft.' At least they'd never been that polite to each other. 'Come and have some with me. You'll not have stopped for anything before coming out, if I know anything about it.'

'You're right.' Cristi, smiling, relaxed a little, and came further into the kitchen. 'Coffee would be great.'

'Oh, I think we can do better than that.'

'But don't let your breakfast get cold.'

'I'd just about finished. Now, there's bacon. Eggs from my own hens. Nasty white sliced bread you'll not think much of.' That helped, taking them back to some familiar footing, and it helped to have something practical to turn to as well. 'Hang on though, I've duck eggs too, you always liked those.'

'I do like them, but they're so huge and filling. I don't think I could manage one on my own.'

'Then why don't we make an omelette, and I'll share it with you. I wouldn't mind starting again, it was pretty sharp out this morning.'

Oh, blessed Dougal, so calm and down to-earth. Cristi, grateful to him, put on hold the memory of that sequence of flaring hope and its swift extinguishing. She knew it would come back to torment her, playing back over and over in her mind. Just for an instant, she had been so sure. For now, though, concentrate on the ordinary, make the most of this brief time with him.

It was good be with him, good to be here in his new home, getting out what they needed as he pointed her to this cupboard and that drawer, looking round the trim, newly fitted and redecorated kitchen, admiring his handiwork and laughing to recall it as the dark and foetid Maclachlan lair.

Watching Dougal as he cracked a duck egg into the bowl, getting a firm grip on the rim and whanging the tough shell open with a crisp blow, Cristi was impressed, and oddly touched, by his new domestic competence. True, Dougal had always been one of those people able to turn his hand to anything, but that had meant outside things about the estate. At home he had been very much the cosseted lad, looked after by his mother as a matter of course, required only to make such masculine contributions as fetching in logs or splitting kindling. Now he was a lad no longer. He was a man, confident and at ease in his own house, more than able to look after himself. In spite of all that had taken place in Cristi's own life recently, she had an odd feeling that the three-year gap between them had doubled in her absence.

'Dougal, it's so good that you got this place.' She looked round her now not to assess the improvements he'd made, but to sense what it must mean to him. 'I was so thrilled for you when I heard.'

'Yes, I've been more than lucky,' Dougal agreed quietly. 'The kind of chance you couldn't dream up for yourself. I've a lot to thank Archie for.'

'By the sound of it he thinks you're doing him a good turn as well.'

'Well, in a kind of way, perhaps, though I expect there'd have been another answer if he hadn't cooked up this one. But I'm not arguing, believe me.'

'And Jean got the house she wanted . . .'

Suddenly there were a dozen things to catch up on, their talk natural and easy, as they grilled bacon to go with the omelette, made fresh toast and coffee, and sat chatting at the table. For Dougal there was such an overwhelming sense of rightness, of this being exactly and only what he wanted, that it seemed every other consideration could be swept aside. Just the two of them, complete and sufficient; all right with the world. As the words were about to burst from him, nothing else mattering, Cristi asked him to show her the house.

Fatal timing, giving him time to remember that he

couldn't think only of his own wishes. Constraint gripping him, he led her upstairs, where walls and woodwork were still stripped, waiting to be decorated.

'Dougal, what magical rooms these could be,' Cristi exclaimed. 'I hadn't realised you'd get this lovely high-perched feeling.' Visions leapt into her mind as she crossed to a dormer window which, glazed at the sides, gave unexpectedly wide views. 'You could run a seat round here, and with this light just think of the colours you could use. I know,' she whirled round, the old eagerness in her face, 'why don't I help? I'm at a loose end and aching to do something with my hands again. Starved for colour too – using colour, I mean. We could plan it out—'

'I'll get round to it sometime.' Dougal didn't meet her eyes. 'Thanks for the offer, but I – well, I haven't decided what I'm doing up here yet.'

Cristi knew she'd been too effusive, assuming far too much, misled by the ease which had re-established itself between them. Even so, it didn't quite seem to account for the embarrassment in Dougal's face, or for the way he turned abruptly to go down, making it clear that the subject was closed.

In a mood perceptibly altered he showed her the work he'd done on the steading buildings, and sketched in future plans. He asked about Brazil, but the questions were more punctilious than interested and Cristi, chilled and puzzled, responded in the baldest terms.

That was fine by Dougal. From her letters, and from news passed on via the family and his mother, he knew pretty well where she'd been and how she'd spent her time. He wasn't eager for more details and certainly didn't want to hear about the ranch. In one sense, of course, it interested him more than anything, but he had too many mixed feelings on that particular subject, and wasn't sure he could deal with them. Ashamed as he was to admit it, Cristi owning that land was a sore tooth which he had no wish to bite on.

The uncomfortable realisation hit Cristi, when the round of the buildings was completed and they were back in the yard, that Dougal was waiting for her to go. No winding up their inspection with more coffee and talk.

Instead Dougal was asking, 'Want a lift back? You'll have plenty to do today, everyone wanting to see you.'

'Thanks Dougal, that's kind.' Had it been obvious that she'd turned towards the house? How awful. 'But I think I'd like to walk.'

'I could put you as far as the village. There's messages I could get.'

'Well, if you're going anyway.'

To her surprise he looked hesitant, almost shifty, a rare thing for straightforward Dougal, and muttered, 'Well, I was thinking of going to Muirend later on.'

A blush rising in her cheeks, which she prayed he couldn't see, Cristi said quickly, 'Then of course you mustn't bother. I know you've got loads to do. And you can't think how I've missed walking while I've been away. This sort of walking, I mean.' She could hear herself sounding prissy and social, and hated herself for it. She felt hurt and rebuffed, desperate to be away on her own, to adjust to this new footing between them.

'There's always plenty to do, you're right.' Dougal glanced around as though seeking help from the bleak stone walls and tidy yard. He felt ashamed, ill at ease with himself; he also felt trapped and helpless.

Cristi, on the other hand, felt extremely exposed and self-conscious as she took the track which curved down the open field towards the village. Was Dougal watching her go? She turned once to wave, but though she could still see him he couldn't have been looking, for he didn't wave back. She seemed to have to walk forever until she was sure she was out of sight.

She hadn't thought what going through the village would mean; it was merely the direct route to Drumveyn. But as this was Saturday morning Ellig was at its busiest, and having run into two or three people and gone through the, 'So is that you home for good, Cristi?' routine, it became clear that she couldn't go home without calling on Jean. Well, she wanted to see Jean, had looked forward to it. But not now. Not with this awful numbness to cope with, numbness which threatened at any moment to turn into unbearable pain.

However, the warm welcome she received kept it at bay a little longer, as Jean, after the barest token enquiries about her time away, dragged her off to examine every inch of the sparkling little house.

'I can still hardly believe it, getting the very one I wanted. And see, it's that handy, everything built in. I've this grand cupboard here, and another one just like it in the wee room at the back. But wait till you see the bathroom, it's that snug I sometimes think I could stay in there all day. But the whole place is warm. No draughts, can you believe that? No draughts at all.'

'And you like being in the village?'

'Oh, do I! No more of that old drive in the ice and snow. The times I've wished I'd lived anywhere else but up that dratted hill . . .'

Cristi felt the immediate irrational defensiveness which any unfavourable comment on Drumveyn could rouse. It reminded her of how Isa's tart comments used to wind her up. But she hadn't expected it from this quarter.

'But now,' Jean rattled on, back in the kitchen and whisking cups and saucers onto a tray, reaching down the familiar biscuit tin, 'I can just walk out the door and be at the shop in five minutes. I'm still hardly used to it. And there's the bus to Muirend once a week, and whist drives now and then, and this winter they've started up the Scottish dancing again. Folk are quite keen.'

'How's Jill getting on?' Cristi asked as they settled in the living-room, where a mammoth gas fire pumped out the sort of heat Jean had never enjoyed at Steading Cottage. No sitting round the kitchen table now; there wasn't room. Cristi was reluctant to put the question, not wanting to dim Jean's shining happiness, but she and Dougal hadn't touched on this thorny topic, and Jean would mind if it was totally ignored.

Jean's face fell at once into anxious lines, but the news, it seemed, was good on the whole.

'She's pretty well settled, as far as I can make out, still

biding with her mother-in-law. There's been no more talk of the bairn being taken away from them, so that's a big relief. Jill's not got a job, but she seems to be managing all right, and she tells me she's finished with that other stuff. I don't know whether to believe her. She won't show her face here these days, so I don't know if she's telling me the truth or no, but there's not much I can do about it one way or the other. She's always gone her own road, that one, and she always will.'

'I'm glad things seem to be working out for her.' It was hard to know what to say, for much as it must hurt Jean to be estranged from her daughter, it was worse to have a grandchild she could never see. Dougal's nephew. Did he mind that too? 'It's great about Dougal, though, isn't it?' Cristi went on diffidently, to turn the conversation in a more cheerful direction.

Jean's anxious look vanished, and she beamed.

'About him and Alison Mowat? He told you then? Aye, it's grand news, I'm fair made up with it.'

Alison Mowat, whose father had been tenant at the Lettoch, a Drumveyn farm. Alison who had been at the glen school when Cristi was there, and who'd gone on to Muirend High with Jill and Dougal. When her father retired the family had gone to live near Perth.

Cristi hoped her face didn't show her shock.

'Dougal met her at his night-school classes. Well, she's studying something different, though don't ask me what. To do with computers, anyway. Everything's computers these days, it's as though folk can't take a step without them. But seemingly Alison's doing very well for herself, working for that vets' practice just down from the Co-op . . .'

Jean saw no need for tact. She had always been very fond of Cristi, who had been a welcome visitor at Steading Cottage through the years. Uneasy at first when her two had started coming and going so freely at the big house, Jean had got used to it in the end. But she had never lost sight of the facts; the Galloways were estate children, Cristi was a Napier.

Though Jean had known the strength of the friendship between Dougal and Cristi, she had also known that was all it could ever be. No matter what Dougal felt, he'd just have to get over it. He wasn't daft; he could see for himself it would never do.

Now, it didn't cross her mind that Cristi might be anything but delighted to hear that Dougal had found himself a girlfriend at last. Cristi had already left him far behind. And now that Dougal had his own place, still a source of astonished pride to Jean, it was natural he'd be looking about him. Who more suitable than a bonnie lass like Alison, a farmer's daughter, brought up in the glen?

'That's wonderful,' Cristi said bravely. Would Jean think her voice sounded peculiar? 'It's ages since I saw Alison. I'm glad to hear she's doing so well.'

Not so hard to find the right words. What was one more shock to chill her heart, which already felt it had been turned to stone?

Yet as Cristi took the old drive to Drumveyn, now no more than a grassy track, and her mind went back over the events of the morning, she found there was all too much to hurt her. No wonder Dougal hadn't wanted her to interfere in decorating his house! Her cheeks burned to remember her assumption that she could turn it into something marvellous for him, something he'd be thrilled with.

In desperation, she turned her thoughts to Brazil, and everything waiting for her there. If she wanted it. And in that moment, walking home in the thin sunlight, raw and lonely, she came to her decision.

In the estate office Pauly was perched on the desk, as close as she could get to Archie's worn leather swivel chair. He was looking up at her with affectionate understanding. If sometimes he could have wished that she didn't flatten so thoroughly those papers he had been unable to scoop out of the way in time, he would never be churlish enough to say so.

'I *know* that's where she's gone,' Pauly wailed. 'It's the first thing she always does, go and find Dougal. She'll be dying to see the croft and the house. I should have told her last night, before anyone else could, but there was so much going on, and after the journey it seemed a bit much to break news like that.'

Archie took her hand. 'Don't upset yourself. If she's found out from Dougal you know he'll have told her as kindly as he possibly could.'

'But to have no warning. She'll think we let her down horribly, letting her walk straight into it.'

'Well, who'd have imagined she'd wake at crack of dawn after a long flight like that?' Archie urged. 'And think of the hour we went to bed. Come on, Pauly, don't blame yourself. It's just the way things worked out.'

'What about the rest?' Pauly asked. 'Do we still stick to what we planned?'

'No reason not to. Telling them all together seems the best way to me.'

As he looked up at her, smiling, she read the happiness in his eyes. He laid a warm palm over her belly, and she leaned down to draw his head towards her, her worries about Cristi receding. As Archie said, if she'd already heard Dougal's news nothing could be done to spare her feelings. And to be fair, no one quite knew by now what those feelings were.

Chapter Twenty-nine

In fact, it wasn't possible to gather the family for any private talk until both Christmas and New Year were over. Afterwards, Pauly couldn't believe there hadn't been a chink somewhere when the six of them could have found a chance to talk, but that was how it was.

When Nicholas came home he brought a friend with him whose parents had been held up somewhere abroad, and before he left the pre-Christmas round of parties, pantomime, school concert and carol service had begun.

There was the usual ferrying back and forth, inevitable if one lived away up a glen with no public transport and most of one's friends did the same. Cristi could be independent, and she spent a lot of time happily catching up with friends, most often taking the hill road over to Glen Maraich where Laura Drummond was home for the holiday at Riach. Nearer at hand she was glad to have Michael and Kirsty Danaher back at Grianan and they, finding the house quiet this year, and saddened by their father's marked retreat into passive introversion, were equally glad to see her.

Cristi often gave Nicholas lifts, recognising his need to shake free of his younger sisters, and also, though it was hard to pin down precisely, a touch of more adult self-sufficiency about him. Among his closest friends were the Mackenzie twins, Laura's half-sisters, so that often fitted in conveniently with Cristi's own plans. But Pauly didn't expect Cristi always to gear her activities to his, and Peta and Josie had invitations of their own, so various Drumveyn vehicles and drivers were kept busy.

A cold spell produced enough snow for a couple of days' skiing, and everything was put on hold for that.

Pauly was also anxious not to neglect Sally Danaher, who wasn't opening Grianan at all this winter, a telling sign of Mike's failing health. While knowing that Mike wouldn't enjoy big noisy gatherings, Pauly didn't want Sally to feel isolated, and made every effort to keep in touch and include them in everything Mike could cope with. Although he chose to spend a lot of time on his own these days, he needed to know Sally was close at hand. She had to be, for as his attention span became more limited and his short-term memory deteriorated, it wasn't safe to leave him alone for any length of time.

Pauly was glad her own parents were on hand, for her father, a neuro-surgeon, was the ideal person to realise what Sally was going through, and he was happy to spend time with Mike in long quiet talks, not minding when they become inconsequent or repetitive.

Not only were Pauly's parents at Drumveyn for

Christmas, but Tom's son Ian with his wife and family were there too. Missing this year was his elder son Rob, now in Mexico, and Madeleine's friend Joss who, though she had a cottage in the village, was still too tied up in her international aid work to get round to settling there. She had vowed she would retire at sixty, but that birthday had come and gone two years ago, and Madeleine was beginning to fear that only exhaustion or ill health would make her return to Ellig for good.

To Cristi's delight Torie managed a couple of days at Drumveyn before rushing back to be with her own family for Christmas in Appin. She had some startling news to impart, news which Cristi found hard to deal with just now. Without a backward glance, Torie had thrown up the job at the Dundee Rep which she'd had been so thrilled to land, and was planning to be married at Easter to the son of a neighbouring landowner whom she'd known all her life. He would, presumably, in due course inherit a chunk of Argyll, and Torie would find herself leading precisely the life her mother led, the only use for the skills acquired in four years of fairly intensive study found in making costumes for the local school play.

Cristi was ashamed to find it hard to be as thrilled as she should. Torie was clearly blissfully happy, and had a future ahead of her for which she was ideally fitted, yet in many ways it seemed such a waste. Then, forcing herself to be more honest, Cristi would acknowledge that guilt lay behind this vague dissatisfaction. She wasn't using her skills either, and it was making her increasingly restless.

At least Isa was sticking to her ambitions, but here too

the news brought small comfort. She had been offered a job in the town-planning department in Gothenburg, and was off to Sweden in January.

'But why Sweden?' Cristi demanded. 'What on earth does she want to go there for? It's so far away.'

'Far away?' Torie mocked. 'And you've just come back from swanning round your hacienda in Brazil! All right, estancia then. It's about furthering her career, gaining experience and earning more money. Remember those details? Anyway, why are you kicking up such a fuss? At least Isa's putting what she's learned to good use, and as you've been giving me such a hard time about squandering my talents you should be glad. Though come to that, I can't say I've noticed you doing much with yours.'

'I know. I'm as bad as you.' The opening in the Edinburgh design centre, once so exciting, seemed far away now.

Cristi hated not being able to feel whole-heartedly glad about these plans, which in their different ways suited Torie and Isa so well. But, with Isa in particular, there was a chill suspicion that this was a parting of the ways. It seemed unlikely that she'd be persuaded to come to Drumveyn again, and Cristi had to accept that the friendship, good as it had been, had had its roots in shared interests and proximity. Letters between them had already become sketchy and irregular, though until now she hadn't let herself admit it. Torie – another Pauly in the making, Cristi foresaw with affection – would always be somewhere in the scene, but the balance would have irrevocably altered.

*　　*　　*

There was no word from Luis. Sometimes that would seem to Cristi entirely predictable. He'd been so angry at her decision to come home that a letter was the last thing she could expect. At other times not to write, not to communicate in any way, seemed incredible, in view of the footing they were now on. Then she would try to imagine Luis sitting down to put pen to paper, and the picture simply wouldn't form. And what footing were they on, exactly?

Round the thoughts would go, increasingly unreal in the environment of home, and often during those hectic days it seemed to Cristi there was simply too much to deal with. She would feel an urgent need to slip away alone, needing time to think. She found herself relishing, in contrast to the climate she had been enjoying so short a time ago, a few wild days of storm before Christmas, with the river over its banks, the loch spreading across the fields; found herself relishing cold, grey skies, bare windswept hills, stone and snow.

She missed Dougal more than she could have imagined possible. They might have grown apart during her time in Edinburgh, but there had never been this bleak sense that he had vanished for good. As long as he'd been up at Steading Cottage, coming and going about the estate, part of it, the contact she depended on had still been in place. Now, though he was only the other side of the village, he could have been a hundred miles away. There was no reason for him to come to Drumveyn, no reason for her to go and see him. How could she anyway, when Alison would probably be there?

Then she would think that was exactly what she should do, go up to the Croft of Ellig, see them together, wish them well, establish an ordinary friendly basis for future meetings. But she wasn't ready for that, and she knew it. Images of the croft haunted her. It was as though she ached with nostalgia for something that had never existed. She would find herself hoping to run into Dougal about the village or glen, then wince with dread at the thought of it.

She had imagined, when she needed time on her own, that her studio would provide a refuge. But it was too much part of the past, reminding her with fresh guilt how far away her creative self now seemed.

During this restless time she often turned to Madeleine for company, finding the quiet room at the old barn a haven after the comings and goings of the big house. Although she had little to say, it was obvious to Tom and Madeleine that she came in search of something. They offered her a loving welcome, trying to let her see that they were ready to help in any way they could.

'If only we could have warned her about Dougal. It was so hard for her to find out as she did,' Madeleine said worriedly one afternoon when Cristi, after prowling about for a while, talking about nothing more pressing than getting the ponies shod and the state of Josie's grazes after falling off her bike, had abruptly taken herself off again. 'I honestly hadn't thought she'd take it so hard. They'd seemed to be drifting apart even before she went to Brazil.'

'It's not only Dougal, though, is it?' Tom said. 'It's my

belief there are a great many things she isn't telling us about her time away. She didn't stay out there for so long without a reason.'

'Well, there's the ranch. It's a big decision.'

'Yes, and I'd dearly like to have a proper talk about it with her. So would Archie. It should be settled. But there's more to it than that. She's come up against things which have moved and disturbed her. I wish she'd come home at any other time but Christmas, so that there was some chance of getting to the bottom of it.'

For Cristi had still spoken to no one about Luis. And though she talked of Jude and the day centre, and more often of Tres Pinheiros, she had found it hard to convey what they had meant to her, or the feeling she had had of belonging to that world as much as this.

Because of the way the holidays fell, the house began to empty on New Year's Day. By the second everyone but immediate family had gone, and dreich weather seemed all too appropriate for the flat feeling which overtook them. There was a universal wish to get the decorations down, sweep up the pine needles, and eat anything but mince pies, Christmas cake or turkey in any shape or form.

It was then that Pauly at last collected the family, not without protests, in the sitting-room at tea-time. On such a day it was already dark outside, and it was with relief that she drew the curtains and enclosed the little gathering in firelight, lamplight and warmth. She had had her usual impulse to make a special cake, then had been impatient with herself. This wasn't a party. Why did her mind never go beyond food?

Archie would have understood that annoyance with herself. He, too, was conscious of how much this moment meant. A moment he had long ago given up hoping for.

'Now please, be quiet for a moment,' Pauly began, when everyone had finally settled down, when those who didn't want tea had gone to fetch orange juice, when a squabble over the occupation of the big floor cushion had been resolved, an extra saucer had been fetched for Broy, and even Archie had delayed matters by putting a couple more logs on the fire. 'And pay attention, because we have something very important to tell you.'

'You're getting divorced!' It was an instant anguished wail from Peta.

What did that say about modern life, Archie wondered with rare anger as he scooped her onto his lap. That any portentous family gathering could only mean its imminent destruction?

'Of course we're not. In fact, it's sort of the opposite,' Pauly started again, slightly flurried by this beginning. She reached a hand down to Josie, close against her chair on the disputed cushion, caught Nicholas's frowning, uncertain look, and hurried on. 'Actually, it's wonderful news. We wanted to tell you when we could be together, with nothing else going on. The thing is, I'm going to have a baby, another brother or sister for you all.'

She heard her voice waver. Damn, she had meant to be

so calm and collected. But meeting Archie's eyes, watching her with love, it was hard to keep her emotions under control.

She's never looked more beautiful, Archie thought. And in spite of the fact that none of the children was hers, she looked so much the mother figure, the natural centre of the circle. Her splendid hair, untidy as usual, glowed tawny under the light of the lamp at her shoulder, and her peachy skin, more blooming than ever in pregnancy, made her seem to his eyes very like the delectable twenty-year-old he had married. Only her body was more ripe, more mature, and it moved him almost unbearably to know that at last, after so many years, it carried his child.

'But you always said—'

Startled, it was Cristi who spoke first. Spoke the inevitable words, as the other upturned faces registered doubt and shock.

'But that's fabulous,' Cristi pulled herself together to exclaim as, her face alight with pleasure, she scrambled up to go and hug Pauly. 'That's so exciting. But it is a bit of a surprise, you must admit.'

'But you can't have babies,' Josie's piercing voice cut across the rising exclamations. 'That's why you have us.' This appeared to her to end the discussion.

'I know,' Pauly said, smiling, blinking back tears. 'It always seemed we wouldn't be able to, but now it's happening at last. Won't it be fun?'

'Then why are you crying?' Peta needed to get things absolutely straight.

'Oh, darling, you know me. I'm one of those silly people who cry when they're happy. Come and give me a a hug and stop looking so worried.'

As Cristi perched on the arm of Pauly's chair and the little girls scrambled onto her lap in a babble of questions, Archie's eyes went to Nicholas, sitting very still, his face uncertain, but his first shock already masked.

'Nick, you know this doesn't make any difference to anything, don't you?' Archie said, reaching to touch his arm, looking insistently into his face till Nicholas's eyes met his. 'You, all of you, are our children, our family, nothing can ever change that.'

Nicholas nodded. 'Yeah, I know. It's great,' he added awkwardly, and Archie wondered if perhaps he should have talked to Nicholas on his own as he had thought of doing. Then Nicholas got up to join the noisy group round Pauly, and Archie let it go.

His eyes moved to Cristi and, catching the look, she distentangled herself and came to hug him too.

'Archie, I'm so thrilled for you. I still can't take it in. But it's the most marvellous news there could be. You must be so happy.'

As Archie produced champagne, as the questioning began about when the baby would arrive and what it would be called, as small hands were pressed on Pauly's stomach and faces grew solemn at this new reality, Archie and Pauly repeated again and again the assurance that nothing would alter, that the new baby would be merely an addition to the family, no different, no more special, no more loved.

But when the group had broken up, Pauly and Cristi going to start dinner, Josie and Peta disappearing to have their baths, arguing all the way about where the baby was going to sleep, Nicholas was left with Archie.

'All right?' Archie asked.

'Fine,' Nicholas replied, and then, sounding as though the words had been wrenched out of him, his voice, suddenly gruff, giving a first hint that soon it would be breaking, he said, 'But you'll be its father, won't you? Its real father.'

'Nicholas.' Archie's face was full of loving concern as he put his hands on Nicholas's shoulders and met his eyes squarely. 'Listen to me. I'm your father. That's how I see myself, how I feel and how I've always felt. Nothing can change it, not in the slightest degree. No other child could be more mine, I promise you.'

Nicholas nodded, his face tight, not willing to risk speaking again, and Archie, hurting to see him hurt, thought it was wiser to leave any further talk until he'd had a chance to assimilate this new development.

Cristi, delving in the freezer for a bag of runner beans, was glad of a moment to herself. Overwhelmingly, she was thrilled for Pauly and Archie. No two people in the world were better suited to be parents, and the prospect of having a child of their own at last must be an intensely joyful thing. She was thrilled on her own account too; what fun it was going to be to have a baby in the house, and how she wanted to be here when it was happening.

But, inevitably, there was the tiny coil of a different

thought. This child would be a Napier; the only one of them all who would. She must talk to Nicholas very soon, she decided, finding what she was looking for and straightening up with a shiver.

Chapter Thirty

It was to Cristi that Nicholas talked in the end. In the general celebrating now that the news of the baby was public his feelings had been successfully hidden. He had always been so easy-going and good-natured, and so grown-up in his approach to everything, that Archie and Pauly believed his initial doubts had been put behind him. Peta and Josie were eager to share the news with everyone, from Ivy Black who came in to clean to Jean in the village, plus of course all the friends they phoned on a daily basis, and in the general pleasure and congratulations it was natural to feel that everyone was delighted.

But Cristi, alone more now that her contemporaries had departed to their own worlds after the holidays, was more observant. It seemed to her that Nicholas was spending more time than usual up in his room. He had a computer there, the weather was atrocious, and as she herself was going out less lifts weren't so readily available, so she thought little of it at first. But when the weather improved and Nicholas showed no interest in getting involved in estate jobs with Archie, and even turned down a day's hind stalking with the keeper, something he normally loved, she became concerned.

Perhaps too, focusing on Nicholas helped to keep her mind off her own affairs. For the feeling of anticlimax after New Year, the emptier days as everyone returned to their normal preoccupations, brought decisions pressing close. Though no one would say so, she couldn't hang around at home for ever doing nothing. She also knew that Archie and Tom were keen to know her plans, particularly for the ranch. They accepted that it was being adequately managed on her behalf, but she was uncomfortably aware that they would regard putting off a decision for much longer as irresponsible. What would they, or Pauly or Madeleine, have said about that other decision which shadowed every thought?

Just when she had talked herself into believing that he would never write, a letter had arrived from Luis, swiftly followed by two more. She found them strange communications from a declared lover. Describing Luis's recent social activities, sending courteous messages from various acquaintances of his, touching on nothing more personal than questions about when she was coming back, they jolted her by their 'foreignness'. When she and Luis had been together they had spoken English or Portuguese more or less interchangeably, so much at ease in either language that Cristi often hadn't been aware of which they were using. But Luis wrote in Portuguese, and his flowing, unfamiliar handwriting with its inverted m's and n's, the fine pen he'd used, the flimsy paper, and above all the formal, flowery style, made it impossible to forget that he belonged to a different culture.

Though Cristi understood that he was merely following conventional written form, the elaborate language was strangely chilling, and it was hard, for this reason and others, to know how to reply.

On an afternoon of pelting rain, when the sodden landscape was dark and dismal, the burns roaring down, Cristi took her chance to try to talk to Nicholas. The house was quiet. Josie and Peta had been hauled off to the dentist, not without much protest at the unfairness of it, since Nicholas had already been given a clean bill of health, and Archie, hearing Pauly bemoaning the length of her shopping list after the inroads of the holidays, had decided to go too. His happiness these days spilled over in protective love for Pauly, never quite able to subdue the nagging fear that things might go wrong, and he liked to be with her whenever he could.

There was no answer when Cristi tapped on Nicholas's door, and fear of intruding almost made her turn away. But the memory of his increasing reserve, so far from his normal cheerful openness, made her try once more.

With relief she heard him call, 'Who is it?'

'Only me. Can I come in?'

'I suppose so.'

The computer wasn't on, nor any light except the bedside lamp. Nicholas was lying on his back on the bed, not reading, not listening to music. As Cristi came in he pulled himself up into an awkward position against the pillows which warned, Don't come too close.

'What do you want?'

He didn't speak rudely, but he didn't sound welcoming either.

'To talk.'

'Nothing to talk about.'

'There's a lot to talk about.'

He shrugged, looking down at where he was tweaking the duvet cover into little starburst creases.

'Can I sit down?'

A lift of his shoulder. Cristi resisted the impulse to sit on the bed, instead turning round the chair at his desk, across the room.

'I just wondered if you were OK.'

'Of course I'm OK. Why shouldn't I be?'

'You don't usually spend so much time up here.' She nearly said 'hide away up here', but realised in time that loaded words should be avoided. 'I thought perhaps you weren't happy about something.'

He shook his head, mute misery in his face.

'Nick, talking can help,' she urged softly.

The bond between them had always been strong. Cristi, nine when Nicholas was born, had adored him from the first moment she saw him. When Peta and then Josie were adopted her allegiance to Nicholas had never wavered, and as the little girls became so much a unit it had been natural for the tie to remain firm.

'There's nothing to say,' Nicholas insisted. He sounded goaded, almost angry, and Cristi guessed – with some trepidation, for the problem might be bigger than she could handle – that given one small push the floodgates would open.

'Do you mind about the baby?'

'Of course I don't!'

It was hard to tell from where she was sitting, but she thought he had coloured at this.

'Is it worrying you,' very carefully, 'that it will be Archie and Pauly's, and Archie isn't your biological father?'

To say 'isn't your real father' was impossible, a betrayal of the love and care poured out on them.

'Well, he's not my father, is he?' Nicholas burst out. 'Why does everyone want to pretend he is? And Pauly's not my mother. They're nothing to do with me. Nobody here is, and I'm nothing to do with this place.'

With a scrambling heave he swung round to sit hunched on the edge of the bed, his hands to his face.

The anguish in his voice brought Cristi out of her chair to come and sit beside him. She pulled him against her and could almost feel the fought-down sobs of a boy who would do anything rather than cry, but who finds it hard to deal with the barely grasped adult emotions besieging him.

'Nick, it's OK. Say whatever you like. There's no one else here, no one in the house even.'

He nodded jerkily, but still kept his face turned away from her.

Cristi could feel his wish to escape her embrace, and also his reluctance to hurt her by pulling away.

'Come on,' she said matter-of-factly, giving him a little hug before releasing him. 'This is eating you up. Why don't we at least try to get it into the open?'

She pulled over the chair she'd been sitting on, not bringing it too close.

'It was you going to Brazil that started it,' Nicholas said unexpectedly.

'Me going to Brazil?' Cristi echoed blankly. 'What do you mean?'

'Well, wanting to find out who you are and everything. Meeting your real family. Thinking you might see your mother.' Deep as he was in his own angst, Nicholas was sensitive enough to check there, looking at her quickly. 'Are you OK talking about that?' he asked. 'I mean, I don't want to say anything that—'

'No, it's not a problem. Honestly. But go on. Tell me what you mean.'

'Oh, I don't know.' He looked around restlessly, as if he wished he'd never started this.

'Come on, Nick, you can't leave it there.'

He put his hands up to his head again, shielding his face, and suddenly the words tumbled out. 'Well, who we really are. This thing about genes. There's so much about it, on the telly, biology at school, all that stuff. I mean, it's who we *are*,' he repeated helplessly, as though he could get no further. Then with a quick embarrassed glance at her he plunged on, 'For you it's – I mean, there's the way you look.'

He paused as if to make sure this was acceptable, and Cristi nodded slowly, saying, 'Go on.'

'For me, as it goes, I look pretty much like Dad, and Pauly too.' Though he sometimes called her Mum, as the little girls did, she had been Pauly in his babyhood, and he used the name naturally. It had never struck Cristi before. 'Peta and Josie could easily be my sisters, come to that. Most people think they are. So it's sort of easy not to think about it. But when you went to Brazil it began to get to me. I couldn't get it out of my head.'

'Wondering about your mother?'

'Yeah. And who my real father was. And wondering if anyone even knew. That's the worst part.' His voice wavered and went deeper. 'Not knowing who you *are*.'

'Yes,' said Cristi. 'I know.' In the silence which fell in the dusky room the rain battering against the window sounded suddenly violent. 'I don't think I know who my father is either.'

Nicholas's head came round in surprise. 'But wasn't it Aunt Lisa's husband? You know his name and everything. Didn't he send you to her when he went off with your mother?' The story was no secret.

'That's what was always said, yes. But when I was in Brazil I had to think again. As you said, you've only got to look at me. Brazilian through and through.'

'But then, who——?'

'Nick, I don't know. And I never will know.'

All reserve gone, they stared at each other.

'As you'll have heard, there was no contact with my mother while I was away, and I've had to accept there never will be. Which means there'll never be any way of finding out who my father was.'

'But how does that make you feel?' Nicholas needed desperately to know the answer to this, and sensed that they had reached a point where he could ask the question without causing pain.

'I minded a lot for a while. Chiefly about not being able to find my mother, of course. But then, gradually – though I suppose it would be different for different people – I began to see there was a positive side to it. Or a bearable side. Although I carry the genetic baggage, I didn't have the emotional baggage to cope with. You know how Tom always says don't give yourself grief over things you can't change? Well, I came to feel – I am who I am. I'm this person, now. It wouldn't add to me, or change me, to know more, and it won't change me if I don't.'

Nicholas nodded, absorbing this. 'But don't you feel you've lost something too, finding that the person you grew up believing was your father was nothing to do with you?'

'Howard? Not really. He just seemed to slip away. Memories of him when I was little, turning up at the house in Rio, bringing presents but then going out again at once with my mother, had been overtaken by other thoughts as I grew up. Realising what he'd done to Lisa. To me. In Brazil, when I came face to face with the fact that he couldn't have been my father, it didn't seem to matter any more. It was as if I'd outgrown the idea of him.'

Nicholas thought this over, finding a bleak comfort in it. 'They must have been a mad lot,' he commented after a moment. So much for the loves and lives of the older generation.

'But it's different for you,' Cristi reminded him. 'Your mother was married to Archie when you were born. Legally he *is* your father.'

'Yup, I know. And I always feel he is. Like I said, if you don't think about it it all seems kind of normal.'

'But you're not happy about it now?'

'It's not just now, not because of the baby.'

Cristi waited, with an ache of compassion that he should have these huge doubts to deal with.

'Do you think anyone still knows where my mother is?' Out the question came at last. 'Would there be any way of finding her?'

God, what have I started? Cristi thought in alarm. I've stirred up my own life to the point where I can barely cope with it, and destroyed Nicholas's peace of mind as well.

'Do you really want to know that?' she asked.

He understood what she was saying, and he turned it over one last time in his mind before answering, 'Yes, I think I do. Just to *know*.' But he couldn't begin to put into words all the things he wanted to know.

'You realise it could be opening a real can of worms?'

Nicholas's face pinched. It was a crucial moment. 'But you've found a way to deal with it?' he asked.

'Yes, I think so.'

That lay ahead, and wasn't up for discussion.

Watching Nicholas's set face Cristi could almost feel the new adult thoughts being taken aboard, and she suddenly saw him with a fresh clarity. How had she, with her eye trained to observe, not noticed the changing structure of his face, the lengthening limbs, the man emerging from the boy's body, as the skeleton of the model's figure is visible to the artist's eye.

'You know, Nick,' she said, 'the best thing would be to talk to Archie. He'd understand.'

'He'd mind, though, wouldn't he?'

'He'd mind a lot more if he thought you were stewing over it and hiding your feelings from him.'

'Yeah, maybe you're right.'

'You know you can talk to him about anything. And if you really want to get in touch with your mother, I'm sure he'd do anything he could to help you.'

'But it's not only about my mother, is it?' The goaded note was there again.

'What else then? What are you talking about?'

'It's obvious, isn't it? Oh look, forget it.'

'Nick, what? Archie is always willing to—'

'I can't exactly talk to him about Drumveyn, can I?' Nicholas exploded, coming to his feet with a violent movement.

'About Drumveyn? What do you mean? What's Drumveyn got to do with this?' Cristi was aware of a chill of apprehension. Would dragging things into the light end in exposing matters better left hidden?

'I can't tell you,' Nicholas muttered. 'It'll sound so naff and awful.'

Apprehension or not, Cristi knew it couldn't be left there. 'You'll have to tell me. What about Drumveyn?'

'Oh, don't be so *dim*.' He was standing at the window now, still with his back to her. 'If this baby's a boy he'll be a Napier, won't he? Archie's real son.'

'So? Oh, Nick.' Cristi went to him, slipping a hand through his arm. 'You mean a boy would be the heir. Would one day inherit—'

'You see, it makes me sound grabby and as if I wanted to take things. But it's not like that,' he protested passionately, knowing he couldn't put this into words.

'I know what you mean. You care about Drumveyn. Being the eldest son is your place. It's not about having or getting. I understand that. But nothing will change that. And what's more, Archie would be devastated if he knew it had even crossed your mind for a second. You are his son. That's how he sees you. And technically, you are, There's no question about it. Nick.' She shook his arm, making him turn to her. 'You know that, don't you?'

For a moment he looked as though he would accept what she was saying. Then he shouted, shaking with a desperate and uncharacteristic rage, 'No, I don't know! This baby is *his*. How can it be the same?'

'You're talking rubbish. Yes, you are. But here's what we're going to do. Are you listening? We're going to say to Archie every single thing you've said to me.'

'*No!*' Nicholas swung round on her in disbelief. 'I trusted you, Cristi. If you say a word to anyone I'll never forgive you.'

'I won't say anything without you there. But you owe this to Archie. Look how up-front he and Pauly have always been about this whole business of adoption and who we were and where we came from. They did it to protect us. There'll be more hurt done if this is brushed under the carpet than if it's dealt with openly. And anyway, all you're feeling, wondering about your mother, insecure because of the baby, is natural. You'll only torture yourself if you go on bottling it up.'

'I told you because I thought you wouldn't tell.'

'Well, now that you have told me I want to help. I'm your big sister, remember.'

'Oh, yeah, look at us,' he jeered, but Cristi knew the moment of helpless rage was behind them and that he would come round. He had been seeking much, much more than the release of telling.

'Look, everybody'll be home soon. I'm going down to get something organised for tea. But remember,' she said, as she went to the door, 'if you want any help, with anything, I'm there for you. OK?'

'OK.'

Nicholas stood very still after she'd gone, trying to work his way back to calm. The room felt charged with emotion, as though some tremendous battle had been waged there. Not a battle perhaps, but some life-altering event. He was glad he'd talked at last. And glad he had Cristi on his side.

Chapter Thirty-one

The narrow lane between its high banks descended at a startling gradient round a series of blind corners.

'Well, I suppose people do come up and down here on a regular basis,' Cristi commented philosophically.

Nicholas tried to smile, but Cristi could feel the tension bouncing off him and made no more attempts at conversation. As she had already found, distances seemed tiny here, so different from the empty miles of home, and in no time they were at water level, making a tight turn into a carpark before running out of road altogether.

'What a fabulous place.' The sheltered inlet was clearly a gift to sailors. Also, to judge from the prosperous-looking bungalows and done-up cottages on the opposite shore, a pensioners' paradise. But Cristi knew, turning to the cluster of houses on this side of the creek, that she was almost as tense as Nicholas.

'I'll ask at the pub. We can check about lunch as well,

then we can always say we've got something sorted out. Unless they go in for total shut-down here as they do in Scotland in January. Coming?'

Nicholas shook his head. Today his face was peaky and vulnerably boyish, as though he'd abandoned the idea of growing into his new appearance.

The pub gave the impression of having opened its doors a couple of centuries ago to a local trade of farmers, fishermen and, no doubt, in this tucked-away corner of the Devon coast, smugglers, and of having resisted change ever since. Bar lunches started at twelve. Blackstone Cottage? It wasn't in the village, but a couple of miles away over the headland.

This small extra delay seemed to Cristi to wring out the last drop of agony. She hadn't been involved in communications about their journey, but she thought someone might have extracted more precise directions. The momentousness of what they were doing struck her forcibly, and she felt shaky as she went to the car.

'Not in the village, it seems. We go back up to the top, then head towards the coast. Not far. You OK?'

Nicholas nodded, concentrating on the boats across the inlet, most out of the water for the winter, a few lying to their moorings with neatly laced covers.

Cristi, glancing at him, didn't drive off at once. 'Look, Nick, we don't have to do this today,' she said quietly. 'If it's too difficult, or if you want more time to think, just say.'

Still he gazed away from her, and she could see the rigid muscles in his jaw. He said nothing.

'Don't think that because we've come so far you have to go through with it. That's all I'm saying.'

'But the letters. It's all arranged.'

'Things can be unarranged.'

Cristi felt that it was Nicholas whose feelings deserved to be considered, not those of the mother who had refused to so much as take him in her arms when he was born.

'We can always phone. You don't have to feel you're committed to anything. It's your choice.'

Archie's lawyer, and Cecil's, had made the arrangements. This means of contact, it turned out, had always been in place. Though he had said nothing, the discovery had shaken Nicholas, increasing his feeling of unknown challenges lurking, stirred into life by his own obscure but compulsive need.

To Cristi it had seemed a cold way to do things, and she dreaded an equally cold reception for him. Yet the message had been unequivocal. Cecil wanted them to come. Silence ticked in the little car. There was no other vehicle in the rough-hewn parking space between cliff and shore. Gulls wheeled with occasional thin cries, and Cristi suppressed a shiver at the mournfulness of the sound over the grey water, against a grey sky.

'We'd better do it.'

'Yes?'

Nicholas nodded more definitely, and she saw with anxiety that his skin had a greenish tinge, last summer's freckles unnaturally visible. A welter of feelings rocked her at this evidence of what he was going through. What would it have been like if she had found herself minutes away from confronting her own mother?

And what must it be like for Cecil, waiting, knowing they were on their way, after the years of silence? Years perhaps of guilt and regret? Fragmented images of Cecil returned: a slim, dark-haired woman, beautiful, groomed and elegant. How odd, it occurred to Cristi, that the impression of slimness had been retained. Cecil must have been, had been, pregnant with Nicholas for the whole time Cristi had known her. Her child's eye had obviously registered no change after the first impression had been assimilated. But the chief memory was of Cecil as someone aloof, a person held in awe, a half-perceived, distant adult who had never descended to a child's level.

She pushed away the shadowy memories. What mattered now was how Nicholas, a boy of fourteen, was going to cope with this meeting. Seeing the state he was in, Cristi asked herself guiltily what she had been thinking of to encourage this journey of discovery, and make it, in practical terms anyway, easy for him to undertake?

But he was clearly determined to finish it. Up the hill they wound, meeting no one, and turned onto an exposed road where the full light from the Channel met them, its waters opening silvery and dazzling after the grey quietness of the secluded creek. Rolling fields, a farmhouse, cottages with gardens protected by thick hedges from the winds which must often buffet over here. It wasn't an environment where Cristi would have expected to find sophisticated Cecil, whose dislike of Drumveyn and rural life had always been part of the legend.

A white-painted name-board, a brief drive plunging to a house set below the brow of the hill, its rear tucked into the slope, its face looking out to sea.

Did Nicholas, getting out, feel his limbs as stiff and reluctant as hers, Cristi wondered, and was his heart thumping too? How would Cecil meet them? Would the remembered aloofness chill and wound this boy, her son, from whom she had so adamantly turned her face?

No vehicle was parked outside. No one appeared or looked from a window. The porch door at the gable end of the house remained shut.

Coming round the car, Cristi reached a hand to touch Nicholas's arm. 'Come on. It'll be OK.'

Because of strung-up nerves the wait seemed endless. Was the bell not working? Cristi knocked.

'Maybe there's another door. Let's go round to the front and have a look.'

'No!' Nicholas's voice was too sharp and high. 'We can't do that. It's all a mistake, let's go.'

'Listen.'

A voice calling. The door knob starting to turn, not going fully round.

They stared at it, uncertain. The voice again, 'Please open the door and come in.'

As Cristi grasped the knob she felt the faint pressure of another hand. She pushed the door open gingerly.

She had remembered Cecil as tall. But then she had been a child. Confusion seized her at the sight of this small, bony woman hunched over two sticks, yet even so there was never a moment's doubt in her mind that it was Cecil. A Cecil so ravaged and altered that Cristi could barely suppress a gasp of shock. The sleek dark hair was white, the thin face, though made up, lined and haggard. But she'd been married to Archie, and Archie was only in his mid-forties. This woman looked twenty years older than him at least. Cristi struggled to adjust.

'I do apologise for the delay. Cristi, how lovely to see you again. And Nicholas.'

Cecil's pleasure sounded genuine, but the words, her manner, were courteous and formal, giving no hint of how painful she had found it to pronounce his name.

There would be no tearful falling on necks in this reunion, was Cristi's first thought. Well, no one had expected that. A little spurt of disconnected nothings about finding the way, asking directions in the village, took them inside. With feelings jangled, the moments a blur as they got the door shut and pressed back out of the way to allow Cecil to turn – unimaginable to think how this must be for Nicholas – Cristi turned right as Cecil indicated, and went down two steps into a room of light and stunning colour which ran the width of the cottage, and gave the impression of being hung high over the gleaming water. Her artist's soul responded with an indrawn breath of delight, then she deliberately set aside its beauty. That must wait its turn. She turned to see if Cecil needed help negotiating the steps.

Nicholas hung back in an agony of uncertainty, instinct and training telling him to help, a less clear instinct warning him not to. He felt doltish, clumsy, too hot in the warm room, desperately wishing they had never come. What did this elderly stranger, dressed in these weird clothes (Cecil was wearing black velvet trousers and an embroidered and beaded waistcoat over a coral-pink silk shirt) have to do with him? She'd greeted them as though they were the most ordinary of callers, and he was beginning to feel the whole thing was some wild dream from which it would be a big relief to wake.

But suddenly, as Cecil reached what was clearly her chair, with a clutter of objects on the table drawn close beside it, and was about to sit down, she paused, making an awkward half-turn towards them.

'Please,' she said, as though she had had no intention of saying this and the words were being forced from her, 'don't think because I greet you in this way that I'm indifferent. Truly, I can't tell you what this means to me, how grateful I am to you for—'

Her voice wavered, and she was unable to go on. She stood bent over the sticks clutched awkwardly in one hand, and began to shake. Her head was down, but she couldn't hide the way the muscles of her face were twisting out of control.

Nicholas, rooted where he stood, swung round on Cristi in urgent, voiceless appeal.

But Cristi was there. 'Oh, Cecil, *please* don't!' The impression that assistance would not be welcome was forgotten. This was too poignant to bear. Cristi leapt to put her arms round those bowed shoulders, horrified, even in such a moment of charged emotion, to feel how fragile and fleshless they were.

Nicholas, too, made a small move forward, his jaw tight, his eyes wretched. He longed to break through his own sense of constraint, but dreaded doing the wrong thing. He could feel pity for this woman, yet how could he feel those things he was supposed to feel? How could he feel she was his mother? His feet seemed too big, his hands inept. He would trip up, knock things over, do damage; yet he wanted to do something.

It all rushed by in a second. Cristi was gently lowering Cecil into the chair, bending over her to say gently, 'It's all right, Cecil. Everything's all right. We're here now. We can take our time.'

'Oh, Cristi.' Cecil sounded as though she was half-laughing. 'You always were so warm and generous. I remember that well. But you won't remember me.' Tense again. 'You were only eight or nine. Why should—?'

'Of course I remember you,' Cristi interrupted firmly. 'You were there the whole of the first summer I was at Drumveyn. How could I forget?'

'Oh, God, it was so very long ago.' Cecil put a hand, crimped into a claw, to her head. Then, as though recalling the purpose of this visit, angry with herself for not having made it her first priority, she lifted her head and met her son's eyes bravely.

'Nicholas,' she said, and the effort she made to keep her voice even could be heard. 'I want you to know how immensely delighted and grateful I am that you've come here to see me. Please be sure of that.'

She held out her hand, and Nicholas stepped forward in one jolted stride, his face colouring, and took it in his, with the look he might have had if someone had given him a new-born baby to hold. Thrilled to find he was trusted, but terrified of doing the wrong thing.

'So much to say.' Cecil's voice was harsh. 'Far too much. So many years. But, for now, I want to tell you that there hasn't been a day when I haven't regretted what I did. I've no intention of putting you through dreadful outpourings of remorse, that would be unforgivable, but I want you to know this — if the time comes when you want to ask me any questions, in order to understand why I did what I did, I shall try most faithfully to answer them. I'm ready to talk now, today, if that's what you'd like, though my own feeling would be that we should try to get to know each other a little before we attempt it.'

For a tortured moment Nicholas couldn't remember how to speak, how to shape words. His tongue felt huge, his mouth stiff. He was conscious of Cristi, ready to leap in to help him, but knew that finding some response was up to him. With an effort, he got out, 'I just needed to meet you. It's great that you let me come. Really. I know it's— I mean, it can't be—' Then the words he wanted suddenly came, as though a separate, more mature part of him had come to life in answer to adult pain and need. 'I didn't want this to hurt you. Coming to see you, I mean. I know I wanted it for me. If it has hurt you then I'm sorry.'

Cecil's lips quivered. She closed her eyes for a second, holding herself very still, concentrating her resources. 'No, not hurt. I feel so thankful that you wanted to come. I didn't deserve it. And when the time is right, we shall talk.' She nodded, a stiff, restricted movement, and could say no more.

The ebbing tension could be felt. Cristi found her muscles uncramping, and was objectively aware for a second of how close, physically, they were to each other, a little knot of oddly linked people. She had been afraid they would never find their way to this point, and then it had rushed upon them out of nowhere, as though the wave of feelings had to rise and break. Now they were freed to find places to sit, give Drumveyn news and greetings, look around them, comment on the lovely room, hear about the alterations Cecil had made to the house, and the wild Channel gales which could assault it.

Cristi, going after a while to make coffee, caught herself thinking how natural it felt to be doing so. Well, we're nearly family, she reminded herself, her mind once more reverting to that summer of her childhood. Then, realising how far she was from taking it in, she remembered that here, in this unknown house, Nicholas *was* family. How strange.

As she found what she needed, her eye was attracted by the superb design and imaginative colours of the kitchen. But of course, that was Cecil's forte. It was she who had designed the kitchen at Drumveyn, with its Portuguese tiles and subtle limed oak, a room Cristi loved. How fabulous it would be to create a kitchen of her own. At the Croft of Ellig: treacherous image immediately springing to mind. But that was not for her.

Flurried by these thoughts, she was struck by the

strangeness of the situation. There, in the next room, was Archie's first wife. Nicholas's mother. A member, in a sense, of the wider Drumveyn family. Cristi listened for voices. Yes, they were talking. She had wondered if Nicholas would follow her out, but though he'd made a tiny movement as if to do so, he had sat back resolutely in his chair. Darling Nick, he was dealing brilliantly with this. The sensitivity he'd shown, gauchely expressed as it had been, was so like Archie's. Cristi checked. The comparison had been so unthinking it had almost passed unnoticed. She was so used to thinking of Nicholas as Archie's son. He so easily could be, both in looks and personality. Nurture and example had to account for it, yet it was hard to believe it was only that.

Taking the tray into the sitting-room, holding it aside to see where she was going, Cristi thought the steps must be a nightmare for Cecil. How did she manage, and why was she living alone in such a remote spot?

Putting the question as tactfully as she could, Cristi was relieved to hear that Cecil was looked after, more or less full time, by the neighbouring farmer's sister.

'So fortunate for me,' Cecil said, a brisk note warning that undue concern would not be welcome. 'They inherited the farm jointly, and when brother married, Olive refused to move out. Brother's new wife, however, made it clear she intended to be boss, so Olive decided to sit tight. She won't go far afield in case she can't get back in, but she'll come this far, because it means she can nip home when she's least expected. In spite of the consequent erratic time-keeping she looks after me well. She's a little possessive, however, and wasn't at all pleased when I said I'd like to be on my own today.'

Cecil's voice, light and ironic as she recounted this, became bleak again, as though the terrors that had haunted her as she waited had flooded back. 'I didn't know, of course, how — how it would be.'

'But as you see, it's fine.' Cristi hated to see that look of self-doubt. Cecil had always been so sure of herself and her views. 'The hard part's over now.'

'Yes.' But the pain behind the smile Cecil summoned gave Cristi a glimpse of what she had gone through, and must still go through. 'Anyway,' Cecil went on more positively, 'Olive left something ready for lunch. You will stay, won't you?'

'No, really, we didn't mean to put you to any trouble. We can easily get something at the pub.'

'I promise you it's no trouble of any kind. Olive and I have the whole thing down to a fine art. I switch on the microwave, she does the rest.' Cecil looked at them in turn. 'I should so much like you to stay.'

It was what Cristi had hoped for. Not lunch prepared by the farmer's sister, but that the visit would evolve naturally, giving Cecil and Nicholas more time together. Cristi had thought, and Nicholas had agreed, that if all went well they could ask Cecil to have dinner with them at the comfortable hotel they'd found in Modbury. It was obviously not feasible, and this drove Cristi to ask, in spite of Cecil's reserve on the subject, 'Cecil, I know you have Olive to look after you, but do you get out at all? How do you manage about that?'

Nicholas had helped to clear away lunch, and was now loading the dishwasher, and Cristi took her chance, more and more worried that these surroundings couldn't be suitable for Cecil. 'Is it arthritis? Please don't mind my asking, but you look as if you're in such pain.'

'I've been arthritic for years.' Cecil hesitated, then made up her mind. 'More ominously, however, I've been diagnosed as having motor neurone disease.'

Unable to hide her dismay, Cristi cried, 'Oh, Cecil, no. That's awful. I'm so sorry.'

She grappled to assemble the few facts she'd heard about this rare disease, hoping the little she thought she knew was exaggerated. But no, as Cecil rapidly and matter-of-factly summed up, the early signs, of drifting thoughts and lack of concentration, were soon followed by the loss of use of various muscle groups, and eventually by a failure of the breathing mechanism.

Cristi stared at her, words sticking in her throat. 'But you'll – I mean, there must be some treatment.'

'No, there's no treatment. All one can do is look after one's general health.' She didn't add that after diagnosis there was rarely hope of surviving for more than six or seven years, usually less.

'But Cecil, living here—' Cristi suddenly saw the cottage as a prison. Cecil couldn't drive, she couldn't walk, couldn't garden. And crucially, she couldn't work, finding fulfilment in the creativity which had given her life meaning in the past.

Nicholas came in. 'I put the food in the fridge,' he said, 'except the cheese. I put that in that larder. Is that OK?'

'What an exceptionally well-brought-up young man,' Cecil said lightly, smiling her thanks at him, and the poignancy of that dealt Cristi another blow. I'm not sure I'm going to be able to get through this, she thought almost in panic.

As though understanding, Cecil said, 'But you've hardly seen anything of the house. I'd love you to see my studio. I can show you if you can bear the slow pace, but if you'd rather look around on your own do say.'

'Don't be silly, of course we wouldn't.'

But the studio was not a soothing place, with its message of impressive talents and a lively artistic imagination laid waste for ever.

'When I first came to Devon I had a flat in Plymouth, down at the Barbican. But it was too tacky and touristy, so I retreated here. Ultimately not wise, perhaps. Apart from the practical difficulties, I see so few people nowadays.'

In such cool phrases Cristi could hear the old Cecil, but now the incisiveness was dulled by a sombre knowledge of having taken too many wrong turnings.

Today, however, was not the time to enter into any discussion about the future. Cristi was only thankful, as she drove away, that the first contact had been made.

'All right?' she asked Nicholas.

She had expected the usual 'Fine' or 'Cool', but to her surprise he clearly needed to pour out his feelings. He talked all the way back to the hotel, about the house, Cecil's paintings which had surprised and impressed him, and about her state of health. His mind, as Cristi's had been, was turning over questions about how she could cope where she was, but Cristi said nothing as yet about Cecil's private revelations.

Nicholas also wanted to hear, reviewing the old stories in a new light, everything Cristi could remember about the summer when he was born. Even more movingly, he tried to express something of his astonished sense of relief that obscure shadows had been lifted for ever.

Chapter Thirty-two

Archie and Pauly lay close in the big bed. Not the one where Archie's parents had lain so rigidly apart.

When Pauly cuddled up she meant it, Archie thought gratefully, as with a cautious movement he tried to get rid of some of the hair between his cheek and her forehead. He had thought her asleep, but she mumbled, 'Sorry,' lifted her head and with a groggy shake sent the hair fanning out across the pillow away from him, then flopped down on his shoulder again.

Good job I'm built on solid lines myself, Archie thought. She'd flatten a smaller bloke.

Whether the humour or his wakefulness transmitted itself to Pauly, with an effort she resisted sinking back into sleep. 'You OK?'

'Thinking.'

She levered herself up with unexpected vigour and leant over him. 'What about?'

'Sweetheart, you might as well lie down again,' he pointed out. 'You can't see me.'

'I know, but it makes me feel I'm taking an interest. And it keeps me awake. No, but seriously. Are you still worrying about Nicholas?'

'I feel so damned guilty. I should have seen how he'd react. And I can't believe I've let him go to see Cecil, even with Cristi to look after him. He's far too young to deal with this sort of thing.'

'Better talk then, if it's worrying you so much.' Pauly lay down again but this time on her back.

'Oh, you've heard most of it. Anyway, my brain's going round in circles, I've thought about it so much.'

'But you've only talked about part of it, haven't you? I mean, you were shattered that Nicholas thought the baby, specially if it's a boy, would alter his future and everything. We've aired that one thoroughly.'

She appeared to weigh this judiciously, as if it could be measured, and Archie grinned in spite of his racked feelings. He knew she was doing her best.

'It was a bit devastating, you have to admit,' he protested. 'To have been so blind and complacent, I mean. It was a natural thing to think, from Nicholas's perspective, though it seems so preposterous to us.'

It didn't occur to either of them that Pauly, who had no connection with Nicholas, might have thought differently, or have had some justification in seeing her own child as Archie's legitimate heir.

'Right,' she said, 'let's have the light on.'

Squaring up for business, Archie recognised in the

brief upheaval. He loved her at such moments, when she recognised that her normal, sweeping, get-on-with-the-next-thing approach wouldn't do, and applied herself to what she called 'getting heavy'.

'OK, we've been there, done that,' she began, settling herself comfortably. 'You put it straight with Nicholas and I talked to him and so did Madeleine. I'm sure he won't worry about that again. I know you're bothered by this sudden urge to meet Cecil, but there's something else besides, isn't there? What is it you're not saying? What's keeping you awake, more to the point? You never have trouble sleeping.'

Archie hesitated for a moment more, his hand cupping her head, his fingers deep in the soft warm hair. 'It doesn't seem fair to talk to you about Cecil, that's all.'

'Well, yes, I can see you might feel that,' Pauly conceded. 'But I don't mind. After all, remember, she was your wife when I first knew you. You were an established, grown-up couple to me. It would be silly to mind you talking about her now.'

'We hardly were a couple.' Archie's face was grim as the memories swarmed back. 'We were miles apart even then, on completely different tacks about how to live, what we wanted about this place, about the baby.'

'She was so beautiful.' Pauly was pursuing her own memories. How dazzling and confident a figure Cecil had seemed to her.

'She was,' Archie agreed. He drew his head back so that he could look at Pauly's face. 'But do you imagine for a second that that cool groomed beauty can compare with

your warm, sexy loveliness? And now that you're pregnant you're even more beautiful, and I love you more
every day.'

The conversation nearly lost its way there, but when
Pauly had made up her mind to get to the bottom of
something she liked to stick to it, and it was she who said
after a moment, 'That's all very nice, thank you, but to go
back to Cecil. You did love her.'

'I did,' Archie said quietly.

'But you're worried about how she'll behave to Nicholas?'

Archie smiled, pulling her close. Pauly saw herself as a
person very much on the surface, good for making
puddings and applying sticking plaster and drying tears,
as she said herself, but she had the astuteness which goes
with absolute honesty and fearless straight thinking, and
had gone accurately to the core of his concern.

'I can't believe I've let him risk being rebuffed, or
treated in a way he won't understand. He's such an open,
direct person himself. Cecil doesn't know him, and
probably won't have a clue how to deal with him. I
shudder to think of him getting tangled in the sort of
emotional hang-ups she goes in for. If he was determined
to see her I should have taken him down myself, and
made sure he couldn't be hurt.'

'No, we agreed that wouldn't have worked. Cristi was
the right person. She understands more of what he's
going through than any of us, don't forget.'

'I know,' Archie groaned. 'And that's another thing
I'm falling down over. Cristi's pretty well gone under-

ground about this whole Brazilian business, yet I've never made the time to talk to her and find out what she really wants to do.'

'I know. I've been worrying about her too. Her sparkle seems to have gone, and that's so unlike her. But there wasn't a minute over Christmas. Anyway,' Pauly dragged the conversation back on course once more. They had to get up not too many hours from now. 'If you had gone with Nicholas, he'd probably have been totally inhibited. How could he begin to make his own contact with Cecil with you there?'

'You're right. I know.' Archie's voice was resigned. 'But Cecil can be such a cold fish. She finds it incredibly hard to warm to people. She always seemed to hold herself on the fringe of whatever was going on, and I'm damned if I ever knew whether she genuinely wanted in or not.'

Pauly didn't feel qualified to comment on this. 'I wonder why she's ended up in Devon,' she remarked. 'I'd have imagined her, if she wasn't in London, somewhere like Paris or Venice or Rome.'

'I wondered that too.' Picturing Cecil in a rural scene had stirred painful reminders of her disdain for Drum-veyn and its way of life. She had only come here during her pregnancy, when she had had to give up work anyway, partly as a healthier alternative to London but also, since Archie had recently inherited the estate, as the 'right' place to bring up their child. Everything thought out. Nothing spontaneous.

Archie pulled himself back to the present, drawing

Pauly against him, his face in her neck, his hand on the swell of a splendid breast. There was warmth, generosity and love here in copious abundance. And this glorious creature was soon to bear his child. He was the luckiest man on earth.

Cecil lay awake, listening to the gusting of the wind against her bedroom window, carefully holding her emaciated body in the position which meant least pain. She knew she wouldn't sleep. After Nicholas and Cristi had left today she had remained unmoving for hours in her big chair, her mind taking a slow, sad journey. Still, now, it ranged through long-ago scenes, played back long-ago conversations.

A life always at one remove from the life other people led; that was the bleak retrospect she saw. The shifting relationships of the adults in her childhood world had left her adrift, turning her into an emotional retard, an emotional cripple. And now she was a cripple in the literal physical sense. But that she had faced, and very soon she would deal with the changes it forced upon her, succumbing to necessity, abandoning this last retreat and adapting to the dreaded proximity of strangers.

That had to come. It was not her chief preoccupation at the moment. What filled her mind in the dragging hours of the winter night was a different decision, different yet in a way the most important part of that old story begun so long ago. Writing the final chapter, as only she had the knowledge to do. Closing the book. For her anyway, but perhaps not for Nicholas.

How extraordinary it was that he should have initiated the contact just now, when she had been, in such an agony of doubt and resistance, approaching the point of doing so herself. And now she had seen him. The tears couldn't be held back as she thought of the tall, open-faced, good-looking teenager, his direct, honest eyes, his air of integrity, and the way he had dealt so sensitively and generously with a scene no boy of his age should have been asked to face.

Her son. For the first time the words had reality, and Cecil wept.

Cristi phoned, as promised, after breakfast. She and Cecil had agreed that it would be be wise to let reactions to the first visit be assimilated before another was planned. But Cristi was positive that Nicholas wanted to come back.

The news shook Cecil with a humble and grateful pleasure. Good as yesterday's meeting with Nicholas had been, better than she deserved or had dared to hope, it had been harrowing too. She wouldn't have been surprised if he'd felt that was enough of raw emotion. After all, he had achieved what he wanted. He had seen her, seen where she lived, made the essential contact.

She took the chance, however, having established that Cristi was alone, to make absolutely sure of certain facts.

'I dread so much making a blunder,' she confessed. 'I just need to be sure of what he's been told.'

'He's been told the truth.' The faint note of surprise in Cristi's voice, though it held no critical overtones, swept Cecil back almost as nothing else had done to the faraway days of her marriage. Of course. With Archie it could not be otherwise.

All the same, it was essential to establish specific facts, and Cecil ploughed on. 'So he knows Archie isn't his father?'

'Of course he does. When Peta and Josie were adopted Archie and Pauly decided it was important to be absolutely open with all the children.'

'They know that Archie—?' Cecil hesitated. Cristi had been a child when Cecil first knew her. They belonged to different generations. It seemed hardly appropriate even now to put such questions to her.

'That Archie was unlikely to have children of his own? Yes, that was explained to them. And Archie felt Nicholas was old enough to know about how you – how you wanted to have your own baby rather than adopt.'

'Right,' Cecil said. Dear Cristi, with her ready tact. And dear Archie too, whose honesty had smoothed the path yet again.

'But look, Cecil,' Cristi said hurriedly. 'I wanted a chance to talk to you without Nick there. I've sent him out to get a couple of things. Although yesterday I know there was nothing in his mind beyond seeing you, and it meant a huge amount to him, there was something else behind it. Something that triggered the decision to come and find you.'

'What else?' Cecil, her own decision pre-eminent in her mind, spoke sharply.

'Pauly's going to have a baby.'

'*What?*' Cecil was rocked by the wash of emotions which surged up at the news. Disbelief, resistance, violent jealousy of Pauly, and an aching sense of loss for something once within her grasp which she had so blindly thrown away. 'Pauly is?' She made a huge effort to bring her voice down to more normal levels. 'You said nothing about that yesterday.'

There was a fractional pause before Cristi replied. 'It wasn't what yesterday was about, was it?'

'Archie's baby?'

'Yes.'

Cecil's brain, having absorbed the initial shock, struggled to take in other implications.

'This is the real reason why Nicholas wanted to find me, isn't it?'

'No, as I said, it was the trigger. He'd been thinking about it long before that because of my going to Brazil, getting in touch with my family and so on.'

Cecil had heard about the Fonseca inheritance and Cristi's travels yesterday, though Cristi had said nothing about the hope that had lain behind them, or the final destruction of that hope.

'Hang on, Nick's here,' Cristi was saying. 'We haven't arranged a time. When would suit you . . . ?'

Cecil lay back in her big chair, her thoughts drifting and swirling. Sometimes she could hardly disentangle which conversations had taken place and which had gone on in her head. Why had the fact that Pauly was to have Archie's child dealt her such a blow? She should be happy for them. Well, she was, but that seemed on an entirely different plane from her bitter, groping sense of loss.

Then, gradually, she saw that nothing could have been more apposite to her purpose. The news, so entirely unexpected, had thrown Nicholas into a turmoil of insecurity, and she was the only person in the world who could offer a counterbalance to this shock.

The moment was close now. To tell at last the secret which only she and one other person knew. To reveal to Nicholas the truth it was his right to learn, the truth which might alter his whole life. Withholding it was to deny him something he should have; revealing it could only enrich him. Only she could give him this, and giving it would enable her, before it was too late, to enter the mysterious, longed-for world of human interaction where other people lived.

As the little car climbed away up the steep drive in the dusk Cecil knew she was more alone than she had ever been before, and nothing would change it now. But in spite of the icy desolation it brought she had been right. That was beyond question. She had seen in time that what mattered, before all else, was Nicholas.

Until the moment when she saw him again, she had been so sure. It was his absolute right to know that, when she and Archie had agreed – no, be accurate, when she had persuaded Archie – to have a child by donor sperm, she had made a private arrangement of her own. No random genetic mix could be risked for her child.

She had always pursued perfection, worked hard for it

and taken for granted that it could be achieved. It had been one of her greatest qualities and greatest failings. However, she had kept that refinement of the plan to herself. How good it would be now to be able to look back and say she had done it for Archie's sake, but it had been because she needed to feel in control. Harsh truth, but there was no point in trying to evade it now.

She had chosen the donor of the sperm. She had selected someone of good physique, good looks and good background. A man of intelligence and ambition; a high-flyer. As a long-time admirer of hers, he had not been hard to persuade. He was a well-known figure nowadays. Someone Nicholas could be proud of, the key to himself. A superb gift, surely, and one in her power to give.

But thank God, thank God, at the last minute some grace had been given her to see past such weighing of material advantages. Face to face with Nicholas's honest eyes, his eagerness to get to know her better tinged with an attractive shyness, she had recognised in time how vulnerable he was, how unsuspecting. As though a shutter had opened in her brain, she had seen with horror the harm the release of this secret could do, its ripples widening and spreading into other lives.

She had discovered at the last moment that the impulse to tell was about herself, not Nicholas. By giving him this information she would bring him nothing but confusion and pain, rocking the foundations of his world, and setting him off, in all probability, on another quest, creating who knew what grief and chaos. He had accepted the facts as Archie had given them to him. That in itself was impressive for someone of his age.

The biggest thing she could do for him, she had realised with appalled shame to have for one moment thought otherwise, was to let him go from here, having made the contact with her which so obviously mattered to him, with his secure and loving world intact.

The biggest thing that she could do for him was to let this secret die with her. He didn't need this knowledge. He had a father. The thought of how her revelation would have affected Archie made her shiver.

As silence filled the house once more, an unfamiliar sensation crept through her. She had thrown away the one major card she had held, the card she had in some warped way believed would win her Nicholas's affection, and give her a place in his life. But it had been a sacrifice made on his behalf, and that brought astonishing comfort.

It helped a little as she had made her painful way down the steps into her empty, waiting room.

Chapter Thirty-three

It was time to go. There was, Cristi knew, no excuse to delay any longer, no further decision to make.

As she walked and rode about the estate and glen, consciously tucking away memories, her thoughts were often on Luis, the ranch, and the dazzling summer heat of another country. Images revolved of the sunlit grasslands, the mountain-ringed beauty of Guanabara Bay, and the friendly city of Porto Alegre where she had felt so much at home. Dougal, so near at hand at the Croft of Ellig, seemed to have vanished into another world.

Nicholas, Peta and Josie had gone back to school. Impossible to lump them together as 'the children' any more. Cristi was still impressed to think of the courage and maturity with which Nicholas had dealt with the trip to Devon.

She had been glad they'd had such a long drive home. Nicholas, after silences charged with thoughts she could almost feel, had at last been able to release them in bursts of talk, saying things he would never have been able to say to Archie and Pauly, or to anyone else, and she knew this had helped him.

Once home, he had left it largely to Cristi to describe Cecil's circumstances, her isolated situation, her changed looks, and the way she had welcomed them. Cristi was able to appreciate, as Nicholas could not, the way this could be told, openly, without fears as to how it would be received.

There would be no jealous resentment from Pauly at hearing about a former wife; she didn't see things in that way. There would be no concealment by Archie of his dismay at learning of Cecil's present plight. Madeleine and Tom, too, were full of concern at the sad story. Everyone agreed that it had been right for Nicholas to go, and Cristi – at present particularly aware of anything which affirmed the attitudes and values with which she had been brought up – was moved by this generosity.

She talked privately to Archie and Pauly about Cecil's illness and its prognosis.

'I haven't told Nicholas. It seemed too much for him to know about all at once.'

'You were right,' Archie said definitely. 'I shall tell him in due course, but it would be very hard for him to feel he's found his mother, only to discover she won't be in his life for very long. Poor old Cecil, nothing ever seems easy for her.'

The unspoken assumption, that with the contact made there was no question of it being broken again, filled Cristi with admiration and gratitude for Archie's steadfast good sense and capacity to give.

What she was not aware of, deep in her own pre-occupations, nearer every day to the moment when she must put her plans into action, were the discussions about what, if anything, could be done to help her. But there was a general feeling that, large as the decisions before her were, she must be allowed to approach them in her own way and in her own time.

The unnatural quietness of the first days of the new term had overtaken the house, just as outside its walls a hard frost after snow held the glen in stillness and silence. Only Broy went ceaselessly about, plopping busily up and down stairs, checking deserted rooms, coming to stand in front of Pauly, gazing at her with sad eyes and girning softly.

Picking him up, cuddling his plump warm body close, Pauly said, 'I feel like curling up on beds and whimpering myself. How I hate it when they go back. It gets worse every term.'

'You'll soon have somebody here all the time,' Cristi reminded her, laying a hand on the lovely firmness of Pauly's bulge. Pauly pressed her hand there, and they stood for a moment in silence, heads bent. It was an extraordinary and tender intimacy, and one Cristi loved, to know that under her hand, in its warm dark floating safety, was a small unknown person who was part of Pauly, part of Archie, who would be dear to them all.

'You know I have to go back, don't you?' Cristi seized the moment of closeness to help her to say this. She had already booked her flight, but had found it surprisingly hard to find the right time to talk about it.

'Yes, we realise that,' Pauly said quietly. She waited, hoping Cristi would add more. 'There's so much still unresolved,' she tried again.

Cristi nodded.

'But we don't *want* you to go,' Pauly couldn't resist adding in a little wail, tipping Broy onto the floor so that she could put her arms round Cristi instead. 'Especially now. I know it's selfish of me, but I'd so love you to be here when the—'

But recalling Archie's admonitions that Cristi must feel absolutely free to come and go, Pauly heroically bit the words back.

With equal self-control, when Archie heard that Cristi was to be off again soon, he forebore to ask if she had come to a decision about the ranch. This, presumably, was what she was going back to deal with. It was hard for him to accept that there was anything in her life about which she couldn't talk to them, for Cristi was by nature a teller, spilling over with eager accounts of everything she'd seen and done. Her present reticence was a worrying reminder of how that eagerness had been quenched when she had first been confronted with the challenges of university life. But he respected her reserve, and asked nothing. It was clear that her experiences in Brazil had had a powerful impact, and while it perturbed him not to share in them fully, he understood that only she could resolve whatever dilemma they had created for her.

Cristi did talk a little to Tom and Madeleine, in the days before she left – days of strangely suspended feeling, as though she was already out of contact with Drumveyn, while everything to which she must return still seemed unreal.

'I know you must be wondering what's going on,' she said, at the barn for lunch one day. It was more than time to say something. She owed them that much. A moment ago Tom had touched on the subject of Tres Pinheiros, then too quickly had moved on to another topic. They shouldn't have to tiptoe round her like that.

'I don't want to shut everyone out,' she added, breaking into what Tom was saying without being aware of doing so. 'It's not that.' She looked at them with an appeal which touched their hearts, but made them feel more helpless than ever. 'I have to sort things out, or sort myself out, first. Out there, in Brazil, there was so much to – well, it was pretty overwhelming, and I don't think I did deal with it, not very well anyway.'

They nodded sympathetically, aching to help, but feeling this didn't take them much further forward.

'I think you've been terribly brave,' Madeleine offered. 'Going out there alone in the first place. It must be so hard to come to terms with something like that, knowing you belong to two such different backgrounds. And for them to be so far apart. Not only in distance.'

She glanced at Tom, afraid of saying the wrong thing, but was encouraged by his quiet nod. She went on, her longing to give comfort clear in her voice, 'Nobody would find it easy to handle. I'm certain I shouldn't. But the main thing to remember is—' and you will *not* let your voice waver up and down so stupidly, she admonished herself 'that we are here for you, always, whatever happens, and we love you dearly.'

Pauly said much the same thing on Cristi's last night at home, swaying into her room like a frilly white tank, in a voluminous Victorian nightgown she had found in some cupboard. As she said herself, it was so peaceful to be *allowed* to be large. Archie hated the nightdress and removed it at every opportunity, saying he couldn't be expected to get into bed with his own grandmother.

'Oh, Cristi, I do so hate this,' Pauly exclaimed, pulling a face at the packed bags.

'Yes, well, don't go on about it,' Cristi retorted ungratefully. 'It's no help.'

'I know I shouldn't. I won't. But look, I do want to say one thing.'

'So long as it isn't something that sets you off, because you know what you're like and I don't think I could stand it tonight.'

'Of course I won't cry. What do you take me for? I'll try not to, anyway. But it's only – I really do need to be sure you know this is home. Your real, forever and always home, that nothing could ever take away from you. You are absolutely sure of that, aren't you? You're not getting any silly ideas like Nicholas did, only thank goodness he seems to have forgotten them now, that you're not proper family any more? Because I simply couldn't bear it.'

'Oh, Pauly.' Cristi got up from the dressing-table and came towards her. 'Pauly, don't.'

'No, I swore to Archie I wouldn't cry. But I had to come. I couldn't let you go without saying that.'

Her voice wavered, and they hugged, everything said between them in that close clasp.

Cristi flew to Porto Alegre this time without a stop-over in Rio. No tangling with Fonseca autocracy this time. It was mildly strange to remember, during the interval between flights, that some of her belongings were still in their house.

Luis knew she was on her way, but she had given him no details of when she would arrive. Landing in the full blast of afternoon heat, almost reeling under it after the stark January temperatures of Glen Ellig, there was nevertheless an exhilarating sense of freedom not to be met, and to be so lightly burdened that it was easy to take the metro into the city. This ordinary act made her feel reassuringly on familiar territory, and that was a comfort, however minor, after the homesickness of the flight and the churning dread of what lay ahead.

Jude, who had proved a surprisingly regular, if terse, correspondent, had found her somewhere to live, not far from the Parque Farroupilha, so she would be central again. Cristi had stipulated that any accommodation must be simple, then realised she needn't have worried. Jude would have no truck with anything else.

After the wrench of leaving Drumveyn — a wrench made harder by the guilt of having kept so much from the people dearest in the world — and the hours of flying, the quarters she found following Jude's directions satisfied her beyond anything she could have hoped for.

In a street of mixed dwellings she located a single-

storied house with a small bright garden. A maid came
smiling to the door and led her to a gate at the side of the
house, which she unlocked, handing Cristi the key and
pointing to stone steps set in a steep slope. Trees hid
what lay above. What had Jude let her in for?

The steps led to a tiny yard, a washing line strung
across it, a stone *tanque* against one wall. A small building
lay at the back. Once a servant's room, it was no longer
considered adequate for its original purpose. It had
white-washed walls with morning-glory swarming up
them, a pantile roof, and shutters of sun-blistered, soft
blue-green. A wooden bench stood under one window.
Dropping her bags and turning, Cristi saw that, sitting
here, one would have a view over the warm colours of
haphazard roofs to the trees of the park.

The door was unlocked. A white-walled room held a
low bed, two chairs and a table. A few wooden pegs were
driven into the wall. On the table, propped against a
chipped enamelled candlestick, was a used envelope.

Jude's message was on it, not in it. 'You did say simple.
Welcome back. J.'

Cristi's eyes smarted: that Jude had taken the time and
trouble to arrange this, had hauled herself in the summer
heat up the steep steps . . . But today, of all days,
emotions must be kept in hand. Concentrate on the
immediate.

To the right two compartments opened, one with
primitive loo and shower, smelling of zinc and cement,
the other with gas ring and kettle, sink and tap. Good
enough. An oil lamp, a few basic utensils, a mesh-fronted

food safe which Cristi decided there and then she would not be using.

This spartan place satisfying some fundamental need in her, giving her, even today, a lift of anticipation to think of paring life down to essentials, Cristi went out to the yard again. The sun made it impossible to sit there at present, but trees shaded the top steps, providing a perfect extra room. During summer – always supposing that water continued to come out of the tap – this tucked-away corner would give her everything she needed.

Cristi took her things inside and, taking the key of the gate, went in search of the nearest *armazem*. She found one on the first corner, poorly lit, its shelves crammed with cheap goods but with plenty of fruit and big baskets of fresh loaves on the counter. She bought coffee, bread, cheese and fruit, and a few household necessities. She would do as she had done before, and eat mainly in *pizzarías* and *churrascarías*, or off the cooked-food stalls which abounded in the city.

After treating herself to a cooling *guaraná* she went back to idle away the rest of the afternoon sitting on the shady steps, for once doing nothing, as the heat took on a drowsy, kindly quality, and the realisation that she was back, the transition once more accomplished, sank in. In this interval of stolen time, before the first voice spoke, before the first contact was made, she also thought, more honestly and clearly than she had been able to achieve until now, about what she intended to do and why she intended to do it.

Then, as that moment came when the orange sun, hanging as it seemed well above the horizon, suddenly dived below it, she had a delicious shower of large splattering drops of luke-warm water, dressed in one of her neat shift-dresses — she had brought nothing more elaborate with her — and went down to the park and the row of public telephones to call Luis.

Chapter Thirty-four

Luis's anger went far beyond anything she had antici-
pated.

When she telephoned, his surprise and pleasure that
she was back were tempered by exasperation on several
counts — that she hadn't let him know her flight time,
hadn't contacted him the moment she arrived so that he
could adapt his plans for the evening, wouldn't let him
come to fetch her now and, finally, that she was using a
public phone which apart from being a health hazard
meant she had to cut him short.

But in spite of these objections, Cristi was left in no
doubt of his satisfaction that she was back. The rest was
mere surface annoyance. He never liked it when she made
her own plans. Of course he'd have preferred to have
come to the airport to meet her (good job he didn't know
she'd taken the Trensurb if he was so excited about the
public phone), and of course he wanted to sweep her into
his orbit again, making the decisions, setting the pace.

Cristi reminded herself, to be fair to him, of how thankful she'd been when he was there to look after her when she first landed in Rio. He had a way of disposing of problems and making things happen. How protective he had been, how generous with his time and attention, and what good times they'd had.

But these were not the most important factors this evening, and Cristi pushed the memories away as she headed for the bus stop. There were always plenty of taxis about, and they were astonishingly cheap, but the crowded anonymity of the bus suited her mood better; perhaps was a reaffirmation of independence, like her basic quarters at the top of the garden. Her life; her choice.

But it was impossible, first jammed in the packed bus, accepting the smiling apologies of those who found themselves obliged to crush against her, then walking along the quiet road in the flowering, tree-shaded suburb towards Luis's house, not to feel excited at the thought of seeing him again.

The memories jostled more insistently – of his caressing voice, the teasing light in his eyes, his strong brown hands, his fit, whip-thin body, his self-assurance and authority. She thought of the way he looked in gaucho dress, his skill as a horseman. She remembered their rides under the huge skies of Tres Pinheiros, the hours on the sunlit rock-slabs cooled by the spray of secret falls, leisurely lamplit dinners when there had seemed everything in the world to talk about.

She had only one moment to set against these seductive memories; one instinctive but overwhelming certainty to bolster her courage.

Luis greeted her with a pleasure there was no mistaking, the formal *abraço* followed by an enveloping hug. Never mind that in the same instant he drew back exclaiming in horror, '*Deus, querida*, what are you wearing? You look like some child off the streets. Where are you staying? I shall have to take you back to change before we go to the club. I'm dining with friends, but they know you're coming and they'll be understanding when we wish to slip away.'

He looked at her with a meaning which brought a flush to Cristi's cheeks. She felt rocked by his vitality and physical attraction. How could she have forgotten the impact they had on her? But she held onto her resolution as he led her in, knowing she mustn't let herself be sidetracked, offering neither defence nor explanations as Luis complained once more about her unannounced arrival, her delay in phoning, and even the fact that she had let the taxi put her down at the end of the road. It was simpler to let him think so.

She asked the obligatory questions about the family, omitting no one; asked, knowing the answers would be as uninformative as ever, about Luis's own affairs. He asked no questions about her time in Scotland. The Napiers as Cristi's family, Drumveyn as her home, didn't exist for Luis.

The blatant omission helped Cristi to keep her purpose in mind. She accepted a drink and they settled on the terrace. The beauty of the remembered view below

them, the city mapped in lights, its sprawl contained by
the dark curve of the river, helped her too. The sight
reminded her that Luis, though calling Porto Alegre his
home, chose to perch up here on its exclusive fringe,
keeping the real life of the city at a distance. While she, in
however limited and transient a way, had come to know
something of its other faces.

'So, Maria-Cristina, you have deigned to return to me.'
Luis, settling in a long chair, raised his glass mockingly.
'What can have kept you away so long? Can you imagine
how I have missed you, what explanations I have been
obliged to give my friends for your absence?'

Light though his tone was, this provided Cristi with an
opening she knew she mustn't miss. Her heartbeat
beginning to quicken uncomfortably, she wished for a
second that they could have spent more time on social
nothings. But they were part of the same family; that
would still remain.

'Luis, I know you're planning to go out, but could we
talk first?'

'Of course we can talk,' he assented, amused. 'We can
talk before dinner, after dinner, all evening and all of
every evening to come. You're back now.'

Back for good. Cristi heard the unsaid words. Luis's
confidence in all they implied increased her nervousness.
Had he taken it for granted all along, in spite of paying
lip service to the idea of having time apart to think, that
they were committed to each other? That marriage was a
foregone conclusion? Knowing Luis, she realised with a
lurch of alarm that this was actually possible. How odd,

though, to have reached such a point with so little genuine communication between them.

'I meant,' she started again, flustered, 'that I'd like to talk properly. Seriously, you know—'

But as she fumbled for the right words, she saw his face darken, become oddly narrower, his eyes fasten on hers with an alert intentness.

'I feel it's wrong to let you go on thinking—' God, this was difficult. 'I mean, there's so much that we haven't—'

Luis came to his feet, startling her, but it appeared he was only going to replenish his glass, glancing automatically at hers but finding she had barely touched her drink. 'Of course we'll talk,' he assured her smoothly, his back towards her, his hands busy. 'There are weeks of separation to catch up on for a start. But not this evening, my sweet,' turning with raised brows and a look he may have intended to be quizzical but which from where Cristi was sitting looked full of warning. 'We have all the time in the world for any discussion necessary. There is a vast amount to arrange, I grant you, but in its due time and place. For tonight, why not enjoy being together again? Celebrate your return?'

Again he raised his glass to her, his face smiling. But there was a clear message in his words, and there was a message in his eyes, which were not smiling.

Cristi, almost without knowing she was doing so, had come to her feet too, and she faced him squarely, her eyes meeting his, intent on total honesty.

'Luis, I'm truly sorry, but it would be wrong to go on under false pretences.' To her relief, her voice sounded steady. 'It's only fair to say now, at once, that I'm afraid I can't marry you. I've thought and thought about it, and I'm positive it wouldn't be right for us. The last thing in the world I want to do is hurt you, but it would never work.'

'My dear girl, you're being absurd,' Luis cut in sharply, and even in the tension of the moment it seemed to Cristi that that struck an odd note. She had caught the leap of anger in his eyes, and this controlled, almost patronising, tone scarcely matched it. 'You're overtired after your flight. You don't know what you're saying. You surely don't imagine you can dismiss our agreement in such a casual way. There was an understanding between us, you will hardly deny that, and I don't accept what you're saying. We'll talk about it, certainly, but at some other time, when you are more yourself.'

Am I in the right century here, Cristi thought, a trifle wildly. Those aren't the words you'd expect from a lover you'd just dumped, today, now. This 'silly little woman, you'll feel better in the morning' speech threw her. What could she say to convince him?

'No, please listen, Luis. I do mean it. It's nothing to do with being tired or jet-lagged. This is serious. This is how I feel. I've had plenty of time to think things over and I'm quite—'

'Precisely. You've been away too long, coming under other influences. Once you've adjusted to being back, when we've spent time together—'

'No, Luis. It really is no.'

She was not prepared for the ferocity of his anger, all

pretence thrown away. He moved suddenly, his hands gripping her arms, his face bent to hers, and the word that flashed into her mind was predatory. No love or gentleness there, no willingness to try to understand what she felt.

She felt a shiver run through her which she knew was a sexual response to his closeness as much as trepidation. The realisation that he could arouse such a response in her at such a moment appalled her but, reminding her of how those feelings had been mixed with guilt, served usefully to toughen her resolve.

'I know I should have said this sooner and not let you go on thinking everything was all right. But it seemed so cold and unfeeling to put it in a letter.' And the letters she had received from him had not encouraged her to write on such an intimate level. 'I thought it would be fairer to come back and tell you properly, face to face. And to thank you for the happy times we had—'

Luis released his grip on her arms and turned away with an exclamation of angry contempt. Cristi, silenced, realised how childish and naive this speech would seem to him. Then she saw him get his anger in hand.

'We'll talk tomorrow,' he said curtly. 'When you're not so tired. And perhaps then you'll have taken more trouble with your appearance,' he added in a little explosion of spiteful disdain he couldn't suppress.

It said so much about his outlook, the value he placed on externals, and of his complete lack of sympathy, no matter how often she tried to explain it, with Cristi's interest in anything outside the pampered world he inhabited. This spurt of anger about something, surely, insignificant in the face of what was at issue between them, made Cristi feel desperately sad.

'You can't walk away so simply from the sort of commitment we made,' Luis was saying, turning to his chair but with ingrained good manners pausing to let Cristi sit down before he did.

'But I didn't feel it was so definite,' Cristi began incautiously, believing as he was ready to sit down again that he was also ready to talk frankly.

She was startled by the fury that flared in his face. 'Not definite? A proposal of marriage? Which you didn't refuse? What planet do you live on?'

'But I didn't accept.' Shocked by his hostility, for a moment Cristi felt she hardly knew how matters had been left between them. 'We didn't enter into any agreement. We left everything open, so that we could think.'

'We postponed our decision. You can't have been in any doubt as to what it would be.'

'But that doesn't make sense,' Cristi protested, with a growing, and worrying, sense of helplessness. Were they talking the same language here? Had they read that final scene before she left quite differently? Had their thoughts since then followed entirely separate tracks? She felt terribly alone.

'My dear Cristi.' Luis, who was having trouble keeping his temper in check, sounded curt and dismissive. 'You must remember that for us such an arrangement has wider implications. It can't be some light-hearted boy-girl affair where nothing beyond feelings is to be taken into account.'

'Why not? What do you mean?' Cristi demanded. 'Are you thinking of our being cousins, and my not being a Catholic? But those were arguments *against* our marrying, weren't they?'

'Cristi, please, be your age,' Luis said savagely. 'Casually as such matters are regarded in your precious Scotland, even you must see the advantages of such a marriage.'

'Advantages?' Cristi repeated blankly. This whole dialogue seemed to be going totally off course. The fact was that she didn't love Luis enough to marry him.

'There is family property involved here,' Luis reminded her, and now he leaned forward, into her space, his eyes fixed on hers, every line of him spelling out impatience with her stupidity. 'A large amount of property, which you cannot have imagined for one second could be yours, personally and exclusively. It's part of Fonseca heritage and history. It could never belong to someone who—'

He broke off, hearing his father's voice urging circumspection. There was too much at stake here to be thrown away by a rash word. Nevertheless, he reached out as he spoke, taking Cristi's wrist in a hard grip.

She gazed at him, half-afraid now, but still believing they could do this in sympathy and goodwill. Especially as she could remove this concern for good. Perhaps, she thought, dredging up a wry humour, that's where I should have begun.

'But Luis, that's one of the things I've been thinking about. I don't intend to keep the ranch. I love it, you know that. It's a magical place and it was the greatest thrill to—'

'You don't intend to keep it?' He repeated her words in a voice that cracked like a whip, and now the look on his face did frighten her. He was a stranger, capable of anything. Cristi tried to free her arm but his hand tightened ruthlessly.

'No, I don't,' she said breathlessly. 'Let go my arm, Luis. You're hurting me. I'll tell you if you—'

He was on his feet, pulling her up with him, and the ease with which he lifted her added to her fear. Cristi was breathlessly aware that as he was dining out there was no one else in the house, no one within call, and then was horrified that such a thought had come into her head.

'You're not going to sell it. That I promise you will never do!' Luis spoke through his teeth, his face thrust close to hers. 'You, the daughter of a tramp, a cheap slut disowned by her family. You think you can come walking in here taking grandfather's money, taking the land which has belonged to the family for centuries, and then decide you don't want it, that you'll let it go, just like that.' He snapped his fingers in her face, his eyes blazing.

'Luis, let go of me. I didn't mean—'

He took no notice. 'Well, my sweet cousin, you will find that such a thing will never be allowed. My father will fight you with all the means in his power. And what hope do you think you would have against him? What hope of winning or even surviving, you little fool!'

He shook her arm and Cristi cried, angry now, 'Don't do that! Let go of me at once.'

His face scornful and bitter, he released her. 'What a little cheat you are. What a sham. Pretending to be in love with me. What did you want? Sex, like your mother? Is that all it was? And do you think I'd want your scrawny little-girl's body? You may be my cousin, but do you think I can forget you were brought up as a foreigner, permitted to mix with all kinds of people? Marriage to you would have meant nothing more than the most effective way of keeping Fonseca land in Fonseca hands.'

Cristi, shaking under this storm of ugly words, wanted to cover her ears. Luis was ranging back and forth along the verandah, his face dark with rage. 'It was to be mine. It was always to be mine. Everyone else in the family had their wealth, their success, but Tres Pinheiros was for me. Everybody knew it. Grandfather had always promised it. But by the end he was mad, ill, he didn't know what he was doing. The will should never have stood, it should have been contested, overturned.'

Rigid with shock, Cristi knew that for the moment she couldn't deal with what he had said about her mother. With a violent effort of will, she thrust it into a dark recess of her mind to wait its turn. Coldly, she made herself accept the facts: the long-term planning of the Fonseca family as a whole, the calculated overtures, the softening-up process of her welcome in Rio, their certainty of success. Many things fell into place.

'You thought I'd be horrified by the state of the ranch, panicked by the responsibility. You thought I'd be grateful to have the family keep it, meeting the costs and tackling the job of hauling it into the twenty-first century. You were ready to take it off my hands as a kindness. And when I didn't react as you expected, when I wasn't desperate to off-load the whole thing and rush back to Scotland, you decided that the only course was to marry me. Or your father decided.' For Joachim's hand in this, his machinations in the background, his driving and controlling at every turn, became all at once blindingly evident. 'But Luis, listen—'

'Listen to you? Who are you to tell me to listen?' The vicious tone startled her, in spite of all that had been revealed. Luis not only didn't love her, he hated and despised her.

Pride stiffened her spine. Such emotions were outside her experience, but it wasn't the end of the world. She'd get over it. 'But I want you to listen, because this is important,' she insisted.

'What can you say that's of the slightest importance to me?' Luis sneered. 'You're nothing. You're a ridiculous child who's caused us a great deal of trouble.' His contemptuous glance raked her, his lip curling.

'I was going to give Tres Pinheiros back to the family.'

He swung round, disbelieving, trying to read her face under the subdued lighting of the verandah.

'You can't mean it.' Fonsecas, even one brought up outside the family aegis, did not make such gestures.

'I do mean it. I agree with what you said – the ranch has belonged to the family for three centuries. I can't live there, and if I can't there's no point in owning it. But I would never put it on the market. Little as you care about me,' and her voice wasn't steady now, 'you can't believe I'd do such a thing.'

'You seriously mean this?' Luis wasn't interested in her principles. 'You'll hand it back to the family? Or you'll give it to me?'

'Oh, Luis.' The soft exclamation, reproaching him for his greed, for all that he had done, unexpectedly reached him. He rubbed a hand through his hair, closing his eyes for a second as he tried to adjust to this new and unforeseen scenario.

'It meant everything in the world to me, you know,' he muttered after a moment.

Being left the ranch, Cristi assumed, deliberately falling back on irony, not their relationship. Well, there had been no relationship. She winced to think of the pain in store as each treasured memory became suspect and devalued in the light of her new knowledge. The pain of trust destroyed wouldn't be easy to deal with.

'We are of course still cousins,' said Luis, with a belated attempt to regain ground. After all, it might be wise to keep Cristi sweet. The British were notoriously indifferent to the things that mattered most in life. At least he wouldn't have to go through with the farce of marrying her. That was a relief.

Cristi, guessing some of this, was interested to find that the balance had swung and she felt in control. Did Luis seriously think he could reveal his opinion of her so crudely (and say those things about her mother), let her see the amount of manipulation that had gone on, and then imagine he made everything all right by reminding her that they were related?

'Not legitimately so, of course, as you have pointed out,' she said, as smooth as he.

Luis shrugged. 'I spoke in anger. You must forgive me.' The tone was perfunctory.

'You spoke the truth. At last.' Cristi allowed a small silence to hang. 'You told me what you are and how you feel about me.' She knew she still had to deal with the way she had felt about him, the powerful attraction he had exercised, and the happiness she had believed they'd shared, especially during the timeless, golden days at the ranch. She shivered at the loneliness ahead.

'I don't think our being cousins means a thing, to be honest,' she said flatly. 'In fact, I intend to have nothing more to do with the family. I'll deal with everything through the lawyers. They, after all, were the ones who summoned me in the first place.'

That went straight past Luis. 'May I remind you,' he said stiffly, 'you haven't done too badly out of us. You still have the money grandfather left you.'

'Yes, I have.' Did he think she should hand that over too? Had he fully taken in what she was doing in returning Tres Pinheiros, or was he so sure that it was the Fonseca due that he'd accepted it without thought? How shallow he was. And evil? Cristi shivered again.

'That's all, really.' She found she was suddenly exhausted. 'Nothing more to say.'

'But we'll be in touch. We must—'

'No Luis. We'll never be in touch again.'

She had made the choice between her two worlds. She had discovered beyond any doubt what mattered to her. The irony was that the place she recognised as hers, and longed for with all her heart, had closed its doors upon her.

Chapter Thirty-five

Without Jude, Cristi wasn't sure how she would have got through the following weeks. Jude and the *casa aberta*. It was a relief to be busy, and to be able to slip back into a life which this time was one unified whole. No conflict now between two different selves; none of the dressing in different clothes, none of the swings between extremes of poverty and wealth which had caused her so much soul-searching in the past.

Now she lived at a level of uncluttered simplicity which appealed to something deep in her. She might not choose to live this way for ever, but she was grateful for the space it gave her to come to some decision about her future. She knew that however hard she worked physically, however long the hours she put in at the hut on the river flats, the vital creative side of her was on hold, and couldn't remain dormant for ever. Too much was happening to her emotionally for it to be a problem yet, but she was confident the old compulsion would return.

It had been profoundly rewarding – and stimulating – to slip the Fonseca leash, and vanish into the anonymous life of the city. On the night she had parted from Luis, a last-minute impulse had made her direct the taxi he'd reluctantly summoned for her to a point far from her new hideaway. She had been shaken, all the same, to see Luis's car turn into the street as she was paying it off.

So he wasn't prepared to let her go. Unable to accept that she could turn her back on the Fonseca connection, or perhaps not trusting her to go through with her plans, he intended to retain control.

That had been scary. Cristi, hardly believing she was playing such a scene for real, had turned without hesitation as the taxi pulled away, and fled in the shadows to the first turning she could find, and away up a narrow alley, her heart in her mouth. She hadn't been familiar with the district she found herself in, but her fear had not been of any encounter in the shabby, ill-lit streets.

It had been simple enough to find a bus to take her down to the city centre, dropping her off near the haven Jude had found her. There had been no way Luis could have run her to earth there, but even so, she had hardly slept, the evening's ugly clash between them playing over and over in her mind. Many hopes, naive as they by this time appeared, had had to be relinquished, and that hadn't been good. When she had fallen asleep at last, she'd been tormented by dreams, jerking awake at imagined sounds.

But in the morning the fears had vanished. There had been leaf-patterned sunlight on white-washed walls, the voices of birds, garden scents intensified by the brief dew, and above all the conviction of having done the right thing. Making coffee, sitting out on the bench in air cool enough to make a sweater welcome, a sense of liberation and achievement had filled her.

Her one fear had been that Luis would track her down. Although she had guessed that his following the taxi to see where she went had probably been prompted by nothing more than anger that she had defied him, she knew if he was determined to find her the day centre wouldn't be hard to locate. Much as he had disliked her involvement there, dismissing it as incomprehensible, he would know roughly where it was situated. But he would also have known, she was sure, within hours if not minutes, that she had been in touch with the Fonseca lawyers the same morning (giving a *caixa postal* number as her address), and hopefully that had been enough to satisfy him. Even so, it was some time before the dread of his suddenly appearing faded.

Cristi had plenty to deal with as it was. The dubious motivation behind all Luis had said and done had to be dragged into the open, faced and put aside. The pretence, the calculation, the disregard for her as a person, had all somehow to be swallowed down. No one could help her with that. Nor could she pretend that the feelings Luis had roused in her had not existed, and it cost her many wretched hours before she could come to terms with that.

It was also hard to accept that she would never see the ranch again. She had not only lost for ever its unspoiled beauty, which had so deeply appealed to her but she must abandon any ideas she'd had about looking after, and coming closer to, its people.

Thinking of Selma, Enrico, Leopoldo, and others who had welcomed and been kind to her, she longed to talk to them directly about what was happening. But she knew in her heart that they would listen without comprehension. To them, whether or not they had been pleased by her appearance at the ranch, or would have liked to have her as their *patroa*, she was a Fonseca. In their day-to-day lives, nothing would have greatly changed. Family feuds and family decisions were far outside their ken. They would assume that she had had some passing interest in the place, and had as swiftly forgotten it. *Então?* And so? Shrug, move on.

It was hard to live with, but Cristi knew it was the price she must pay. Hopefully, knowing Luis's contempt for grandfather's antiquated methods, he would take the first opportunity to get the place into shape, even if his aim was only to make it pay better, and that would improve the situation of everyone who worked there. But would their circumstances be of primary concern to him? Or of any concern? Would he tolerate anyone not capable of full employment occupying one of his houses?

Knowing his ruthlessness, Cristi would wonder guiltily if after all she had made a cowardly decision. Also, turning her back so comprehensively on the Fonseca world, at a time when it was so impossible to return to her own, could make her feel alarmingly adrift.

Thank God that Jude, as long as no needy child was claiming her attention, was prepared to listen to much of this. She and Cristi almost always had supper together these days, at a fishermen's café on the docks, or picking up something in the covered market on the Praça 15 de Novembro to take back to Jude's room.

Jude was outspoken in her relief that Cristi had freed herself from the ruthless grasp of the Fonsecas, and even, to Cristi's surprise, approved of her returning Tres Pinheiros to them. Cristi would have thought her more hard-headed.

'You don't think I should have sold up and put the money to good use?' she asked.

Jude sniffed. 'That ranch was nothing to do with you and you know it. Oh, you liked it all right, I think I've got that much straight. But your grandfather only left it to you to spite the rest of them. You don't want anything to do with that sort of carry-on.'

'Or perhaps in the end he regretted quarrelling with my mother?' Cristi knew she still wanted to believe this. 'Perhaps he really loved her. Well, I know he did when she was little. So in a way it was giving it to her . . .?'

Jude snorted. 'Believe that if you must. But it's a damn silly way of making it up to her, if you ask me. Don't tell me he couldn't have found her long before if he'd wanted to.'

Cristi said nothing, her lips tight. Then, with difficulty, she voiced a thought much on her mind recently. 'They're not a very agreeable lot, the Fonsecas. But I am one of them.'

Jude shot her a quick look. 'Fair enough, I can see that would bother you. We can't change who we are. You have that blood in you. What about your dad?'

Cristi looked away, not finding it easy to reply. She saw nothing of the ugly little room where Jude kept her few battered possessions and spent so little time. Her face was pinched and bleak. Jude waited.

'I don't know who my father was,' Cristi said at last. 'It can't have been the person I was always told it was, Howard Armitage, Lisa's husband. You've only got to look at me. And now that I've learned more about my mother I can't go on accepting that convenient answer. My father could have been anybody, and I'll never know who.' It still wasn't easy to say this. 'Just as Nicholas will never know who his father was.'

Jude guessed that Cristi's thoughts were far from her present surroundings, and she said nothing. No words would help.

'How weird, really,' Cristi went on at last, 'that it should be the same for both of us. And that we should both be brought up at Drumveyn by Archie and Pauly. I mean, to end up with such amazing people, and be given so much by them. Not just things, but values, integrity.'

Jude nodded. 'Seems to me, love, you haven't got much to worry about when all's said and done. Wherever you came from, you fell into good hands, and by the sound of it they're hands that'll never let you go.'

Cristi's head came round. 'You think that? Just from what you've heard me say?'

'Don't be daft,' Jude said.

Cristi laughed at her tone. Of course Jude was right. Nothing was surer. She'd just needed to hear it. Relaxing, she reached to cut a couple of slices from the perfect juicy pineapple in front of them.

'OK,' she said. 'We've got that clear. Now I've got to decide what to do.'

'Yes, I think you have.'

'You know I'd like to go on helping you for a while, if you want me. But it won't be for ever.'

'You do talk a load of nonsense sometimes, for a person I'd call halfway sensible. Yes, I want you, for as long as I can keep my hands on you. And no, there's no way you'll stay for ever, that's plain. But what you're not telling me is what's keeping you from that glen of yours.'

She looked at Cristi's glossy head, ducked quickly to hide her face at this blunt attack and, as so many people did, marvelled in passing at the graceful slenderness of the flower-stalk neck.

'It's that lad, isn't it?'

For a second everything in Cristi resisted replying, then with a rush of relief she realised she could talk about this at last, releasing some of the pain and regret which ate at her.

Reading this in her face, Jude thought wryly, Goodbye to my early night. But she didn't mind. Cristi was a willing little trooper, and though she might be better off materially than Jude thought any single individual had the right to be, she'd had a fair bit to cope with one way or another.

Well, might as well get on with it. 'He's still the one, isn't he?' she asked. 'All this faffing about with Luis – and you were lucky not to get your fingers burned there, my

girl – has been more to do with getting your chum
Dougal out of your system than anything else. That's the
bottom line, isn't it?'

Jude was familiar by this time with what she called the
set-up at Drumveyn. She had the names more or less
straight, and she'd heard a good many of the stories, past
and present.

'Of course it wasn't!' Cristi was instantly on the
defensive. 'Dougal and I have never been – I mean, there
was never – we've always been friends, that's all.'

'Oh, yes?' said Jude. 'I haven't got all night, remember.
Here, have the last of the coffee and get on with it.'

'There isn't anything to – oh, well.' Cristi accepted
defeat. 'It was just that Dougal was always *there*. Part of
everything, from the very beginning. It started to go
wrong somehow when I went to art college. I think he
minded that. I don't mean that he was jealous, he's not
that sort of person, but it must have seemed so easy for
me, everything I wanted handed to me on a plate. His
own life was pretty grim just then, his father ill, his sister
always in trouble, his elder brother refusing to help out.
He had to give up his own plans to stay at home. Then I
suppose he found it hard to see me with other friends,
from uni, I mean. Not boyfriends, I never took boyfriends home.'

Cristi paused, considering that. Why had she never
invited male friends to Drumveyn? She'd have to think
about it properly when she was on her own.

'Torie and Isa came quite often. I think we drove him
mad when we were together. Well, I know we did. Girlie

stuff, arty stuff, gossiping for hours in the studio. Neither of them was specially keen on estate things, the sort of things Dougal and I used to do together. Then when he heard about this Brazilian business, I suppose it was hard for him.'

'Chip on the shoulder, has he?'

'Of course he hasn't. He's not a bit like that,' Cristi flared up, and missed the gleam in Jude's eye. 'I hate that expression. Dougal doesn't think that way.'

'But you lived in the big house and he was the shepherd's son. And you got handed a few thousand hectares and a stack of money, and he has some crummy job he hates and has to do his studying at night-school.'

Cristi wished Jude didn't have such a good memory. 'Yes, but you've got him all wrong. None of that was important to him.' But it had been important. Cristi couldn't pretend any longer. It had slammed shut a door which had already started to close.

Then once more that moment returned which was burned into her memory, the delight and certainty she had felt, and had been equally certain he felt, as she had walked into the kitchen at Croft of Ellig and Dougal had realised who was coming in. However brief, however swiftly suppressed as the true state of affairs between them had been recalled, that mutual reaction had been unmistakable. And in that moment she had known what she must do, about Luis, about the ranch. Then she had called at Jean's . . .

'All right, so it wasn't important.' Jude's dry voice cut across her thoughts. 'But tell me this. When you were home for Christmas was Dougal in and out of the house as he used to be? Did he and his mum have their Christmas dinner with you? You'd go to call on her, no doubt, in her council house in the village, and you wouldn't bother picking up the phone first. Did she drop in on you?'

The colour rose in Cristi's cheeks. 'But that's how it's always – Jean wouldn't think of—'

'That's what I'm saying.'

'In any case,' Cristi argued, trying not to sound defensive, 'it's different now. Dougal's engaged.'

Now we're getting somewhere. 'Is he now? And who's the girl?'

'She used to live in the glen. We were at school together.'

'Don't give me that. You don't mean at your posh boarding school, I'll bet.'

Cristi's blush deepened. Too many things always taken for granted, yet uncomfortably demanding re-examination in recent weeks, were being tossed at her. 'At the village school. We all went there.'

'And where did this girl live?'

Cristi was beginning to wish she'd kept her mouth shut. 'On a farm.'

'Yes?'

'All right, her father was tenant farmer on a Drumveyn farm. He's retired now. They've moved away.' She thought of Dougal's views on tied houses.

Jude watched her, her face full of an affection, and a sympathy, which Cristi didn't see.

'You don't need me to spell it out, do you?' A small silence stretched. 'You say he hasn't got a chip on his shoulder, and you'll know best about that, but he's got his pride, hasn't he? He knows your lives will follow different paths. And be fair, you did come in for a pretty good whack of the earth's riches, which you'd done nothing to deserve. You let him alone, is my advice. If he's found some girl that suits him, and he's got his start with that smallholding or whatever it is, you're just going to have to bite the bullet and leave him in peace. Anything else will only bring him grief.'

'I know.' Cristi's voice was muffled and there were tears on her lashes. 'I know it's great for him, and I'm glad, truly. But Jude, it makes me feel so *empty*. There's this huge aching space inside me. At home, at Christmas, I couldn't take it in that he could be there, only a couple of miles away, yet completely separate. It felt so weird that I couldn't go up to see him whenever I felt like it, or blether to him on the phone every day, telling him everything that was going on. It was as if—' she paused. This wasn't easy. 'It was as if he'd become a person I only know in a general way. He can go into his house and shut the door, just like other people in the glen I know but whose houses I never go into.'

I thought we'd done that one. Never mind, she's getting there in her own way.

'I can't just go and dump myself down at home,' Cristi argued, as though Jude had suggested she did. 'Not only because of Dougal. I'd have to have a job. I can't hang around doing nothing.'

'But you need the comfort of being at Drumveyn.'

'Silly, isn't it? The only place I can't be. Part of me longs for it all the time,' Cristi confessed. 'Yet I want to be here too. I know that getting in touch with my Brazilian family hasn't been the biggest success you could think of, but because of it I've found a lot of other things that matter to me. It was right to come. The ranch was a fabulous experience, and the glimpse I got of that whole gaucho world is something I'll never, ever forget. Going to the day centre, working with you, living in my own way, has given me so much too. Even the time in Rio was part of the picture. Whatever happens, I could never altogether turn my back on this country.'

'But you know now which is your true home?'

'I do.' Cristi smiled ruefully. 'One cold winter's morning walk up the glen was all it took. It made me realise how much Drumveyn had given me. I arrived there at an age when I was ready for every new experience, short on affection — except from Isaura — and short on company, stimulus and fun. I was used to being dressed up like a doll, spoiled and indulged, but never allowed a moment's real freedom. Then suddenly I was in this new world. I still remember that first morning, shoved into jeans and a sweater borrowed from Jill, and allowed to play in the snow. To get wet, get cold! You can't imagine what a revelation it was. And there were Dougal and Jill, puppies, animals, miles of hill and moor, a new school. I was allowed to do things, learn things, try things, ride, row a boat, swim in the loch, go round the sheep with Donnie. And I was surrounded by people who were kind, good-tempered and above all consistent. People who enjoyed things and laughed.'

'Humph,' said Jude, who'd heard most of this before. 'Sounds like a bloody fairy story to me.'

Cristi laughed, coming back to earth. 'But you know what I mean.'

'Oh, I get the rough idea. And you see now that falling in with that lot, no matter how unlikely the way you got there, was more important than the dosh and the land and all the rest. I'm with you there.'

Although it had changed nothing, and nothing could change, it had helped to talk. The step of freeing herself from the Fonsecas was behind her, she had a roof (a delightful one in her view), occupation and friends. Decisions would have to be made, but she could take her time over them.

The students were back after the summer, and it wasn't hard to pick up the easy friendships of the spring. The unravelling of the ownership of Tres Pinherois rolled ponderously on, but seemed scarcely to concern her. She signed what had to be signed, refusing to go to Rio and letting the lawyers come to her, but most of the time managed to put the whole thing out of her mind. Decision taken.

News from home, though it could make her restless and filled her with longing to be there, could be shared with Jude, and that helped.

For, as the weeks passed, some of that news was startling indeed.

Chapter Thirty-six

Archie had been down to Devon to see Cecil. That was the first piece of news to rock Cristi, and she read the fat letter in Pauly's sprawling hand many times. She could so well imagine Archie and Pauly, unable to dismiss the disturbing picture of Cecil which she and Nicholas had brought back, talking over the problem with concern and compassion. Archie would have found it impossible to do nothing, and Pauly would be ready to support him in whatever he decided.

In their quiet way they were remarkable people, Cristi thought, filled with love and admiration for them, as she sat with the letter on the garden steps, in the golden warmth after a hot day, a supper of her favourite savoury pasties and salad and fruit beside her. Remarkable not just because they were ready to help where they saw help was needed, but because they weren't influenced by conventional arguments.

The fact that Cecil was Archie's ex-wife, who had

abandoned him and Nicholas in a way which at the time had seemed both ruthless and unnatural, wouldn't deter them. Simply they would see that Cecil's present situation, isolated and alone, an incurable disease taking its slow course, was intolerable, and that something must be done about it. They might see the irony of the fact that, with Cecil's fatal incapacity to build relationships, to give or receive love, she had washed up on such a lonely shore that the closest links she had left in the world were with the Napiers, but it would be a mere passing thought.

Pauly would have no hang-ups about Archie going to see Cecil. She wouldn't be doing battle with secret jealousy or resentment. Having gone through so many emotional hoops herself in the last few months, Cristi felt humbled by Pauly's commonsense approach. For the first time she saw with real understanding how it must have been for Pauly, falling in love with Archie while he was still married to the cool and beautiful Cecil, crushing down her feelings and getting on with her job – which had included looking after Cecil's child. Until, convinced that Archie would never look at anyone so young, slapdash and scruffy as she was, she had left Drumveyn in despair.

Until now it had been one of the stories of the past, to do with a previous generation, like Madeleine's romance with Tom, or Lisa's odd triangular relationship with Stephen and Joyce. Never before had Cristi tried to think herself into the skin of the cheerful, smiling nineteen-year-old she had first known.

What lay behind Pauly's warmth and readiness to give,

Cristi pondered, still holding the letter like a talisman? Was it the deep security of what she and Archie felt for each other? That must also have underpinned Archie's decision to go to see Cecil. They wouldn't query each other's response, or waste time on doubts. They would say what they felt, and believe what they heard.

It sounded so simple. Cristi sat on till the shrill voices of the cicadas fell silent and the soft darkness, almost unbearably sweet with garden scents and thickly patterned with enormous stars, descended around her.

She hadn't given herself much time to think lately, plunging into work at the day centre, spending as much time as she could with friends, and enjoying more of the cultural offerings of the city as the new season began, going to concerts and the ballet, and also spending solitary nostalgic hours looking at the work of gaucho artists in the Museu de Arte.

It hadn't been easy to shake off the memories of her last encounter with Luis. She still had dreams about it, waking convinced that it couldn't be that simple to get clear away from Fonseca control, dreading some backlash. Then she would remember that she had, after all, given up Tres Pinheiros. There was no reason for them to hound her. On the contrary, they must be as glad to be rid of such an undesirable family member as she was to be clear of them. It could still shake her to think Luis had actually been prepared to marry her to get his hands on the ranch, and she would be overcome by shame to imagine ever having been attracted to him.

But gradually, as her dealings with the lawyers went

forward with surprising dispatch (Fonseca greed spurring them on, no doubt), and as good sense told her that Luis had nothing to gain by tracking her down, she began to look more seriously at her own future.

She had had to come back to Brazil to see Luis, and she had had to get away from the glen, but these were both in a sense negative reasons for being here. In real terms, her life was on hold, except for one reassuring thing – almost without her being aware that it was happening, her eyes had begun to look and see again, her hands itch to record what she saw. Once more a sketch-book went everywhere with her, and the pleasure it gave her tempted her to try some watercolours. With the same reawakening need for creativity in any form, she began to make her own clothes again and, with the abundance of beautiful material on hand, couldn't think why she'd waited so long to do so.

Day after day the sun poured down. Minimal clothing, minimal possessions and the simplest of food gave a sense of light and freedom. The *casa aberta* kept her in touch with reality, its chief lesson being to live in the moment. Repining over yesterday's failures or worrying about tomorrow achieved nothing.

It wasn't always easy working with Jude, however. Though she rarely complained, it was obvious from her movements, especially in the mornings, and the wince of pain she often couldn't hide, that she was suffering the aches and pains of an ageing body which had never been well treated. At such times her temper could be chancy.

She flared up one evening, after a busy day, when she

found Cristi letting one of the children draw on their precious store of paper.

'For God's sake, do you think I beg and cadge for that stuff for you to doodle all over it? Go outside and draw in the mud if you must.'

Cristi apologised hastily, then realised this could be an opportunity to broach something she'd been wanting to say for some time, and she took her chance.

She had been growing increasingly uneasy with the contradiction that, while they scraped for every penny to keep the centre going, she had plenty of money. As long as she owned Tres Pinheiros she had seen her Fonseca capital as indivisibly tied to it. Now things had changed and, after weighing the matter conscientiously, she had decided there was no obligation to return it to the family. She had expected some demand via the lawyers but there had been silence on that point.

From the beginning, when Jude had sent her out touting for cash and goods, she had slipped in contributions of her own, but she had always been sure Jude would resent it if she knew. It was hard to say why. In general, Jude had few qualms about grabbing anything that came her way if it would keep the centre going for a little longer. But Cristi had had the feeling that if she came swanning in, as Jude would have put it, doling out largesse, then some delicate balance between them would have been destroyed.

She almost wished she'd let sleeping dogs lie when, having said diffidently that, with the matter of the ranch now settled, she could offer financial as well as practical help if that was acceptable, she found she had opened the door to some searing revelations.

Jude's first response was anger. 'I don't want your money. Keep it. I get along all right as it is.'

'I know you do. But wouldn't some extra cash mean you could do more for the children?'

She was startled at the effect of touching this nerve. Jude, drawing a harsh breath, almost broke down and Cristi, not daring to interrupt, found herself listening to confessions she would never have dreamt of hearing from her.

'I know I'm potty, you don't have to tell me. There's no excuse. I've been getting so frustrated with myself lately. I guessed you'd been chipping in, and I knew I shouldn't have a problem with it.'

Cristi hesitated before asking carefully. 'But why is it a problem?'

'Hah.' A sound of bleak self-contempt. 'You may well ask. You'd think I'd be glad of anything that would help the kids, wouldn't you? Well, the only way I can explain it is that I need to be battling, or I don't feel I'm achieving anything. It's about me, that's what it comes down to, me. Maybe it always has been.'

'Jude, you can't think that,' Cristi protested. 'You've spent your whole life helping other people.'

'Maybe. But I got my kicks out of it being hard graft, and somehow thinking of you being able to hand over a pile of cash, and not even noticing it had gone – well, I just wasn't big enough to accept it. I'm the one that gives, see. Ego. Sad, isn't it?'

'So help from me, financial help, would seem to make your efforts pointless?'

'That's about the size of it.'

Cristi put her hand on Jude's gnarled, work-worn one. 'You may say you do this for your own gratification,' she said, looking round the battered hut and its sparse contents and thinking what they had meant to so many desperate children, 'but you must know in your heart how much you've given. There must be hundreds of people who remember you with gratitude.'

'Huh.' Jude pulled her hand from Cristi's. 'I'm not into this touchy stuff, remember.'

Cristi thought of that hand turning bruised and swollen faces to the light, cleaning festering wounds, binding knife-cuts, treating lice-infested heads; thought of Jude's skinny arms enwrapping small, half-starved, trembling bodies. 'Sure you're not.'

Letters from home, apart from telling of Nicholas's successes at rugby, of Tom walking down from the barn with a single stick, or Broy accidentally catching a mouse and, after carrying it about for a while in embarrassment, stuffing it under his beanbag to shut it up, brought graver news.

At Grianan Mike Danaher was failing rapidly. Michael and Kirsty were home every weekend, and Sally's friends were giving her all the help in their power. She felt committed to opening Grianan for the summer, as so many people came year after year and she didn't want to disappoint them, but it was going to be a difficult season for her.

More arresting, yet after the first shock no real surprise, was the news that Archie and Pauly had persuaded Cecil to come and be looked after at Drumveyn, and that it was even now being arranged. Cristi shed tears over the letter, written this time by Archie. The magnitude of the gesture, not proposed until it was clear that it was also what Nicholas truly wanted, said so much of the values of home, and increased her aching longing to be there.

Nostalgic images beset her, giving her no peace, and in spite of all her efforts most of them inevitably circled back to Dougal. Unable to banish them, and concerned by the sense of living a mere temporary, holding existence which they created, she did her best to analyse objectively why he still meant so much to her, after the estrangement of recent years.

The instant answer that came was that he felt part of her; that without him there was a perpetual sense of loss and incompleteness. Other men, beside him, were ordinary mortals, separate people, strangers. Delving deeper, Cristi realised – something she saw she had taken for granted until now – that physically he satisfied every sense. There was a pleasure in his nearness which was nothing like the brief, heady, half-guilty attraction she had felt for Luis. Not only were his looks right and satisfying, but the very texture of his skin, almost as familiar to her as her own, the way he moved, the clothes he wore, his aura of competence and strength, woke a deep response in her.

There was that same quiet strength in his character

too, an integrity and sound sense in which she had trusted without ever being aware of it. But above all, it had been such fun to be with him, so natural, the best part of being at home. He had teased her, roughed her up when he felt like it and kept her in her place, but goodness, how they'd laughed together, how they'd talked, about everything under the sun, and how good they had found each other's company.

Memories she hadn't thought about for ages, and which she could have done without, swarmed back to torment her. How protective Dougal had been during those first weeks at the glen school, and how utterly she had taken for granted his watchful care. And later, when she'd gone away to school, how marvellous it had been to slip back into instant companionship, with or without Jill. Somehow he had always known where to find her. How often, setting off at a run to go up to Steading Cottage, she had found him coming down to meet her, his face lighting up with his cheerful grin at the sight of her, and how, almost without discussion, they had set off together to pursue some favourite ploy of the moment.

Clear, disturbing vignettes of those times presented themselves with a poignancy it was hard to bear. Chilly, motionless hours waiting at the badger setts in the wood as a grey dawn slowly lightened, and their smiles of delight to each other as at last their wait was rewarded; Dougal, laughing, wading to fish her out when a loose stone had turned under her foot and she'd gone down in the burn; the two of them bringing the pony down from the hill on a hazy, mellow late afternoon of August, pleasantly tired after a long day, with the vehicles carrying the guns and the other beaters disappearing down the track ahead of them, leaving them on their own; and Dougal, always, at her shoulder when they stopped for their piece during the day's grouse driving.

That particular picture arrested her, and she looked at it with new eyes. They had been part of a group of estate employees and other glen children, with the family lunching on the other side of the dyke. Yet Dougal had never shown the least self-consciousness at being beside Cristi, always. Had he come in for much ribbing? He must have done. She'd never thought about it. That was just the way it had been.

One question she knew she must ask. Had her developing interest in all things connected with the arts really been the element which had alienated him? No, looking back with a new bleak clarity from this distance, she knew they had had far too much in common for that to be the crucial factor. Dougal had an enquiring mind and plenty of interests of his own, and his range of knowledge had always impressed her. It wouldn't have mattered what her choice of subject had been – far more fundamental issues had driven them apart.

And she saw at last, with wincing shame, that putting the problem right had been down to her, and only her. How could she have expected Dougal to sort things out from where he stood? All it had needed was for her to have been a little braver, to have trusted him a little more, and that appalling chasm between them would never have widened and widened till matters came to this.

It had been upon shared attitudes and outlook, as well as strong affection, that the solid basis of their friendship had been founded, and she had understood it too late. Way, way too late.

Still no word came of Dougal being married, and Cristi found herself torn between longing to hear a date had been set for the wedding, so that at last it would be definite and inescapable, and dreading the news with a cold anguish which would literally send a shiver over her skin.

Until he was married, and thoughts and longings had to be put out of her mind for good, she couldn't trust herself to go back. Once it was a fact, and Dougal and Alison were established at the Croft of Ellig, then perhaps she would finally be able to make decisions about her own future.

Chapter Thirty-seven

As often happens, the most startling piece of news arrived indirectly, as little more than a chance remark by someone not thinking of its possible impact. Sally Danaher occasionally exchanged letters with Cristi these days, needing contacts outside the enclosed world of Grianan, and it was she who wrote, assuming that Cristi would know about it already, 'What a shame Alison Mowat's so adamant about not living in the glen. Says she's had enough of being stuck miles away up some farm track, apparently. So sad if Dougal has to give up the croft, after all the work he's put into it. I shouldn't think Archie will be too happy about it either.'

Then she skipped on to other matters – anything to avoid dwelling on what was happening in her own life – and Cristi was left, shaking and breathless, to try to take in the implications of what she'd said.

Dougal, asked to give up the dream which had meant more to him than anything in the world? Dougal obliged to give up his one chance of working land that belonged to him, no matter how small a patch, and the animals it supported? Dougal leaving behind the environment he loved, understood and was part of, for the noisy, polluted, soulless life of town?

Even more unsettling was the thought that Dougal and Alison were embarking on a future together with such different aims. Cristi had seen Alison, a farmer's daughter – hard not to mind though it had been – as well suited to life at the croft, more than capable of sharing with Dougal every aspect of life there. But now she remembered how happy Alison had been with the move to Perth when her father retired, rejoicing in the prospect of at last being within reach of all the things taken for granted by her friends: shops, cinema, clubs, cafés, with public transport making accessible the even greater delights of Glasgow and Edinburgh. If Alison liked that scene, then living at Croft of Ellig might very well feel like stepping back into the despised past.

But, disquieting though it was to think of Dougal's satisfaction in his new life being jeopardised, behind these thoughts a new, tentative realisation was taking shape. If, for whatever reason, Dougal decided to abandon the deal with Archie and leave his precious toehold of land, awful as it would be for him, it would mean that she herself could go home. There would no longer be any danger of chance encounters about the glen, nor would she have to put herself through the torture of meeting Dougal and Alison as the established couple.

For the irony remained. Though Glen Ellig and

Drumveyn might hold the core of her greatest pain, it was still the only place to run for comfort. But nothing was certain yet. She couldn't act on Sally's passing comment, huge though its impact had been. Still she must wait. She couldn't risk going back until, one way or another, Dougal was committed.

It was in one of Pauly's cheerful, loving, rushed letters, taking half a dozen attempts to finish, written in half a dozen different pens, that definite news came. Alison, according to the account a much distressed Jean had given Pauly, had delivered an ultimatum – life in the glen was not for her. The Croft of Ellig was too remote, too primitive, not her scene.

'Of course, to quote Jean, "there's nothing to be got out of Dougal",' Pauly wrote. 'But it must be dreadful for him. We did so hope he'd be happy.'

But Pauly was only repeating the version which Dougal, thinking it no one's business but his, had allowed Jean and the glen at large to believe.

After the first excitement of the engagement, the happy visions of the future, and delight in their good fortune to have a house of their own straight away, there had been a less euphoric phase when Alison – aided by her mother and her elder sister – applied themselves to the serious business of equipping and furnishing the house, deciding on colour schemes, making noises about double-glazing, and arguing about which kind of central heating to have. Could oil always be delivered in winter; how long, away up here, might power cuts last?

Weekends had been taken up in choosing carpets, curtains and a three-piece suite, without which, Dougal gathered, no one could seriously be considered married. There were visits of inspection by Alison's family and friends, who of course had to be fed and entertained, and he in his turn had to attend the weddings, birthday parties and other rites which seemed to come up with great regularity in her large clan.

Dougal had accepted this as a necessary part of the whole. He had taken Alison to tea at Jean's, and been shown off to her married friends, sitting through more indifferent meals in 'smart' hotels than he ever had in his life before. His wardrobe expanded to meet the new calls upon it, though it bothered him to spend money, so urgently needed elsewhere, on inessentials. But Alison was spending her own savings on equipping the house, and it would have seemed more than churlish of him to complain. In the traditional glen way, he comforted himself that a dark suit was always handy for funerals.

Money wasn't the only worry, however. Time, more precious as spring approached than at any other time of year, was being recklessly squandered, a thousand jobs clamouring for attention. It wasn't only his own longing to get on with them either; he had his obligations to Archie. But these concerns he kept to himself. It wasn't fair to grudge Alison her special time. Everyone wanted to make a fuss over an engagement; things would calm down soon enough, and in the long hours of light soon to come he'd no doubt be able to catch up.

In any case, once they were married Alison would be

there to share the chores. With two of them to see to everything they'd make nothing of the work. And they'd be able to take in more livestock, get the garden going.

He hadn't bargained, though, for the time consumed by planning the wedding, or for the scale the wedding was taking on. It was hard to argue. Alison's father was being more than generous. It was her day after all.

There never seemed to be time to stand back and look at what was happening to his life; or perhaps he didn't want to examine it too closely. There was always the next step waiting to roll him forward, and it was not in Dougal's nature to do anything half-heartedly. If this was what Alison wanted, then she should have it.

But he couldn't blind himself to the gradual, almost imperceptible at first, change in Alison's attitude, the first signs of impatience with the drawbacks of living 'so far from everywhere'. It began as small jokes, ironic comments like, 'I must need my head examined to be coming back here again,' but soon moved on to unconcealed petulance about having to open gates in the rain, the mess the wind made of her hair, the state of her shoes and, with real anger, the fact that after going up and down that damned track she'd had to have a new exhaust for her treasured car.

These complaints, which Dougal tried not to take too seriously, merged with ominous speed into the inference that naturally putting up with such annoyances was 'just for now', that 'once they were on their feet' they'd do better for themselves. In other words, move to some nice little house in Muirend, handy for

Dougal's work, handy for going to see Mum at the weekends. Alison's Mum.

They had it out one evening when they drove up to the croft just as a wild squall of rain battered down. Dougal told Alison to stay put, he'd do the gate, but even so when he got in again, soaked, she burst out in undisguised frustration at the absurdity of anyone even thinking of living in such a place.

Dougal sat for a couple of beats of taut silence, then quietly told her that this wasn't going to work, he couldn't marry her. He dealt as best he could with her shock and distress, and with the increasingly hysterical arguments about the wedding preparations, the bridesmaids' dresses being ready, Alison's own dress costing the earth, the presents, the shame of having to cancel everything, tell people. Somewhere at the back of his mind, as Alison first wept then raged, he wondered wryly how many people had been bowled forward into matrimony on the basis of just such considerations.

But all the latent strength and resolution of his character came to his aid. He had entered into this whole thing for the wrong reasons. He had 'chosen', not wishing to be alone, a girl he had thought would fit into his environment, give him the children he wanted, and make the sort of life with him that his parents had had, her parents had. In a determined bid to stop hankering for a world he could never enter he had, whether consciously or not, turned back to his own roots. But somewhere, at some time, without even realising it, he had moved on from them, and he would never be satisified now with what they offered.

Sitting in the same spot a couple of hours later, after taking Alison home, his only regret was having hurt her so badly. But he couldn't let her, or her family, or his mother, channel him into being someone he was not. He was himself, his own person, and tonight he had taken a decisive step to affirm it. Better to spend all his days alone up here than enter into some unsatisfactory compromise, after the glimpse he had had of what could be. In time, he would find contentment of a kind.

Shaking, her hands crumpling the pages even as she tried to smooth them out, Cristi read Pauly's words again and again. Was this mere glen gossip? It couldn't be if it came from Jean herself. But would Alison have changed her mind? Or would Dougal have decided to go along with what she wanted after all? Perhaps by now the sunny, high-perched house was bare and silent again, its buildings deserted, its fields empty.

But if it were true? Cristi knew now – she had had more than enough hours and days to mull over it – that she had let Dougal slip away through her own naivety and lack of initiative. When he had appeared to withdraw she had been baffled and dismayed, and had done nothing to put matters right between them. How easy it was from this distance to see where it had all gone wrong, to look at the situation from Dougal's angle and recognise the obstacles which would loom for him. He had needed reassurance and she had been too immature and unsure of herself to give it. She had let the rift widen, and though she had been wretched about it she had done nothing.

But how could she be sure that Dougal would still feel as he used to? Time had moved on. He'd fallen in love with Alison, had wanted to marry her, and must now be devastated by her leaving him.

Cristi saw in time the danger of thinking like this. It was precisely what had driven them apart before. To her rescue came the memory, clung to with tenacious need, of that moment when everything between them had seemed plain beyond all doubt, the moment when she had walked into the croft kitchen and seen the blaze of delight in Dougal's face, and known that it reflected everything she felt herself. That moment, and her trust in it, must carry her home.

She walked to the croft, as she had done before, her mind unable to fix on what lay ahead, allowing her attention to be caught by the sights and sounds around her. The year was on the turn, when the evenings lengthen visibly from day to day, when snow lying at dawn is gone in a couple of hours, when temperatures are zero one day and nine or ten the next – then frequently zero again.

Below her spring ploughing alternated in severe dark patterns with pale over-grazed winter fields. Mounds of pussy willow glowed gold along the burn, and the late sun drew a red sheen from the birch buds. The air was full of the calls of curlew and oystercatchers, the thin mewing of a buzzard high above. As the light took on the blue tinge peculiar to March evenings – blue hills, smoke-blue clouds — fear and excitement gripped her. This familiar beauty suddenly meant too much. Was she about to make some terrible mistake which would exile her from it all over again?

Heading up the exposed track she began to wish she'd brought the car. It was still light. Dougal was sure to be outside somewhere. He wouldn't fail to see her. Yes, he was at the gate already, leaning there motionless, watching her come. She should have phoned, at least giving him the chance to decide whether he wanted to see her or not. That would have been only fair. It was hard to walk the last few yards under his eyes. His face was expressionless, and as she came to a halt in front of him her own face was as set and unsmiling as his.

'Cristi.' He ducked his head in a quick nod, but his eyes never left hers. No reassuring blaze of pleasure this time.

'Hi.' What an absurd syllable, after all the longing and loneliness and doubt.

'I didn't know you were expected home.'

She heard in his voice that he was finding it as hard to get words out as she was. She stood for a moment more of tense silence, aware of the cool touch of air on her cheek, of the light draining from the dusk and the stark outlines of the snow-covered ridges above the house.

'I came back because I wanted to see you.' It was said.

Dougal straightened, his eyes still fixed on her face. 'To see me?'

'Yes. To talk to you.'

Silence. No, not silence, but the movement of the light

wind in the tips of the firs, the throaty sound of the burn gorged with snow-melt, bird-calls.

This was hard. The closed gate between them. Dougal had made no move to open it. But Cristi had come a long way to say this.

'I heard about Alison.'

Dougal's eyes narrowed. He didn't help her out.

'Dougal, I'm so sorry it didn't work out for you.'

Cristi meant it from her heart. Seeing him, she couldn't bear to think of him unhappy. At the same time hot embarrassment swept her to realise how selfish and insensitive she had been to come rushing up here like this. Dougal must be hurt and heartbroken. If only she'd let him believe she was home on a visit, simply walking up to say hello on her return in the ordinary way. Dougal was a stranger now, nothing to do with her life.

But no, such doubts had done their damage before. Honesty was vital now. A true instinct told her so. Also, she knew Dougal well, and nothing about him told her he was stricken and grieving.

In that instant, before Dougal had said a word, Alison faded like a wreath of hill mist and was gone.

'I'm cold,' Cristi said.

Dougal took one look at her face and reached for the catch of the gate, fastening it behind her as she waited, then walking close at her shoulder towards the door.

'We'll put the kettle on,' he said.

Divine ordinariness. Fly halfway across the world and put the kettle on. Tears – though for what she couldn't have said – sprang to Cristi's eyes as she walked with him through the neat steading yard, breathing in the nostalgic smells of pine resin, dung, wet straw, dank stone, and spring.

In the now more elaborate kitchen they made tea. Jean gave him that pot, Cristi thought. Such details had an unbearable poignancy. Where to begin? How to put into words the thousand thoughts which had brought her to this moment?

Dougal was stirring his tea. She looked at his broad capable hands, at the brown hair soft and shiny under the worktop light, at the weather-tanned skin of his neck against the thick wool of his sweater. She looked at the stocky, powerful body in the work-clothes he'd changed into to do the evening feeding, and she knew that every detail of this was what she wanted – this quiet, self-contained man of proud independence and integrity, this simple place, this way of living.

'Dougal, I've been such a fool.'

He turned quickly, a light in his face which made all the words, all the explanations, superfluous.

'You a fool. God, Cristi, I think there's been a pair of us.'

She thought he would take her in his arms then; that with the truth so clear between them there'd be no need for further discussion. But at the last moment he checked, turning his head away with a frown.

'Still, we were probably right enough in a way.'

Cristi, beginning to tremble, could hardly believe her ears. 'Right?'

'I mean, it's good to be friends, isn't it? That'll never

change. It was—' he clearly chose the word with care 'great to see you coming up the hill just now. It's great to have you home . . .'

Cristi was so chilled that for a second she almost forgot all the hard lessons she had learned. But only for a second.

'I'm not having any of that,' she said. Her eyes fell on a Tesco's carrier bag on the table. 'Supper? Enough there to share? Because we've a good bit to sort out – starting with your boring old stiff-necked pride.'

'What are you talking about?'

This wasn't a joking matter to Dougal. He stared at her, jaw jutting.

'I'm not sure you deserve an explanation, you're such an idiot.' Cristi was high on confidence now. She knew why she'd come. It might not happen instantly, not before supper anyway, but this time he wasn't going to escape. 'Come on, let's get cooking.'

'Cristi.' His tone arrested her. He couldn't treat this lightly. He was torn by love and need and doubt.

Well, it wasn't a light matter for her either. She went to him quickly, putting her hands on his arms, looking into his face.

'Dougal,' her voice was soft. 'I'm back. Just me. As I am, as you've always known me. Glen Ellig is my world, the place I want to be. The Brazilian part is over and done with. I'll talk to you about it soon, and all it meant to me, but for now it doesn't exist. I've given the ranch back to the family. But what no one knows yet, no one here, I mean, is that I've given away the money too.'

'To the family?' He was clearly startled.

'No, to someone else. To that – sort of charity I was involved with.'

'To a charity?' He was too dazed to relate the reference to anything.

'The money was never really mine. Fool's gold. And we shan't need it.'

'Cristi?'

She nodded. She could feel the tension in the muscular arms under her hands.

'Are you saying what I think you're saying?' His throat felt tight; he could barely get the words out.

'You know I am.'

Almost gropingly his arms came round her, and he pressed his cheek against her hair, as though he wasn't ready yet to let her see his face. 'Do you mean it?'

'I do. I was so stupid and self-engrossed—'

'You're never that.' Smiling, he drew back his head to look at her, gently touching his fingers to her cheek. 'God, I can't take this in . . .'

Laughing, shy suddenly, she burrowed in against him. 'I think we'll have to come to it gradually.'

'You know it's all I've ever wanted, don't you?' he demanded with sudden fierceness, taking a grip of her arms that almost lifted her off her feet.

'I wasted so much time for us.'

'No, I don't think that's true. You'd always have needed to know about that other side of you. But you seemed so swept away by it. I thought you'd gone for good. Listen, though, this giving away all you inherited, are you mad? And what's Archie going to say about it?'

She laughed at him. 'It's nothing to do with Archie, nothing to do with anyone but us. If I'd kept it it would only have got in the way. We're going to dig our tattie patch and keep our puckle hens, and you'll have to go on earning an honest wage.' Cristi had no idea of the plans for Dougal and the management of Drumveyn over which Archie and Tom were quietly biding their time. 'I'll get to work in my studio and who knows what I'll produce.'

And she'd have to do something about this kitchen, and the rest of the house too if it was anything to go by, though it was a bit soon to say so yet.

'God, Cristi.' Dougal hugged her in a soaring delight which quickly turned into something more serious and intent.

Pauly's baby would be arriving soon; she'd need help as well with looking after Cecil. Sally could do with all the support they could offer as she faced the tragedy that was coming. Drumveyn, the family, friends, the glen – they would all be there as a familiar background to the new life here in this perfect little house – a life shared with the one person who made her feel complete, who felt truly part of her, in the one place she wanted to be.